HOLIDAY MYSTERY

By Charlot King

THE CAMBRIDGE MURDER MYSTERIES SERIES:

Book 1: POISON

Book 2: CURSED

Book 3: BLOOD MOON

Book 4: A CHRISTMAS MYSTERY

Book 5: VALENTINE'S DAY – KISS OF DEATH

Book 6: HOLIDAY MYSTERY

Book 7: Coming soon!

COPYRIGHT

First published 2023
Published by: Beautiful Day Cambridge Ltd
ISBN: 978-1-8384781-3-1

Illustration: Robin Howlett

DEDICATION AND THANKS

I thank the NHS for helping me with my recovery from long covid. Thank you to the two Robins, who are both excellent! I dedicate this novel to my son, who is the best. Finally, my books would be nowhere without you, readers. I hope this one does not disappoint. Cxx

PROLOGUE

Consider the value of a diamond. Now consider the value of a person, an animal, or nature. What we put value on, we protect. But what we put value on, becomes a resource. Everything is traded. Everything is sullied. How did I wind up here? Climbing a tower, and for what? To be richer? But what riches? Are they truly to be found in diamonds? Or, the glimpse of spring through the tower window, noticing the wisteria in bloom down below, the stone wall with delicate erigeron clinging and turning its daisy heads towards the sun? I know which I would prefer to set my eyes upon for eternity. When did I miss the moment to make a conscious choice? Was I hard wired the wrong way? Now fate has taken grip and I am the passenger.

1 CLEANING AWAY THE SPARKLES

Inside a fancy art gallery situated down a narrow street right off the upmarket Piazza della Signoria in Florence, Italy, an exhibition of sparkly jewels can be ogled at by those coming home from night shifts in the early hours, but only if they peek from the dark pavements through the metal chainmail and iron bars crisscrossing the windows to protect against any ramming of exhibition space frontage. The transparent surfaces in this minimalist and dazzling space focus all eyes towards tiny objects behind glass plinths. Rubies, emeralds, sapphires and diamonds all blazing under multiple lights like the eyes of dragons and unicorns.

Inside, a cleaner moves his bucket closer to a cabinet. Behind the framed straight glass edges, each jewel is cushioned on a tiny velvet pillow as if in slumber. He takes a closer look at a ring with the most magnificent red gem he has ever seen. He leans in, his nose accidentally huffing up the glass. He pulls up his sleeve to rub the surface clean, glancing back onto the gloomy street to see if anyone has noticed, then back at the precious rosy light splintering shards of scarlet across the room. It makes him tremble, knowing the possibilities such wealth could offer. He could start again. Somewhere else. Fly his own plane. Not that he wants to. Buy an expensive car, though it has never been up there on his list of ambitions. No, it would give him time. In the bank. To choose to do anything or nothing. Make him controller of his own destiny. Not beholden. To stick it to the man. Break away from work, eat, sleep, repeat. Have time to love, rest and love again.

The cleaner looks up at the surveillance camera and then walks out of the exhibition room to the toilet. From his pocket he pulls out a hat, sunglasses and a mask. He removes his overalls to reveal his jeans and black jumper. With his face covered, he wanders back into the exhibition room. Then, bending down he pulls out a small hammer from his bucket of water. He smashes the glass and hears the alarm go off. A metal gate falls to hinder his exit, but he places a device at the bottom which explodes and he is able to walk through. His red hair poking out the back of his jacket.

2 EASTER HOLIDAY

Professor Elizabeth Green, a sweet pixie faced lady with pinched shoulders, congenital poor posture and a mass of unruly brown curls, is shuffling towards the front door at Foxes' Haven, followed by her best friend, Professor Emily Masters.

"Is that all you're taking? And why are you leaving so early? It's the crack of dawn!" Emily asks, a little worried.

"Godric insists only one small bag, so–" Elizabeth dumps a red carpet bag and a briefcase by the front door, narrowing her beady green eyes. "It's more than enough. We're only going for a couple of weeks. And he wants to get through the tunnel before it gets busy." Elizabeth's grey linen trousers hang too long over the old walking boots she is now pulling on over thick socks.

"Whatever will you wear to the opera?" Emily is aghast. Her own blue silk dress with hand painted orchids, and not a hair out of place, are very different to her friend's attire.

"You need something nice to wear while you're away. Even just for Easter," Emily despairs.

"We'll use hotel laundry. Please, stop fussing," Elizabeth's usual booming voice a little quieter than usual. "Clothes are made to keep us warm or protect us from the sun." Elizabeth knows her favourite cardigan, a little worn and thin at the elbows does neither. Still, it has been her armour since her husband, Sir Gerald Green and original wearer, passed away nearly two and a half years ago. It has been a particularly harsh and cold spring in Cambridge, with easterly winds nipping noses, toes and fingers. But Elizabeth has worn this cardigan most days. This holiday is especially needed after the past few months when Elizabeth has not quite been herself. With almost no energy to even speak, she hopes this journey which she is taking as much for her grandson as for herself, will put distance for them both between the murders on Valentine's Day.

Elizabeth strokes her hands through the dogs' hair as they follow their pack leader, hoping her existing activity indicates impending walkies. Hector and Monty, the Afghans she has just brushed this morning, and Clive, the Old English Sheepdog, who has had a super short haircut for Emily's sake, bang into the telephone table, knocking over the umbrella stand in a state of building excitement. She leans back to give Bertie, one of the cats who share Elizabeth's home, a kiss on the head as he watches from the bottom of the bannisters. Elizabeth then picks up a small flower press her father made her decades ago and tries to squeeze it into the top of her carpet bag, but it won't fit. She shakes her head and stuffs it under her arm. "You sure about the dogs?" Elizabeth finally asks Emily before opening the front door.

"I've already used them as an excuse to upgrade all the carpets on the ground floor. I've told Cuthbert we're having them, like it or not."

"They do get quite dirty," Elizabeth warns.

"Oh, not yet. After I hand them back to you."

"They're not allowed upstairs. Just tell them no."

"We'll see. You know Pepper's all over my bed."

"Where will Cuthbert sleep?" Elizabeth asks.

"He can move along the landing," Emily chuckles to herself. "Anyway, now you're fussing."

Elizabeth pulls a face. Emily is right. Both friends step out onto the gravel driveway and see Elizabeth's nextdoor neighbour, Mrs Cloud, putting some scraps into her bins.

"Good morning. You off then, on your Italian adventure? Getting an early start." Mrs

Cloud asks enthusiastically.

"Just waiting for Godric. He telephoned half an hour ago. Said he has a surprise," Elizabeth replies, a little preoccupied with the dogs in her life, all gathered around her feet. "You know where the cat treats are, don't you? And don't shut the airing cupboard. Bertie likes to sleep in there, and Soot likes the garden pod, so I've taken the door off so he can't get trapped inside. And Fred sleeps in the summerhouse. I've–"

"I've got your list, Professor Green," Mrs Cloud kindly interrupts, quietly dropping the bin lid and pulling her hands from her marigolds. "It's very comprehensive. You've left no stone unturned," Mrs Cloud raises her eyebrows imperceptibly, hiding a smirk.

"Godric rigged up a camera, so just ignore it. It's in the drawing room. In case we miss the cats. Actually, I miss them already." Elizabeth looks back into the house, sadly shaking her head, wondering if she is doing the right thing. "I'm not sure I want to do this," she whispers under her breath.

"Sounds like a lovely idea," Mrs Cloud smiles, not having heard Elizabeth's doubts, knowing she had better keep all the cats alive as they mean so much to Elizabeth. "I'll phone if there are any issues, but I'm sure there won't be."

"Thank you, Mrs Cloud. You have Godric's

phone number?"

"Yes, yes, that's right. I have your grandson's and yours too, Professor Masters. And I have all the codes to all the locks and doors, and all the keys. I think I'm set." Mrs Cloud looks at Emily. Emily smiles back. They both wonder if Elizabeth will ever leave.

"Right, thank you," Elizabeth sighs. There is no room for error. Not when it comes to the animals. "And you have the lists of what they eat and when. No dry biscuits for Bertie," Elizabeth frowns. Mrs Cloud can see the worry on Elizabeth's face.

"I'll go and sit with them, with my knitting, every now and then to keep them company." Mrs Cloud winks. "Anything to get away from Mr Cloud and his football. He has it up so loud it hurts my ears. I'll enjoy the peace and quiet at yours. You can watch me knit one, pearl one. On your camera. Tell me when I've dropped a stitch."

"Will you?" Elizabeth is overwhelmed. She tries not to cry, just from the kindness of her neighbour. "That's very kind."

Elizabeth pops back inside, coming out with a bag she gives to Mrs Cloud.

"The contents of my fridge. Don't want it going to waste. Couple of peppers, some rocket, organic apples, vegan cheese, oh and soya milk."

"Hmm," Mrs Cloud replies. "I love an apple

with my afternoon tea. Thank you." As Mrs Cloud holds up the apple they all hear a pop, pop from a small car engine as Godric pulls into the driveway. Elizabeth's friends' jaws drop.

"Good gracious. You can't seriously be going in that?" Emily cannot stop her thoughts from tumbling out, shocked by the size of the little car Elizabeth's grandson, Godric, has pulled up in. "That's a dreadful idea. No, no, no."

"What ho!" Godric beeps the little horn.

"What is it?" Mrs Cloud asks. Godric has the window open and hears. He jumps out of the car to give his nanna a squeeze, Emily a kiss on the cheek, and a scruffle of the dogs' heads.

"It's a Fiat 500, 1975. Sunroof, radio and CD player. Luxury, Mrs Cloud, and it's been converted. All electric now." Godric looks excitedly back at Mrs Cloud with his large grey eyes sparkling like sunbeams across the sky. He smiles at her, then back at his nanna, his beauty far surpassing most humans that both Mrs Cloud and Emily have ever seen, and not of this era or world.

"Where are the airbags? You're driving to Italy you know," Emily questions and reminds Godric. Meanwhile, Elizabeth smiles at Godric, puts her bags in the back using the sunroof. Godric's tall frame bends low to lean back into the car door, and he grabs the flower press and his nanna's briefcase off the back seat and opens it.

"I said one bag. He pulls out his nanna's passport and wallet. Anything else you need for holiday travel in here?" He asks.

"My reading," Elizabeth insists.

"You will be people watching and talking to me. If work comes on this holiday, then I will have to go back for my collection of single malts and travel roulette. You're coming on holiday with me," Godric replies matter of factly, his natural tan and blonde curls making him look less undergraduate and more movie star who has just been on the beach.

"What a lovely chance to relax," Mrs Cloud nods before popping the vegan cheese in the bin while no one is looking. "You'll have fun, the two of you."

Elizabeth sighs and shakes her head. Godric shoves the briefcase and flower press into Emily's arms, then gives Emily a big kiss and holds her gaze. "Thank you." They both share a look, knowing Elizabeth needs this time to finally accept the death of her husband. So much in one look, but they both have witnessed the slow crumbling of Elizabeth around the edges until the edges have started to become the important bits and not just the edges anymore.

"Okay. I'm ready." Elizabeth climbs into the passenger seat. She likes the tiny size. It makes her chuckle. "This is going to be an adventure. Goddy, and you won't be able to speed."

"Why would I? When I want to look around me on our hol-i-day," he replies, emphasising the word. Godric puts on his hat then looks at his nanna to do the same. "Hat?" Elizabeth looks back at Godric, confused.

"It's going to be hot," he advises, waiting for her to respond.

"Why didn't you say before I got in?" Elizabeth starts to unbuckle her belt.

"Ooh, lovely! Heat. We can only dream here," Mrs Cloud says encouragingly.

"Stay there!" Emily shouts, keen to get Elizabeth on her way before she has a change of heart. "I'll get it. Which one?"

"The green one, hanging by the door." Emily comes back out with Elizabeth's brown hat, which she passes through the sunroof, then grabs the dogs' leads so they don't chase the car. The dogs kissing Elizabeth through the car window, wanting to get in. Elizabeth can feel the start of her tears.

"You're not wearing that green thing. It's only fit for the bin!" Then Emily sees Elizabeth start to wobble. "They're in safe hands. Go and have a wonderful time. You deserve it," Emily says, getting emotional herself.

"Take a photo, would you?" Godric hands Emily his mobile.

"I hope you're not going to take photos

every time we cough," Elizabeth frowns.

"Smile," Emily says. Godric smiles for the camera. Elizabeth looks sadly at the dogs then up at the camera, pensive. So Godric puts his arm around her, and finally she melts. Emily takes the photo and then hands back the phone. Godric starts up the car.

"Bye! Bye! Toodle pip!" He shouts. Mrs Cloud waves and smiles from over the fence.

"Bye! Have a lovely time," Emily smiles and waves, holding three leads with the other hand as all the dogs bark at the car.

"Well, off we go," Elizabeth looks at Godric uncertain, then glances out the back window at her friends and animals.

"That's the spirit. We're going on our spring, Easter, nearly summery holidays! It's going to be wonderful," Godric beams as they pull away and drive down the hill, past the spires and Colleges of Cambridge, bound for Italy and good times. Elizabeth wondering if they are doing the right thing.

3 TUSCANY

A couple of miles outside Florence, a car heads down a quiet lane. On either side, Cyprus trees and rolling vineyards climb to the skyline and a rising orange sun. The cleaner from the art gallery is on the phone, his mask discarded on the seat, a caffeine drink held between his knees. He looks down inside his open bag on the passenger seat, the jewel poking through, casually still stashed on its black velvet pillow. He wipes his brow with a handkerchief and shakes his head.

"It's done. Yes, I have it. No, I'm fine. Fantastic, aren't I? I mean, how easy was that?" He holds his phone to his ear, listening to the person at the other end as he changes gears with the other hand. "Well, I'm halfway there. Yes of course, I left straight away." He listens again, then replies. "Like I said, as soon as I got the diamond. Precision timing. No, no one saw me. Geez," he replies, slightly manically, then cuts the call.

As he does, he shakes his head again and

blinks, screwing up his eyes, his car veering to the wrong side of the road and back again. A lorry driver heading straight towards him slams on the brakes and beeps his horn as the cleaner lifts his head as the truck passes. He then drives past hedgerows full of sparrows, his windows open. The sound shakes him awake momentarily and lifts his spirits. It is going to be a good day. He then drops his drink on the floor, the car veering from one side of the road to the other again as he tries to retrieve it.

4 REIMS

Elizabeth and Godric have made it onto the train journeying through the tunnel joining Kent to France under the English Channel. The classic Fiat 500 sits stationary in the carriage which is moving at nearly one hundred miles per hour. The little car is currently overlooked by a large four-by-four in front with children pulling faces at Elizabeth from their back window as they scoff crisps and sweets. Elizabeth sticks out her tongue at them. Behind, Elizabeth glances in the Fiat's side mirror to see a couple in a soft top sports car shamelessly making out and in a state of semi-undress. Godric laughs, having spotted the same thing. Then realises the children might be able to see right through to the other car, so opens a map to try to block their view. The children blow raspberries at Godric.

After thirty-five minutes of waiting, the train emerges from the tunnel and into the bright sunshine of France. Godric turns on the car radio, an upbeat presenter babbling in

French plays lively poppy jazz.

Elizabeth shakes her head as Godric beams. “Bonjour, madame.” An old red van that looks like it should have French breadsticks poking out of the window, trundles around a roundabout nearby.

*

A couple of hours or so later, Godric is driving through tree-lined avenues in the centre of Reims, a town still quiet and not quite woken up yet.

“This is the splendid life, isn’t it?” Godric beeps the horn.

“It’s perfect, Goddy. I love it. But what is this noise?” Elizabeth feels the warmer sun on her face as she listens to the music in the little car.

“Daft Punk isn’t noise, darling Bunny. It’s legend,” Godric smirks knowingly. Elizabeth rifles through the CDs in the tiny glove rest. Debussy, Ravel, Bizet, Satie.

“And you’ve picked daft punks?”

“Exactly,” Godric turns up Digital Love, shouting over it, “Thought we’d stay here in Reims tonight. It’s not about rushing anywhere, is it,” Godric suggests.

“Thank you for taking care of everything,” Elizabeth replies, “this was a good idea.” She glances at the trees. Just the lightest breeze in the blue sky, she takes in a deep breath.

Her department said she must take a sabbatical for the summer term. She thinks back to the awkward conversation. Were things really that bad? After turning down the Master position at Granta and admitting to the Dean it feels like everything is slipping away. Perhaps. But Reims? A holiday for two weeks with her grandson. She looks across at him as he concentrates on the satnav on his phone and turns into a narrow road with rows of cherry blossom trees. Elizabeth rests her head on the window and stares up into the bows. The music still on the radio, she feels like she's left her own life and moved into another's, as if in a dream. But whose life is this?

Godric finds a car park directly opposite a smart looking hotel. Elizabeth's eyes widen at the grandeur.

"Let's just say I've dipped into my trust fund, which is bottomless and to be enjoyed," Godric grins, tapping his nose then turning off the engine and cutting the music. The art deco hotel on the corner of Place Drouet-d'Erlon stands proudly before the two travellers. Elizabeth has never been here before. It all looks so, well, French. Sophisticated, beautiful.

It is not long before they have checked in, paying the extra to do so this early, found their adjoining rooms, compared bathrooms with marble floors, and then left to wander the pavements for an early brunch. Not a stone's throw from the hotel they find a line of pavement tables, large cream parasols and lavender in oversized pots spilling out from a fancy restaurant. It catches Godric's eye. He stops to look at the menu in a glass display.

"Vegan. This'll do nicely."

"This'll do?" Elizabeth looks up in wonder at the peaceful spot. Roses adorn two pillars as they enter, and a maitrê di nods and Godric points at a table in the corner, where the sun beams through some honeysuckle but also gives a good view of the boulevard.

"People watching time, beer, heavenly." Godric breathes in and then stretches his arms out. He reflects on how far they have already come. "The dear car is awfully nice."

"Suits you. Though I think we are still a little early for people watching." Elizabeth and Godric observe the empty street and notice many places are still closed. Elizabeth then checks in lightly with Godric, not wanting to bring up all the death and murder they escaped at Valentine's, the brutality of the past month or so, but also not wanting to bury it. "I'm glad we set off early. A good decision. You okay?"

"I think that gorgeous little car is going to be the star of our trip. I mean, come on, we're headed to Italy. Everyone will adore us," he grins, then pulls down his sunglasses to look at his nanna more seriously. "Everything'll be okay. What's not to be okay about? Whether

I'll have the vegan burger and hand cooked chips, or the chickpea tofu stir fry, or, yes. I'm having the vegan dumplings and noodles for breakfast!" Godric pours over the menu.

"Vegan?"

"On this holiday, sure. Why not? How hard can it be? One for all and all for one." Godric waves the menu about.

"This is not going to be a chip filled holiday," Elizabeth screws up her face at some fries being carried to a nearby table. Then pushes a little more at Godric's defences, "But really, after everything in February, just weeks ago? You're bound to still be in shock."

"Frites, Bunny. Frites. I shall eat them with French mustard tucked in a French baguette, while watching *Monsieur Hulot's Holiday*." Godric then thinks some more and adds, "I might stay home next year and not get involved in any plays." Godric looks into his nanna's eyes. "But we both went through something there, didn't we."

"I don't know what I would do if anything–"

"Nothing happened. I'm here, eating breakfast. I'm here," Godric says, interrupting.

"Will you choose for me then?" Elizabeth smiles.

"Sure." Godric looks at what to choose for his nanna from the menu.

"But no aubergines. No chips. No–"

"Please, you pick." Godric gives her a knowing glare.

*

After their second cup of coffee, Elizabeth and Godric head towards the imposing and impressive Reims Cathedral, where they sit outside for a while before moving across to the Place Martyrs de la Résistance to drink Orangina at the Guiuleton, with its hundred-and-eighty-degree view of the French square, its trees and benches effortlessly blending into the foreground, the huge backdrop of the cathedral behind. Elizabeth wonders how Emily and the dogs are getting on. She already worries about Bertie.

"We're going to do a lot of sitting and watching people on this holiday," Godric announces, looking at a man dressed in a black polo neck and blue jeans. The man smiles at Godric, the most beautiful man he has ever seen. Godric, as cool as a cucumber, lifts his shades and acknowledges the moment. "Just so you know, Bunny. I intend to spend my time practising the art of doing nothing."

"You don't need my permission to have fun," Elizabeth replies, noticing the silent exchange.

"Nope. While we're away, I'm strictly all yours." Godric lowers his sunglasses and takes a long slurp from his fizzy orange. “Wherever we are on this holiday, let’s drink Orangina.”

“Hmm. What if there is no Orangina?” Elizabeth asks.

“Damn, I hadn’t thought that far ahead. Well, we will stop what we are doing and pause. Pause to look, pause to feel, to see what is right in front of our noses. Not think about the past. Not think about the future. Not think about exams, or work. We will just, well, be!”

“To being.” Elizabeth raises her drink to Godric’s, and they ‘cheers’ to mark the moment.

The two sit in silence for some time. Elizabeth tries to stop thinking about things from the past and future. She relaxes her shoulders and looks up at the blue sky, tiny white puffy clouds hanging high above.

“I like the shape of these bottles,” she says to Godric.

“That is the eight-year old in you talking. She needs this holiday,” Godric replies, He lifts his paper straw, sucks up some malt whisky from another glass and then lets it go. Whisky runs down into the orange bottle.

“Thank you for, you know, persuading me to get away,” Elizabeth looks sideways at Godric, his sunglasses reflecting images of the huge cathedral across the square. She knows better than to comment on his morning drinking.

“I did it for me too. All that business, it’s

left me," his thoughts drift into silence. Then he looks back at Elizabeth. "In need of this. It's about all I can do right now." Godric does not know what else to say so takes another sip of his whisky Orangina mix.

"Your grandfather. I know it's been," Elizabeth cannot acknowledge the time that has passed, as it will take Gerald further away. "Having you stay has–"

"Given you a different kind of grief?" Godric interrupts and smirks but then feels more serious. "I think I understand. What happened at Valentine's Day certainly made me grow up fast."

"Well, this is a nice break before your exams," Elizabeth says, trying to lift the conversation but failing.

"Shh, never to be spoken about again while on foreign turf. And anyway, geniuses never revise," Godric is aware he has made it known that he is a genius. But right now, he feels anything but. Elizabeth nods. She cannot believe how Godric has managed to continue on his course, seemingly doing so little work.

"At least you have Alex now. He seems like a nice young man."

"Oh, him?" Godric pauses. "Toast."

"Wait, what?" Elizabeth is confused, sipping her drink through a straw.

"He drinks too much. I couldn't date someone who does that. His job as a barman. I

should have guessed."
Elizabeth splutters out her drink, biting her tongue.

*

The two finally prise themselves out of their seats and meander along streets and alleyways, popping into shops now opening to browse, looking up at the architecture. They see an old red van.

"Hey! Didn't we see one of those already?" Godric watches the van goes by.

"Gerald would have loved that," Elizabeth replies. "Take a photograph." But before Godric can pull out his phone, the van has turned a corner.

"That's a Renault, I think? You said you hoped I wasn't going to spend the whole holiday taking photographs?" Godric smiles.

"Yes, alright."

They find an avenue, Cours Jean-Baptiste Langlet, entirely covered in grass and decide to explore. A tram trundles slowly past them down the middle of the avenue, tracks hidden between clover. Happy faces inside look back at Elizabeth. It lifts her mood and she notices a bumble bee travelling around some daisies in a huge pot. Things feel peaceful here. Godric finds a shop selling quirky things and pulls at Elizabeth's cardigan. They enter, and he hones in on a rug with three-dimensional knitted field mice climbing across it, running towards a knitted bottle of spilt whisky.

"I have to have that," Godric says.

"Space," Elizabeth reminds him.

Godric sighs, remembering there is no room in the car and quietly chats to an assistant, asking her about delivery options and taking a card. Elizabeth buys Godric a tin of car sweets instead, with a pale blue and grey butterfly painted on the outside of the lid.

"If you were a butterfly, that would be you," she says as Godric looks at the tin.

"Rubbish, I'd be an Atlas moth."

"Ha! You'd never. They don't eat. You have hollow legs."

As they continue their walk, they see two miniature poodles sleeping in the spring sunshine in the window of a bookshop. Elizabeth walks into the shop and enters the window display to stroke them before anyone can stop her. She pretends to read some Tin Tin to the dogs, to make Godric laugh. Godric whips out his mobile and takes a photograph. He watches his nanna for a while, then turns and looks up at the day. It is so quiet, and the sun feels different. Warmer than in Cambridge.

His mind tries to shut out the events of Valentine's Day. Those deaths, murders. He wonders if he will ever be able to block out those terrible memories. He looks back at his nanna, engrossed in talking to the dogs. Godric wonders how his Bunny can help the police and still be standing, walking, talking. Tears spike as he smiles through the window at her. He wants to grab her and tell her he will always be there to protect her. Elizabeth looks up, and sees her grandson on the pavement. What are they doing here, in Reims? She feels so far from home already, and anxious about the road ahead.

5 SAN GIMIGNANO

Now more than a yard's arm above the horizon, the sun drenches fields and valleys in warm yellows and pale greens. The cleaner thief from the art gallery parks his car beside the outer wall of San Gimignano. As he stumbles out of his door, he looks out across the valley. The car parks are still empty. Too early for tourists. Up high, this hill town has a three-hundred-and-sixty-degree view of miles of rolling Tuscan fields, vineyards, Cyprus trees, the first red poppies of spring, winding lanes which weave between, and which mainly stand empty under the morning sky. The cleaner smiles, grateful to be alive, to be here this early in the morning. But then suddenly feels a sharp pain in his chest. He grabs the bag with the diamond, stares down at the cobbles beneath his feet then starts to climb the tight alley through a town archway, heading towards one of the towers that still possess the skyline since medieval times.

Holding onto bricks in the town wall, he catches his breath, beads of sweat clinging to his forehead and top lip. Finally emerging into a piazza where the one restaurant opposite is still shut, the cleaner slips through the entrance to a tower in the corner, checking his bag and the many steps ahead that he has to climb. It feels like a gargantuan task. He is nauseous as he lifts out his phone to dial a contact, but they do not reply, so shoves the bag over his shoulder and starts to slowly ascend. His phone rings.

"Yes, yes, I'm here. I just called. I know you wanted to celebrate, but you could have picked somewhere closer to the ground." He listens as he climbs. "Yes, a bit dizzy. Probably the adrenalin. Just pumped." The cleaner stumbles, grasping the handrail, narrowly avoiding a fall back down a section of thirty or so steps but dropping his phone down the well of the staircase. It smashes a few seconds later below. He cannot find the energy to go back for it. He makes a mental note to pick it up when he returns.

As he climbs out through a small door onto the roof of the tower, the fresh air hits him and the early morning low sun, feeling so close up high, makes him squint a little.

"I made it. A very clever Peter, reporting for duty," he smiles blindly into the face of the person he agreed to meet, already waiting here for him. But instead of the expected greeting, Peter feels his arm grabbed and the person pulling him towards the edge. “Hey, slow down. I’m just getting my bearings.” Then he feels his feet being lifted. “Hey! Stop! What are you doing?” He feels the bag grabbed from his shoulders as he is lifted into the air. “Put me down. Who’s? Hey, who’s that?” He makes out another person behind him. But, before he can catch a look at their face, Peter is staring over the edge of the tower, looking back down at the closed restaurant and cobbles. Seconds later, he knows he is falling to his death.

6 PENNY IN THE FOUNTAIN

After having gone back to their hotel for coffee and a map, Elizabeth and Godric step out again into the delightful Reims' day. Trees line avenues full of restaurants now crammed with diners, laughter and frivolity spilling out into the glorious April day. Hungry again, the two pause at a crepe stand and order two vegan chocolate with banana.

"This is very uncouth."

"What?" Godric asks, his mouth full of crepe.

"Eating snacks and walking."

"Nonsense, it's holidaying."

Elizabeth insists they find somewhere to perch to eat, so they roam back over to the Cathedral and sit on the large stone seating. Others with the same idea are also snacking and taking photographs of the spectacle. Elizabeth feels suddenly adrift, far away from home and the familiarity she craves, the love from her animals, her own armchair. She observes the people sitting either side, relaxed, having a good time, talking small talk, and somehow finds this reassuring. Perhaps the familiarity of watching the father open a packet of crisps for his son, the husband holding open his wife's bag so she can find her lipstick. The universal in the everyday things we all do for each other.

"Come on, let's mooch," Godric says as he takes Elizabeth's napkin and watches her put the last piece of her crepe into her mouth on his instruction.

"Where to?" Elizabeth tentatively asks.

"Anywhere." Godric throws up his arms. They wander further and then come to the Statue of Winged Victory on the Sube Fountain in Place Drouet – d'Erlon. Elizabeth crosses the street to look at the magnificent glimmering bronze angel. She pulls out a Euro and throws it into the fountain.

"Did you make a wish?"

"No." She replies.

"Here, make a wish." Godric hands Elizabeth another Euro. Some people start to watch, and Elizabeth wonders if they will take out the coins after she has thrown another, so waits for them to pass. Then she thinks of a wish and throws in the money.

"What did you wish for?" Godric asks.

"I can't tell you that, or it won't come

true," Elizabeth shrugs and smiles. "You have to believe for it to come true. Then it will come true."

"What, and if you don't tell me then it will come true? Honestly?" Godric smiles, then throws in a coin. "Okay, there. I'll tell you my wish if you tell me yours."

"You first."

"I wished that you'd tell me your wish," Godric looks at his nanna dead pan.

"Darn it!" Elizabeth realizes she now has to spill. "I wish we have a happy and peaceful holiday."

They stand for a while with their thoughts, then step back across the road. Engrossed, Elizabeth forgets the cars are travelling the wrong way around the roundabout. A red van comes around the bend and drives past nearly clipping her, but somehow this action stops her from walking right into the path of a larger white van. Godric quickly pulls his nanna out of the way of the white van just in time, and they both look at the little red van disappearing into the night. The larger white van having only just stopped in time on the roundabout in front of Elizabeth, the driver staring blankly ahead. Did he nearly just kill this woman? Elizabeth and Godric's eyes are still on the little red van. Godric can feel his heart pumping and struggles to catch his breath. Just as they expect it to turn a corner and be out of sight, the red van stops, and a man gets out and looks back, too far away to see his face. He stares at them for a while, then gets back in and drives off.

"I have a feeling we should get going," Godric gasps, desperate to protect his nanna from any sign of trouble.

"Back to the hotel?"

"No. I'll check if we can go a day early at the next place," Godric replies, unsettled. "Check out of here. We don't have to stay. Let's get moving."

"Okay, it's okay," Elizabeth agrees, a little more aware of her mistake of not looking properly. She can sense his unease and is fully aware his quick reaction would have protected her had the large van not been able to stop. "Thank you for saving me there."

"No, let's move on. This next place is nice. You'll like it. Smaller. Quieter. We can spend more time there."

They walk back together to the hotel in silence. At one point, Godric puts his arm around his nanna, still looking over his shoulder for further danger. Elizabeth, aware how easily shaken Godric is at the moment, wonders if coming away was such a good idea after all. Elizabeth knows that Godric, her only grandson but also a soulmate, understands at least a little of what is going on under the surface. There were, after all, significant pointers. He could not ignore her emotional breakdown over Valentine's Day. She heard Godric knocking as she would not leave her bedroom for days. She also knows it frightened him and imagines that is why he felt he had to do something. This holiday is his attempt to put things right for her. She knows it is why he is keeping the itinerary secret, to take away any possibility of responsibility. Anything to divert her attention for a little while, to cushion or place something between February and now. She sighs and breathes deeply as they walk under a line of cherry blossom trees, which seem to touch the bright blue sky above her head. Soon summer will take hold. She wonders back at her younger self. Was she more sure of things then? Once an oil painting, now a pale fading watercolour? A frail version of herself, slowly turning into a ghost.

7 SUNRISE ESCAPE

San Gimignano is now fully awake. Dew on the grass long evapourated, and the spring day warms the air. Birds are singing out their hearts as shutters open, carpets are beaten, washing hung, and tourists have parked and made their way into the centre, hoping to climb towers, eat ice cream and sit and watch the world go by.

None of this surrounding beauty matters to the person whizzing over cobbles on a scooter, leaving as quickly as possible, their rucksack in a basket covered over by a blanket, bottles of wine and a stick of bread poking out and masking the real cargo. As the scooter winds down and out through an arch in the town wall, three police cars pass with their lights flashing but no sirens. The scooter indicates left and takes the road towards Castagno Val d'Elsa.

8 BEAUNE

Having calmed down from the earlier roundabout and van near miss, Godric finds a Willy Nelson's song, 'On the Road Again', and plays it for his nanna as they leave the wide avenues and grand buildings of Reims and head for their next destination, further south and in the direction of their final stopping off point, Italia.

Elizabeth has not had any input into the itinerary, however, as Godric is keeping everything as a surprise. He assures her this next bit will be very different, and Elizabeth reminds him that Reims was lovely and she should have looked more carefully where she was going.

As they relax into the next part of their journey, Elizabeth's mind wanders. The past few months have hit her like a bolt. Waves of grieving and the rug unexpectedly pulled from under her by something as seemingly innocuous as bunches of flowers sent posthumously by her much beloved

Gerald a few days before Valentine's Day. Like a polar bear on melting ice, every step since feels trepidatious. Over two years after losing her husband, she is now also being visited by lady insomnia. How much life all now seems out of her hands. So, not knowing where they are going is a mere footnote on the huge stratospheric chasms of uncertainty that surround her. She closes her eyes and sees Gerald, his roguish smile and hears his bellowing laugh.

It is true, for the journey, at least today, the uncertainty feels quite liberating for Elizabeth and makes looking out the window at the wide expanse of French cornfields and vineyards even more magical. Elizabeth glances across at Godric, driving carefully for his nanna. She vows not to bring it up the past while they are away. Godric sings along to Willy. The tiny car has thrown them both much closer than usual, a mere foot between their noses. She wonders if this song will be a recurrent theme. Godric glances across, all dimples and bright eyed.

"You okay?"

"I'm more than okay," she replies.

*

A little later, Godric pulls into a service station to charge the car at an electric point. They wander into a café packed with families stopping off from their journeys. Most are

French, but there are a few Brits. Something about the pasty looking skin or the louder voices when answering if they want more chocolate on their waffles. Elizabeth notices so many children are looking at their electronic devices rather than at each other. Godric manages to find a table outside in the sunshine then pops back in to pick up their order. Vegan waffles with dark chocolate, plus hot chocolates.

"Did you bring water?" Elizabeth looks at all the sugar and worries for her arteries. Godric pulls out two bottles of water and places one beside her hot chocolate mug, which is big enough for any fly to compete in the fly Olympics should they dive and fall.

They tuck into their waffles, chocolate oozing out from the imprinted squares of the waffle iron.

"Do you see that man over there?"

"Where?" Godric follows his nanna's finger and sees a man standing around the back of a small red van. The back doors of the van open to reveal sacks of something and a small refrigerator. "Is that–"

"Must be the same one, surely. A Renault, you said?" Elizabeth lowers her pointing finger.

"Well, this is a main road out of Reims, and we are in France, the home of Renault. It's possible there may be at least two?"

They both stare at the classic red van, just

like the one outside the Channel Tunnel and seemingly exactly like the one that nearly ran Elizabeth over in Reims. Godric frowning.

"What's he selling?"

"His van says fromage. So, cheese is the safest assumption," Godric stuffs an overly large piece of waffle into his mouth as dark chocolate drips down his chin while he searches online for Renault vans. "Here, look. It's a Renault 4. 1980s. Wow, that's really old." Elizabeth glances at Godric's phone, then back at the man.

"Some of us were already adults then. And, if he's selling cheese, what are in those sacks? Cheese would need a larger refrigeration unit than that."

"Perhaps he's an unsuccessful cheese seller, or they're crackers," Godric replies. "Shall I march over there and have words? He nearly killed you."

"We don't know it's the same van." Elizabeth leaves half her waffle, glad of the apple she stuffed in her cardigan pocket. Gerald's cardigan pocket.

*

They head back out on the road and notice how many people wave at them. Godric reassures his nanna that it is the car they are happy to see. Not going much faster than forty miles an hour, it is overtaken multiple times. Children stare as Godric wobbles his head and pulls faces back at them. Elizabeth wishes Godric would just keep his eyes on the road but reassures herself that they are moving so slowly that she could easily grab the wheel and guide them to safety. So, it is with some surprise then when the man passes in his red Renault 4 van and doffs his cap to Godric.

"It's him!" Elizabeth yells, pointing and making Godric jump in his seat. "I supposed at least he isn't following us. Hopefully, that's the end of it."

"Fromage man. 'A cheese for all occasions'", Godric says, interpreting the French sign on the side of the van as it passes.

"He's not selling cheese."

"What's he selling then?"

"I don't know. But there's something about that van and that man."

9 COMMISSARIO LORENZO AND SERGEANT ANGELOU

Behind police tape, at a crime investigation scene, Commissario Lorenzo Bianchi stands in a piazza below the tower in San Gimignano, with one hand picking at his teeth and the other holding a half-eaten croissant and coffee. In a baggy linen suit, with crumbs in his beard, his dark thick hair slicked back behind his ears and the sun reflecting in his sunglasses, he strolls over to the restaurant to see if anyone is in, then walks away, but not before looking at their menu in a glass box beside the door, quietly saying to himself. "Huh, that's new." Heading back to directly under the tower, he makes a mental note to visit the restaurant sometime soon. Officers have already covered the dead body of a man and are now taking photographs and searching for evidence in the surrounding area. Bianchi nods at them all encouragingly, as deferentially they nod back.

"Lorenzo! Where do you want me to take this? Siena or Florence?" Shouts the chief pathologist, now standing not far from police officers redirecting tourists and gawpers away from the vicinity.

"Florence."

The pathologist shrugs, then indicates for his assistants to lift the body, which they do with little fuss as they are used to this kind of thing and are already otherwise entertained, laughing about something they saw in a bar last night as they swing the body into the pathology van. One slams the back of the van shut while the other climbs inside the driver's seat, and they speed away. Lorenzo looks up at the tower looming over him then across the piazza below.

"Hey, Angelou!" the Commissario shouts over to a tall, slender man in his twenties, wearing a leather jacket and black jeans.

"Hey!" Angelou holds out his arms, to warmly greet his Commissario.

"Did you eat?" the Commissario asks. Sergeant Angelou Rossi shakes his head. So the Commissario adds, "Me neither, come on."

"You have a croissant?"

"Just warming up my pipes. This isn't food."

Commissario Lorenzo Bianchi and Sergeant Angelou Rossi walk away from the tower towards the Piazza Della Cisterna and spot two men they know outside a wine bar mid argument.

"I told you to keep away!" One shouts at the other.

"Go home, granddad." The other man replies.

The Commissario and Sergeant make their presence known.

"What, you can't keep the peace when a man has just died, Marco?" the Sergeant waves his arms at the men, attempting to break up the argument. The Commissario puts the rest of his croissant in his mouth and looks about the piazza. He notices the ice cream shop selling the 'best ice cream in the world' according to the sign above the door, opening its shutters. A few tourists are already queuing. Opposite Marco's wine store, the Commissario can see another restaurant is just opening as well.

"Like that's gonna help business," replies Marco, his black hair and almost black eyes made all the more noticeable by his black trousers and black shirt. Marco brushes off the other man and starts to carry a sign advertising his restaurant and wine store, and places it near some tables, then starts to lift chairs down and wipe tables.

"You just stick to business and leave Isabella alone," the other man tries to get in the last word.

"Stefano, come on." The Sergeant tries to halt the bickering. Stefano Esposito glares at Marco as he starts to head towards the other opening restaurant in the piazza. Stefano is older than Marco, perhaps by twenty years. Dressed in tatty clothes, he has a warmer face, with many crinkles around his eyes and dimples where he has laughed many times.

"I get coffee." Stefano lifts his chin then points at Marco's wine café "but he leaves Isabella alone. He leaves her alone!"

10 FROMAGE MAN!

In the wine region of France, surrounded by the Côte d'Or vineyards and vino growing villages, is the cobbled town of Beaune. Elizabeth and Godric amble through a communal square within their hotel grounds, crammed with blossoming trees. Under an arch they are led by a receptionist to a private courtyard, where for the next eighteen or so hours, they will be able to enjoy their secret grand apartment with private terrace brimming with pots of geraniums, alliums and Sicilian honey garlic bells. French doors open into expansive rooms with white linen beds, original oak wood wall panelling and high corniced ceilings. Elizabeth raises her eyebrows at Godric.

"My trust fund is vast." He defends his choices.

"Your mother is a wealthy woman." Elizabeth picks up a chocolate on bed's pillow.

"And she hardly treats her mother to anything. So, this is me just moving some of the money around," Godric replies, then hugs his nanna.

"If you put it like that," Elizabeth smiles naughtily, secretly happy they left Reims too, perhaps admitting to herself now that the incident with the van shook her a little too.

"Shall we go and stretch our legs and find a drink? That was a lot of driving. We can come back for a nap before supper," Godric suggests.

"Five o'clock-zees," Elizabeth smiles.

The two dump their bags and wander back through the courtyards. Content looking guests mooch across the hotel grounds. A husband and wife in their seventies, two women in their twenties, an elderly gentleman wearing a snazzy looking summer wide brimmed Panama hat while carrying a French newspaper under his arm, all nod and smile as they pass. Elizabeth wonders if she will ever feel like they look.

Godric finds a pretty bar on Petit Place Carnot and a table outside under the awning.

"I think we should play a game. Mark people out of ten as they go by."

"That's an awful game, on so many levels."

"Well, he's a nine." Godric's eyes open at a man wearing a gold kaftan topped by psychedelic sunglasses and a long blonde beard. "I wish I could grow a beard like that."

"I'd cut it off in your sleep." Elizabeth stares at the bearded man.

"He's a nine," Godric looks at another man, this time wearing a pink jumper and white jeans, with long brown hair."

"Well, if you're only going to give everyone nines, it's not a game either, is it."

"Oh, so you agree there are sixes, fives, fours?"

"Goddy, stop it." Elizabeth watches at a man picking his nose as he walks by, then back at Godric.

"Definitely a three," Godric pulls a face, then starts searching for more beautiful people.

"There. Look." Elizabeth points. "There he is."

"He's not even a six," Godric squints.

"Fromage Man! The man not selling cheese from the red van." Elizabeth realises she's being quite loud and animated with her pointing, so slides down in her chair so as not to be noticed.

"Maybe he's on holiday?" Godric shrugs.

"I think he's selling something on the black market." She is convinced.

"Ooh, there's a term. Marché noir."

"Let's go and investigate."

"I've just ordered a beer?" Godric protests.

"You stay here. I'll be back." Elizabeth gets up. Godric watches as she skulks across the square pretending to look at paintings in a gallery window then walking closer to the man. She stops again to admire some window boxes until she has positioned herself just behind 'Fromage Man' without him noticing. She pretends to read some postcards on a stand outside a gift shop. Godric sees Fromage Man leans over the top of his van to speak to someone standing in the street, and Elizabeth taking advantage of the moment and peering inside the van. But then, the man in the street looks at Elizabeth, causing Fromage Man to turn around. Elizabeth has to look away quickly and decides to return to Godric.

"What did you see?" Godric asks when Elizabeth returns.

"He's definitely not selling cheese." Elizabeth frowns.

"Right."

"He's definitely doing something illegal." Elizabeth narrows her eyes as she sips a peppermint tea.

"What though?"

"What illegal things do you know that are traded frequently?" She asks.

"Drugs, animal parts." Godric says matter of factly. Elizabeth shudders, so Godric tries to distract her, not wanting them both to spiral. "Look. Surely, he's a nine. Godric nods towards a young man dressed in a grey coat, wearing black jeans, with a mop of brown hair. But Elizabeth won't take her eyes off the van until it has gone.

After they have sat for a while and Godric has eaten some fries, much to Elizabeth's disapproval, they decide to explore more of Beaune, Godric hinting that they will be somewhere completely different tomorrow and to make the most of the peace and quiet.

It is true that as soon as they leave Place Carnot, with its carousel, bandstand, small parade of boutique shops and pretty individual cafes and restaurants, they do reach streets of this small French town where nothing is happening, apart from a local washing his windows, two people walking their dogs, others are just chatting on corners, and the only cars are those that are parked. At the end of every lane is a view across a valley of vineyards. They come to a walled garden, where benches and flowerbeds are evenly spaced around a gravelled courtyard. As they lean on the wall to stare out across the fields, they begin to feel raindrops on their cheeks.

"Poo, rain won't do. Not on our hols," Godric frowns, looking around for possible shelter. A small local bar, much less showy than all the others, set back in the downstairs of a mid-terraced stone row of tiny cottages, has just one door open almost as if to dissuade tourists from popping in. Godric can see a gathering of three or four gentlemen, probably in their eighties, with wrinkly creased suntans and knowing eyes peering out as they hold their beers. The rain starts to increase in droplet size and pace of falling. "Here, let's take cover," Godric can see Elizabeth shivering and whips off his only holiday jumper and gives it to her to cover her shoulders from the rain. Godric's shirt sticks to his chest as the shower rapidly turns into a heavy downpour. They make it across the square, but not before becoming soaked to the skin. As they enter the bar there is a loud cheer. Two beers are immediately placed on the bar for them to drink, followed by the question, "English?" Then laughter and some shots are placed beside.

It isn't long before the sun returns, and Godric is playing boules outside with the locals. Elizabeth takes a stroll with a man called Jean, who for the past hour has been trying and failing to persuade her to drink Absinthe.

"So, holidays with your grandson?" Jean asks.

"Yes," Elizabeth does not going to give up information about her life freely but is interested to learn what this man might know about cheese sellers. "Tell me, we have come across this van. Bright red, a little rusty around the edges. It is, I am reliably informed by my grandson, a Renault 4."

"Ah, magnificent. They do not make them like that anymore. Built to last." Jean sounds pleased to be talking about classic cars.

"Do you know anyone with one?" She persists.

"No, sadly. Why? Are you looking to buy?"

"Oh, we already have one classic car on this trip. Another would be completely unnecessary." Elizabeth wonders whether to share her curiosity about this mysterious Fromage Man. "It's just that. How can I say this? The man who is driving it. He looks like he's not selling cheese."

"Right. And you like cheese?" Jean asks.

"No, no. I'm a vegan."

"You do know you're in France, Madame," Jean mocks.

"Just tell me this. Are there many independent cheese sellers in France that you know. And who might drive a red van?"

"The country is full of cheese sellers. Wine sellers, good times. Good times."

"Right," Elizabeth sighs.

"What's the matter?" Jean asks.

"There was just something about this man. He was acting suspiciously."

"What was he doing? Eating cheese?"

"It wasn't what he was doing. It was his van. It advertised cheese, but he had this tiny fridge which could only fit a couple of cheese in. And then all these sacks."

"Maybe they were baguettes?" Jean smiles in disbelief that this charming woman can be so preoccupied with the sale of cheese.

Elizabeth decides to give up on Jean. She turns abruptly and heads towards the hotel to read, with just the smallest possible wave goodbye. As she wanders alone, she comes to square and is completely taken aback. It is covered in grass, with a mass of daisies growing up through it. She has never seen anything so beautiful. It stops her heart in its tracks. The square is silent, not a soul about, just the sound of the breeze in the grass and buzzy bees going about their business. Elizabeth spots a bench and sits quietly, staring at what must be ten thousand daisies. It isn't long before she starts to notice all the other insects and butterflies. Gerald would have loved this. She can feel a faded Gerald sitting beside her but she cannot see him, cannot touch him. She tries to remember. It makes her feel panicked. She takes out her purse and opens it to see his photograph.

"Look, Gerald. Look at the daisies." Elizabeth points the photograph towards the daisies, so Gerald can see them.

11 A FLORENTINE WIDOW

Commisario Lorenzo Bianchi and Sergeant Angelo Rossi arrive at the dead man's apartment. With paint flaking off a wooden front door, high up overlooking the Arno River and a stone's throw from the Ponte Vecchio Bridge.

"Let's see if the Englishman's wife is in?"

A petite woman opens the door to the Commissario and Sergeant. Her tiny pinched face scrunches up under a childlike fringe, wondering what the police are doing at her door. When she walks back into the room, the Commissatio and Sergeant notice her almost translucent skin.

"Nice place."

"What is it? Why are you here? Is everything alright?" The woman asks in her soft Devonshire accent. They look around the apartment, with its radio tuned to the BBC World Service and British newspapers spread out on the dining table. A jar of marmite open next to some buttered toast.

"Are you Mrs Mia Jones?"

"Yes."

"Mrs Jones, please may I ask you to sit down."

The small woman sits on a chair at the table.

"Will someone please tell me what's happened? You're freaking me out."

"We found a man." The Commissario pauses. "He had fallen from one of the towers in San Gimignano. We believe it might be your husband."

"What? What are you saying?" Her tiny frame shrinks with dread and panic.

"We need you to come and identify the body as we believe–"

"No, no, no, no, no. No!" The small woman stands up and rushes to the window. She looks out across the river and lets out a groan as if all the air is leaving her body.

"We believe your husband may have fallen from the tower," the Sergeant finishes the Commissario's words. Mia Jones turns to look at the young Sergeant in disbelief.

12 FAMILY TIME

Elizabeth got up early to have one last walk around Beaune. Back at the hotel, she plonks the paper sack with food gathered from a local shop, as Godric opens his eyes.

"It's nine. I brought snacks for the car."

"What?" Godric screws up his eyes, still sleepy. "Pm or am?"

Elizabeth sits in the courtyard to wait for Godric to get ready. It is so quiet. Just some laughter behind shutters and someone sweeping up further away. A short time later and they are on the road. She makes Godric take a detour and drive through the daisy square, which he agrees is magnificent. He jumps out and takes a photograph of Elizabeth in the car with all the daisies and French homes in the background.

*

Soon they arrive beside the clear waters of Lake Annecy. Godric's eyes light up.

"This is officially my favourite place ever."

"We haven't even looked around yet?" Godric keeps his eyes on the road as the traffic is much busier than in Beaune, but he cannot fail to glance to his left where he can see almost within touching distance the turquoise lake below a blue sky with just a few puffy white clouds almost painted above hanging about doing nothing. "That's what I want to do," he whispers to himself under his breath. Little white boats, not more than ten feet long, bob under their white covers, looking almost new. People wander along the promenade with ice creams piled high on fancy cones.

"I can't believe I've never detoured here before?" He says to his nanna.

Getting to their hotel proves a little trickier, however, as it is in a pedestrian only area. They park on the front and walk across several bridges.

"It's around here somewhere?" A little lost, Godric stands on a bridge on the Rue Perrière in Vieille Ville. Elizabeth points up at a grand old hotel overlooking the bridge with a view of the lake and the alps in the background.

"Is that it?" She is asks.

"Yes! C'mon. You deserve it. I deserve it." They find reception and are taken to the first floor and adjoining rooms with balconies overlooking the bridge they were just standing on, the epicentre of Annecy. Godric walks out onto his balcony, looking up at the alps, when he spots the red van. He is going to tell his nanna, instead watching it drive away around a corner. It could have been a different one. It could. But he knows it was not.

*

After a hot drink, Elizabeth and Godric take a stroll down by the lake. They find some boardwalks stretching out across the water at right angles from the path. They must be used to moor boats, but right now are completely empty. Elizabeth and Godric walk down to the end of a narrow boardwalk until they are at least twenty metres off the shore, right out onto the lake. It is peaceful. Godric lies down then looks up at the sky. The two relatives remain silent, the only sound being gentle ripples kissing the wood beneath them and the little white boats bobbing on their moorings.

"I think I want to go on one of those." Godric looks across at some pedalos and then back at Elizabeth. He sits up, walks back up the boards, having spotted a pontoon where a row of white pedalos are being hired out. Elizabeth watches as Godric steps into a pedalo and chugs out across the lake. What is he doing? She can see larger boats and the pedalo man waving for Godric to come back closer to the edge. A large holiday steamer passes just feet away. Godric's little craft is violently shaken from side to side and nearly capsizes, but Godric manages to keep balance, only to get in the path of three swans.

"Pedal faster!" Elizabeth shouts as the swans' beaks start to peck at the back of the pedalo. Godric's back is now inches away from being pecked.

"Ow!" Godric arches his back as he feels the first peck. He decides to stop pedalling and stand up. But then he is pecked on his shins, so he dives into the water. The pedalo owner shouts at Godric and the now captainless pedalo. He voices some expletives about Godric not getting his deposit back as he watches his craft drifting. The man jumps in a speed boat and retrieves the pedalo while Godric makes it by a whisker up onto the boards before the swan can peck again. As he jumps out of the water, Elizabeth finds some baguette in her pocket and feeds the swan. Godric laughs out loud that he made it.

"Poor swan. He's just hungry." Elizabeth looks at the swan, who she thinks seems thin. She then opens a small paper bag in her pocket containing seeds. "There you are. Bread and seeds. One is bad for you, but you like it. These are good for you, and you can take or leave them. That's right. Not so different, are you." Elizabeth continues to talk to the swan as Godric rests his head on her lap, making it damp. "My grandson here. He is taking me on a holiday." Elizabeth says to the swan, squinting in the sunshine. "And so far, it's the best thing that's happened in a long time," Elizabeth continues. The two now sit for a while, motionless.

*

Elizabeth and Godric have to drag themselves away from the idyllic spot after an hour or so, to make the most of their visit. Godric suggests they climb up to Place de Château. They first meander along the canals, with their cafes and bars and beautiful people sitting and soaking in the day. They pass a sunglasses store and Godric makes his nanna try on a dozen or so until she finds a pair of seaside green art deco shades she can settle on.

"Brilliant!" Godric pulls out his phone to take a photograph and hurriedly buys them, then pulls Elizabeth out of the shop. They buy some patisserie cakes, climb the hill, then sit to watch the boats down below moving slowly about on the lake, and tourists who now look like ants wander between the lanes and canal lined streets.

"Our five o'clock-zees moment," Godric reaches across to his nanna and pulls her to him for a hug. Elizabeth looks at her watch, about to say something, but it is near enough.

Later, they come out when it is dark and

after having devoured some local food in a restaurant around the corner from their hotel, they stroll back to the lakeside.

"I want to live here forever," Godric sighs. Elizabeth pulls out something from her pocket and puts it around his wrist. "It was Gerald's favourite." Elizabeth ensures it is secure, lifts Godric's wrist, kisses the watch then squeezes Godric's hand. "Make sure you find time to do what you want with your life." She looks thoughtfully at Godric as they sit on a bench facing the alps. "It goes by so fast." There are hardly any people, and there is a bit of a chill in the air, so Godric wraps his arm around his nanna and hugs her close. He cannot find the words to tell his nanna how uncertain he feels about everything. Elizabeth looks at the beautiful evening and knows who would have loved it. Her heart aches so badly. As they sit in the quiet darkness, Godric's phone starts to ring. He looks down. Inspector Bob Abley. What does he want? Godric cuts the call. Whatever it is, his nanna is not helping him this time.

13 WHATEVER SPARKLES

On the Ponte Vecchio Bridge in Florence, under one of the arches close to the centre, a person in silhouette stands looking out across the river. They pull something out of their pocket and hold it up to the moon. It sparkles. It is a huge red diamond ring. They quickly pocket the diamond and disappear among the milling tourists into the night.

14 ON THE ROAD AGAIN

Elizabeth and Godric leave Annecy behind and head for the Mont Blanc tunnel. Snow-capped Mont Blanc and adjacent mountains tower over their little car, making them feel quite insignificant below.

"I've not seen them from this angle before. I'm usually up there." Godric points to what looks like a ski resort perched on the side of a mountain.

"Just stay focused," Elizabeth replies, watching the road snake and curl, hugging the edge of steep cliffs, only to cross a ravine and everything fall away either side, the tarmac lifted onto stilts. They cross one long bridge after another, quarry rocks beneath. The mountains soon start blocking out the sky, and everything finally turns dark. The little car feels vulnerable between big lorries as the winding queue waiting to enter the tunnel comes to a halt. It is cold so they both close their windows, spring not finding a space here. Nothing like playing boule or sitting in a pedalo, Godric thinks. Their teeth chatter a little, so Godric tries to make Elizabeth laugh by seeing how many vegan marshmallows he can stuff into his cheeks.

"You'll need a dentist, or worse. You'll choke and we'll go hurtling down the ravine." It is not too long before they are through passport control and entering the lengthy tunnel, half an hour's journey under the mountain. They are pleased to be able to open the windows when they come out into the light of Italy.

"Buongiorno!" Godric shouts. He beeps the tiny horn of the classic Fiat 500. Elizabeth shakes her head. "What? Everyone is noisy in Italy!" Then he beeps again, and just to confirm his point, cars start to beep, mainly for him to get back into the slow lane as he is driving at fifty miles an hour. "Only priests and pregnant women drive slowly here. And that's only when they are carrying a carload of small children with tadpoles in bowls," he says as he watches many Italian cars race off down the hill.

"It's warmer?" Elizabeth unwinds the window and drops her arm outside the car. "It's like summer? How can that be?"

In the rearview mirror, Godric spots a red van. Surely not. He glances at his nanna, who hasn't seen it yet. The last thing he wants is to have it upset his nanna again.

"D'you have your pocket map? Let's get it out. In case my GPS breaks down?"

"It's in my bag down by my feet." Elizabeth rummages, and as she does, Godric slows the car down to let the red van pass. He turns up the radio to try to muffle its distinctive engine noise.

"Is it down there?"

"Yes, I have it."

"We need it to know where we are going."

"Maps do that."

"Open it out." Godric tries anything to encourage Elizabeth from looking out the front window as they are right behind the red van. She pulls out the map and opens it up on her lap.

"Where are we going next?"

"There is a pretty place not far from here. A comfort break before we head to Pinkham's place in the North Tuscan mountains. That's all I'm saying."

"I like the sound of that. You said no holidaymakers, hardly any people. Not what Tuscany is known for."

"It's the furthest point in Tuscany to the North. Well, almost. Can you find it? Patigno."

"I didn't appreciate there were mountains in Tuscany. Or are they large hills?" Elizabeth starts to look up, so Godric points at the map.

"Pinkham says it's his emergency

hideaway. Look for it. You know, if the world ends and he has to be self-sufficient. He says he had a lorry to get all his stuff up the rickety road."

"You think we will be okay in this?" Elizabeth asks.

"It's his car. He's taken it there before. Anyway, one stop before there." Godric watches the red van disappear up ahead of them, hidden by other cars now. "We don't have to drive fast, do we? We're not in a rush?"

"I couldn't agree more." Elizabeth pauses, then asks, "You think you'll look up Valentino while we're here? I know you liked him the most."

"Don't be silly. I like you the most."

"He was rather lovely, though."

"He cheated on me," Godric sighs.

"I hate him," Elizabeth replies bluntly.

*

They arrive in Ivrea, and everything is shut. Half day closing, they are told when they try to order a meal in a pizzeria. The high street is empty, all but one bar bucking the rule. A single patron sits smoking and reading *'Three Men in a Boat'* translated into Italian. There are no cold soft drinks. Only Campari. They both sit in the sunshine of the empty street and order Camparis. Old buildings with crumbling plaster and painted signs from decades ago line the empty parade. But both of them are hungry and when they ask the barman if they serve food, he shakes his head. All out of peanuts too!

With Campari lined stomachs, they continue wandering up and down the unspoilt streets, with only a few locals popping their heads out from Siestas to chat in the square or take a dog for a walk.

"What are we going to do for food?" Godric asks his nanna. They peer into closed shop windows and local stores. They find an alley with hundreds of steps down, which looks like it runs from the top of the city to the bottom. As they start their descent, a group of men appear from the opposite direction – their black hair, black leather jackets and sunglasses, like cawing crows at a funeral.

"Just try to look relaxed and carefree," Godric whispers quietly to his nanna as the men approach, mildly aware they are alone with no one about and what looks like the Italian version of a group of Hell's Angels about to surround them.

"Where's that map?" Elizabeth replies, retrieving a small handbook of Italy from her bag with a pullout map at the back.

"Put it away."

"Oh, it's hardly going to have street details on this for Ivrea. I just wondered if there might be tips on opening times." Elizabeth holds up the little book of Italy and stretches out the map to see it properly. As she does, the men are now just steps away.

"English?" One asks with a grin to the others as he sees what Elizabeth is doing.

"Yes, as a matter of fact. And hungry," Elizabeth replies tersely.

"Everything is shut today," the man grins. "You came to the wrong place, haha." The others laugh. Godric notices at least two have teeth missing.

"But this is a beautiful city. I am glad my grandson brought me–"

"Your grandson?" The man clad in black leather head to toe nods, interrupts Elizabeth, removes his sunglasses, and then stares at Godric with a bemused face, observing Godric's effete gentle soul. Elizabeth then moves into the group of men, twirling her map around their heads.

"Isn't there anywhere where we can buy some food?" The testosterone flies around Elizabeth, hitting the walls. One takes out a cigarette as all the men stop on steps and surround her.

"Nanna? Nanna?" Godric calls.

At that moment, a black cat starts to climb the steps, having jumped down from a wall. Immediately, Elizabeth bends down to say hello. The cat winds itself around Elizabeth's legs. One of the men kisses the air to say hello to the cat, breaking the tension.

"Franco, is your mother's place open," one looks to the other. Franco stares at Elizabeth, then at Godric. He says nothing. "Franco!" the man talking then bends down to say hello to the cat with Elizabeth. "This is Marlon. He lives next door to my mama. The man grins at Elizabeth. "Marlon, Marlon. Here boy."

"Ci," Franco replies. For a short second, Godric envisages Franco might pull out a knife so rushes to stand between them.

"What are you doing?" She asks him. Then Franco beams the warmest smile. "Mama has her shop, just down there on the right, then left, then right again."

"Take them, Franco," the other man orders, pointing.

"But I will have to walk down and all the way up again?" Franco looks at the many steps to the bottom.

"Franco!" The leader of the pack growls.

"Ci, ci." Franco leaves the large group of leather clad men and peels off, waving at Godric and Elizabeth to follow.

"Thank you," Elizabeth looks at Franco, who nods. Then Franco leads them to a rather beautiful and, more importantly, open delicatessen. He points for them to go in, only to follow and be hugged and kissed by his nanna, who pinches his cheeks and tells him he is not eating properly, then stuffs food into his pockets. Franco beams at his nanna.

"I wondered where he was taking us for a minute," Godric sighs.

"Godric, really." Elizabeth waves to Franco. "Choose what you want for your tea. This one is my treat," Elizabeth says, looking at the juices, fruit, soy yoghurts, fresh bread, humous, nuts, seeds and more. Godric heads right for the wine chiller, lifts out two bottles, some beer, and then heads to the checkout.

Half an hour later, they are sitting on Godric's bed in their hotel, tired, watching some Italian afternoon television game show. Open jars of pickles, tubs of humous, olives all nestled on a towel-makeshift-table in front of them, Elizabeth having refused such crumbs on her own bed.

"This is going to be such a wonderful holiday, Godric. Thank you for this mystery tour. I am already relaxing. And, not a red van in sight," Elizabeth adds. She makes a mental note to eat more, relax more. She wonders if this is her new life. If it is, she wants more. But what will she do when Godric moves on after university, as he must? She tells herself that she can't think like that. Can't worry about the future. This is her and Godric's time now. Their holiday. And it is going to be wonderful.

"Exactly, a lovely holiday. You deserve it." Godric looks at his nanna, his nerves frayed. Just seeing those men was a trigger.

He remembers the deaths at Valentine's. He picks up two breadsticks and passes one to his nanna. "To us," he says, as they knock together the breadsticks in a toast.

"To us. Aren't we lovely?" Elizabeth raises her eyebrows.

Godric leaves the room and looks in the bathroom mirror. He stares back at the man standing in front of him. He feels so guilty for being alive. To be alive, when so many died at Valentine's. His phone rings again. It is Inspector Abley. Godric answers.

"Stop calling. We're on holiday." Then Godric cuts the call.

The TV entertainment show ends, and the Italian news replaces the light, bright snazziness with a serious tone. An Italian diamond ring has been stolen, worth millions of euros, from a gallery in Florence. Godric and Elizabeth watch the bulletin as the newscaster is replaced by an image of the diamond ring.

"Ooh, look at that. Can you get red diamonds?" Godric asks.

"I believe they are the rarest type of diamond in the world. I would imagine one that size would indeed be very hard to find."

15 COMMISSARIO LORENZO BIANCHI

Commissario Lorenzo Bianchi stands over the dead body of Peter Jones in the pathology laboratory at Florence's central police station.

"He may well have been pushed," the Commissario says, waiting for a confirmation.

"Hmm." The pathologist, Roberto, scratches his head. "Well, I've taken a look."

"Yes?" the Commissario raises his eyebrows. "Go on."

"There are bruises on his arms and ankles," Roberto explains.

"Like a struggle?"

"Could be."

"Likely?"

"Look, I'm just telling you there are bruises," Roberto replies forcefully.

"Alright. Anything else?"

"It appears he was already dying from organ failure. The oxygen levels in the blood were very low at point of impact. His heart was oversized."

"Wait, what are you saying?" the Commissario is surprised to hear. They peer at Peter's face, his mottled skin, and his sticky hair full of dried blood.

"It would appear there were drugs in his system before he fell."

"He died twice?"

"That is your job, Lorenzo. Not mine. A man who was killed twice? Now that I haven't heard before. You have your hands full," Roberto, replies. The Commissario nods, disappointed this is not an open and shut case.

"He was an anthropologist, according to his wife. What was an anthropologist doing falling off a tower?" Lorenzo asks himself. "Look, I've got enough on my plate, trying to solve the theft of a diamond. Isn't this just a case of a man who wanted to end his life? I mean, we all know what that feels like every now and then, don't we?"

"Maybe he didn't fall. The bruises. Maybe it was someone who wanted to make sure he was really dead, no?" Roberto smiles. "This is your job, Lorenzo. Stop leading me into this."

"So, you do have opinions?" The Commissario laughs at Roberto.

"No. I'm just playing with you, Lorenzo. You owe me a meal, by the way."

"I owe you a meal? I'm always inviting

you round." The Commissario corrects his pathologist friend, knowing full well he just wants another invite to his home so he can eat the best food in the region cooked by his wife and grandma. "You don't think it could have been suicide? Honestly? He took drugs, he jumped?" The Commissario asks, hoping this is just a simple case to wrap up.

"He fell head first. Most suicides jump and impact their legs. You know that."

"Yes, yes, yes. Alright, Ro. Thank you. Always good to remind me, no?" The Commissario watches the pathologist start to cut open the cadaver. Pulling a face, he decides to leave. "I must go. I've been chasing around all day over this diamond theft. The boss wants my head on a plate if I don't turn something up soon. My diet is all over the place. And I'm none the wiser." The Commissario pats Roberto on the arm, continuing, "and Gino's is closing in half an hour for siesta." He looks at his watch.

The two nod at each other, then the Commissario walks out and across the square to Gino's, where he is met with a warm welcome and taken into the restaurant to eat the largest meal anyone could ever imagine. But as he is about to put the first mouthful in, his Sergeant, Angelou Rossi, comes rushing in and sits down beside him. He nods and opens his phone. The Commissario shakes his head and stuffs food into his mouth.

The Sergeant plays a video on his phone of CCTV inside an art gallery.

"What are you showing me?"

"Keep watching."

They watch a man wander about, cleaning the floors and then staring at paintings. Then disappear, only to come back in, disguised, and steal a diamond.

"Hang on? It's the same guy? It's the tower fall guy. It's Peter Jones. He's an anthropologist, and a cleaner? What?" The Commissario holds the phone still. "So, our anthropologist was moonlighting as a cleaner and manages to steal a very expensive diamond and then falls off a tower? Is this best and worst heist ever seen?" Then the Commissario picks up a large potato covered in creamy tomato sauce and pops the whole thing into his mouth.

"It looks like Peter Jones was an anthropologist and a cleaner, and he stole the diamond. It's the same guy! No mistake. Wonder what else he did." The Sergeant picks up a potato from a dish and also pops it in, munching and smiling.

"Hey! My food! Get your own." The Commissario smacks the Sergeant's hand, then watches the Sergeant just lean in with his other to pick up more food and grin back at him. The Commissario then pauses his eating and thinks. "What was he doing stealing a diamond in Florence and driving to San Gimignano to throw himself off a tower?"

16 PATIGNO

The next morning Godric and Elizabeth cannot wait to leave their hotel. They get up as early as Elizabeth can wake Godric without it being unkind, then head down for the hotel breakfast. But, in the far corner of the hotel breakfast room is a face Elizabeth cannot forget.

"Look."

"What?"

"Fromage Man," Elizabeth hisses. Godric tries to turn surreptitiously and notices a man in the far corner, eating what looks like ham on toast.

"Why is he not eating cheese on toast?" Godric quips.

"You don't think he's following us?"

"He'll have trouble following us to Patigno, that's for sure," Godric replies, although having sighted the red Renault 4 in Annecy and through the Mont Blanc tunnel, he does begin to wonder. "His cheese will roll down the hill."

Elizabeth frowns. Before Godric can stop her, she stands to go and have a word with Fromage Man. Elizabeth is already looming over the man's table before he can look up.

"Good morning," she says.

"Buongiorno," the man replies, a little puzzled why this proper looking English woman, most probably a tourist, has come over to greet him. He looks at his table and passes her the salt.

"Excuse me. But well, we have come from England. Three days ago, or was it four? It's all beginning to blur. We're on holiday."

"Ci, a beautiful country."

"We saw you in Calais."

"Yes, yes. I come from England."

"Yes, but we saw you in Reims, then in Beaune?" It feels like too much of a coincidence?

"We are going the same way," the man shrugs.

"Would you mind me asking, as we are curious," Elizabeth looks back at Godric, who waves, mildly embarrassed, "what are you selling? We saw the fromage, but, well, your van doesn't look built for long hauling cheese. With chillers and everything."

"Ci, formaggio, yes, cheese. Parmesan, gorgonzola, pecorino, mozzarella. The English, they like my cheese, and I see my sister. She lives in Kent."

"Yes, but doesn't cheese need refrigeration?"

"Ci, frigo. Yes."

"How do you keep it so cold?" Elizabeth asks, biting her tongue, not believing a word he says.

"With a frigo."

"Do you sell anything else?"

"Sometimes yoghurt."

"But, your frigo. It's so tiny?"

"Huh?"

"Surely, you sell other things?"

Godric can hear that his nanna is getting dangerously close to potentially pissing this man off.

"Nanna, I think your beans are getting cold!" Godric shouts over.

"Look, madame, I do not know what to say. I sell cheese."

Elizabeth glares at the man, but he takes a large bite of his ham on toast and nods, so she has no choice but to return to her seat.

*

Not long after breakfast, Elizabeth and Godric's little car turns left at a crossroads and starts to climb a hill. As they ascend, the road begins to narrow and hug the cliff. For a while, they travel in silence, aware that the scale of the drop into a ravine is just a foot or two away.

Godric has to change down a gear until they are climbing in second.

"You should have let me talk to him," Elizabeth starts up on Fromage Man again.

"I thought we were over him. We've talked about him for at least half an hour already. You made me turn the music down. Anyway, as I said, he didn't look that friendly, or like he was keen to share his business story. And today is Saturday. Tiswas day. Spit the dog. Fun time."

"He's certainly up to no good."

"We don't know that." Trying to change the subject, Godric looks out his window to the right, "Quite a view," Godric glances across the valley, with its tall trees and large boulders, which look like they have fallen from the cliff to their left. The road narrows again. A car comes hurtling down from the top of the hill kicking up stones which they can hear hitting the bonnet and door.

"Maybe just concentrate on the view above," Elizabeth says as kindly as she can, aware how small this car is, as Godric has to change down into first gear.

They come to a platform where the road expands on a corner, and space to park. There is a fence and what looks like a viewing platform, so Godric decides to stop.

"Give the car's engine a breather." Godric can feel his palms sweating and heart racing at the dramatic drop so close to the edge of the road. They step out of the car on the narrow space beside and look back at the view for miles across the northern mountains of Tuscany.

“Your grandpa would have loved this. So clean and wild.” Elizabeth turns from the spectacular view to look at the road and the steep hill they have yet to climb. “I know I’m not allowed to ask exactly where we are staying, and you said it was rustic, but it is not a tent on the top of that hill, is it?”

“I can promise you it isn’t. Pinkham did say it is a bit of a shack. Ramshackle, I think was one word,” Godric gulps. Where *is* he taking his nanna? “Perhaps I should have investigated first. He’s always inviting me. But, somehow, he’s never sold the prospect well enough before.”

“Ramshackle?” Elizabeth repeats Godric’s word.

Godric nods. Elizabeth says nothing. They get back in the car and start to climb again. This time, there are rocks on the road that Godric has to navigate around. By the time they reach their destination, they are so relieved not to have suffered being buried under a rock fall they breathe a sigh of relief at seeing the hundred or so homes that make up this hill village.

“Pinkham is proud to be the only Englishman to own a property here,” Godric says, pulling over and looking at some photographic directions from Pinkham on his phone.

"What's the address?" Elizabeth asks.

"Ah, well, there is the peculiar thing. It doesn't have one."

"Goddy?" Elizabeth looks around.

"Apparently so. We have to go right down a track past the zebra crossing."

They drive around for a good ten minutes. They stop at a butcher's to ask if he has seen an Englishman's house and for any directions. But the butcher only seems to want to sell them lamb, so Elizabeth has to explain they are vegans.

In the end, a local appears from the only restaurant in the village and asks them if they are lost. There are a few words in Italian, and what turns out to be the restaurant owner, Flavio, jumps on his bicycle and beckons them to follow.

"Is this where we disappear into the woods, never to be found again?" Godric jokes.

"Not funny."

The man signals for them to park on the road and leave the car, as they will have to walk the final steps. They wander under a few stone arches until they arrive at a small courtyard. Flavio waves goodbye. Godric and Elizabeth cannot believe their eyes. It must be the biggest home in the whole village.

They use Pinkham's key left under a plant

pot and open a huge wooden door. Wandering through numerous open plan living rooms with guitars, large saggy sofas, floor to ceiling windows with panoramic views across the valley. Godric opens doors to balconies, verandas, a roof terrace. Elizabeth flops into a chair on a balcony, looks at the view and forgets about everything. Just for a while.

"Here." Godric passes Elizabeth a lemonade, "Pinkham left supplies. He flew over last week, he said, just to open the house for us, make sure everything was ship shape after winter."

"Ramshackle? I'll take this ramshackle any day. Cheers." Elizabeth smiles.

Godric finds the bottle of single malt his friend had left him, grabs a blanket, then plonks himself down on a sun lounger.

"Wake me up when it's time to go to Flavio's for supper," he shuts his eyes. Elizabeth breathes a sigh of relief. What an adventure.

*

Elizabeth and Godric spent the next day just relaxing and watching the sky change colours, the sun cross the horizon, then stars come out. Neither able to speak about what happened in Cambridge. Neither wanting to spoil the happy mood. Both still feeling so close to sinking below the surface, clinging to the normality to keep them afloat. The habits, the routines. The cups of tea, sandwiches for lunch, brushing of teeth. There is not much laughter, but there is peace. Watching the sunsets, spotting a butterfly and talking about it. Wondering if the heavy cloud means rain or if it might travel elsewhere.

After twenty-four hours in Patigno, doing as little as possible, Elizabeth decides to explore the area surrounding the home. Godric makes it clear he is studying all the different malts left by the host for him to taste test.

Elizabeth sets out and finds some fallen Cyprus cones to take home as she would like to plant one in her garden. While she is walking, she notices a tiny creature in a hedgerow. At first, she wonders if it might be an ill fox, all brown and muddy. But then, she soon realises it is a little dog. Elizabeth tries to say hello, but the dog hides further in the bushes. She rushes back to find something for the little thing to eat, but Godric's friend has only left non-perishable items, understandably. So, she hot foots it to the one butcher shop in the village, which is about to close.

"Stop! I need to buy some meat."

"We only have some steak and these sausages," the butcher says, "I thought you said you are vegans?"

"We are, but–"

"You must eat this if you buy it. You cannot free it now. It is too late," the butcher laughs.

"I saw a little dog. It looked in trouble. Is there a vet here?"

"In Zeri. Down the hill." The butcher waves his arm in the direction of the steep hill. "Well, if it is for the little dog, you must buy the sausages."

"We'll have the steak, please, and the sausages," Elizabeth replies, not knowing if the sausages might have ingredients which might make the poor thing sick.

"Lucky dog."

"Do you know this dog? It is this high. Is he or she homeless?" Elizabeth holds her hands up off the ground to indicate the height. But the butcher is uninterested.

"You worry too much. It gets scraps. It likes it up there." The butcher nods up towards the woods. She grabs the last two steaks, handing over euros, the butcher looking confused by this eccentric lady. By the time Elizabeth gets back close to the house, Godric has heard her commotion and is now outside, the blanket around his shoulders.

"There's a little dog," Elizabeth replies, distressed, holding what Godric can only presume is a bloody dead dog in her hands. Elizabeth sees his misunderstanding. "No, this is steak. The dog is up there."

They walk up to the same hedge where she saw the little dog half an hour ago, but he or she has gone. Elizabeth's heart sinks. They wander along the hedgerow, calling gently and waving the steak about in case the smell attracts the dog. They sit down on a mound and Elizabeth puts her head in her hands, despondent.

"Are you sure it was here?" Godric gets up to look about, then glances back at his nanna. Not sure she is okay, not sure he knows what to do. It is then that they hear a rustle, and a tiny, black, dirty, scrawny dog emerges slowly, sniffing the steak.

"Should we have cooked this?" Elizabeth asks.

"Nah, meat is meat." Godric pulls a piece of meat off a steak to make it easier for the little dog to swallow. The dog wastes no time and eats the chunk. "You're a cutie pie." Godric smiles. This continues for at least half an hour until the dog runs off before they can grab him or her. "Let's go and cook this, we can come back later." Godric holds the rest of the steak and sausages. "This isn't what I had in mind for my tiffin."

As the day ends and night falls, they can hear the little dog howling. It breaks Elizabeth's heart and so they wander back out. This time, Godric takes some water in a bowl and the dog reappears to eat the rest of the now cooked steak. But what they do not expect is for the little dog to follow them home. They open the door, the dog rushes in and jumps on

Elizabeth's bed and falls asleep on Elizabeth's cardigan, or rather her favourite cardigan of Gerald's. Now what do they do?

As Godric prepares for bed, he checks his phone. Inspector Bob Abley has texted him. That's all they need. "I need to speak to your nanna urgently. If you get this, please call me." Godric deletes the text then turns off his phone. Stuff him. This time the golfing Inspector will have to deal with things himself back in England.

Godric looks at his nanna, asleep on her bed along with a very dirty dog. He smiles, unsurprised by this turn of events and somehow feeling even happier to be with his Bunny. He walks to the kitchen and looks for the bowl of water they used earlier. Finding it, he runs the bowl under the cold tap, carries it into his nanna's room, puts it on the floor, then turns off the light and quietly closes his nanna's bedroom door. They all need to sleep. Godric picks up the bottle of whisky and carries it to a sofa where he settles in for the night.

17 A VERY ENGLISH INSPECTOR

The sun is out, but there is a chill in the air at the Gog Magog golf course in Cambridge, England, this morning. Inspector Bob Abley stands on the fourth tee. His collar is turned up on his sports jacket, his tanned skin and kind face looking happy with his lot. He is pleased as the nip in the air keeps all but the serious players off the greens. He does not like that his game is to be interrupted by work. He has gone out with his favourite buddies, but cannot ignore the call from Superintendent Raynott. He hands out some sweets from his pocket to his friends. They busily unwrap them, as does he, while he holds his phone with his shoulder to his ear.

"Yes, Super." Inspector Abley rolls his eyes at his friend, notices there is no one behind them, so indicates he will be a moment and walks over to the long grass to take the call in private, popping in his sweetie. "No, I'm not. I'm standing in my garden. I did get your messages about the apparent English jewel thief. Yes, you mentioned from Cambridge. But it's Sunday morning, and to my recollection this case isn't active in Cambridge?" Abley sighs. "Yes," Abley scratches his head, looking at his moccasins getting dew on them. "No, that wasn't the point. I'm in Grantchester, yes," Abley covers his phone but it is too late, as on the other side of the rough where he stands is another hole and someone has just shouted very loudly, 'Four!' Abley makes his excuses. "No, it's the television while I catch up on paperwork. No, I'm not slurring my words. I'm sucking a sweet!" Abley crinkles up his face, his bushy eyebrows dancing with bemusement at the ridiculous expectations of this horrid little boss yapping in his ear. "Yes, I have tried to reach her already when you told me to. She doesn't own a mobile, or I would have shared her number with you." Abley listens to his Superintendent repeat the news that a Cambridge man, who may or may not have been responsible for the biggest diamond theft in Italy in a decade, is recently dead in Florence and that the Italian police have requested help from the Cambridgeshire police. And now the Super is piling the pressure on the station's favourite Inspector to get their favourite consultant involved. She is over in Italy, after all, the Super bends his Inspector's ear to the effect, but Inspector Abley grows more irritated. Does his Super not care that Elizabeth is in a fragile state? "I'm not sure what I can do about it?" As soon as Inspector Abley utters the words he regrets it, and he has to hold the phone away from his ear for a good minute, checking every other sentence and then hold the phone away again. "Alright, I'll try again, but like I say, she's on holiday. Holiday, Sir. I feel very–" Abley is interrupted again. "I'm just saying, I know you want me to see, but–" Abley gets another lecture, then replies. "Alright, okay. Okay, I'll do what I can." He listens again. "Yes. Yes. Bye."

Inspector Abley turns off his phone and frowns. How can his Super be so inconsiderate? After everything Elizabeth has gone through. It makes him angry. So angry at that snivelling waste of skin. He is not going to have any more interruptions from that eejit again on this round. He walks back onto the green, shakes his head at his playmates, then takes his putt. His friend holding the flag. He misses, the ball rolling past the hole by a foot. He groans and takes a second shot, this time putting the ball into the hole. His friend pats him on the back, another friend pulls his club trolley for him, allowing him to calm down. But Bob Abley cannot stop thinking about his dear friend, and what she is about to walk into. Thankfully, he has more sweets for now, and his friends remind him they have tip top refreshments waiting for them all at the nineteenth hole.

18 ONE ITALIAN COMMISSARIO

Commissario Lorenzo Bianchi is sitting in a café drinking a small beer this Sunday morning. He is pondering what to eat for breakfast. He has been working hard on the stolen diamond case, but as yet he has no leads other than a dead 'anthropologist cleaner' who falls off towers. And that is making him hungry.

"Let me do my eggs parmesan, a little ciabatta on the side with my roasted tomatoes and some prosciutto," the restaurant owner suggests, having come out from inside the back and is now leaning on the chair opposite Lorenzo.

"Have you got some of those little salsiccia?"

"Ci, I can do that and–"

But the restauranteur is interrupted by the Commissarrio's mobile phone. The Commissario makes an apologetic face and opens his eyes wide to indicate to the restauranteur just how much he hates taking calls over breakfast.

"Buongiorno," the Commissarrio listens. "Yes, that's right. I'm he." The Commissario listens some more, "Ah, Inspector Burb Abley!" The Commissario repeats what he hears and mispronounces Bob, then crunches on a croissant he has taken from a basket on the table, now talking fast to Burb with a mouthful. The restauranteur leaves to prepare breakfast, realising that their conversation about food has come to an end, as the Commissario asks the question, "What can you tell me then, about your Professor Elizabeth Green?"

19 THREE MUSKETEERS

In the morning, Elizabeth and Godric drive down the treacherous cliff hill to visit the veterinary surgery in Zeri. A nice young man examines the dirty blackened stray, explaining that he himself is from Patigno and knew this dog's owner, who died six months back. That he has himself tried to catch the dog to put her out of her misery, as no one wants her, and how perhaps the little dog is smart for hiding, knowing what might happen. Elizabeth gasps. The vet gives her an expression of what they can do.

"We cannot be overrun with strays. They bring back parasites to the domesticated dogs."

"We'll take her with us," Elizabeth replies adamantly. "She is very much no longer a stray!"

"If you're going to take this dog back to the UK, you'll need a pet passport and rabies vaccination," the vet opens his eyes wide, incredulous that anyone would want to rescue such an unappealing canine. "Is that sensible?"

"Vaccinate, please." Elizabeth looks at him crossly.

"You'll have to wait twenty-one days before you can take her into your country." The vet wants to make sure Elizabeth is serious. "A dog is not a toy."

"Finally, something we can agree on."

The vet shrugs, then opens a drawer, searching for the right vaccines. It saves him a job he was not looking forward to. Then, he finally vaccinates the little dog that Elizabeth will not let go of all the time, stroking her trembling skin.

"And the tick and other medicine. It will not be cheap," he adds.

"I'd also like her chipped. Can you do that?"

"Yes, of course. Not a problem. If you want to pay the money."

"And one of these. And this. And some food." Elizabeth starts removing food and treats from the shelf.

"Of course. Start her off with as plain food as possible. She has lost a lot of weight and been through quite a drama. What name shall I put on the pet passport?"

"Patty," Godric chimes in. Elizabeth looks at him as he smiles. She wants to cry at the sight of this little dog. "Patty. You're coming on holiday!" Godric says excitedly.

Elizabeth cannot help a tear running down her cheek, but wipes it away quickly. She knows she is going to have to be strong to take care of this little life. Eventually, the vet smiles.

"I think Patty just got lucky."

*

After seeing the vets, Elizabeth, Godric and Patty drive back up the hill to Patigno. Elizabeth walks out onto the terrace to calm down. Godric pulls over a sun lounger for his nanna, who sits, then Patty climbs onto her lap and the two doze. Godric could tell that Elizabeth was stressed in the car. He wonders how they will cope with a dog on holiday. And, how is his nanna going to stay in France on the way home without him, as he cannot stay twenty-one days, what with exams looming? For now, he decides not to worry, instead taking action on those things he can control.

"You must not call again. She needs rest," Godric says after he's pulled out his phone and dialled Inspector Bob Abley.

"Godric. Don't hang up."

"I don't want to know. She's fragile. We're on holiday. Please, no more," Godric replies.

"Let me explain. We need your nanna's help to find the diamond. The Italian police will be–" Abley starts, but before he can finish, Godric cuts the call. He has his nanna and now

Patty. They just do not need anything to do with the police.

20 PISA

Later that morning, Elizabeth, Godric and Patty leave Patigno. Rescuing Patty made it feel like the best destination so far on their holiday, as well as it being a place with a complete absence of any sightings of a certain little red van. The sunshine pours in through the sunroof, and Elizabeth holds Patty's paw through the gap in the seats. Godric has made an exception to his journey of surprises and reveals they are headed to Pisa, which is just as well, as when they are stopped by the police at a toll to check their papers, Elizabeth is not completely clueless as to where they are going. Also, thank goodness Patty has her passport, as the police explain quite curtly that they would have had to confiscate the animal 'if that's what it is' as they look into the back seat of the car and wonder if dirty Patty isn't a giant ferret 'as they cannot allow vermin in the city'.

The whole thing puts a bit of a dampener on their morning and prompts a now completely preoccupied Elizabeth to make Godric drive directly to the pet pooch parlour on the outskirts of Pisa, even before they check into their hotel so that Patty can look like a dog and be safe from any other unwanted police interventions. They use the opportunity to buy some toys, a bed and a blanket. Once Patty has been cut and groomed – Elizabeth staring through the window and refusing to leave her sight for the two hours it takes, much to the annoyance of the groomer staff, who are placated by the handsome Godric, who makes them laugh in equal measure – they leave with one white dog, who smells of strawberry shampoo. The staff inform them they have a 'proper Italian Bolognese!', and a very pretty one at that. That the hair will grow longer, but they had to cut it short as it was matted. When Elizabeth asks if the dog is a puppy, she is told that Patty is most likely a young dog, yes. What a start she has had already. Lucky dog! They exclaim.

After the haircut ordeal, the three walk to the Leaning Tower of Pisa and sit down with ice creams. Godric tries to take the perfect photo and captures one of Patty seemingly licking the tower with her doggie ice cream. The sun bakes down on them, and tourists everywhere search for the shade of trees. They are relaxing when Godric's phone rings. Bob Abley again. He cuts the call.

"Was that Bob?"

"What?"

"You're not very good at hiding your screen." Elizabeth raises her eyebrows.

"He was just talking me into golf when I get back," Godric hangs his head covering.

"Has the house burnt down? Are the dogs okay?"

"Emily texted us yesterday. They're fine. You're on holiday."

Elizabeth pats her lap for Patty to jump up, and she soaks in the atmosphere of Pisa. There are couples wandering hand in hand, families, young children with lollipops. Everyone looks so happy. Everyone wants to be here. Some stare up at the tower. A lot take photographs. She looks at Godric, who is trying to take an arty panoramic photograph.

Elizabeth ponders what to do about her friend. If they call Bob back, then what? What does he want? She shuts her eyes for a while and opens them again. A nearby fountain scatters droplets onto the pavement in an adjoining garden. The only clouds in the sky are tiny and puffy. She looks down at Patty. This little creature who was in the bush a day ago is now curled up refusing to leave, clinging on to hope. She strokes Patty reassuringly. Patty opens her eyes and turns to try to kiss Elizabeth. Elizabeth feels the warm wet tongue on her chin and wonders if the little dog is thirsty again. So pours more water into her little bowl. But Patty just looks at Elizabeth with round scared eyes. Elizabeth sighs.

"I don't want to speak to Bob. Thank you for shielding the calls," she finally says to Godric. "I'm just–"

"Happy here." Godric smiles after finishing his nanna's sentence. Elizabeth nods. "Time for scones?" Godric smirks. They both know they won't find scones here, but she knows what he means, as they get up to find more treats.

As they wander, Godric and Elizabeth pass a shop selling women's clothing. Godric sees a very delicate and pretty green cardigan in the window.

"Back in a mo'," he says, nipping in. Elizabeth does not pay much attention, instead looking back at the Leaning Tower, which keeps appearing between buildings. "There," Godric says, coming out quick as a flash with the cardigan.

"What's this?"

Godric doesn't say anything, knowing she has given up Gerald's precious cardigan to keep Patty warm and how Patty has more or less destroyed it, sucking and chewing on the corners, not to mention the smell and mud. Godric indicates for Elizabeth to put it on.

"Have we got space in the car, especially after all of Patty's things? We could throw out a CD, maybe?" Elizabeth says, immediately falling in love with the chartreuse colour.

"We have room," Godric replies, ignoring his nanna's protests about his music choices. He watches her run her fingers over the tiny honeybee patterns hand stitched into the cuffs and collar that appear here and there, raised up as if they could take off, and notices how her face beams like a child. How this strong, fierce and formidable woman is transformed into someone so young and innocent in front of his eyes. An immediate desire to protect her wells up in his chest. Just a green cardigan. Such a fragile heart.

"I don't think I'm ever going to take it off. Even in the heat."

They both feel the heat of the sun on the pavements. Godric puts one arm around his Bunny, the other holding Patty's lead.

*

After checking into their hotel and Elizabeth taking an afternoon nap while Godric laughs at yet more Italian TV game shows, they wander out for supper. The day's heat is still hanging heavy, but rain showers have gathered and finally release their load. The three get caught, so rush to the first restaurant they can find on the stretch by the Tower of Pisa.

Under parasols and somewhat unwanted heat lamps, they order food. Most of the tourists have left, driven away by the rain. They are the only ones sitting outside. Patty sits on Elizabeth's lap. Just for a moment, Elizabeth feels okay. Perhaps the freshness of the air making her wake up to what surrounds her, how far they are from home, how completely at ease they all are, how it all fits together.

Time ticks by as the rain continues to patter on the canvas above their heads. Godric tells Elizabeth countless jokes until she cannot stop herself from laughing. Elizabeth orders Patty her own dish of chicken and rice. After they finish eating, the rain stops and they are able to take a stroll around nearby streets. Patty smelling all the new fresh smells. Godric and Elizabeth looking at some of the grand houses and wondering who chooses to live two streets away from one of the most visited towers in the world. It is only when they return to the hotel a couple of hours later and the concierge follows them to the lift, is the holiday spell abruptly interrupted.

"Excuse me, madam, a Commissarrio from Florence," he looks down at his scribbled note. "Commissario Lorenzo Bianchi is trying to contact you and has asked for you to call him immediately on this telephone number."

"Who? Wait, what?" Godric asks, mildly concerned about the tone of the receptionist's voice, which sounds trembly.

"What's happened? Does he say? Is

everyone okay?" Elizabeth asks, grabbing the note from the concierge's hand. She looks at it. Three missed calls. She can see the times.

"I think it's important. I have a telephone back at reception. Would you like to borrow it?" The man in an ill-fitting black suit asks, beckoning her back and leaving her little choice.

"You go up. I'll catch you in a minute," Elizabeth instructs Godric, passing him Patty who she's been carrying for the past two blocks.

"Not bloody likely." Godric frowns, unsure about all this.

They both wander back to the telephone and the concierge dials the number for Elizabeth.

"Can you put it on speaker, please," she asks. "I want my grandson to hear." Elizabeth takes a deep breath and Godric holds her hand, knowing that his nanna is concerned this person will want to take Patty away. The phone rings and a man who sounds like he is eating picks up on the other end. The concierge babbles in Italian and says, "Professor Green."

"We can speak Italian," Godric shakes his head, understanding every word.

"Hello, Professor."

"Hello," Elizabeth replies.

"Sorry to interrupt your holiday. Are you having a lovely time in Pisa? It is so beautiful, no?" The Commissario asks.

"Are you sorry?"

"Right, yes. Well. Your name has been given to me by a police Inspector in the UK as someone who may have some expertise on a delicate matter. An Inspector Burb Abley," The Commissarrio pronounces the name Bob as 'Burb'.

"Yes?"

"You are renowned for being an expert in solving impossible cases, I hear."

"And?"

"You are a woman of few words, I like that," the Commissarrio chuckles. There is a long pause.

"Why are you calling me?" Elizabeth sounds a little frustrated. "We were stopped outside Pisa for our papers by the police. They kept us there for a good twenty minutes. They let us go, but without any explanation." She shuts her eyes.

"Your colleague, Inspector Abley. He suggested you might be able to help us."

"Please, just spit it out, would you? You've said that already."

"Yes, yes. He said you are the best expert he knows on poison."

Elizabeth looks at Godric in disbelief and he shakes his head and rolls his eyes.

"What is this? Why is he telling you about me? Make your point."

"Have you been watching the news while you are in our country?" The Commissario munches whatever food he is eating, sounding very relaxed for someone with such high stakes with which to contend.

"We hear enough ruddy news when we are back in England," Godric chimes in.

"Why we should want to up our threshold while here on things we can do even less about goodness knows," Elizabeth adds to Godric's comments, irked that Inspector Abley has sprung whatever this may be on her.

"Well, how do you say, to cut a story short, a diamond thief has stolen a very valuable stone here. One of the most valuable ever stolen in Italy."

"We did see that a diamond had been stolen, yes," Godric replies. "But that's your funeral, not ours."

"It turns out the thief is an anthropologist from your country. From the United Kingdom."

"How unfortunate. But, still."

"Yes, yes. He was from Cambridge, England. He's dead."

Elizabeth does not want to give this man any more energy than she absolutely has to, so remains quiet. After a moment of silence, and the concierge's eyes widening even further due to the shock of being party to this intelligence, the Commissario continues. "He's dead, and we don't have the diamond, and it looks like he has been poisoned."

"Poisoned?" Godric asks, looking at the

concierge, who is entirely gripped by the news.

"Yes, so if we find who has poisoned him, then we find the diamond. It's simple," they can hear the Commissario stuff more food into his mouth.

"If it is so simple, as you say, then I wish you all the luck. Now, if you will excuse me, I've had a very long day and am tired. Good day to you, Sir." And Elizabeth hangs up.

"No one hangs up on a Commissario," the concierge says under his breath. "On the Commissario from Florence. in the biggest case in–"

"Are you coming?" Elizabeth interrupts the concierge to speak to Godric, then heads for the lift. "My feet are aching." Then she shouts back to the concierge. "No calls and no visits. We are not to be disturbed."

The concierge has not moved, his eyes still wide.

When Elizabeth and Godric are in their room, Elizabeth fills the dog water bowl for Patty and then falls back on her bed to relax.

"Now we know why Bob Abley was calling me," Godric says.

"I don't want to know," Elizabeth replies, covering her eyes with her arms and sighing.

"Did he say one of the most expensive diamonds ever stolen?" Godric asks.

"Yes, I believe so," Elizabeth replies from under her arms.

Godric looks at his mobile and searches the news. He sees a photograph of the diamond they saw on the television the other night. "Whoah, it looks bigger here!" Then sees Elizabeth open her eyes so shows her the photograph. "Burb is out of order, though. Passing on your deets."

"Oh, we know he's been strong armed." Elizabeth tries not to think about this prospect but cannot help herself. Her heart sinks. She can imagine how it has gone down in Cambridge. A local man has stolen something from Florence. The Italian police are leaning on the Cambridge force to share any details on him. They are probably coming up short, so Superintendent Raynott thinks why not give them her? Bob must be under pressure.

"Call Bob," she suggests.

"What? You said you didn't want anything to do with it?"

"I don't, but I need the facts."

"Is this the time to break the surprise again and tell you I've booked us a week in Florence?" Godric says sheepishly, then defends his decision. "How was I supposed to know that you'd be asked to find a diamond thief in Florence." Godric strokes Elizabeth's arm. He cannot cancel now as he booked a hotel right under the Dome and called them already to check if dogs were allowed. "It's the highlight of the trip."

"Goddy, that sounds wonderful," Elizabeth leans across to give Godric a hug, quite moved by his generosity and thoughtfulness. "We're definitely doing that. Your grandpa would be so happy." Then she leans back and explains. "I want to know what we're walking into."

"It's late."

"He's an hour behind."

The phone rings, and they both hear Inspector Bob Abley's voice.

"Godric, thank god! I've been trying to reach you. How are you? I hope you are having a lovely holiday?"

"You're on speakerphone, Burb," Godric replies. Both Godric and Elizabeth wait for Inspector Bob Abley to speak first. He has some explaining to do, so there is an awkward silence.

"Hello, Elizabeth."

"Hello."

There is more silence.

"Are you having a lovely holiday?" Inspector Bob Abley asks trepidatiously.

"We were, until the police accosted us at a toll, and then a friend of yours, a Commissario here interrupted our nightcap."

There is more silence. Elizabeth can picture Bob rubbing his forehead with guilt. As he should!

"Did they tell you about Peter Jones? He was caught on CCTV stealing a six million euro diamond and was then poisoned. He's dead. They don't know with what," Bob Abley explains.

"Why are you giving them my details? You're not suggesting the Commissario is winging it? Surely they don't need any help?" Elizabeth asks.

"They only have your name. I didn't give it to them. Superintendent Raynott–"

"Can you stop them, please!" Godric says crossly.

"Stop them? I–" Bob sounds confused.

"Yes, tell them to leave us alone. We're on hol-i-day," Godric interrupts, emphasising each syllable of the word holiday to the Inspector.

"Godric is right, Bob. I'm here with my grandson," Elizabeth grabs Godric's phone and tries to cut the call. There is some fumbling. "How the hell do you cut this call?" She gives it back to Godric to cut.

"Elizabeth–"

Godric cuts the call and Inspector Abley off mid-sentence, confused. Did his nanna not just say she wanted to find out the facts? Why hang up now? Godric decides not to throw more rocks into the pond, instead picks up the phone in the room and orders 'anything vegan on the pudding menu. Yes, two of everything'. Elizabeth is too tired to do anything but stroke Patty and wonder whether this is the end of their holiday.

21 FLORENCE

The next day and the journey from Pisa to Florence is very pleasant. Elizabeth and Godric both had surprisingly good sleeps and hearty breakfasts. Everything has been quiet. No police checks, no police calls, no mobile phone calls. Godric even starts making jokes again, until finally.

"Knock knock."

"Who's there." Elizabeth asks.

"Rough."

"Rough who"

"It's your dog."

Elizabeth tells Godric to stop.

Driving into Florence proves harder than Pisa as, rather like Cambridge, the city entirely discourages the combustion engine altogether. Their classic car with its converted electric engine does not wash, so Godric suggests they park and catch the tram instead. And, as they sit on the crammed tram heading into Florence, locals stare at Patty as she rests on Elizabeth's lap looking back suspiciously at all of them who might try to take her from her new family.

"We're staying in such a lovely location," Godric reassures Elizabeth, but they are both already nervous about heading right into the Commissario's patch and where this diamond was stolen. "I couldn't change the dates. I tried," Godric adds knowing that perhaps if they'd gone to Rome or San Marino they would have been further from the eye of the storm.

Worries dissipate when they step off the tram and find their hotel not a hundred yards from the magnificent Duomo on the Santa Maria del Fiore Cathedral. Even better, when they open the hotel apartment balcony the view not only of the Duomo but the bustling streets below, with so many people completely uninterested in diamonds or anything other than shoe shopping or eating ice cream, transports them into holiday mode again. A throng of holidaymakers pack the streets. Artists with their paintings and memorabilia of the Duomo standing on every corner, hoping for sales.

Elizabeth walks into the kitchen and explores the ridiculously lavish rooms Godric has booked.

"How long are we staying here exactly?" She asks.

"Enough to forget time and what day it is. For a while, at least."

Patty jumps up on Godric's bed and starts to dig at the pillows, so Godric jumps up on the bed and starts to bounce, making Patty fly up into the air, then back down again, where she returns to digging, then the cycle continues until there is a knock at the door.

"Ah, our elevenses. They have quite a selection of dairy-free cakes here," Godric explains as he opens the door to find a slender man still wearing his sunglasses inside, which are surrounded by a mass of curly black hair and black beard.

"Good day to you, Godric? Ah, Professor Green. So lovely to finally make your acquaintance, no?"

"Hello?" Godric says, taken aback by a stranger knowing their names. Is he from the hotel?

"We ordered brunch?" Godric asks him.

"We all make good decisions sometimes," the man looks behind him to see if brunch is arriving, quite hungry himself. "Commissario Lorenzo Bianchi. We spoke yesterday on the phone. Just call me Lorenzo. No problemo."

"Excuse me?" Elizabeth, eyes widen, "This must be breaching some kind of international harassment law. We have, to my knowledge, not broken any law nor made any indication of where we might be travelling."

"Professor Green. I'm sorry. I did not mean to give you a surprise. But I really do need to speak with you." The Commissario walks further into the room.

"I cannot help you," Elizabeth replies. "You're scaring my dog."

"Aww, who is this little cutie? A Bolognese. I have two of these," Lorenzo picks up Patty, who proceeds to lick him. He takes a dried piece of liver biscuit out of his pocket, and Patty scoffs it down.

"What was that?" Elizabeth asks, perturbed he is feeding her dog without permission.

"I hold many weapons about my person, Professor Green. And one of them is my 'no biting' weapon." Then he looks at Patty, "But you're so beautiful. You're not snappy. Is that what you say? Snappy?" He then kisses Patty. This makes Elizabeth soften towards him a little, although she does wonder if Bob told him that would be how to win her over, so remains on her guard. "Let me show you the best place in Florence to have breakfast," he says.

"We have had breakfast and are waiting for brunch." Godric replies.

"So, have a second breakfast. You're on holiday?" Lorenzo looks warmly at Godric.

"We're vegans," Godric replies proudly, protecting his nanna.

"They can do that. What is that, no egg, no dairy? Yes, yes. Not a problem. We're not in the dark ages. Come. Let's eat. You're in Italy. It's

always time to eat. Fantastico!"
Elizabeth and Godric look at each other, acknowledging that perhaps the best thing for this man to go away is to eat with him and make it plain.

"If it makes you leave us alone then we'll come and see this so called best place to eat in Florence. Then, we are here to enjoy ourselves. Alone," Elizabeth replies firmly.

"I guess I will let reception know to hold our brunch?" Godric says to Elizabeth

"Get them to put it in the fridge. Don't cancel. Gino makes the most wonderful cherry crostata. Have you ordered it?" Lorenzo kisses his lips. "They always run out here. Get them while you can."

Elizabeth and Godric look blankly. Lorenzo grabs the phone in the room and speaks quickly in Italian to the reception. While they can speak Italian, they cannot understand his bullet speed order. They hear 'fridgo' and 'crostata', and are quite taken aback that he is already organising everything. "Ci, ci. Ciao."

Godric says quietly to Elizabeth, "If you say Ciao to say both hello and goodbye, isn't it hard to ever end a conversation? As, you might be saying goodbye on a call, but someone thinks you are saying hello again, and then the whole conversation has to repeat again? Ciao, how are you? Yada, yada."

"Goddy, stop."

*

Out on the pavement, it is immediately apparent that everyone knows the Commissario. As he leads them to this supposedly fantastic place to eat, people constantly tip their hats or nod hellos. Some even stop to have a chat. Elizabeth and Godric cannot help but notice how warm and kind he is with his responses. Soon the Commissario is taking them down a tight alley entirely off the tourist grid, with washing strung out from one side to the other above their heads, Vespas and old beaten-up cars parked right up against front doors. The Commissario stops.

"Momento." And he unlocks his forty-year-old Fiat 600T van and pulls out his battered briefcase. "I forgot it this morning," he says, holding it up. "Was in a rush. But it's all in here." He pats his briefcase and winks, then keeps walking down the alley with no doubt that they will follow.

Eventually they enter a piazza, far off the beaten track and approach a café. Flower tubs and small olive trees in pots huddled around the entrance. A pastel awning hangs over four or five tables, and all the tables are full, bar one. This is a local café, full of Florentines. The Commissario is warmly greeted and they are led to the remaining table set out on the pavement in the morning sunshine.

Elizabeth and Godric notice the 'reserved' sign on the table. The Commissario sits, then starts the conversation by shaking his head and complaining to the café proprietor about his Questore, the local head of police, who, as an aside he explains to Elizabeth and Godric, manages the police in accordance with the Prefetto, the principle of government. He looks at the menu and orders for everyone, including a treat for Patty. He continues speaking very quickly in Italian – which Godric understands, and Elizabeth tries – then starts to speak in English once again.

"He cannot find me here, so I'm safe," the Commissario chuckles to himself, then touches his nose while looking at Elizabeth.

"We know someone in the same boat," she replies, thinking of a certain Inspector and Superintendent she knows. "Is this vegan?" Elizabeth asks as the café owner, who has walked out with a tray of savoury pastries, together with some warm baby new potatoes and fine beans in a garlic sauce.

"Ci, no meat, no dairy," the café owner replies, adding, "but your dog, carnivore, no?"

"Yes, all good," Elizabeth replies.

"Don't worry, I was listening, Professor," the Commissario reassures her. He bites into a pastry, then takes off his sunglasses. Elizabeth looks at his overly long eyelashes and wonders if they are made from the legs of tiny spiders. His chocolate brown eyes stare at her thoughtfully for a moment. “So, you see, I have this problem. I’m temporarily hiding from my Questore because he wants my head on a platter as I haven’t yet found the diamond.” Then he pauses, waiting for a reaction from Elizabeth.

“Yes, I can see you have your hands full,” Godric replies, wondering how the Commissario has time for a long brunch.

“You should try this,” the Commissario puts his sunglasses back on, then hands Godric a small side dish containing pastries full of spinach and pine nuts. “This sauce is the best in all of Tuscany. Dip it, dip it, go on, dip it.” The Commissario points for Godric to dip a pastry into a small bowl of mint green dip, then he shoves his own large fork into his mouth and chews on some ravioli while speaking. “Peter James was very likely poisoned. If we find out who poisoned him, then we find the diamond. Until then, I have to watch my head.”

“And we, meanwhile, need to continue our holiday. So, while this food looks good, and we might come back here before we leave if we can ever find it again.” Elizabeth thinks of all the narrow alleys the Commissario took them down before they emerged into this picturesque square, “We have said we cannot help you.”

"Professor Green," Commissario again removes his sunglasses and stops chewing. He looks intensely at Elizabeth, "If Peter James was murdered, then a killer is out there. We are doing everything we can, but they could strike again. Someone might die. Your Cambridge thief might be causing a spate of deaths in our country, and–"

"Don't try to guilt trip my nanna," Godric raises his voice, "you should do your job. And don't blame one rotten apple. I'll have you know Cambridge has very low crime statistics," then Godric thinks of all the murders recently, "most of the time."

"We are, believe me. We have a team back at the office doing all they can." The Commissario pauses and watches Godric eat. "That's good sauce, isn't it?"

"Yes!" Godric is munching the food dipped in the green sauce. "Is that lime? And saffron?"

"Yes, yes, it is." Then the Commisario looks back at Elizabeth. "Please. I'm just asking you to meet once with our pathologist. That's all. Just see what you think." Commissario Lorenzo Bianchi pulls a file from his briefcase, puts it on the table, then pushes it across to Elizabeth. "There are witnesses to show that Mr Jones was staggering when he arrived in San Gimignano. We think he still had the diamond in his possession before he died."

"No CCTV?"

"It had been damaged. Deliberately most probably."

"Just because someone's staggering, doesn't mean they've been poisoned. He could have been drunk and giddy at the prospect of what to spend all that money on from stealing such an expensive diamond. All the peace and quiet that was to come," Godric replies.

"Perhaps he was, but my pathologist says his cells were dying."

"Really?" Elizabeth's ears prick up for the first time. "How so?"

"I'm not an expert. It's all in there. Please, I'd be so grateful for your help."

Elizabeth looks at Godric and then at a wiry man approaching. He is wearing a leather jacket and aviator sunglasses and has thick black hair.

"Bonjourno."

"Angelou. Come and meet Professor Green," the Commissario introduces his Sergeant. "Sergeant Angelou Rossi always knows where to find me."

"I just have to smell the best pasta being cooked, and there you are," Sergeant Rossi looks at his boss through his mirrored shades. Then the Sergeant leans in to kiss Elizabeth twice, once on each cheek, before she can stop him. Then he moves to shake Godric's hand, but Godric stands to kiss the Sergeant on the cheeks, and an awkward handshake happens instead. Sergeant Angelou Rossi turns to Elizabeth again. "You know, Lorenzo, he always eats where I cannot park, so I'm always late, and he's always eaten the best dishes by the time I arrive."

"Your fault for driving such loud beasts of the road." His Commissario replies.

"My Ferrari purrs. She's not a beast but a thing of beauty." The Sergeant corrects his Commissario. "I'm just stating pure fact." Then the Sergeant asks Elizabeth. "You're going to help us find out who killed Peter Jones? Peter was an academic studying fieldwork in Siena. You're also an academic. He was an anthropologist. You are a botanist. He was studying olives. That's botany. You had so much in common."

"I was coming to that, Angelou!" The Commissario says, irritated, chewing on another mouthful of pasta.

"You snooze, you lose," Angelou replies, sticking out his chin at the Commissario, then looks back at Elizabeth, waiting for her response.

*

Elizabeth and Godric finish their brunch then leave the square, where the Commissario and Sergeant remain seated in the sun. They wander into the Piazza della Signoria, stopping to look at the replica Statue of David. Elizabeth then wanders towards the Fountain of Neptune in front of the Palazzo Vecchio. She remembers this fountain from when she visited Florence with Gerald many years ago. It has been renovated. It glistens, and the water gushes more violently than she remembers.

She stood in the same spot all those years ago. She looks at the horses and wonders what Gerald would say if he were here. But she cannot hear him. He is fading backwards, behind her. Shadowy. She is cross with herself and tries hard to remember something. His laugh, his smile. She grabs hold of the memory, closes her eyes, then opens them again. Somehow the horse statues seem colder. She feels distraught that Gerald is not here. Angry at that Commissario for invading their holiday, their time, time to think, not think, just to be. Guilt tripping her into helping. The more emotional she feels, the more Gerald fades from her mind.

Elizabeth looks up at the blue sky. Even though still early April, it is very warm here in Florence in the sun. Her cheeks are burning a little after sitting with the policeman in the café. Godric touches her shoulder.

"He wanted me to come back," Elizabeth explains, coming out of her thoughts and returning to the present with Godric. "I told him I liked the horses. When we came here before. But he wondered whether they looked unhappy, and decided they were raging. He said we should return one day so I could rescue them. How do I rescue statues?"

Godric cannot bear to see his nanna like this.

"Shall we go and rest for a while? Come back out this afternoon?"

"Yes," Elizabeth stares at the horses.

"Hey, we still have weeks left away. This little blip is nothing. You have a new friend," Godric picks up Patty, whose little legs look tired. "I think I need to find one of those baby papooses for dogs so that I can carry her across my stomach."

"I don't think she'd like that."

"We need to find something with all the walking we'll be doing."

"She likes the way you are holding her now."

"Yes, but my muscles are getting tired," Godric smiles at Patty.

"Not as tired as Patty's," Elizabeth kisses Patty as they enter the lift to their apartment.

Opening their apartment door, they see a handwritten note stuffed underneath. It does not look like something the hotel would write as it is a little scuffed and the handwriting poor. She opens it and reads it aloud for the benefit of Godric.

'Dear Professor Green. Please forgive me,

but Commissario Lorenzo Bianchi told me you were staying here. I am Giuseppe Esposito. I have been in touch with the Commissario many times to get to the bottom of my friend's death, Peter Jones. He is my best friend, and now he is no longer, and I want answers, and the Italian police don't have any. I managed – by way of bribing with a large tiramisu - the Commissario to tell me that he was going to be asking you for help and that you are from the Cambridge police. I am from Cambridge, or Ely, to be precise. Please, will you meet me this afternoon at the Pop Café? I would really like to speak with you. It is so good to know you are here as I fear for my life. I heard Peter was poisoned, but the police won't tell me anything. I am very fearful that I will be next. Please, help me. I hope to see you soon. I will wait all afternoon. Giuseppe.'

"Can't people just leave us alone?" Godric takes Patty's lead off and goes into the kitchen to fill her bowl with water.

"It's rather dramatic, isn't it? But, in the circumstances. What kind of poison stumps a pathology lab? Cell death, it's true, can be caused by so many different poisons. But, still."

"You're curious?" Godric looks at his nanna.

"Why can't they find the poison? I mean, this is Florence, not some small provincial town. They must have people with far more experience than I."

"You're interested." Godric does not know if this will be good or bad for his nanna. He has not seen this glint in her eye since she solved the Valentine's Day murders. She has been a ghost of herself for so long. But there it is, that piercing look. He has been trying to shield her from this because he wanted to make sure she got some rest. "But, if you think taking a look will, well."

"Make me better?"

"No. I don't mean that. You just look–"

"I know, and I don't like it."

"Well, then throw this in the bin. Why don't we rest for a while, then stroll around some of Florence's finest gardens this evening before supper?"

"Where is this *Pop Café*?" She asks. Godric looks up the location on his mobile and shows his nanna.

"It's in the same direction as most of the greenery?" Elizabeth replies. Godric's heart sinks for his nanna as he knows this is her addiction she cannot shake, and he knows she is not yet better.

"I can think of a thousand things I'd rather do."

"I'll go. You stay."

"No, I'll come."
"Stay."
"Okay, I'll stay with you."

22 A MAN CONVINCED HE'S GOING TO DIE

A few hours later, Godric and Elizabeth have stepped back out onto Florence's streets, still heaving with tourists. It seems everyone is either walking off their afternoon ice creams or just stepped off a tour bus on Via dei Calzaiuoli to see an evening performance somewhere or other. But as they move across the Ponto Vecchio Bridge and head towards the Piazza Santo Spirito, Godric wavers, worried about his nanna meeting this stranger.

"D'you think this man is who he says he is?" Godric asks.

"I don't know. Thank you for coming with me. I just have to find out if he's from Ely and why he wants to meet me."

They enter the piazza, and people thin out significantly. A local plays ball with his dog, and a couple sit on a garden step eating a sandwich. Elizabeth and Godric find the café and see a rotund man waving at them. Sweaty, perhaps from sitting in the direct afternoon sun. He stands up, spilling his cola all over his chips.

"Bongiorno," Giuseppe extends a hand. "Thank you for coming."

"You said your life was in danger?" Elizabeth asks, not taking his hand, instead looking with disdain at the massive plate of burger and chips this man is about to consume and noticing the three doughnuts on a side plate.

"I've been going out of my mind." He wipes the cola off the table with his hand and then brushes his wet fingers through his hair. "But, discovering you were here, I just had to talk to you." He beckons them to sit and clicks his fingers for the waiter, who comes over, despite the rudeness.

"Might you have peppermint tea?" Elizabeth asks.

"Ci, of course."

"Beer, please?" Godric says quietly, still wondering what to make of this man.

"Large or small?" the waiter asks.

"Large," Godric replies, "and some of those, please." He looks enviously at the chips. Elizabeth grabs the waiter's attention and declines all chips for Godric and herself.

"We are not staying. We'll go elsewhere for supper. We haven't come here to eat chips with

Mr Esposito," Elizabeth explains quietly.

"Here, what is mine is yours," Giuseppe nudges his chips closer to Godric, hearing Elizabeth's whisper. "Call me Giuseppe, please I'm English. My mother was Italian, like Peter's. We have–" Giuseppe corrects himself. "We had so much in common. I cannot believe he's gone."

The three of them pause their conversation. Guiseppe, seemingly thinking about Peter. Elizabeth and Godric wondering what this man expects them to do about it, Godric a little more uncertain about how safe this whole thing is. Patty spots a cat under the next table. She pulls on the lead as the cat's eyes narrow. There is no question that this bruiser of a white feline, well fed and unimpressed, lives at the café or nearby and takes advantage of any dropped delicacies. The staring contest continues until the pussy hisses, showing his fangs. Patty decides any possible altercation is not worth it, especially when Godric takes one of Giuseppe's chips and gives it to her to scoff.

"Why do you say you are in danger? And why d'you think we can help?" Elizabeth asks, getting to the point.

"I'm being followed. I know it. Whoever is after the diamond, maybe they think I have it? I don't. I don't know anything about the diamond being stolen."

"So, your friend who died really was tied

up in this jewel theft?"

"I don't know. I couldn't believe it. I read it in the papers yesterday. The CCTV from the art gallery where it was being exhibited. It's unfathomable. It is so not like Peter. I mean, he didn't steal anything?"

"And you do?" Godric asks asks.

"What? You know the art gallery is not far from where you're staying. You should have a look. He was an academic studying the history of olive groves in Tuscany. And I'm supposed to believe he was a cleaner?"

"You know a lot about him," Elizabeth comments.

"He was my best friend, Professor Green." Giuseppe stuffs a handful of chips into his mouth, having swished them around in the bowl first with his fingers to gain purchase. Then he offers the bowl again to Godric.

"It's okay," Godric replies, a little grossed out.

"Are you a thief?" Elizabeth repeats her question.

"You shoot from the hip." Giuseppe stares at Elizabeth, wondering if he was wise to ask for her help. "Look, if I see a ten euro note on the floor, I'm not going to hand it into lost property. Come on. But, Peter, he would. He was so honest. It's all unreal. I mean, this is a crazy big diamond."

"What can you tell us about Peter?"

Elizabeth asks.

"Why? I'm the one in danger here." Giuseppe crams in a large mouthful of burger, the ketchup dribbling down his chin. "I'm alive. He's dead as a dodo. There's nothing you can do for him now. I'm the vulnerable one."

Elizabeth looks at the huge weight of Giuseppe, his thick neck and bulging eyes. Heart disease is going to get this man, she thinks, before any murderer.

"We're on holiday, Mr Esposito. If you're not going to answer my Bunny's questions, then perhaps we should go. Nanna?"

"Yes, I think that might be a good idea." Elizabeth and Godric make to stand up.

"Alright, alright. Sit down. Please. I'll tell you about Peter. But then, please, you need to help me."

"We'll see," Elizabeth replies. The waiter brings Elizabeth her peppermint tea and Godric his beer, so they decide to stay for those at least.

"His mother was Italian, like mine." Giuseppe glugs some cola, realising he is not in the presence of pushovers. "I met him in Cambridge. He gave a lecture on Italy. I was going to live here, so after the lecture I went up to him and we got talking. Then we went for a beer. And when he came out to do his fieldwork, I got back in touch. We'd go for meals, for drinks. That sort of thing.

Okay? I mean, I don't know his inside leg measurement, but I know, knew him pretty well. He lives not far from here. Lived. Or, his wife does. In his mother's old apartment. His mother passed, and they were using it as a holiday home, but then moved in when they came over, you know, to study anthropology and olives."

"You say Peter was an anthropologist? Why do you think he stole a diamond?"

"I told the police it was murder, not suicide. It was me who said Peter must have been poisoned. They weren't sure at the start."

"What do you mean? They weren't sure?"

"They were going to announce a suicide until I kept on at them. I threatened to tell the press he'd been murdered." Giuseppe clicks his fingers at the waiter.

"Threatening the police. An interesting choice," Godric looks at his nanna, his eyes wide.

"I think they wanted to close the case. Or, that part of it. They need to find the diamond, but what happened to Peter? I mean, getting chucked off a tower. It will be me next. I know it."

"Wait, what?" Elizabeth looks at Giuseppe. "Chucked off a tower?"

"Yes, the suicide. Only I think he was pushed."

"Wasn't Peter Jones, as you say, your

friend, poisoned?" Godric asks.

"He was, but then he was pushed off a tower in San Gimignano. It's not on the news. I only know because I heard Sergeant Rossi talking about it. They all go to the bar across the street from their station. I've been going in there, well, to pick up what I can about Peter. Until they kicked me out, that is. Barring me for harassment. I mean, my friend has been murdered, and I'm next! I'm the one being harassed! Hello."

Elizabeth looks at this man and thinks perhaps he is not telling the truth. "Do you have the diamond?" She asks.

"You think I'd be badgering the police to find Peter's killer if I stole the diamond?"

"You say you are from Ely?" Godric asks.

"He was the reason I made my big move over here. I read his book, 'An Englishman in the Chianti Fields'. D'you know it? Now he's gone, I think I'll go home."

Godric looks at this fat short bald and sweaty man in a stained shirt and thinks he might give Chianti a swerve for a few days.

"Might you have a copy I can borrow?" Elizabeth asks.

"I do, but my copy is in my home in England. But I'm sure Mia will be able to help. She'll have one."

"Mia?"

"Peter's wife?" Giuseppe looks at Elizabeth

and frowns. "And you're a detective?"

"I'm not a detective. And I'm on holiday." Elizabeth drinks her tea and looks at Godric. She has had more than enough of this odious man.

"They were so in love," Giuseppe says while chewing his burger.

"So, it's likely she knew about the theft?" Godric asks.

"I doubt it, but who knows? Who knows anything."

Elizabeth shakes her head. Without explanation, Elizabeth gets up. Godric pays their bill. Elizabeth gives Giuseppe the hardest stare. "I just need to be with my grandson. If you need to talk about this, don't come to me. Speak with the Commissario. Do you understand?" She gives Giuseppe a hard stare to make it clear she wants nothing to do with him. Giuseppe, at first looks confused but then shrugs.

"But you're involved now. You're here," he replies.

"I'm not here. I'm a ghost about to disappear and have a proper Italian supper."

Elizabeth turns and heads for the piazza gardens with Godric and does not look back. Looking forward to a relaxing evening which does not include diamonds or death.

23 FIVE THINGS YOU CAN SEE

The following morning, Professor Elizabeth Green leaves Godric sleeping and takes Patty out for a constitutional. She decides to walk back to the fountain with the four horses outside the Palazzo Vecchio, wanting to throw in a penny for Gerald. Only once standing there, out the corner of her eye, she notices the red Renault 4.

Reims, Beaune, Ivrea, is there nowhere this van is not? She picks up Patty and runs across the piazza to see if she can catch it in time before it turns the corner. She just makes it to the edge of the piazza, only for it to disappear again. But there is no mistake, the writing on the side, the man's face in the driving seat. Elizabeth feels unnerved and a little queasy. She cannot shake a constant feeling of things feeling off kilter.

Suddenly, the world begins to spin. She puts Patty on the ground and leans against a window, but she can feel herself going. She fumbles for her purse and pulls out a little note from her best friend, Emily. The little piece of paper is folded and shoddy, but the handwriting is familiar and feels like home to Elizabeth right now as she struggles with her breathing and the dizziness envelopes her like a black cloud. Elizabeth reads it out loud, her breath panting and exaggerated, 'Tell me five things you can see', it reads. Elizabeth looks around. She can see a man on a bicycle, stopped, talking to another man holding a dog. They are laughing. She can see steam coming out of a coffee shop doorway. An older woman, hunched, carrying shopping bags that look far too heavy. That's three. She frantically looks for two more. Elizabeth feels faint and clammy. Two more. Her eyes dart about. She can see a discarded disposable coffee cup near a drain. Look up. The blue sky. Elizabeth looks again at Emily's note from her wallet. 'Tell me four things you can touch'. Elizabeth feels herself sliding down the window. She can touch the ground, that is for sure. She can touch Patty. Patty kisses and licks her face. Patty. Elizabeth can touch her fur. Four things. Four things. She can touch her green cardigan Godric gave her. Yes, the bees on it. Embroidered. She can touch the bees. She can feel the bees. Elizabeth looks for a fourth thing to touch. She can touch the lead. It is a soft velvety feel and leads her eyes back to Patty. She sits with Patty on the pavement. A tear falls down Elizabeth's face. Elizabeth holds the little note her friend gave her, her hand trembling. 'Tell me three things you can hear'. Elizabeth tells Patty she can hear her panting. Hear a small car bumping over the cobbles. Two things. One more. Her heart beating fast in her ears. Elizabeth catches her breath and is finally able to take in a deeper breath. She looks again at the little piece of paper. 'Tell me two things you can smell', the note reads. Elizabeth shuts her eyes. She can smell the dust on the pavement. She puts her face in Patty's hair. She can smell that. Elizabeth takes a deep breath. 'Tell me one thing you love'. She thinks how much she loves her best friend for writing this note to help her control her panic attacks. Elizabeth sits on the pavement for a while with Patty before a young man stops to ask if she is okay. She nods and is ready to accept his helping hand to get back onto her feet. She makes an excuse, and walks back to the hotel apartment. In her pocket, she can feel the penny she was supposed to throw into the fountain for Gerald. Gerald won't leave her. Elizabeth enjoys the pain she feels, as the pain makes him real and close.

*

When Elizabeth arrives back at the hotel, Godric is still fast asleep in bed. Patty jumps up and lays so close to his face giving him breathy carbon dioxide kisses that Elizabeth wonders if they will both pass out. But after seeing Godric move his face in his sleep, she heads for the police station. Something draws her to the police pathology unit. The whole thing is putting her on edge. She has not spoken to Inspector Bob Abley today, as she does not feel she has fully forgiven him for this. She aims to return to make the most of the day with Godric before he even opens his eyes. Just one tiny peek at why they seem unable to solve it themselves, she tells herself, that's all, to put this to rest.

When Elizabeth arrives, they must have been expecting her as the Commissario is standing on the step of the station and welcomes her in. Elizabeth is rushed to the pathology lab, where she is introduced to an older man with bushy white eyebrows, wispy hair and wearing a white coat. Roberto. He greets her gruffly and clearly does not want her help but shares data that he has run and finally allows her to look at the blood results.

Left to her own devices for an hour, Elizabeth sees that this pathologist has been very thorough. She grows more intrigued. What did kill Peter? Yes, his body has impact trauma from the fall, but the bloods clearly show he was already dying. They have looked for the obvious poisons too. Prescription drugs, illegal drugs, insect bites. Damn, Elizabeth thinks. She was hoping this might be easy and quick. Frustrated, she leaves with more questions than answers. She simply shakes her head at the Commissario, who is still on the steps and now eating a pastry.

"See you again tomorrow," he replies. "If you have any needs for your holiday, let me know."

Elizabeth would like to be left alone, to be on top of a hill with a view of the Tuscan valley, under the sunshine, watching the birds fly in a blue sky. She knows the Commissario has other things in mind for her now.

24 SAN GIMIGNANO

"I don't know why you went?" Godric asks, as they trundle along in the old Fiat 500 out of Florence and towards San Gimignano, playing his favourite music again.

"I just want them to leave us alone. I thought it would help. Do we really need this on?" Elizabeth tries to turn the CD off.

"Help them leave us alone? By you helping them?" and "Yes, hands off. Me drive, me choose." Godric keeps his fingers over the CD players so his nanna cannot change the music.

"I found nothing. I was more than useless." Elizabeth sighs. "The Commissario gave us the pass to park the car in the city." They both look at the police 'access-all-areas' car pass in Elizabeth's hands which she has just pulled from her pocket.

"We can park anywhere we like in Tuscany?" Godric is thrilled!

"And I only have to spend a few more hours looking for poison. I don't even have to find it. And you were asleep until eleven," Elizabeth replies.

The little car climbs the road approaching San Gimignano, and the towers begin to peer down from the sky through the sunroof. Patty lifts her nose to smell the warm spring day. Godric looks ahead at the rolling hills full of vines. They hear a dog barking from a farmhouse a few hundred yards away. Patty barks back.

"There might be fourteen towers in this town, I'm not sure, but there used to be around seventy-two at one point. I've been reading the guidebook. But I don't remember exactly. I mean, it all blends, doesn't it? Towers, families at war, arguments over resources, and now we all gawp at them." Godric chuckles.

"Thank goodness that never happens anymore," Elizabeth replies, raising her eyebrows. "We had better not see the red van here."

Godric drives up into the square with their access all areas car pass, even though the whole of San Gimignano is a car-free zone. Godric has no shame. He parks below the tallest tower.

"Let's stretch our legs before we do anything like tackle climbing that," Godric falls out of the car, his legs far too long. He takes Patty's lead. The three wander around the piazza, then up and down Via San Giovanni, with its little tourist shops. Godric steps into one which just sells lavender and buys Elizabeth some soap. They walk into a glass shop only to be told no dogs allowed. Then they turn down along an alley that opens up and find a pretty wine shop with a café and tables overlooking a beautiful view of the valley below. They sit and order some food. But, when it arrives, it is clearly not vegan. The waitress is rude and snatches the plates away and shoves a bill in their face. Elizabeth decides to only pay for the drinks, and they leave. Unfortunately, the owner chases after them a few minutes later.

"You run away without paying. You owe me money!" He shouts.

"We paid for our drinks."

"Pay now, or I'll call the police!"

At this moment, a classic red Mondial Ferrari pulls up into the Piazza della Cisterna, right next to where they are standing. Out steps Sergeant Angelou Rossi. Elizabeth spots this and decides to call this grumpy offensive café owner's bluff.

"Okay, call the police. Call them. I'll tell them how you robbed me of my plates before we could even decide whether to feed the meat to our dog. We ate none of the food. It was taken immediately and nothing was offered in its place. I will tell the police how incredibly poor the service was, how I paid for the drinks, and how we were treated. Call them.

Call them now." Elizabeth stares at the café owner, his huge brown eyes and handsome tall physique ablaze with anger and affronted at the customer who dared to walk away and now dares to question his authority in his town. Patty barking at Marco with all her might. After Elizabeth takes a breath, she thinks how dangerous this man looks. What was she thinking? Godric is also a little nervous about his nanna's tactic and does not fancy a night in the cells all over missing payment for a meaty salad.

"Is everything alright, Professor Green?" Sergeant Angelou Rossi looks back at his Ferrari and the gathering tourists who have come to witness the argument or admire his classic car. He walks closer and stares at Marco, who has been pointing his finger at Elizabeth. He glances at Patty, still barking at her least favourite café and wine shop owner.

"No, not at the moment. We ordered what we thought was vegan food and were brought meat." Godric explains. "Paid for our drinks, and then this man chases us, threatening the police on us."

"Marco. What's this?" the Sergeant sticks out his chin and narrows his eyes.

"This woman did not pay for her food!" Marco shouts. Patty lunges for his ankles and catches his trousers. Marco begins to shake Patty off. "Get off!"

"Don't shout at my dog! You're much bigger. She's just defending me from you, you nasty man! I shall have to call the police for animal cruelty." Elizabeth finds that she has to shout over the noisy crowd that has gathered to watch the showdown.

"Marco, is this true? I came for a drive in my Ferrari. I could have brought out the Lambo Jarama for a test run. She's been in the garage all winter. But she sings when–"

"She ordered food. She pays for it!" Marco interrupts the Sergeant talking about his cars, now watching the crowd peering into the windows of his favourite motor vehicle.

"This is outrageous, and what treatment." Elizabeth raises her hand, now quite cross. Patty starts barking again, looking very cute. A woman in the crowd pulls a face and mouths what an 'adorable' dog.

"Marco, you chase this woman into the street?" The Sergeant looks back at Marco.

"She pays, or the police," Marco shrugs.

"This is Professor Green. Professor Green is helping us solve one of the biggest robberies this country has known. Yes, call the police. They will lock you up," the Sergeant laughs at Marco and then winks at Elizabeth, showing his dimples.

"She pays."

"No!" Sergeant Angelou Rossi's smile drops, and he starts to shout quickly in Italian.

Arms flail, and Marco begins to crease up his eyes. But when the Sergeant pauses for breath, Marco kicks off with a retaliatory diatribe. Elizabeth and Godric step back and sit on the square steps, as no one is now paying attention to anything but Angelou and Marco. They hear the Sergeant shout, "Maximilius Romano!" and then some Italian expletives. Finally, the Sergeant stretches out his arms and adjusts his neck in his jacket while Marco throws his arms up into the air and walks back to the wine shop. The Sergeant follows. Godric and Elizabeth wait for what seems like a very long time – probably five minutes – until the Sergeant appears, clearly eating something. In his hand, he carries a serviette with a sausage poking out the top.

"Are we going to be thrown in prison?" Godric asks, mildly worried about this escalation and wishing that perhaps his nanna had just paid the bill and not been so stubborn.

"He's such an idiot." The Sergeant grins, then drops his hot dog for Patty to take a bite from. Patty wastes no time and takes a big chunk out of the sausage. Elizabeth and Godric then watch the Sergeant put the rest of the hot dog in his own mouth.

"You told him that we were looking for the diamond of Maximilius Romano and that Maximilius would not want to know that Marco was obstructing the investigation? Who is Maximilius?" Elizabeth pauses. Waiting for the Sergeant to reply. Sergeant Rossi pauses, surprised they heard every word.

"Keep a distance. He needs to calm down." The Sergeant tries to hide his anger and stress and ignores Elizabeth's question about Maximilius. "You had ice cream? The best in the world. You been up a tower?"

"If you're going to ignore our questions, perhaps you can show us the tower where Peter Jones fell?" Elizabeth asks.

"What?" the Sergeant is surprised Elizabeth knows about the fall.

"Why the secrecy? Giuseppe Esposito told us," Godric says.

"We don't want to spook all the tourists, do we?" The Sergeant explains quietly. Though, Elizabeth does not believe this is the real reason. "I can show you if you like?"

"I think Patty and I shall join the queue for a rum and raisin. Take good care of my nanna." Godric signals to his nanna that it is okay if she wants to look up the tower with the Sergeant first. "I can go when you get back, maybe?"

"Call me Angelou. Yes, she's very safe."

"I'll have a quick look." Elizabeth begins to walk with Angelou. "Is it a crime to be a vegan here?" Elizabeth has taken a liking to this young Sergeant, who fought her battle when she really did not have the stomach for it today and shared his sausage with Patty.

"I had to pick up some wine for my brother. Marco does have the best. But we're not all like him. Far from it. He likes to think he's all powerful, you know, connected. Throw his weight around. But Marco is nothing but a small-time crook." The Sergeant spits out the words.

"A crook. Why don't you arrest him, Angelou?"

"Seriously?" The Sergeant relaxes a little, then smiles. "He fears Maximilius. They all do. It is what keeps him in check." The Sergeant grabs Elizabeth's hand, which shocks her. "We go up." He flashes his badge at the front desk, and they breeze through. Elizabeth can only see hundreds of steps above them, and the Sergeant races up the first section holding onto Elizabeth to help her but sees that he needs to slow down. They pause to look at some of the paintings and wall art to give Elizabeth a chance to catch her breath. But then, he grabs her hand again and finally, they make it to the top of the tower.

Still breathless from being pulled at a pace, Elizabeth looks down at the ant sized people below. The Sergeant points out Godric and Patty, now sitting on a bench below, eating ice cream. They wave up at Elizabeth, who waves back. The Sergeant laughs. Elizabeth glances at this Ferrari driving 'just call me Angelou' Sergeant, barely the same age as Godric but already with a police badge and wonders how this confident young man copes with seeing death. He lights a cigarette, so Elizabeth walks away to look across San Gimignano to the other side of the roof. It is breathtakingly beautiful. The other towers, fields and undulating valley.

"The Ferrari is just gorgeous, isn't she?" The Sergeant walks over to Elizabeth and points at his car. "She gathers a crowd wherever she goes."

"What happened to Peter, Sergeant?"

"He fell here over this bit. It's Angelou." Angelou, the Sergeant, points his cigarette matter of factly over the edge back down at the piazza side of the tower, then chucks the butt down.

"That could land in someone's hair?" Elizabeth says, flabbergasted. Angelou laughs then makes the sound of a bomb falling and then exploding, to illustrate Peter Jones's demise.

"Do many jump?" Elizabeth peers over the edge and sees the cigarette land safely on the street, not hurting anyone.

"That's why we thought it was suicide at first. But–" Angelou sticks out his chin and turns down the corners of his mouth. "It wasn't."

"How could anyone lift someone up and over this wall? The edges of this viewing platform are quite high?"

"If they were drugged?"

"Wouldn't that make them heavier?" Elizabeth questions his logic.

"Doesn't that depend on the drug? You know, whether they were high?" Angelou takes off his sunglasses and looks straight at Elizabeth. His green eyes matching her own, almost too wise for his body.

Elizabeth looks down at where Peter Jones fell. She cannot imagine how painful a death that must have been and hopes that whatever he was poisoned with made him less aware.

"You have to find the poison, Professor Green. You're a wizard by all accounts. I looked up your record."

"My record?"

"The one your police sent over. A Mr Raysnout."

"Raynott."

"You solve all the crimes. I respect that." Angelou looks at her with very serious eyes. Elizabeth almost laughs at this young man who is trying to perfect his stare. "You look like a clever woman."

"For argument's sake, just tell me what you can about the case. I'm not working. I'm on holiday. But, for a moment, you have a captive audience." Elizabeth tries to get the Sergeant to say more. But the Sergeant is more interested in what has parked beside his Ferrari.

"Oh no. Why does he drive that?" Angelou

looks down at an old banger and tells Elizabeth that the driver knew Peter. "That man there wearing a bright red neckerchief. Him." They watch this man walk across to a bar in the square and sit down among some empty tables. The Sergeant tells Elizabeth that Peter was, "wasting that man's time. He was supposed to be researching him, when all he wanted to do was steal our diamonds." The Sergeant then tells Elizabeth that Marco was there, in the piazza, when they were covering up Peter Jones's body. "He lives here. Nothing escapes him."

As Angelou speaks, Elizabeth can almost feel herself detaching from her body and lifting up then falling down over the side of the Tower, just as Peter Jones had. Before she feels herself falling, she sees that Godric has spotted her looking over the edge again and is waving, but she cannot see his smile. She needs to see his smile, needs to be with him. She feels a panic growing. She must get down.

"I have to go down. Quickly."

25 ICE CREAM, OLIVES AND STEFANO BRAMBILLA

After Elizabeth descends the tower, she begins to feel much better. She turns and says goodbye to the Sergeant, who walks off to pack his wine into his Ferrari. Elizabeth and Godric hear him loudly leave the Piazza della Cisterna.

"Patty had ice cream too?"

"Doggie ice cream, and they have vegan ice cream to die for. I got you one but had to eat it as it melted. Here let me go and get you one. The queue has gone down. What flavour?" Godric jumps up and is already walking over.

"I don't mind." Elizabeth sits on the central monument steps and soaks up the ambience of the Piazza della Cisterna. Milling tourists look up at the thirteenth-century buildings, as surprised as she is that they survived for so long. Wondering what secrets the walls could tell if they could speak. The sun floods the cobbles, so when Godric returns, Elizabeth is grateful for the tutti-frutti two-scoop ice cream with hundreds and thousands all over the top and a toy unicorn on a stick poking out.

"It looks so gorgeous. A little girl was walking out with one," he says. Elizabeth would have preferred a sharper flavour but only has herself to blame for not choosing. She pulls out the toy unicorn and holds it away from Patty, who wants to chew it. As she tastes the ice cream, she is surprised by how refreshing it tastes. She looks at Godric and smiles. The two sit in silence on the steps, Patty dozing now by Godric's feet while Elizabeth finishes her cone.

"I'll stay here while you go up the tower. The views are incredible," Elizabeth finally says. Godric checks his pockets and hands over Patty's lead.

"Okay, I'll be careful not to fall off the top."

"Stop it!" Elizabeth replies crossly.

Godric smiles and wanders off.

*

Godric runs up the steps two by two, passing many older and younger explorers. He bursts out onto the roof, causing a young couple to step back in shock.

"Yay! We're all on holiday!" He shouts to them.

"Ci," they reply nervously.

Godric jumps up on the inner wall to look over. There is another wall below, but not much protection. He dangles his feet over for a while to take in the view. He cannot quite believe just how beautiful it is. Finally, he drops down and walks over to the other side, the side where Peter Jones fell. Godric can see his nanna and Patty. He waits for them to look up, then waves vigorously. He sees his nanna waving back.

Godric starts to take tilt-shift photographs. He tries to include one of all the tourists below as they already look so tiny. Suddenly, through the lens of his camera, he can see the man from the café, Marco. He takes some tilt-shift photographs of Marco's café. But then he notices Marco walking over to his nanna again. Godric turns and runs down the tower, jumping chunks of steps to get out to his nanna as fast as he can.

*

"Now the police have gone, and your grandson has left, you are enjoying our hospitality?" Marco sneers at Elizabeth, looking down at her on the steps.

"I beg your pardon?" Elizabeth tries to look up at his face, but he is standing in front of the sun. Patty starts barking at Marco, clearly a man she does not care for.

"No one comes here and tries to rob me. No

one," he threatens.

"You're a very rude man. Cease with your macho antics and leave my poor dog in peace," Elizabeth replies firmly.

"Why are you still here?" Marco continues to poke at Elizabeth. "What are you doing in my town? Angelou, he said you're looking for the diamond. You won't find it here."

"Perhaps you should go back to your wine shop and have a cup of tea to calm down."

"You're not welcome here." Marco lifts his chin and sneers. Patty grabs hold of his trousers again only this time will not let go, and Elizabeth makes no effort to stop her.

"No one tells me what to do. Certainly, not a rude man like you."

"Control this mutt!" Marco glares at Elizabeth, then continues to shake his leg.

Now back at ground level, though still from a distance, Godric can see the altercation and picks up speed running towards them. From a hundred yards away, he can see another man, dressed in tatty clothes, clearly walking over to join his nanna and this Marco man.

"Hello," the second man, now with Elizabeth and Marco, gives Elizabeth the broadest smile and extends his hand to shake Elizabeth's. She looks at it but doesn't respond. "Is this man bothering you?" The second man eyes up Marco, still with a piece of his trouser in the small dog's mouth.

"He's proving to be a bit of a bother, yes. But nothing myself nor Patty cannot handle."

"Marco, what are you doing to this lovely woman? And stop upsetting her dog." The man turns to Elizabeth, holding no grudge that she did not shake his hand. "I'm Stefano," he says.

"She's poking her nose here looking for the diamond. She won't find it here. I told her, I cannot have rumours destroying our reputation!" Marco shouts.

"This gentlewoman does not look like someone who would poke her nose into anything. I was watching. She was sat here quietly with her dog, eating her ice cream."

"Did you know Peter Jones?" Elizabeth looks carefully at Stefano, noticing the red neckerchief around his throat that the Sergeant had pointed out earlier from the tower. Stefano pauses, curious about who this woman is.

"How did you know? Yes, yes, I did," Stefano smiles again, utterly uninterested in Marco all of a sudden.

"Great, now I have two people who don't like parting with cash," Marco is cross and gesticulates at Stefano and Elizabeth.

"You don't look strapped for cash," Elizabeth replies, observing the shiny front of the restaurant wine store.

"You have no idea how hard it is to make a living here!"

"Ha!" Stefano laughs, trying to block

out Marco, only eyes for Elizabeth. "Would you like to see the most beautiful view of San Gimignano? We can leave this man to remain grumpy alone." Stefano grins. There is something about him which reminds her of Gerald. She cannot put her finger on it. His kind face, the curls on the back of his head, winding their way back towards the front of his face around his ears, his kind eyes.

"I will if you tell me how you knew Peter Jones."

"He was my friend."

"Nanna?"

"This man wants to show me the most beautiful view of San Gimignano. I suppose with a promise like that?" Then she looks at Stefano, "Stefano, my grandson, Godric. Godric, Stefano–"

"Brambilla, Stefano Brambilla. Pleased to meet you, Godric."

Patty lets go of Marco's trousers when Godric returns, pleased to see him.

"And, he did rescue me from a barrage of abuse from that man."

Godric watches as Marco throws up his hands, shakes his head, and walks back to his wine bar. "Why is that man so cross?" Elizabeth asks Stefano.

"I think he's worried about Maximilius Romano. Yes. He was there the night," Stefano makes the noise of someone falling with a whistle, then smacks his hands together to indicate the impact of Peter Jones on the cobbles.

"He was there? He witnessed the death?"

"I don't know about that. But someone saw them talking in the Piazza Del Duomo. Marco and Maximilius. That's all. But Marco is sensitive because Maximilius is a very powerful man."

"Maximilius?" Godric asks, completely confused.

"It was his diamond. Or, more accurately, his wife's." Stefano curls the corners of his mouth down and shrugs.

Elizabeth and Godric follow Stefano down the Via San Giovanni towards a grand looking hotel and watch as he says hello to the manager, who leads them all through to the restaurant.

"Wow! Totally worth being screamed at by an angry Italian for." Godric immediately starts taking photographs of the panoramic view of San Gimignano. Like a painting, endless vineyards, small woodlands, undulating fields, all spilling out across the valley with tiny country lanes winding through until they disappear on the horizon. They sit and pass the time sipping small beers while Patty curls around Elizabeth's feet. Time passes until Stefano suggests they move off for another adventure.

"So, you will come and have lunch at my olive grove?"

"Thank you, but we have just come from Florence for the day," Godric replies, giving his nanna a sideways glance about this forward invite from a total stranger.

"How long are you in Florence?" Stefano asks.

"Only a few nights," Godric fibs a little, so this stranger does not know their business. Godric cannot stop taking photographs, his bendy tripod now attached to the window.

"Fine, you have plenty of time to come back here. You come."

Elizabeth and Godric are flummoxed. Who is this man?

"We don't know you," Elizabeth replies, shaking her head.

"I think you've had a hard time with Marco, and I want to show you that not all Italians are as unfriendly. You are on holiday, no? Most won't get to see an authentic olive grove. You like olives?"

"Mostly." Elizabeth replies.

"Have you tasted fresh olives?"

"Yes."

"From the tree to table?"

"Well, no, because they must be pressed. They're bitter from the tree. I have an olive tree in my garden at home, as it happens," Elizabeth replies knowledgeably.

"You passed the test!" Stefano beams. "Please come. Drink good wine. Eat. See some beautiful countryside from a local's tour, and I will get you back here for tea. Perfect, come on. Look, you know my hotel. You know I knew Peter." Stefano leans across to the head waiter and asks, "Am I a good man?" The waiter smiles and nods, 'the best'.

"Okay, you got me at good wine," Godric rolls his eyes at Elizabeth, then looks back at Stefano. "And you don't seem like a serial killer, so if you can just confirm that, then I'm in."

"I'm not a serial killer. I want to cancel out your experience from your encounter with that very bad man." Stefano nods up towards the hill where Marco has his restaurant and shop. Then turns to the head waiter and speaks quickly in Italian, and says 'Marco' at least three or four times. The head waiter frowns and shakes his head.

"We don't want to be driving back to Florence in the dark." Elizabeth presses. "Just for a couple of hours tops then," unsure of what they are walking into and aware she is acting entirely out of character, putting her trust in a stranger like this. But Stefano does not feel like a stranger. In fact, it feels like they have known him all their lives. His belly laughs, his crinkly smile, his gait. But, more than anything, she can feel his kindness. Not in what he says, but how.

Stefano leads them back through the hotel lobby to the banger of a van. He opens the boot and lifts out a crate of olives, hands them over to the hotel manager and then opens the passenger door. Elizabeth and Godric are surprised when they are encouraged to get in. What is it about old vans? Their expectations drop as to the size of this so-called olive grove and the quantity of wine on offer. But Stefano is insistent, and Elizabeth is intrigued to hear more about Peter Jones. However, she is unsure about leaving their own Fiat in San Gimignano with Marco roaming, so they agree to move it a short distance away from the centre, and then all finally swap into Stefano's. During the swap, as both cars are parked beside each other, Stefano looks into the back seat of the Fiat 500 and notices an old cardigan that Patty has been using to sit on.

"You know, I have something better back at home I can give you? You can throw out that old rag?"

"No!" Both Godric and Elizabeth shout at the same time. Stefano holds his hands up to gesture that it was just an idea, and Godric ushers them all into Stefano's van. Before they know it, they are on their way, all three in the front on one big seat, Patty looking out the front on Godric's lap. On the road again, this time with a complete stranger, who somehow feels so familiar it is almost unsettling.

26 WHISPER IN THE ALLEY

After Elizabeth and Godric have left San Gimignano with Stefano, the Piazza del Cisterna outside Marco's wine café starts to fill up. Marco is placing wine bottles from a box onto a shelving unit to create a display, his hands treating the bottles like he has done this a million times before, almost throwing them into place when someone taps on the window from outside. Marco looks up, and a man is staring at him and pointing to the door. Marco pulls back his ears and sighs. He looks around to see if any of his staff have spotted this man, but he is the only one in the wine shop, so he shouts down to the restaurant floor below and says he is stepping out for a moment, hurriedly taking off his black apron, the pocket of which contains his cigarettes. No time for one now. Marco turns the sign on the door to 'closed', locks it behind him, and then follows the man down an alley. The two men shaking their heads and whispering as they look about to see who else can see them.

"Maximilius, I had nothing to do with it. I saw him, yes. But he was already dead."

27 SIENA AND THE OLIVE KING

Despite Elizabeth and Godric being fully aware they are beholden to a stranger, Stefano has an ease and warmth which spreads through the car in no time. He says all the right things and makes the sun come out on the inside. Elizabeth listens to her grandson conversing with Stefano about Italy, Cambridge, Fiats, dogs, and spring. From starting out as a young irresponsible bacchanalian louche, she smiles realising that without her even noticing that Godric has grown into a decent, kind man with wonderful qualities. So much that she can feel life tipping in his favour. He is looking out for her, watching over, being the responsible one. She did not even notice the tilt. Just like that, they are all grown up. On loan for such a short while.

It was Elizabeth who got into a car with a stranger. Godric was unsure, and she can tell from his subtle line of questioning that it is he who still has his wits about him. Elizabeth tunes out. He has it in hand. Sunshine floods fields either side of the road, contributing to her general state of felice. And when Godric tries to open the window in Stefano's van for Patty, and the handle falls off the door, Stefano just roars with laughter, making Elizabeth smile.

"Oh, it always does that," he explains, putting the handle into his pocket, then leaning across Elizabeth and Godric and pushing the window down by pressing against it, the van swerving a little as he does. "You've just got to push it in place. See?" Patty sticks her head out, her ears now flapping, breathing in the sweet smell from an avenue of orange trees in blossom, bees buzzing along to feed.

"Well, I think we're going to see the real Italy," Godric whispers to Elizabeth.

The van trundles down the hill and out into the countryside. Elizabeth feels the front sofa seat bounce as she is squished between Godric and Stefano with no seat belt. Every time Stefano changes gear, his hand gets very close to her knee.

"Is it hard making a living from olives?" Godric makes more small talk as he looks down at a one-inch gap between his passenger door and the rest of the car and wonders if that is supposed to be there.

"It's tough work. I wish my daughters would help now they have grown up. But they're not interested in olives. What can you do?" Stefano says and then laughs.

"So, what happened to Peter Jones?" Elizabeth finally decides there has been enough small talk.

"A tragedy. I knew Peter well."

"Really? How did you become friends?"

"Yes," Stefano takes his eyes off the road and looks at Elizabeth. "Good friends. We were. Very good."

"How did you meet?"

"It's no secret. He asked me if he could study my family. Our olive grove goes back many generations. He was making a study of our family." Stefano waves his arms about, letting go of the wheel.

"An anthropologist."

"Yes, he was from England. Just like you," Stefano smiles at Elizabeth and leans into her, thankfully putting his hands back on the wheel. Elizabeth points ahead to try to make him focus.

"It's okay. I know this road. I could drive blind." Stefano shuts his eyes and continues to drive for a couple of seconds.

"Not funny old bean," Godric pipes up. "You're making my driving look tame."

"Don't worry, I will look after your nanna." Stefano nods, "Anyone who can stand their ground with Marco deserves a medal. Formidable," Stefano replies, having opened his eyes and is now staring at Elizabeth again. She points at the road ahead.

Having left thick hedgerows, the road starts to open out, and they can see an expanse of sky. Huge groves of olive trees line either side of the lane, which appear to go on for acres. They drive for minutes before anyone speaks. Godric and Elizabeth are both thinking what a lot of olive trees.

"There must be a lot of olive farms around here. Do you find it very competitive?" Godric asks, noticing a goat below an olive tree, munching on grass.

"Not so much," Stefano says.

"I've never seen so many olives." Godric blinks and shakes his head.

"Well, you're in Tuscany. In fact, not far from Siena."

"Does his magical mystery tour include Siena?" Elizabeth says quietly to Godric.

"It might," Stefano says quietly to Elizabeth, his beard almost tickling her ear.

"Not today, thank you." Godric makes it clear no moving the goalposts. "Just the olive farm for now."

"How long did you know Peter?" Elizabeth asks, changing the subject back.

"Ooh, let me think. Are *you* Peter's friend? I saw you speaking with Angelou. I knew

Angelou when he was just so little." Stefano puts his hand down to the floor of the van, indicating the size of a young child.

"No, we didn't know Peter," Godric replies. "We don't know anyone in Tuscany. We're on holiday."

"What were you speaking with Angelou about?" Stefano asks.

"He came to defend us from Marco." Godric replies.

"Oh, I thought you knew him."

"We met Sergeant Angelou Rossi in Florence," Godric explains. "But, no, we don't know him."

"Well, this is a very explosive case. My advice is to steer clear if you want a peaceful holiday." Stefano nods and smiles at Elizabeth.

"Is that a threat?" Elizabeth glares at Stefano. Stefano glances back at her, surprised by her question.

"What? You think I want to threaten you?" He smiles broadly. "No, there are a lot of egos involved. It is the biggest diamond theft Italy has known for decades. Peter was English. If I thought you knew him, then others who are not such a teddy bear as I am might also make the same conclusion but with a different outcome. I want you to be safe, is all." Stefano looks at Elizabeth warmly. "But don't worry, don't worry. Just be careful, is all I'm saying. Don't go how d'you say, don't go 'poking the bear'?"

"You haven't answered my question about when you first met Peter? I'm allowed to be curious. What are you hiding?"

"Should we be getting involved?" Godric whispers to his nanna.

"Come and enjoy some lunch on a real farm first." Stefano looks at his watch. "I'm late. We'll get to Peter soon. But let's not spoil the journey or our food."

They continue in silence for a little longer until Godric has to comment on the number of olive trees again.

"I'm sorry, but I feel like we are in a maze or something. How many olive farms are there around here?"

"Just one," Stefano says quietly. Godric looks at Elizabeth, realising this is a lot of land they have driven by for the past ten minutes. Stefano turns down a small lane and onto a track. The van bounces about and Godric offers Elizabeth his jacket to put under her to cushion the lack of suspension. Finally, they see a small house by a gate, a two-up two-down, but in very good condition. There is no sign of lunch or anyone home. Godric feels a little worried now. What have they let themselves in for? But his nanna seems okay, so he tries to push aside any fears that they are maybe in the car with a serial killer after all.

Stefano drives straight past the little

house and enters what looks like a golf course, but slowly Elizabeth and Godric realise the manicured greenery is someone's front lawn, with sprinklers everywhere, and the house they passed was just a gatehouse.

"Such a contrast from all the olives. What's all the netting?"

"Stop the wild boars. My wife would have them dealt with more swiftly if she was allowed," and Stefano makes a gunshot sound in his mouth, "but I say they won't bother us if we keep them out. And, yes, I feel a bit guilty about watering the grass, but it keeps people in work, so–"

"Wait, this is yours?" Godric looks at the lawn which seems to stretch out for a mile and then at the van they are sitting in.

"Welcome," Stefano says quietly. They continue to drive past stables, picket fences, parked-up horse boxes, and statues with fountains until they arrive at what can only be described as a mansion. Two supercars are parked on the gravel, which snakes around an impressive central fountain with many cherubs looking rather pleased with themselves and down at any guests as they arrive. Stefano pulls up beside and steps out to speak to a gardener, then turns to Elizabeth and Godric.

"Lunch is usually on the terrace." He guides Elizabeth and Godric around the side of the building, their feet crunching on gravel as Stefano's frame seems to grow even more relaxed as he chats to a butler and they catch only a few words, including 'vegan', then the butler hurries off to the kitchen. Stefano then turns back to them both. "I just need to find my wife. This way."

Following Stefano, neither Elizabeth nor Godric could have expected to see gardens which sweep down to a view of Tuscany that could merit the front of a postcard. To the right an infinity pool, and the left a huge terrace flanked by oversized pots full of gardenia and geraniums spanning the length of the back of the house. But the central view is of a sweeping valley full of an intricate lattice of fields, vineyards, country lanes, and Cyprus and umbrella pines.

Sitting at the table is a leggy and tanned woman with long brown hair which has sun-kissed highlights. Stefano calls out to her. She looks up and smiles, noticing the guests and then standing up to welcome them.

"Bongiorno," she says, as her large brown eyes hold their gaze on Godric. Godric shakes her hand, and the two are invited to sit down. "I'm Aurelia. Very pleased to meet you."

"They're hungry because Marco didn't feed them."

"Hello," Elizabeth says.

"Ugh," Stefano's wife replies. She shouts

into the house at someone, who comes rushing out. "What can we get you to drink? Champagne?"

"This is Professor Elizabeth Green and her grandson, Godric."

"Yes, please," Godric says, "and water."

"Might you have peppermint tea?"

"Yes, of course."

"Did you know Peter Jones well too?" Elizabeth wastes no time, staring at Aurelia. This throws Aurelia a little, and she looks at her husband.

"Oh." Aurelia glances at her husband and then looks back at Elizabeth. "Were you his friend?" Aurelia asks Elizabeth, but Elizabeth waits for her answer, so Aurelia continues, "Yes, we knew him. It is so awful. I cannot believe it. He was such a nice man. He was here just last week?" Aurelia looks at her husband again. "He knew my husband more. I didn't really know them much. Peter and Steffy would go off together, but they would come to eat. He and his wife. He was a nice man. Both quiet, reserved, very–"

"British?" Godric asks.

"Well, I suppose we're all different. But he did not seem like someone who would, well, steal a diamond. We were both very shocked," Aurelia crosses her legs and offers a bowl of nuts to her guests which were on the table beside her cocktail. "Food is on the way, I promise."

"What does someone who steals a diamond look like?" Godric asks.

"Well, I don't know. You know. Someone who looks like a thief, I suppose?" Aurelia shrugs. "He was, well, he seemed to be educated. You know, brought up right."

"What did Peter look like?" Elizabeth asks Aurelia pointedly.

"He was a nice man," Stefano jumps in. "He was a bit creased around the edges, just like me. Just the normal battle scars. But a good man. Aurelia is right. He did not look like a diamond thief."

"You have those photos, Stefano. Show Professor Green those of you in the trees with Peter," Aurelia suggests.

Stefano gets out his phone and opens the photographs. He hands Elizabeth his mobile, and she and Godric look at pictures of Stefano and Peter up in the branches of a large olive tree. "They climbed to the top," Aurelia adds. Elizabeth cannot really see Peter's face but has already seen it in the paper. "They were two peas. Is that what you say?"

"Two peas? So, you are a diamond thief too?" Elizabeth asks, looking at Stefano.

"Gosh, I thought the British were backwards in coming forwards?" Aurelia recoils a little. Stefano politely continues.

"He was interested in our family. In its

history. I think I did mention that." Stefano smiles then pauses, thoughtfully, adding, "I think he wanted to make a contribution." Stefano looks at Elizabeth. "To understand why we farm olives. He was very interested in why I came back here after studying in England. I took a horticulture course in Kent. Yes, I know your garden of England. And I would catch the train to London as a young man. Go to parties. It was lively!" Stefano thinks about his younger years and stares out across the garden. "He wanted to understand what had drawn me home, Elizabeth. What made the family business a stronger pull than anything else in the world."

"And, did he find his answer?" Elizabeth asks.

"I don't know? I'll tell you what I told him. I'm an olive man. Cut me open, and you'll find olives moving around in my blood."

"Why you? Why was he looking into you?"

"We have the biggest farm in Tuscany, one of the largest in Italy," Aurelia replies, looking straight at Elizabeth, then smiles, "My husband is a modest man."

"It does seem to be a very large farm," Godric adds, sipping his champagne. "We drove past a lot of olives. I like olives, well, some olives, to go with things. Not just a plate of olives."

"My husband won't tell you, but you can

walk from Siena to Florence on our vineyards and not have to step off for one minute," Aurelia boasts. "Though my husband does like to plan his expansion."

"I want to get that patch down by Poggibonsi. The soil is good," he nods at his wife, then smiles at her and shrugs.

"You know that will encroach on Marco's," Aurelia raises her eyebrows and frowns a little.

"He should leave my daughter alone then."

"Do you know anything about the funeral?" Elizabeth asks Stefano.

"I imagine it will be after the autopsy. You could ask his wife, perhaps?"

"Where did you study in England?" Godric asks.

"Near West Malling. It is so green there, but not many olive trees."

"Do you know Giuseppe?" Elizabeth changes the subject, not needing a geography lesson on Kent from an Italian.

"Not very well. I know who you're talking about. Peter's friend."

Two young tall, thin, beautiful Italian women turn up at the table, all dressed to go out. They kiss their father.

"Isabella, Sophia, say hello to Professor Green. I had to rescue her from Marco. Huh!"

"Ugh. Papa! Don't say that," Isabella replies. "We're going into Florence. Catch you later," she adds. Both daughters kiss their mother. Sophia speaks very quietly to her mother in Italian, and then they are gone.

"Children," Stefano says, listening to one of the supercars start up in the driveway and leave with his daughters.

"You can lead a horse to water. Isn't that right, Professor?" Aurelia looks at Elizabeth.

*

The four eat lunch under the shade of the terrace pergola, and Godric begins to slip down into his seat.

"Would you like to see my stables, Professor Green?" Aurelia asks.

"Yes, though I'm sure the horses hate being ridden and left in stables."

"They are my babies. I look after them well. Have you ridden before, Godric?"

"Yes, but I stick to things much lower to the ground."

"Oh? Are you not a sporting man?"

Elizabeth gives Godric a sideways glance. Godric chooses to remain quiet, not really caring to expend any energy in the heat of the day, and full from stuffing in a lot of pie and drinking far too much champagne over lunch. He spots a hammock under some trees.

"I love horses. Though today, they are close, but no cigar." He looks at the hammock longingly. "Think we might go and see how my balancing skills are right now, actually," Godric says, carrying Patty.

"Your grandson is very tired?" Aurelia asks Elizabeth as they wander off towards the stables.

"He doesn't want to see horses in stables."

"Why not."

"Because, like me, he thinks it's cruel."

"They get carrots and fresh hay."

"They should be free."

"Then they would starve."

"We have wild horses in England. They don't starve."

The two women wander around, looking at the horses, with Aurelia greeting each one and Elizabeth stroking their noses and putting her head against their necks. But the tour is not going as Aurelia expected, with Elizabeth pointing out several animal welfare issues until finally, after a while, Aurelia suggests that perhaps they should return to the house.

"Why are you really here?" Aurelia asks.

"Your husband invited us. I think he was trying to balance out our impression of Italian men. As he explained, we had just had an altercation with–"

"But why did you say yes? I mean, you don't know my husband?" Aurelia interrupts.

"I've been asking myself the same thing. Your husband–"

"Is very persuasive. I suppose I knew the answer. A man of the soil, Professor Green. And you and your plants."

"And you do not like either?" Elizabeth is curious.

"I grew up in Florence. And he invited me out for lunch, just like you today. I came despite the land. I came to be with Stefano. And if you love Stefano, you must love olives," Aurelia smiles as they arrive back on the terrace. Stefano has been on the phone and has papers from his briefcase spread out on the table where they earlier ate lunch.

"Are you ready to go back? Have you seen enough of the horses?"

"They are beautiful. You need to make their fields bigger. They only have a tiny place to relax."

Stefano looks at Aurelia, who shrugs and smiles, "Goodbye, Professor Green. Please do say goodbye to your grandson. I have to go and change to pop into Siena, darling," Aurelia looks at Stefano.

"Here, let's take some water and find Godric on the way," Stefano kisses his wife, then picks up the water for Elizabeth to drink. "It is hot today, no?"

Stefano and Elizabeth find Godric asleep under a hat that he found on the hammock. Elizabeth pushes the side of the hammock to wake him up, making it sway. Patty jumps down.

"Ooh, keep going," Godric says, peeping

out from under the hat at his nanna, then does a full roll and falls out onto the grass and picks himself up.

"Let me show you the olive groves here," Stefano suggests. "We can take the van. It's on the way back."

The three plus Patty climb back into Stefano's old van again, and he starts to take a detour down a tiny lane.

"This definitely is not on the way back," Godric says, holding onto his nanna so he doesn't fall out of the door, which this time isn't even closing properly. "And, Stefano, this is an interesting choice of vehicle, given the size of your estate?"

"I like her. She has been with me for years and years," Stefano replies, patting the old van's dashboard. "This is nice, speaking English with two new English friends, no?" Stefano smiles at Elizabeth.

"The police think Peter was poisoned. They seem convinced he didn't just fall from the tower. They didn't tell me he had actually fallen. Why are they keeping his death from the tower quiet?"

"Tourists," Stefano replies, immediately more subdued, flicking his indicator on from habit to turn left at a junction, despite there being few cars on his estate.

"It is quiet out here, isn't it? Apart from the crickets, who are so noisy," Godric puts his arm on the door to stop it from rattling.

“Do you know who killed Peter?” Elizabeth asks Stefano again.

“I feel like you asked me that on the way over here,” Stefano replies warmly. “I wish I did. I would seek revenge, Elizabeth,” Stefano says angrily. “He was such a sweet man. As I said, I cannot believe he stole the diamond either. It is, how do you say, ‘a bit fishy’.”

“But there is CCTV. We saw it on the news. The police released the footage.”

“Yes,” Stefano shakes his head.

“So, where do you think this diamond is hiding?”

“I have no idea, and I really don’t care. It is just a shiny piece of stone. Does it feed anyone? Does it care for anyone? No, it just brings trouble. I hope it’s at the bottom of the ocean.”

“But your country seems only to be talking about the diamond. It’s on the television, on the newsstands.”

“The world has gone crazy, don’t you think?” Stefano looks at Elizabeth and holds her gaze for longer than is normal.

“That is the kind of thing my husband used to say.”

“Where is your husband? Why is he not on this trip?”

Elizabeth cannot find any words to reply. She struggles to say those words from her lips, not wanting to make them real. But the silence is deafening.

"My grandfather passed away," Godric fills the silence.

"Oh. I'm so sorry." Stefano slows down the van, turns around, goes back the way they came, and then turns right up a tiny track, changing his mind about their destination after hearing of Elizabeth's loss.

"He would have loved it here too, even the missed turns," Elizabeth looks out at the valleys covered in Chianti vines, olive groves, Cyprus trees and even small woods as the little van climbs to the top of a hill. Stefano slows down and pulls up next to a white cottage. They all get out and stretch their legs, Patty happy to sniff new places, so long as Elizabeth does not stray too far.

Stefano opens the cottage, pulling back some double doors so the whole building is open to the view. Inside is a central wheel. He grabs a sack of olives from a fridge and puts them in the top of the contraption.

"An olive press?" Godric asks, taking some more olives and chucking them in the top.

"It was my grandfather's. I couldn't lose it, so I built this little cottage around it. In case he ever wants to come back and press some olives with me," Stefano looks at Elizabeth.

"It's all squirty," Godric says, looking at the machine crushing the olives. "Did they already lose their stones?"

"Yes, they're already pitted by this." Stefano points to a small hand worked olive destoner, which looks like it destones a dozen at a time. Then he turns his attention to Elizabeth, staring at the beautiful view of the Tuscan fields which stretch on for miles. "My grandfather would get me to press the olives. When I was a troublesome teenager." Stefano laughs. "I think I drove my mother up the wall. Or, at least, that is what she tells me when I go for lunch with her."

"You lost your father as well as your grandfather?" Godric looks at the photographs on the wall. "I'm not sure my father or grandfather did anything like this when I was troublesome."

"When you were troublesome? You were never troublesome," Elizabeth looks at Godric, knowing full well he still has the capacity to be mildly troublesome on occasion.

"Yes. I come up here when I feel like I want to be close to my grandfather, and my father. I don't see people up here."

"Did Peter come up here?" Elizabeth asks.

"No."

"But I thought he was your friend. Your good friend."

"He was."

"Studying your family."

"Nobody comes up here apart from me," Stefano replies firmly.

Godric turns the manual olive press after Stefano shows him how to, and they all watch as the olives are crushed.

"From here, the paste needs to go through malaxation, where it is slowly churned and has to be warm, allowing the smaller oil droplets to be released. It's not something you can hurry. While you turn, I will show your nanna something outside," Stefano explains. Godric pulls a face, not keen to continue any manual labour, but his nanna gives him a look that suggests she would like to speak with Stefano alone. Godric sighs and nods to his nanna, then watches her and Stefano leave the cottage and step out into the bright sunshine on top of the hill.

"I find it hard to understand you not showing this to Peter Jones when he was studying your family's heritage."

"It is a very private place," Stefano shrugs.

"What do you want me to look at," Elizabeth replies as Stefano starts to walk down a hill to a bench. He sits and pats the bench.

"I want you to feel the peace and quiet." Stefano puts his fingers to his lips to indicate that they should say nothing.

Elizabeth sits and tries to find the peace he is talking about. But all she can think of is what the hell is she doing here? Why even entertain this stranger? She should be with Godric and his magical holiday. She looks at Stefano's face, and realises that he is a kind man who having heard about Gerald is just trying to make her feel better. So, she looks back at the view, for a minute, to humour Stefano. Then, it hits her. It is the best view she has seen since they arrived in Italy. It is all at once overwhelming. Vast sweeping sprays of poppies, blossom forming circles around large cherry trees, tiny lanes winding here and there, long hedgerows, small wooded areas all glow in the warm sun. What she cannot see are homes or people anywhere. They stare at the view in silence for what feels like moments, but is more than ten minutes. Birds singing, bees buzzing, until finally Elizabeth cannot help herself from breaking the silence.

"Where is everyone?"

"This is my land. This is how this view looked when my grandfather was a boy. I have a photograph."

"This is all your land? But it goes on for miles."

"It's so peaceful, apart from over there. Can you see?" Stefano points into the farthest distance, frowning. "Can you see the tractors?" He stands up, animated, jabbing in the direction of where he says there are tractors.

"No," Elizabeth squints. "I can just see a tiny bit of dust rising on the horizon, I suppose."

"They're cutting down trees, clearing hedgerows. Just to put in more vines. We have enough!" Stefano shouts and smacks his hands together.

"I thought we were sitting peacefully?" Elizabeth asks.

"Marco bloody Conti. He's encroaching on my land, my grandfather's view!"

"Quite the popular man."

"The field went to auction, and he beat me to it," Stefano turns to look directly at Elizabeth with a face full of confusion. "And now, he takes my daughter? He's an old man." Stefano waits for a reaction from Elizabeth. He stands, his arms tanned from the sun, his linen jacket crumpled from sitting in his old van.

"Takes your daughter?"

"The more I protest, the more she runs into his arms."

"Ah, daughters," Elizabeth responds, thinking of her own and how rarely she sees her.

"What can I do?"

"I'm afraid my daughter and I do not see eye to eye."

Stefano throws himself back on the bench and stretches. "I think we have a lot in common."

"You do?"

"Yes," Stefano smiles. "Shut your eyes, just for a moment."

Elizabeth is not used to doing as she is told,

but this experience feels warm and safe, so she shuts her eyes. As soon as she does, she hears crickets so loud that they become almost overwhelming.

"How does that happen?" Elizabeth asks, opening her eyes, the crickets sounding a little quieter. She shuts her eyes again and the crickets sound even louder. She laughs. Elizabeth isn't sure about this man. Why is he being so friendly, why invite them to lunch? She does not really know why she accepted. It is not like her. She feels like she is drifting, and now she can see Gerald in this man's eyes as he smiles at her. He has such a warm smile. Elizabeth is overwhelmed and has to look away. She is grateful for the sunglasses Godric bought her in Annecy that she can hide behind, as she can feel the tears welling up in her eyes. Patty jumps up on her lap and tries to lick her chin.

"This really is beautiful," Godric says as he wanders over to stand behind them, picking up Patty to give her a kiss and saving his nanna from revealing her emotions.

"Have you brought your wife up here?" Godric asks.

"Once or twice. But she doesn't like it. Too hilly, too many stones for her horses. I sometimes sleep up here out under the stars. She complains about the wild boar. Tells me I could get trampled."

"Could you?"

"No."

"She is very beautiful, your wife. She does like her horses," Elizabeth says.

"Thank you. Oh, she is always with her beloved horses," Stefano leans forward. "She used to breed them to race. Did she tell you? Quite successful at one time, racing them in Siena. But every horse is different, and the ones she has now. Not so fast. I think she finds her horses quite frustrating."

"Do you watch the race in Siena?"

"I've never had the stomach for it. It's quite brutal when they fall, you know?" Stefano replies.

Elizabeth immediately wonders if this man has cottoned on to her love of animals and is saying things in an attempt to get her to let her guard down. She regrets her thought. Why is she so untrusting?

"You never really told us where we are?" Godric questions, now sitting beside his nanna on the old wooden bench.

"Two miles north of Siena," Stefano replies helpfully.

"What is this called? This area?" Godric asks.

"Verernuso. I named it Verenuso. It really didn't have a name before."

"This is all Stefano's land," Elizabeth explains to Godric.

"Crikey."

Elizabeth is still curious about Stefano.

"Why don't you want your daughter mixing with Marco Conti? Is he as unpleasant as he seems?" Elizabeth wonders if Stefano is trying to tell her something.

"Ruthless." Stefano smacks his hands against each other again. "Come on, I will take you back to San Gimignano," Stefano jingles his van keys in his pocket. "We need to find you some friendly refreshments before you return to Florence. I know just the spot." Stefano pauses and lifts his sunglasses to look at Elizabeth more closely. "And, you simply must come with us to Siena for Maundy Thursday evening supper. First, we passeggiata, then supper in Monti's, before a choir in the Duomo di Siena. It's truly magical. We go big at Easter, Professor Green."

"We're not religious, nor do I wish to watch others eat a sacrificial lamb."

"Oh, there will be no sacrifices, just a lot of fruit and vegetables. It is a plain supper." Then Stefano lifts his nose to the air as if breathing something wonderful before continuing. "But, a candlelit walk on the edge of the city afterwards. Now that is something not to miss."

Stefano drives them back to the edge of his land, near San Gimignano and stops off at his own delicatessen shop. He gifts them a large hamper full of picnic food. Bread, biscuits, juices, nuts, fruit, crackers, olive treats, and some dried beef for Patty. Elizabeth wonders if she will ever be able to look at an olive again in the same way after the day they have had.

28 INSPECTOR BOB ABLEY CALLS

When Godric and Elizabeth arrive back in Florence, they are so tired they can hardly speak. Godric has to lift Patty off the backseat of the Fiat, already fast asleep. Elizabeth notices Patty's tiny dirty paws sticking out from Godric's arms, her paw pads all scratched and sore from living rough. Such a small creature, with so many stories she cannot share, now entrusting her future so willingly into the hands of two strangers. Godric slows to allow Elizabeth to kiss Patty's head. Patty's eyes open to see where she is being taken, back into a building where she recognises the smells.

"We're home, Patty. Home now."

Their newly given 'access all areas' police parking badge, enabling them to pull up right outside the hotel, makes it easier for their new family member's comfort. Mere steps before Patty is cushioned on plump warm pillows like puffy white clouds compared to the thorny brambles of Patigno's cold hedgerows.

The idea of helping the police tomorrow, taking her away from Godric and Patty, makes Elizabeth shiver, so she starts unpacking the food basket gift from Stefano in the kitchenette to distract herself when Godric's phone rings. He shows his nanna the caller, 'Burb Abley', which Godric renamed after listening to the Commissario. She rolls her eyes and nods for Godric to accept the call.

"You have caused untold disruption to our holiday," are Godric's first words to Bob's face as he appears on Godric's phone.

"Hello, is Elizabeth there?"

"Er, you called my phone?" Godric shakes his head, turns the phone to his own face, waves, then points the phone at his nanna.

Inspector Bob Abley speaks again in Elizabeth's direction, only making out her silhouette in the dark. "How are you? I've been trying to reach you. I wanted to find out how things are going with Commissario Lorenzo Bianchi. I hear you're helping him on the case. That it's official? The Commissario said you are not leaving Florence until you find the poison. Please can you buy a mobile phone, Elizabeth?" Inspector Abley says, trying to be friendly and upbeat. "Lovely to see you."

"We're still on holiday," Godric reminds him, turning the phone camera back to face himself. "Why don't you wait for a postcard, like other people?"

"I hope you're getting to see the sights," Abley continues, ignoring Godric's barb, so Godric keeps the phone deliberately pointed at his own face, giving Elizabeth a chance to continue unpacking.

"We were shouted at, threatened with arrest, then taken to an olive farm by a stranger who knew the jewel thief. It messed with the itinerary I'd planned for Bunny. San Marino for the night. A hotel on standby which thankfully I was able to cancel," Godric rubs his face. "You do remember Valentine's Day, don't you? And, the whole reason why we wanted to get away? It wasn't just to look at buildings," Godric raises his eyebrows at Inspector Abley. They needed the break and Abley knows it.

"San Marino? That sounds wonderful." Disappointed, Elizabeth pulls an 'I'm sorry' face, deeply touched by his efforts to make this a holiday to remember. Then changes her tone to be short with Inspector Bob Abley. Shouting across at Godric's phone – Godric having laid back on the bed next to Patty and holding the phone above his head – she yells, "Look, Bob. We've had so many intrusions! Can you tell Superintendent Raynott that he should not have shared our information without our permission. That breaches all kinds of laws. The police here are not even telling me all the facts!"

"Peter Jones, you mean?"

"They fail to tell me that Peter Jones fell from a Tower. A tiny little detail. And, I did not agree to stay in Florence until the poison is found, as you put it! Who told you that?"

"He told me he told the Commissario that we were lending you to them for the duration." Abley shakes his head.

"He did what? What's his number?"

"Don't, Liz. I'll let him know," Abley sighs.

"Awful. We are having an awful time. Awful!" Elizabeth shouts, smirking at Godric, knowing it's only been partly awful and seeing that Bob would not be able to see her face. "There is this horrid man in San Gimignano. Nasty. Threatened to call the police on me because I wouldn't pay for a meat dish he gave me. It's true. We have met a friendly man. His name is Stefano. But can we trust him? He's being very friendly for a stranger. He saved us from the other man, Marco, but why? Why, Bob?"

"I don't understand?" Bob replies.

"Neither do I. Neither do I! Why is Superintendent Raynott giving out my name without permission to the Italian police who, by the way, were thinking about detaining us hours before at a car toll? Why are we not allowed to be tourists?!"

"Oh, Elizabeth. You have my word. I'll do

my best to get to the bottom of this. I have a call with the Commissario tomorrow. Can I see you? I can't see you?" Bob Abley pauses momentarily, then adds, "he always appears to be eating when I speak with him. Is he a big man?"

Elizabeth stops what she is doing and walks over to sit next to Godric, who hands her the phone. She holds it next to her ear, Bob can now only see the curls on her head. "Don't bother. I'm going to look at the bloods and cell analysis as they still haven't found the poison," she says. "Then, I'm out. If he doesn't listen to me, then I'll get you to speak with him then."

"Are you sure?" Abley asks. There is a pause.

"What are you going to do? You're miles away," Elizabeth shakes her head at him.

"The parking permit is useful," Godric says quietly.

"I do know. You went to, well, get away from everything." Bob Abley pauses again. Elizabeth winces that the phone is loud in her ear. "Let me see you. You have to hold the phone in front of you."

"I know that," Elizabeth replies, irritated by Bob bringing up her mood, irked that he is also calling her when she was unpacking, and when she was trying not to think about the sadness of missing Gerald and instead bury her thoughts in olive groves.

Godric and Bob know about Elizabeth's breakdown. Like a tank of water filling up around her head, and all she could do was blink. And all they could do was watch her suffocate. But Superintendent Raynott knows nothing of the sort. Bob Abley wants to shield his friend and feels like he has failed. Elizabeth does not want to discuss. Meanwhile, Godric whispers if he should take the phone back.

"Once I have identified the poison, I mean if I can. Once I've done that, I'm done with this. We're back on our holiday. Capeesh?" Elizabeth replies, finishing the conversation in her mind and handing the phone back to Godric, then getting up to return to the kitchen.

"When are you coming back?" Inspector Bob Abley replies but can now only see Patty the dog, sleeping on the bed now. Even Godric has no energy for this conversation. His tone changes. "You know I've been, well, worried about you. I care, Elizabeth." Abley's words take Elizabeth and Godric a little by surprise. Why bring that to the table tonight? Not appropriate. Especially in the mix of all this.

"Who knows," Elizabeth replies, but not shouting anymore, causing Bob to strain and Godric to have to repeat Elizabeth's words. Elizabeth knows she has a sabbatical from college. That things got a little complicated after Valentine's Day when she withdrew. Elizabeth does not wish to remember any of it.

She looks at Patty asleep on Godric's bed.

"My arms are aching," Godric takes the phone and props the phone up against a bedside table light.

Elizabeth finishes unpacking the gifts, lays down and nuzzles her face into Patty's. She listens to Inspector Bob Abley's small talk emanating from the phone. About the golf courses he's played on just outside Florence with the best seventeenth hole with this view over Tuscany that takes your breath away. About the driving ranges really close, how he knows they'd enjoy it if they went, and how it is very relaxing and a good idea to try on holiday. How he has finally had his kitchen fitted out in his new home in Grantchester, but he had to do a lot of the work himself as the builders kept disappearing. Elizabeth shuts her eyes. Godric walks into the kitchen to get some orange juice for them both, some of the olive bread he can eat with fresh humous from the hamper. He fills Patty's water bowl with fresh water, her other bowl with food, then picks the phone back up, Bob still talking about how he has set up a putting green in his garden as his neighbour has some excellent tips about how to grow the perfect putting lawn.

"Thanks, Bob. We'll come and look when we get back. Got to go now." Then after Bob Abley continues to talk about his putting swing, Godric increases the volume of his voice, “We have to go now, but can’t wait to see your new green!” Bob Abley finally hears and laughs with a goodbye. Godric hangs up and looks at his nanna. “That’s obsession, right there.”

Godric sits down on his bed next to Elizabeth and Patty. This apartment is the only one where they have not had separate rooms. Earlier, he enjoyed watching Patty jump between the beds, but Patty is not moving now, and seemingly neither is his nanna. He gets up quietly, picks up a blanket to cover them both, then walks back and settles down to watch a film on his phone with his headphones in on the other bed. Godric looks around the room and smiles. No matter what happened today, San Marino or no San Marino, he is happy to be here with his and nanna, who he knows loves him more than anyone in the world. He’s the lucky one. He tucks into the olive bread, humous and some of the vegan cheese and crisps from the hamper. “Nice one, Stefano,” he says quietly as he munches and turns his attention to choosing a film. As he takes a sip of red wine and scrolls through a search of Italian and comes across *‘La Dolce Vita’*, he presses play, putting in his headphones so as not to disturb his two most favourite people in the world.

29 POISON IN POLICE PATHOLOGY

The next morning, Elizabeth wakes early. After taking Patty out for an early pee-mail roam, she heads to the pathology lab at the police station. A few police officers recognise her, and her temporary pass gets her in without any issue or required conversation. The pathologist she met before, Roberto, is not there. Instead, a younger assistant is sat at a desk, studying DNA data on the computer while dunking biscotti in his morning coffee.

Elizabeth nods, then sits down beside him. She asks him to call up some files as she wants to investigate the possibility of olives being used as a poison in any form. But no matter what they look into, it appears even wild or uncooked olives will not kill alone and were not found in any blood works or cell autopsy. She is not writing off Stefano just yet, however, as who would be so nice to a stranger for no reason? A nice man, perhaps. She shakes her head again at her doubt and mistrust. 'Stick to the facts', she can hear Bob saying. What evidence does she have against Stefano? None. What about Marco? None. Although didn't Sergeant Rossi say that Marco was there at the bottom of the tower when the police found Peter Jones's body? Yes.

Elizabeth spends a while longer, making a deeper investigation into the data already accrued by the pathologist. Could he have missed anything? Doubtful. She notices a clock on the wall. Already two hours have gone by. This is not even her case. Elizabeth reminds herself that all she is doing here is agreeing to look to see if she can identify a poison. Today, she has not. Elizabeth tries to tell herself that it is not her fault. But the voice in her head is growing louder. Not only from what, but why did Peter Jones die?

"This is quite the challenge you have here," Elizabeth says to the assistant pathologist.

"We've tested for everything", he replies, munching, looking up at Elizabeth, his brown eyes like two cups of espresso, "and tested for drugs again yesterday. No drugs, alcohol, or prescription meds, like the report said. No spider bites. Nothing obvious. Perhaps it was a virus. I'm looking at that again now." He waves around another biscuit.

"What caused the immediate organ

failure? There are low to no autoimmune markers. No sore throat, no marks on the skin, nothing in the phlegm. I've read your colleague's report," Elizabeth replies, too tired to allow this seemingly friendly new person to know her. Everything is too complicated to let down her shield. Instead, the two of them nod, and the young man scratches his head.

"I've got to look anyway, so."

"Right ho." Elizabeth leaves the laboratory frustrated but determined not to spoil Godric's holiday.

*

Elizabeth, Godric and Patty meander through the streets of Florence. At the bottom of a steep hill, below the Piazzale Michelangelo and on the Viale Giuseppe Poggi, they stop at a corner restaurant that juts out into the fairway of an old cobbled street and independent boutique shops. With its wobbly leg, their street-side corner table overlooks milling crowds who head up the hill. Patty jumps up onto Godric's lap as they collapse into their seats.

"Isn't this relaxing," Godric says, sipping a glass of ice-cold vino brought to the table moments before. "I could do this forever."
Elizabeth closes her eyes and opens them again to look at the view. Holidaymakers wandering slowly, locals with newspapers and dogs on

long leads greeting others. People looking into shop windows full of mirrors, children staring longingly at knick-knacks on corner stalls, an old lady with a walking frame inching her way across the street. Vespas and trucks stopping and waiting patiently for her to reach the other side. A beautiful young woman, taller and thinner than anyone, smiling at a young man who turns once she has passed to wonder what might have happened had he had the guts to say hello.

"This is such a contented city," Elizabeth observes.

"The sun is out. What's not to love?" Godric looks at a handsome Italian man walking past, pushing a bicycle.

"I had the best sleep," Elizabeth admits to Godric, nodding to the waiter for bringing a plate of freshly made spinach and vegan cheese ravioli. "If only I could stop thinking about this wretched jewel thief."

"I have an idea to help you forget. Let's go up the steps after this and have pudding up there?" Godric opens his eyes wide. Elizabeth looks up the hill, where brave souls are already embarking on the climb.

"One of us will have to carry Patty," Elizabeth says, realising with those words she's agreed to take on an almost vertical climb.

"I'll carry Patty."

"I wish I'd identified the poison this

morning and could be done with it. It's staring me in the face, but I just can't see it," Elizabeth prongs a piece of ravioli with her fork.

"Maybe he wasn't poisoned. I mean, he was pushed. They seem to be overcomplicating the whole thing," Godric suggests.

"He suffered multiple organ failure at least an hour before he fell. Classic poison. Even an autoimmune response like Lupus wouldn't be that quick."

"Maybe mull it over but give yourself a cut-off time. We move on. We leave this behind." Godric stuffs so much pasta into his mouth Elizabeth observes a possible choking hazard, cheeks like Dizzy Gillespie, but is relieved when somehow it disappears with speed.

"What I don't understand is why Stefano was so nice to us?" She waits to hear if Godric has a reliable answer.

"Yeah, and boy, what a big place he had there."

"How did he happen to be there when that dreadful Marco Conti was shouting at us?" Elizabeth tries not to think back too much about the incident. "Could they have been playing us? Nice man, horrid man? Do you think they are in this together? This Marco seems to be connected to Stefano's daughter?"

"It's a small place, isn't it, San G. Let's face it, most of the people out and about are tourists. Did you notice that?" Godric continues to watch the tourists go past as he shovels another fork loaded with far too much farfalle.

"Stefano didn't look like a killer. But working with the Inspector has taught me that they never do. He can't be that nice all the time." Elizabeth pauses, unsure whether to say anything more. "You know, it felt like we'd met before. He was so familiar, wasn't he?"

"He said he liked the English," Godric acknowledges, taking a sip of wine, missing her cue that he might resemble his grandpa in some way.

"Yes, that must be it." Elizabeth decides not to tell Godric what she is thinking. How Stefano has an uncanny smile just like Gerald's, and how she finds it most unnerving. Could Stefano be channelling Gerald from wherever he is? Oh, what rot. Clinging to magical thoughts like this. She prides herself on being rational. Is it the Italian air? She looks around again. Everyone really does still look happy. Can she feel happy too? Breathe, she thinks. "Are you sure this is vegan?" Elizabeth asks Godric after tasting the pasta.

"Yes, see? Both are 'Vegano'. Can I try some of yours?" Godric picks up the menu, pointing, then prongs some of Elizabeth's pasta ravioli before her reply.

"This is delicious," Elizabeth pops more food in. "What is Patty eating?"

"She ate a lot this morning. Her tummy is like a drum." Godric feels Patty's tummy.

"Maybe we can ask for a carrot? I hate to see her left out, salivating over our food." Elizabeth strokes Patty's head.

"Stefano invited us to that supper thing. Let's go, and you can see if he gives any clues away, can't you," Godric smiles, "and Patty might get a steak out of it." Patty licks Godric's chin almost as if she understands. Godric whispers to a waiter, and soon they come over with a peeled carrot, chopped into thin sticks. Elizabeth's mind is racing ahead.

"Sergeant Rossi said Marco was there when the police were sifting for clues after Peter's fall. What was he doing? Am I getting too involved?"

"No, you're just trying to help," Godric replies. "But when it's time to go, it's time to go, okay?" Godric is concerned that his nanna is becoming way too involved in the case, but he also knows that she must realise that for herself. He cannot pressure her at all, as she is full of self-doubt.

"And Giuseppe." Elizabeth is not listening, too wrapped up in this case. "They're coming out of the woodwork." Elizabeth pops another ravioli into her mouth. Godric beams to see her so animated. But he also knows what this means, so he reiterates.

"When it's time to go." Godric looks at his

nanna. "Steps next, then?" Elizabeth nods, then watches Patty crunch carrot.

*

The steps up to the Piazzale Michelangelo are crowded. Everyone hoping to see the spectacular view across Florence, politely trying not to bump into one another. Elizabeth remembers how she had meant to climb them with Gerald and how they were going to count the steps, but they never made it. Gerald had said he would take her back, and they would drink champagne as the sun went down. She does not tell Godric, but this is the place she has been dreading visiting the most. The view that Gerald never saw and will never see. This time, with Godric, they climb the steps quietly. After a while, Elizabeth has to pause to catch her breath. Many are doing the same thing. Street sellers have placed their drawings, postcards and other objects for sale in places where they know there will be a good excuse to browse. When Elizabeth and Godric finally get to the top, they notice how busy it looks. Godric leads Elizabeth across to the railings, where everyone has congregated to look at the view.

"Your grandad and I were going to come back here to drink champagne and watch the sunset. He wanted to come but I was in a hurry to look at something else. Some seed collection, if I recall. So, we never got to see the changing light that he wanted to take me to." Godric listens to his nanna, seeing the angst across her brow. "It was my fault," she laments.

Godric wants to make her feel alright, to take the pain away or numb it at least. His eyes dart about, across to the refreshment area. The most expensive looking restaurant on the highest point looks completely full. One of those places where booking is essential. Ugh. But then he notices a couple about to leave and rushes to secure their spot. Not waiting to explain to Elizabeth. Before anyone can question whether he is next to be seated, with confidence, he orders their most expensive bottle of champagne. This beautiful, tall young man, leaps and bounds more handsome than anyone in the vicinity. Perhaps the restaurant thinking he might be a famous actor or model, takes his order.

Elizabeth spots what he has done and walks across with Patty, smiling. Godric sees her smile and beams, holding out her chair. They sit and watch the afternoon play out across Florence, Godric fully aware of the bittersweet emotions passing across Elizabeth's face. The nostalgia of her last trip to Florence leaving her wounded. Even though Elizabeth would rather chew off her own hand than converse with tourists about what type of breed Patty is, she finds herself doing so just to bury heavy feelings about Gerald. Finally, the long line of people adoring Patty slows, and Elizabeth looks out across the city and starts to count the beautiful buildings that jump out of the skyline. Godric orders himself some expensive whisky to wash down the champagne then squeezes his nanna's hand.

"Watch this," Godric takes a treat out of his pocket, throws it into the air, and Patty catches it. He does it again. This time he throws the treat higher, and she catches it again. "I think we have a cricket leg fielder here."

"Remember, she's not a performing monkey." Elizabeth smiles. She shares her other, more pressing distraction. "I'm not surprised they can't find a diamond. It could be anywhere."

"Something tells me you're going to find it, if you want to," Godric replies, then throws a peanut from a bowl on their table up into the air and catches it in his mouth. Then throws another higher and catches it again. Patty jumps to try to beat him. So he throws a dog treat up for her.

"I'm just going to look for the poison," Elizabeth says to her two performing monkeys, perhaps trying to convince herself about the turn of events. "And then we're gone." She looks at Godric. "I do listen."

"Maybe that's all they need to solve it." Godric pauses and remembers the film he watched last night. "Maybe the jewel thief, like Marcello Rubini in *La Dolce Vita*, was so wrapped up in a world they didn't enjoy and yearned for a simpler life that they took it to escape Florence?"

"First, *La Dolce Vita* was set in Rome. Second, the poor neglected girlfriend committed suicide. She wasn't poisoned?"

"No, but perhaps we should be looking for the decadence in Florence. Perhaps decadence is where you'll find the poisoner. You know, sex, drugs and rock and roll. Who steals an expensive red diamond from an art exhibition? Someone who knew it was there. Your average Joe wouldn't, would they? It's quite the sexy theft, isn't it? Look at all this wealth. Like I say, like in *La Dolce Vita*."

Godric and Elizabeth stare out at the beautiful city, full of many opulent properties. There is no sign of sex, drugs, or rock and roll. Just rooftops and pale brickwork, spires and the Dome. They stay for ages and watch the sunset, ordering more food, as tourists mill below taking endless photographs. Try as she might, Elizabeth cannot feel less like one of them. With no Gerald and already pulled into what is impossible not to think of as a murder case, she has foreboding that the only way out of this trip is to speak with the Commissario about the missing diamond and a dead diamond thief.

30 THE FIRST WHIFF OF DECADENCE IN SIENA

The next day, Elizabeth and Godric manage to get at least some time to themselves during the day, Elizabeth writing postcards to Emily, Mrs Cloud and Bob Abley among others. Godric sleeping, teaching Patty more tricks, and watching Italian gameshows on the television with the sound turned down. As the heat of the day departs Florence, the sun soon to leave the pavements and climb up the walls, in an attempt to keep the holiday feeling going before they drive to Stefano Brambilla's dinner invitation, Godric takes his nanna on a short stroll with Patty to a 'wine window'.

"I remember this," Elizabeth smiles, reminiscing how Gerald had taken her to one of these before as they stand beside a beautiful old building with flaking paint and sun-bleached shutters.

"That's why I thought you'd like it. Wine or by the glass from a window." As they arrive, there is no queue, and Godric picks up two full-bodied reds in paper cups and they perch on steps beside the window with a bag of peanuts, catching the last rays in this piazza full of tall old buildings, most of which look like residential homes.

Elizabeth looks at her grandson, sipping wine, enjoying the moment. She notices geraniums in bloom in window boxes and a local woman leaning out of a first-floor window beating a mat stretched over a washing line which hangs across an alley. How pretty and peaceful the small tucked away piazza seems as they celebrate this timeless tradition. Elizabeth shuts her eyes in this transient moment and can picture Gerald. Telling them about the buildings and their history. Chatting with the local proprietor and already building such a rapport that he knows their first name and where their children go to school.

"Follow me," Godric stands up after the wine. They wander through to the next piazza, Mercato Nuovo. There Elizabeth sees the bronze statue of the wild boar, Il Porcellino, his nose shiny from all the rubbing by tourists. "You came back," Godric puts his arm around his nanna.

"Ah." Elizabeth smiles fondly at the boar

standing proud on a plinth, and walks across. She remembers Gerald telling her the tale that if you rub the nose of the boar then you will return to Florence. She remembers distinctly that Gerald had not rubbed the nose all those years ago. He was so busy looking for a coin for Elizabeth to put in the statue's mouth that he forgot. Elizabeth tries to avoid Godric's eyes in case she cannot control her feelings. Instead, she leans down to Patty and strokes her head. "Isn't Goddy kind, bringing me here," she says, still looking firmly at Patty. Finally, Elizabeth glances at Godric, who can see how close her emotion is to spilling over. He takes her hand and they wander out of the piazza, the warm glow of the sun now just clipping the rooftops.

*

By the time they arrive in Siena, it is almost twilight. Parking outside the city they head through imposing gates and up the Via Pantaneto.

"I have this hotel booked for a bit next week. I might as well tell you now we're right here." Godric stops outside a hotel frontage, with its two olive trees in large pots either side of the entrance and lights within the leaves just starting to twinkle. Patty sniffs and finds something on the pavement which she starts to eat.

"Ah, what a lovely idea," Elizabeth looks up

at the stone walls and shuttered windows.

"Shall I postpone it?"

"Definitely not. It will be wonderful."

"Maybe I will find where you've hidden my music by then. Hmm?" Godric raises the issue of his missing Daft Punk CD he was looking for.

"I don't think you'll get lucky," Elizabeth smirks.

They pass the hotel and turn left into Via Rinaldini to Ill Campo. Bleached stone buildings with shutters and window boxes make it feel romantic as the piazza opens out into a vast space. Godric takes Elizabeth's arm and folds it over his own as the two stand in the middle of Piazza Del Campo taking in the evening, Patty nudging into Elizabeth's leg. The floor is sloped down towards the Palazzo Pubblico. People squat down on the warm cobbles, still emitting heat from the day, and look up across the tall tower, the last pigeons perched high who themselves are observing all human activity in case of the chance of final pizza crumbs before they settle to roost, coo-cooing out the last of the spring sunset.

"Have you been here before?" Elizabeth asks Godric.

"Only on a stag do. I think I was in a coma for most of it," he looks around, this time in awe. "Where are we supposed to be, exactly?" Godric asks. Elizabeth points behind them.

"I think that's us. Looks like we missed the

passeggiata." They both look up to the top of the piazza at Ristorante del Monti's. There must be thirty people all standing, drinking apéritifs and clearly in a group. They see Stefano, who then spots them and starts to wander down. "And there is our charming new friend," Elizabeth whispers.

"Well, they look like a jolly bunch. Free booze. Warm evening. I say let's do this," Godric replies under his breath.

Stefano ushers them to meet his friends and reacquaint themselves with his daughters and wife. Godric picks up Patty to protect her from the bustle.

"That is Octaviarius, Ock. He is dating my daughter, Sophia." Stefano points to a large tall man with blonde curly hair, tattoos, unnaturally white teeth, and ostentatious designer clothes.

"And you are singling him out first because?" Elizabeth asks.

"It was his mother's diamond. He comes from one of the richest families in Italy," Stefano shouts to Elizabeth and Godric over the noisy group.

"And he is dating your daughter," Godric nods. As if Ock can feel his ears burning, he turns. Sophia too. They make their way over to Stefano, clearly having yet to speak to him this evening.

"Papa! You're looking gorgeous," Ock

shouts, looking down at Stefano's black jeans and floppy linen jacket, wobbling his head in disapproval. "Listen, you could wear a bin bag and look wonderful!" Ock goes in for a huge hug and squeezes Stefano, towering over his girlfriend's father by half a foot, even though Stefano is probably over six foot himself.

"How are people getting taller and taller?" Stefano asks, glancing back at the very tall Godric and then at his daughter, Sophia, who has to bend in her heels to kiss her papa. "Ock is in the fashion biz. So, I have to take his words about my clothing as genuine, Professor Green," Stefano explains, leaning right into Elizabeth's ear to bring her into his confidence, putting his arm on her shoulder, then whispering, "Or at least it will all be his – the fashion empire - when he hits twenty-five. It's all trust fund for now. He's just playing at being a grown-up right now."

"Quite a connection, the families then," Elizabeth replies.

"My daughter, Sophia. Isn't she beautiful?" Stefano hugs his daughter.

"It's nice to see you again. Are you enjoying your holidays?" Sophia asks Elizabeth and Godric, beaming a youthful smile at Godric.

"Yes, we are," Elizabeth replies.

"It is certainly nice to have left the English weather behind," Godric adds trying, to be agreeable even though he's not immediately taken to either Sophia or Ock. Something about their air of superiority.

"I've never been. I would love to see London," Sophia says.

"Then I'll take you," Ock kisses Sophia in front of Stefano. "Shall we take our seats?" Ock suggests to Sophia, looking across her shoulder at the cooler group beginning to sit down.

"Professor Green, Godric, you must sit with us." Stefano beckons them further down the table, where Aurelia is already sitting. Once he has them all seated, Stefano walks away momentarily to greet someone else, leaving Elizabeth and Godric wondering about the people in front of them.

"Why has Stefano invited us to this?" Elizabeth shakes her head at Godric, leaning in to speak quietly over the din around them. "He comes to our rescue in San Gimignano. It's quite the coincidence, isn't it? That he happened to know Peter Jones, the dead man. The man who stole the diamond from Stefano's daughter's boyfriend's mother?" Elizabeth whispers to Godric, hiding her mouth with a napkin.

"But why use Peter Jones at all?" Godric asks quietly. "If Stefano stole the diamond? Wouldn't he just have made some excuse to pick up his daughter from the house and taken it himself? Why wait until it is in an exhibition, and then push a man off a tower?"

"But that would leave a link back. No, we must keep Stefano close. This man is too perfect. Did you hear him telling me Ock still needs to get a trust fund? He has a trust fund? And what's that got to do with anything anyway? Is he trying to suggest that Ock stole his own mother's jewellery?"

They watch Stefano walk back to them, carrying a bottle of champagne and three glasses.

"We will have wine soon, but here. Let's celebrate." Stefano pours, "To new friendships."

Nothing about this meal feels Maundy Thursday. Wine flows, and the quality of conversation from the guests declines proportionally. Attentions dwindle so much that Patty is able to take a steak from under a guest's nose without them noticing. All but Ock, who spots the action.

"How shall we punish this dog?" He jests, jumping up and pointing at Patty finishing the meat, both front paws on the table, having found an empty chair to reach across to the ignored plate.

"With love," Elizabeth replies, not liking the spoiled young man.

But Ock does not listen to Elizabeth. He lunges and grabs Patty, holding her up, her back legs dangling, and starts to shout across the table in

Italian to his young male friends that perhaps he should shoot the dog for stealing the steak. Aghast, Godric stands up and holds his hands out for Ock to return Patty.

"You'll have to shoot me first!" Godric screams.

"Hey, hey. Everyone, calm down. Ock, that's not funny. Come on, what's got into you?" Sophia asks.

"Oh, I don't know. Let me think. You're sitting with the English and they just robbed my mother." Ock holds Patty for too long until reading the room and seeing the level of disapproval, so reluctantly hands Patty back to Godric, while at the same time looking at Stefano. "It's true, is it not?" Ock throws away the line as he returns to his seat.

"Professor Green, please accept my apologies on his behalf. He is just a spoilt brat, with more airs than sense," Sophia shakes her head.

"Are you happy he is seeing one of your daughters?" Elizabeth, now cross, asks Stefano.

"Grown women know their own mind." Stefano sighs. "Or, at least, that's what my wife tells me." Stefano looks at Aurelia.

"Grown women do, darling. But she will always be your baby," Aurelia replies, then continues speaking with the man sitting beside her.

"People who are cruel to animals are

cruel to people," Elizabeth replies, observing Ock from across the table as he piles glasses high and pours champagne into them, only to let them fall all over his friend, soaking his trousers.

"I fear he's not a fan of the English. As it happens, I don't think they like his fashion empire, the clothes. He's tried to sell in London but has had to close the stores," Stefano pulls the side of his mouth up.

Elizabeth takes a strong dislike to Ock, continuing to stare as he grabs hold of Sophia's chin, not letting go, then ruffling her hair with the other hand while laughing, before pushing back her face. Ock looks back at Elizabeth, noticing her eyes on him. Elizabeth picks up a carrot from a side dish and gives it to Patty and then stares back at Ock, who holds his hands in a shape as if he's strangling Patty, then sticks out his tongue to the side, making a face as if being choked, before turning back to his friends and laughing. Elizabeth wonders if she should have riled up this young man. She watches Patty munching on the carrot, perhaps a little unhappy that it does not taste like steak.

Just as the tiramisùs are brought out, Stefano stands and says he will be back in a moment. They watch him cross the piazza and stop outside a café. Moments later, Marco Conti appears, mingling out the front between the patio tables, speaking to diners and filling up wine glasses.

"What? Look at that. He must have a wine store and restaurant here too?" Godric says surprised.

"This is such a complicated family," Elizabeth observes. Then they see Isabella, Stefano's other daughter who is dating Marco, emerge from Marco's restaurant.

"Uh oh," Godric comments, "Papa isn't happy."

Stefano starts to gesticulate at Marco, and they see Isabella trying to separate them as Marco puffs out his chest and pulls Stefano away from his customers and out into the piazza.

The two men are far more animated now, jabbing at each other. Elizabeth looks around at the table where she is sitting. Everyone is still chatting and laughing, not noticing what is happening less than a hundred feet away. She looks back and sees Isabella following the men and pulling at Marco to leave her father alone. Stefano starts to prod at Marco's chest and push him backwards. Marco doesn't retaliate at first but then starts to shove Stefano backwards. The two men begin to shout. Marco shoves Isabella to stay out of it, which prompts Stefano to punch Marco. Both Elizabeth and Godric watch as Marco falls back onto the stones and stays down. Then right in front of Stefano's eyes, his daughter, Isabella, falls to the ground and kisses Marco where her father punched him. There are gasps, as it is clear some closer to the altercation have been watching. Elizabeth then sees it, out of the corner of her eye, parked up along a street which enters the piazza. She stands up. Godric looks at her.

"Do you see it?!" Elizabeth shouts.

"Bunny?"

"There. There. Look! The red van. Look!"

Godric sees it.

"Yes!"

Elizabeth rushes out into the Piazza Ill Campo, leaving Godric with Patty, unsure what to do for a moment. He picks up Patty and follows as Elizabeth rushes across the piazza. They both hear the tell-tale red van's engine start and it begins a clumsy three-point turn. Elizabeth is almost across the piazza and feet from the rear window as it makes the final turn before it zooms away. Godric following after her. They look at each other. There was no mistake. That was the red van that has been following them.

"You saw that, didn't you?"

Godric nods. For a moment, they are completely caught up in what that means. Elizabeth shakes her head. They start to walk back, almost forgetting the fight that just happened between Marco and Stefano.

In the middle of the piazza, they watch now at a close distance, as Isabella gets up, leaves Marco sitting on the cobbles, and wanders back to the restaurant, not looking back at Marco or her father. Marco shakes his head, still stung from the punch. Finally, he gets to his feet and disappears into the back of the restaurant. Stefano sees Elizabeth and Godric, thinking they have rushed out to him. He joins them in the middle of the piazza, now bustling and alive again with a generally convivial atmosphere of holidaymakers having gone back to their relaxed dinners and drinks.

"Please accept my apologies, Professor Green. I didn't mean for you to see that. Not my finest hour. Also, for leaving you here. I'm sorry. But I must take my daughter home. May I call upon you tomorrow and take you to see some more of our beautiful countryside in an attempt to salvage our earlier time together? You're my guests. Everything is taken care of." Stefano gesticulates towards the restaurant. "I do hope we can meet again."

"I did not expect to witness violence this evening," Elizabeth states disappointedly.

"Another day," Stefano shakes his head. "Good night. Good night, Godric."

Elizabeth and Godric watch him retrieve his daughter, Isabella, and then leave the Piazza Ill Campo from the top corner. Isabella, with her arm around her father's shoulders, kissing him on the cheek.

Feeling more exposed to Ock and his friends, who grow more riotous, Elizabeth and

Godric decide not to return to the restaurant without Stefano.

"Well, that was something else," Godric laughs nervously as he places Patty gently on the cobbles to stretch her legs.

"Fathers and daughters."

"Notice his right hook? I mean, kapow."

"Certainly a heightened reaction." Elizabeth is puzzled by Stefano. "He seems to have two sides. Did you hear him apologising that we saw his violence but not for actually hitting Marco?"

Godric watches Patty sniff a post. He bends down to pat her head. "Good Patty, yes you are, yes you are."

Elizabeth and Godric decide to take a wander around the edge of the piazza, still a little shaken. Somehow, stretching their legs before they get back in the car to Florence seems the wise decision. Siena's sunshine has been replaced by twinkling lights from restaurants and outside fires from the pavement cafe patios. With each step, a calm feeling envelopes them once again.

They come to a standstill outside a corner cafe at the very bottom of the piazza, far enough away from where they ate earlier, and decide to perch for a while. Two vegan hot chocolates come in large art deco cups, which Elizabeth secretly wants to take home—looking at the bottom to see where she can buy them later. With Patty on Elizabeth's lap, they sit in comfortable silence and watch a group of children play ball, which keeps running down the piazza slope. No older than ten or eleven, so full of life.

Then, from the top of the piazza, a graceful woman wearing an extravagant sparkling midnight blue ball gown, with a long train, glides straight through the children, ignoring their tackles and kicks. They weave around her as if used to such a vision every day. She pauses at the bottom of the piazza for a moment, right under the Tower. Elizabeth and Godric are at once mesmerised, the lights from the restaurants bouncing off her glittering gown. From the far side of the piazza, another woman appears, wheeling out a harp. The beautiful woman in the dress stands for a moment, almost as if staring at the boys scoring and defending goals or perhaps possessed by some invisible otherworldly goddess leader. People walk past, busy in their conversations, some not noticing at all. Others, seeing and then in hushed tones whispering to their friends and lovers about the famous lady.

Then spontaneously, the woman bursts into singing Puccini's Gianni Schicchi '*O mio babbino caro*'. Elizabeth feels overwhelmed by the acoustics of the piazza and the strength and beauty of the woman's voice. The sloping piazza carries the music into the air, circling above their heads. People immediately stop to listen. The harpist like an exquisite creature. Some appear from their homes above restaurants onto balconies, windows thrown wide. There is a hush from the restaurants as almost everyone stops their chatter and clanking of forks. The music enters their hearts and transcends, sending joy soaring into the night sky.

After the opera singer finishes, there is a round of applause, and then the singer and the harpist leave the piazza, walking right past Elizabeth and Godric as if they were just out on an evening stroll. The singer smiles at Godric. They are gone, then people continue enjoying another extraordinary evening in Siena.

"See, all these things I arrange for you," Godric says jokily, as surprised as Elizabeth by what just happened. "How are you feeling?" Godric asks his nanna? "Was this a good idea, or what?" Godric lifts his finger to the waiter to bring two more hot chocolates.

"This was a very good idea." Elizabeth smiles, momentarily caught by the beauty of music.

"What a night." Godric references in his voice all things that have gone before. "That kind and generous man we were sitting with at dinner punched a man so hard he fell to the ground and stayed there for rather a long time? We haven't seen an ambulance, so I suspect he's okay. Though that must have hurt," Godric makes a punching noise and flicks his face to the side.

"It seems there are too many suspects who could have taken the missing diamond. Stefano, the friend of the thief, a violent but kind man? Marco, the nasty restaurant owner from San Gimignano, very close to the tower where the jewel thief died. Now the son of the woman whose jewel was stolen. And what about Ock's possible fashion sales failing in London. Are we led to believe he did it? Then the panic-stricken Giuseppe, who thinks he is next, but who is still very much alive? And, why do I feel like we are being dragged more and more into something which far from resembles a holiday." Elizabeth tries to keep hold of the music in her heart, but it has already disappeared for anxiety to take its place once more.

*

Godric drives his nanna and Patty back in the dark to Florence. The scents of jasmine and honeysuckle from the hedgerows waft into the windows on the shortcut route Stefano showed them earlier, with only stars and an occasional roadside restaurant lighting their way. The small Fiat 500 classic headlamps, grateful even for the help from the smallest glowworm. Despite being nearly midnight, people are still out eating and drinking as the air remains warm. Villages come and go until finally the lights of Florence begin to flicker on the horizon.

Still happy with his free parking pass, Godric drives to their hotel and into the car park bay. Once again, they both collapse into their hotel apartment. Patty jumps up on Godric's bed, and he lifts her onto Elizabeth's. As Elizabeth brushes her teeth, Godric notices a note come whizzing under the hotel apartment door. He walks over and opens the door to see who left it, but no one is there.

"Curious?" he says to himself. Godric opens the note and continues talking to himself as he walks back into the room. "What is it about these Italian men and notes? Why can't they leave my Bunny alone?" Godric reads the note, then makes a paper aeroplane out of it and throws it towards Elizabeth's bed, watching it glide across onto her duvet. He is pretty happy with his aerodynamic skills and nods his head. Elizabeth walks out of the bathroom, notices and picks it up.

"Are you taking up origami now?"

"Maybe, with all these invitations being thrown at us like darts. You're cordially invited to attend some event tomorrow night with Giuseppe Esposito. Yada, yada."

"Ugh. I find that man completely devoid of charm. Do me a favour and make that plane fly again right out the window."

"With pleasure," Godric replies, grabbing it back off her bed, reassembling, then taking great joy in watching it fly out into the dark sky.

"What is the Crocioni Castiglione di Garfagnana anyway?" Elizabeth asks rhetorically. Godric checks his mobile.

"It's in Grassina, about fifteen minutes outside Florence in the car. Apparently, they put on an Easter passion play. Oh my. It says around five hundred locals reenact the Passion of Christ. A three-hundred-year-old tradition in the evening by all accounts."

"Does Giuseppe not know I'm an atheist?"

"No, but it is Easter Friday tomorrow," Godric shrugs. "Maybe he is?"

Elizabeth goes to bed hoping tomorrow that their holiday can return to normal, at least after she's tried to look for poison one last time in the police pathology laboratory just so Godric can keep his free parking.

31 FRIDAY I'M IN LOVE

Morning in Florence, and Elizabeth repeats her early rise to try to go into the police pathology lab before Godric stirs. She walks Patty first, noticing the paper aeroplane from last night still on the pavement beneath their window outside the hotel. With a heavy heart, Elizabeth picks it up. Not knowing why but thinking she might need it later.

She looks around at the people walking by. A few are rushing, perhaps to shop jobs or offices, most just ambling, contented, stopping to window shop, or to listen to the busker further up playing Spanish guitar, or even maybe choose what type of croissant to buy from a breakfast café which seems to have at least twenty different kinds of pastries photographed and stuck on the wall, with smells of coffee and sugar pumping out onto the pavement.

Unlike the happy people, Elizabeth feels uncomfortable, aware of some uncommon fragility that has settled inside. In her mind's eye, her own heart is circling a drain. Elizabeth stops in the middle of the pavement and puts her hand to her heart to check she can still feel it beat. At first, she cannot find the pulse. She slips her hand through the buttons of her blouse, still nothing. She shuts her eyes and drops her chin. Is this where she is? Finally, there it is. Not like an elephant's booming rhythm, nor that of a mouse, whose frantic beats would enable flights of speed. Instead, faint, ghost-like, disappearing. All the grief molding into a dark mountain.

Elizabeth opens her eyes and looks down. Patty has just been standing, doing nothing, waiting patiently for Elizabeth to move. Why is Patty's life so vulnerable to Elizabeth's own levels of joy? It feels so unfair that she can wield such power over an innocent creature whose life is much shorter than her own—with no time to go over and over things or waste minutes, days, months, years lamenting, broken. Elizabeth spots a sports shop and wanders in. Before any staff can protest about Patty, she has purchased a tin of tennis balls.

"Patty, you want to play ball?" Elizabeth lets Patty off the lead in a small piazza. She laughs, watching Patty run after a ball, return then drop it beside Elizabeth's shoes, only to repeat the exercise again and again. Clearly not Patty's first time at this game! Finally, Elizabeth ruffles Patty's fur, kisses her on the head, takes out another clean tennis ball and drops it down. Patty is overwhelmed with joy. Two balls!!

*

Bank holiday Friday means the police reception officer at the front desk is surprised to see Elizabeth but waves her into the station. The pathology laboratory, however, is completely silent. Elizabeth sighs. Being on a supposed holiday herself means that every day feels like today, although she spends a good hour or two looking at samples, testing blood for different compositions and opening up the computer software to rerun sample analysis. She still finds nothing and leaves the station, the reception officer now watching a football replay on a small screen in the front office.

When Elizabeth arrives back at their hotel apartment, Godric is sitting in bed watching a film on his phone. She suggests they have a tourist morning when he's ready, and switch off from all the recent shenanigans. It takes a while for them to leave the apartment, but when they do they ask the hotel reception for the best pizza restaurant in Florence where the locals eat. First, they wander along Dei Neri heading to the Basilica of Santa Croce and notice little churches with flowers on pedestal displays. Godric spots another classic Fiat 500, probably from the 1960s. This time black and more beaten up, with no sunroof. Finally, a rain shower and petrichor bouncing off the cobbles drives them into the recommended eatery, and they sit and share the largest pizza, giving Patty some of her own food in a bowl. By the time Elizabeth and Godric are on their lemon sorbets, they have forgotten all about Commissario Bianchi, Stefano, Marco, Giuseppe and the dead Peter Jones.

Once outside, beneath a rainbow, they wander along the banks of the River Arno and stop to watch a boat chugging up towards the Ponte Vecchio. Another short but heavy rain shower makes Godric pick up Patty and suggest they take cover in a shop selling pet toys. It is tiny, but Godric manages to eke out twenty minutes of joy squeeze-testing all the rubber chickens and mice. In the end, they leave with a dog blanket and a toy duck to add to her favourite tin of tennis balls.

"Dead duck," Elizabeth says, holding the toy. "Patty, you have a dead duck, dead duck." The fluffy orange and green piece of material sewn into the shape of a duck, but with an elongated body perfect for little teeth, is grabbed by Patty who tries to hold it with her feet and kill it.

As they continue along the riverbank, they notice more flower displays in grand homes and little churches—Godric comments on the lack of Easter bunnies or chocolate eggs. Finally, the sun pours down beneath the clouds. Patty stops to sniff a lamppost, and they come to a standstill at a pair of large shiny metal gates, through which they see a driveway with three supercars parked outside.

"Boy, someone knows how to take more than their share," Godric says, looking up at the windows. "Hey! Isn't that the Maximilius chap from the papers? The diamond owner and presumably that Ock bloke's father?"

"Where?" Elizabeth looks up at the house, but Maximilius has disappeared from the window.

"Oh, where did he go?"

Then, to their surprise the Commissario exits the front door, speaking with a beautiful woman who resembles something of a movie star from 1950s Hollywood glamour. The Commissario spots Elizabeth at the gate. She is unsure whether to run or pretend to be someone else as she was so enjoying her holidaying with Godric. He waves at her, indicating for them to wait. The Commissario nods his head at the woman, and they shake hands. She returns inside but not before pressing a button on the gates so that the Commissario may depart. Elizabeth and Godric watch him pick up speed and only just make it through the gates before they snap shut. The Commissario laughs as it is not his first time.

"They got me last time. Vicious." Then he smiles. "Is this a coincidence, or were you looking for me? Good timing, as I'd like to speak with you. There's been a development."

"It was a coincidence," Elizabeth says, not smiling. "And what gives you the right to say to my Inspector that I was staying in Florence to find the poison and wouldn't leave until it's found?"

"Come on, let's get you some of our famous ice cream to put a smile on your face."

"Are you just going to ignore my question?"

"I will answer, but first, ice cream." The Commissario takes them across the Ponte Vecchio Bridge, which is very busy and for a split second, Elizabeth wonders if they could accidentally on purpose lose the Commissario in the crowd. But he keeps turning around, making sure they are still with him, holding up his arm and pointing in the direction they all should head, and Elizabeth, disappointed with herself, feels like she has no resistance against this man's plans. Crowds start to thin out on the other side, and after a few streets they reach the Pritti Palace and the sloping pavement outside, all the glorious gardens hidden behind its high walls.

"The best view is inside," the Commissario explains, "and the best ice cream."

"But Patty isn't allowed in the Boboli

Gardens? No dogs?" Godric is confused about why Lorenzo should lead them here. The Commissario smiles, and as they approach the entrance he nods at the man next to the gates inside the ticket office who waves them all through. The Commissario then nods to Godric that he can put Patty down and let her off the lead.

"I'm famished. Lucia Romano is a wonderful host, but I'm not a fan of caviar." The Commissario sees a stall selling cones of chips and orders one for himself, and Godric nods for another. Elizabeth winces at the idea of chips, and certainly not double-fried chips! They sit on a bench nearby as Patty rolls on the grass behind them. After the Commissario finishes his chips, he returns to the stall to order two hot dogs.

"These are the best hot dogs in Florence. Well, I'm not sure about the vegan ones," Lorenzo smirks at Godric. They see he has also bought a large bag of sweets to stuff into his jacket. Once eating has finished, the Commissario stands. Now ice cream. The Commissario comes back with three.

"Shall we walk? Patty can stretch her little legs?" The Commissario does not wait for them to agree but starts walking, turning his back on them. Elizabeth raises her eyebrows at Godric, but they are both clearly happy to be in the Boboli gardens with Patty, so choose not to complain about his bossy ways, instead soaking up the thousand colours of green in the borders and lawns while they lick their rum and raisin. The Commissario leads them past the Neptune Fountain, and a little water carries in the wind and kisses their faces. Elizabeth remembers coming here with Gerald many years ago.

"I hear you've been to San Gimignano, Siena, and a certain olive farm. You're seeing the sights, no?" The Commissario asks, waiting for a reply.

"We do seem to have rather been pulled into life with the locals," Godric replies, seeing his nanna looks tired.

"And, how is your research for our poison?"

"Not going so well," Elizabeth sighs. "And you have not answered my question. What gives you the right to tell my–"

"Have you been in today?" The Commissario presses, interrupting.

"Are you checking up on me? The audacity. I see no reason why you should have been led to believe that I am helping on this case. I'm merely looking for poison for a while. If I don't find it, I don't find it. That's it. Nothing more. If you're to suggest otherwise, then I shall stop."

"I'm a Commissario, Professor Green. I do not check up on anyone. Or, I would have been a Questore with bad breath and no sense of humour." The Commissario thinks of his own boss and frowns. "But, I have just been asked by the lady of the Romano, the owner of the ring, if there is any chance of finding it. So, here we are. Bonded by a common goal. I have not asked you help on the case more than to help me find the poison. We are bonded in that goal."

"We are not bonded to your goals," Godric laughs sarcastically, looking about to see if he can see a stall for water for his nanna.

"And what about the man who died? Did she ask about him?" Elizabeth wonders.

"I cannot understand why she would?" The Commissario pauses. "My Sergeant had to intervene to stop you from getting arrested for not paying a bill?"

"They served me meat. I ordered vegan."

"You walked away."

"I was cross. And what is your point?" Elizabeth feels annoyed with the way the conversation is going.

"That's okay then." The Commissario looks around, taking in the day.

"The police had already stopped us outside Pisa at a toll. We were harassed and kept there for at least twenty minutes," Godric adds.

"Are you enjoying your holiday? Is this not beautiful?" The Commissario ignores Elizabeth and Godric, stopping on the path to take in the view.

"This is beautiful, but I don't thank you for

making me feel stressed about what happened in San Gimignano. The waitress was so rude. And we came home last night and Giuseppe is saying we have to meet him in Grassina. That it is very important. What are you actually doing about all this?" Elizabeth is cross with the Commissario for lulling them into a false sense of security, only to put her on edge.

"All I'm saying is help us find the poison and don't get involved in the case."

"Hey! You came to us!" Godric can feel his blood beginning to heat up.

"I don't want to get involved, believe me," Elizabeth replies. "At first, you said it might not be murder, but it looks that way to me. You failed to tell us about the pushing and the tower completely. You keep me in the dark but expect me to help you."

"Look, I do not want to upset you, Professor Green. I'm just warning you away from some unsavoury characters. You look, you are, well, very English. And, with an Englishman having stolen millions of euros. I feel responsible. I got you involved, no?" The Commissario opens the packet of sweets in his pocket and offers one to Elizabeth and then to Godric. Both decline. "I think you misunderstand."

"I don't understand. That's for sure," Elizabeth replies quietly.

"My godmother was English, you know.

She died when I was a small child. That's all I remember—sticky toffee pudding and custard," the Commissario reminisces.

"This is ridiculous. Come on, Bunny," Godric says, still mad and starting to walk away.

"You know, maybe go to Grassina with Giuseppe tonight. He's an Englishman. He might admit to you more than he's telling the police."

"You just said to stay out of it?" Elizabeth says, flabbergasted.

"I changed my mind," the Commissario wobbles his head, smiles, then stops under a beautiful cherry blossom. "Giuseppe is harmless." Then the Commissario stops walking. "Shall I leave you here to enjoy the gardens? I can let the staff know to not disturb you." He bends down to stroke Patty.

"The leaving us alone part would be a great idea," Godric replies.

"I didn't mean to offend you," the Commissario adds. "By way of a thank you, I'd like to invite you to lunch."

"More food?" Elizabeth shakes her head.

"Not now. But soon, yes? At my home."

"I can't see us doing that anytime soon," Godric huffs.

"Please do enjoy the gardens" Commissario Lorenzo holds out his hands, then claps and points at Elizabeth. "Don't give up on finding the poison." Then he turns and walks. They watch as he puts more sweets in his mouth.

"That man." Elizabeth takes a deep breath. "Grassino?"

"Us, at a religious event? And, on Good Friday? Talk about fish out of water. Or turning water into fish or whatnot." Godric is not in the least pleased.

*

After wandering around the Boboli Gardens for another hour, Elizabeth and Godric head back to the hotel for a rest. They cross the Ponte Vecchio bridge, stopping to look at the expensive watches in the tiny jewellery shops and wonder who must buy such things. Over the bridge and closer to the hotel, they stop again, this time outside a shop that only sells orange things. Orange mugs, cushions, wall art and more. Godric takes a photograph. The owner tries to persuade Godric to buy Elizabeth an orange costume ring, but Elizabeth stands outside vigorously shaking her head. Godric laughs and shrugs. They move on and stop outside a shop selling chocolate balls. Red ones, yellow ones, white ones, green, orange. Godric picks up an orange one and suggests it is in the wrong shop. He finds a tray of vegan balls and loads up a bag for them to eat later.

They wander on and Godric poses for

photographs under statues with a somewhat unwilling Elizabeth, who advises him that giving his phone to a complete stranger to take the picture might not be the most sensible thing. Godric replying that is why he always chooses women with short legs so he can catch them if needs be. Elizabeth points out that the short-legged woman could hand the phone to a long-legged man. Godric enjoys the banter with his nanna, photographing her face mid-lecture.

As they approach their hotel apartment, not a hundred feet from Ill Duomo they hear the bells ring for Good Friday. Many stop what they are doing and stand in the square out of respect. Godric takes the opportunity to record the bell ringing on his phone. Neither he nor his nanna speak of their general unease about being pulled further into what clearly is now a murder case in a foreign land, and this when they are already both so exhausted that they still have not spoken properly about what happened back at Valentine's Day.

32 GIUSEPPE, THE LAST MAN STANDING

Much later and Elizabeth, Godric and Patty arrive in Grassina. It is already dark this Easter Friday evening. Up a hill, with its narrow streets, groves and vineyards surrounding, the old buildings make it feel eerie. Unchartered territory, anticipated drama, and a large group begins to congregate.

"Patty's our barometer," Godric agrees as they mingle with what must now be a couple of hundred people dressed in costume around the largest wooden cross, tilted on its side for now. But no Giuseppe Esposito. "If this gets too loud, we're gone."

"He said eight o'clock under the crucifixion on the hill. Which hill?" Elizabeth looks around at sloping hills in every direction.

"I suppose we follow the procession up that way," Godric replies, noticing the crowd has started heading one way. They walk for five minutes, Patty in Godric's jacket seemingly okay for now, when Giuseppe jumps out of the crowd, looking even more sweaty.

"It's not hard to find that blonde mop!" Giuseppe shouts to Godric across the heads of people wearing sheets and Jesus creepers.

"Why are we meeting here?" Elizabeth shouts back, somewhat annoyed by all the unnecessary intrigue.

"Safety in a crowd," Giuseppe shouts back, pulling them both aside, looking around, and taking Elizabeth's arm as he declares, "I've been sent a death threat." Giuseppe hands Elizabeth the note in Italian, but she can decipher that it warns him how he is living on borrowed time and that he should hand over the diamond or he will find a 'cavalla' head at the bottom of his bed. "I haven't been home since. I'm out of my wits," he adds, his eyes darting about the procession, looking for his killer.

"Have you been to the police?" Godric asks.

"How do I know they will protect me? They haven't so far. I don't think they take me seriously. They might have connections," Giuseppe replies.

"You should tell the Commissario. He would take this seriously," Elizabeth suggests. "We're not the right people to help."

"I need to go back to England. I need my passport from my apartment, but I can't get it. It's too dangerous for me. Will you help one of your own in dire need?" At that moment a car backfires, but the crowd gasp as if it might be a sign from a higher being. Godric strokes Patty, who still seems fine inside his jacket.

"One of your own?" Godric frowns.

"Where are you staying?" Elizabeth rolls her eyes.

"In a hotel, under a false name. I was in a hurry."

"I can't believe anyone would want to hurt you. Why do you think they would? This isn't the first death threat?" Elizabeth asks.

"Please, Professor. I'm losing my wits." Godric and Elizabeth look at each other. This is all they need. This man in front of them, however, seems so scared that he might suffer a heart attack.

"Calm down, Mr Esposito," Elizabeth says firmly.

"That looks really life like?" Godric says, in shock, watching the procession overtake them and a man dressed as Jesus being dragged up the hill.

"It's time for us to be anywhere else," Elizabeth remarks.

"You have to help me. Get my passport."

"You must have other friends," Elizabeth asks, wanting to leave before they are consumed and carried up the hill by the sheer number of people joining the procession.

"Peter was my friend. I keep myself to myself. Please, you are my only hope," Giuseppe

implores.
Godric looks at Elizabeth, unsure what she wants to do. Elizabeth thinks perhaps visiting this man's apartment might unlock a clue to help her identify the poison so they can high tail it out of this tangled mess.

"Okay, we'll go. You need to tell us where to leave it," Elizabeth replies.

"You will? Thank you so much! Oh, thank you. I can come and get it from your hotel."

"No. You must tell us where you are staying, so we can reach you," Elizabeth replies.

"I haven't told anyone," Giuseppe replies reluctantly.

"Have a nice life." Elizabeth starts to walk away, pulling Godric.

"Okay, I'm at the 'Last Man Standing'!" Giuseppe beckons them back.

The level of the procession noise begins to build, and Godric starts to walk away. Giuseppe hands Elizabeth his key and thanks her again before disappearing into the crowd. A line of men carrying poles with papier-mâché snakes hiss at Elizabeth.

"'The Last Man Standing'? Really?"
Behind them, lower down in the hill, a red van is parked in the shadows.

*

Elizabeth and Godric return to Florence after their Grassina excursion, Godric shell-shocked from the noise and commotion, Elizabeth notices and suggests they walk out for a nightcap in the Black Cat café in the Piazza della Signoria before turning in, partly to calm Patty's nerves, partly their own. Neither know what to make of Giuseppe Esposito.

"Why did you say you'd get his passport?" Godric asks, shaking his head.

"I seem to be involved whether I want it or not. Anything to help me find the poison so we can be on our way. I'm not sure Commissario will make it easy for me to leave."

"I'm not letting you go into a strange apartment alone, which could be a set-up. We should tell the ruddy Commissario that this is a poor show."

"We will. But first, I want to look, in case Giuseppe is right and someone in the police might tip off whoever Giuseppe thinks he is hiding from."

"He was really scared, wasn't he?"

"Or, a good actor." Elizabeth looks at Godric. "Are you okay?"

Godric asks. Elizabeth looks at her grandson. She can see that he is not. His usual beaming smile has not been out for some time. Elizabeth sighs and looks out into the dark night. Again, the beauty of their surroundings could not be further than their moods right now.

33 SNAKE IN THE GRASS

Easter Saturday, Elizabeth wakes early to pay another visit to the main Florence Police Station. While in the pathology lab, she finally breaks into a smile. As she is running tests to confirm her deduction, in walks the Commissario.

"What are you looking so happy about?" the Commissario is munching a packet of biscotti sticking out of his jacket pocket.

"I know what poisoned Peter."

"Fantastic! Hold that thought. Let's go and celebrate with some breakfast." No sooner than the Commissario has walked in, he spins on his feet and starts to leave. "I got up and didn't have time for much breakfast."

Elizabeth follows the Commissario out across the piazza to his favourite restaurant, or one of them, as he seems to tell all the restaurant owners that every one is the best in all of Italy. They are seated and have to go through the whole ordering process before the Commissario will let Elizabeth spill the beans.

"Okay, I'm ready for your good news," he smiles as he tucks his napkin into the top of his shirt.

"Peter Jones was poisoned by snake venom."

"What?" the Commissario puts down his fork.

"Yes, I looked at the most likely and deadly here and it appears to be the vipera aspis."

"Snake venom? Wasn't that one of the first things our pathologist would have looked for?"

"That's why it threw me, and I suspect your staff. The autopsy ruled out insect and spider bites, so I didn't think of such poisons. Strictly speaking, I'm a flora expert. There were no actual snake bites, but the bleeding, kidney failure and the fact that eyewitnesses said he was clutching his eyes and staggering. He was dizzy and had blurred vision. He was puffy and had necrosis. Your pathologist ruled out snakes because there was no bite, but he didn't check for snake venom. I just ruled it back in and checked it. It's snake venom."

"What on earth made you think of it?"

"It's Easter, and being in Grassina. The city and surroundings are awash with Christ and the Bible. There were snake costumes, snakes on poles. It is a poison of choice, is it not?"

"But how can you be sure?"

"When I looked again, I found traces of vipoxin and ammodytoxins."

"How did we miss that?" The Commissario shakes his head.

"It surely confirms you're looking for a murderer, as I believe snake venom deaths are extremely rare in Italy. We all suspected, but it leaves little room for doubt. This was an unnatural amount of venom, and no bites. So, unless he chose to steal a diamond and then kill himself twice?"

"Twice?"

"The tower fall?"

"Right, right, right." Then the Commissario pulls apart a croissant in a basket on the table, puts some in his mouth, chews, then pauses for a while before he swallows. "D'you think the poison was a message?"

"It always is. Peter Jones stole a diamond and then was pushed off the tower. I'd say that's a strong message not to steal. Could the Romanos have done it? Caught him in the act? Maximilius and Lucia Romano?"

"I wouldn't go about saying that loudly. We need evidence before making accusations against the richest family in Florence, or one of them."

"You have the theft on CCTV, so this wasn't a very clever thief. Someone who didn't know what he was doing. Perhaps his first time?"

"Hmm, these are good," the Commissario

takes time over chewing the rest of the croissant. Elizabeth wonders if he is even not more bothered about the jam he is slathering on his pastries than her news. Elizabeth looks around at the piazza. To the left is a small green space, at most fifty feet square. Elizabeth can see pigeons and some sparrows in a tree. A child sits on the steps with his mother, blowing bubbles from a pot. Behind them, four women carry a huge floral display and stop to prop it up on a plinth in the centre of the small park. "What do you think of our city, Professor Green?"

"The flowers are beautiful. They're everywhere."

"They take over at Easter. Oh look, isn't that your grandson?" The Commissario says. Elizabeth notices Godric walking Patty into the piazza and starts to wave. She knows he will not want to eat with the Commissario, so she quickly stands up ready to leave. However, perhaps Godric is super hungry or just out of fight as he chooses to sit, ordering a lot off the menu.

The three of them stay there long enough for people to start coming in for the lunch settings, and Elizabeth does wonder how this Commissario solves any case, given his appetite for food. Though, she does notice that he is often just picking his teeth with a toothpick and chatting with the restaurant owners.

After some time, and after Godric has eaten a cooked breakfast and at least five pastries, Elizabeth can finally stand up again.

"Well, I think I might stretch my legs and do some sightseeing," she says, knowing Godric will surely want to escape the Commissario now. But before she can leave, the Commissario has taken out his phone, dialled and is speaking.

"Burb Abley? Yes! Yes, your Professor Green has done it!" The Commissario hands over the phone to Elizabeth to say hello to Inspector Abley.

"Happy Easter, Bob. Yes, No. No. Well, I'm off now. I'll hand you back. Speak soon." Elizabeth doesn't want to speak to Bob in front of the Commissario and abruptly halts the conversation. The Commissario makes his excuses and cuts the call.

"Well, if you won't talk to your Inspector, you must come with me, the three of you," the Commissario looks at Patty and pats her head, "and see Lucia Romano. I need to update her on the case and tell her we're getting closer. You should come. Her house is spectacular and only open to the public once a year."

"Open to the public?" Godric asks. "Does she live in a museum?"

"It's one of the largest homes in Florence. I think it has over thirty bedrooms. Come, you'll see. She has a fantastic cocktail bar," the

Commissario grins at Godric. "You have seen it from the other side of the lethal gates but not inside."

Elizabeth looks at Godric. Though not keen to get any closer to this case, especially now she has found the poison, she can see the idea of a glamourous home with cocktails has lit up Godric's face.

"Is she a hostess with the mostess?" Godric asks.

"You know, I think she might just be a woman living the high life, for sure." The Commissario grins at Godric's thirst for alcohol after all that eating.

*

The four of them, three humans, are buzzed through the gates, and immediately Elizabeth and Godric feel like they are entering a rock star's home. The gravel on the drive, the huge fountain of some goddess or other and two giant panther statues on either side of the front door on plinths, wearing sparkling collars. As Elizabeth passes, she wonders if they are real jewels. The front door opens, and Lucia stands at the door wearing a bikini and heels as high as the Eifel Tower, having just swum in the pool, her hair still dripping down her back, her shirt open showing off a natural tan.

"Come in again, Lorenzo. I'm just taking brunch. Join me. And your friends?" Lucia waits to be introduced.

"This is Professor Elizabeth Green and her grandson–"

"Godric, pleased to meet you. Nice pad you have here," Godric grins at Lucia.

"Thank you, Godric." Lucia turns to Elizabeth, "Any friend of Lorenzo's is a friend of mine." Lucia squeezes Godric's arms. She observes the blonde curls tucked behind Godric's ears, his white teeth and saucer sized grey eyes.

"Oh, we're not friends," Elizabeth corrects Lucia.

"Are we not?" the Commissario looks at her, a little taken aback.

"I've been helping the Commissario briefly on the diamond case. But that is now over," Elizabeth clarifies firmly.

"My diamond. Ah, if only I had it back. Come in, won't you?" Lucia starts to speak fast to the Commissario in Italian, then in English more slowly to Elizabeth. "I'm sorry, I was just telling Lorenzo that I've just bought a new painting and was asking him whether I should tell the police before it goes missing." She raises her eyebrows.

"Is that a Turner?" Godric asks, staring at a large painting on the wall in an even larger reception room. "Great Yarmouth. Strange that you have it here."

"Not strange. Money." Lucia looks at

Godric kindly. "I have too much of it. The least I can do is preserve fine art."

"Shouldn't you give it to the people of Great Yarmouth?" Elizabeth suggests.

"I might, in my will. I'll have to see how good they've been before I go," Lucia replies as they move through several rooms and out onto a veranda. "It'll soon be too hot to sit outside. But we may have an hour. Enough for a good 'brunch', d'you call it?"

"To make up for the small jentacular," Godric suggests.

"We've just had an extensive breakfast," Elizabeth frowns at Godric.

"We always have room for Lucia's brunch," the Commissario sits at the table and spots a napkin. He puts it in the top of his shirt, ready for round two. Something Elizabeth notices is beginning to feel like his trademark. Lucia whispers to the butler, "they're vegans,", having quietly been informed by the Commissario on the way in. The butler looks confused.

"We don't eat animals," Elizabeth replies, adding, "and yes, that does exclude fish, eggs and dairy."

The butler raises his eyebrows but says nothing. He looks at Lucia, who just smiles so he walks off, unsure what the cook will say.

"So, have you come here with good news? Have you found my diamond?"

"This is now definitely a murder investigation," the Commissario sighs.

"Have you found my diamond?"

"The man who took your diamond has been murdered," Elizabeth replies.

"And I care because?" Lucia sips her drink and leans back in her chair, revealing her toned body in her bikini.

"Because it might be harder to find your diamond if the thief can't talk," Elizabeth replies, adding, "Because it puts you in the frame as a suspect."

"Don't you just love the English for their diplomacy?" Lucia looks at Godric.

"I should point out that Professor Green discovered Peter Jones was poisoned by snake venom."

"He was bitten by a snake?" Lucia looks confused. "Well, he was the viper who stole my diamond," she adds, holding up a knife to check her appearance.

"No, it was ingested or perhaps injected. More tests will have to run on how it was administered," Elizabeth explains, not warming to Lucia, who seems a little frivolous.

"Could he not have tried to kill himself?" Lucia puts down the cutlery and picks up her drink, signalling for the drinks butler to come to the table. "Godric, what would you like? You look like a whisky man. We have a fine forty-year-old single malt."

Godric's eyes sparkle and widen as he nods.

"What, straight after a robbery? He steals a diamond then throws himself off a tower, but not before ingesting some snake venom. Really?" Elizabeth asks, irritated with Lucia.

"Why not?"

"Or, he steals your diamond. You get it back and kill him in revenge. Surely, that's less of a stretch of the imagination," Elizabeth gives Lucia her beadiest stare.

"I don't think Professor Green thinks that for one moment," the Commissario jumps in. Elizabeth looks at the Commissario. It is his case, and it is no skin off her nose whether he finds the thief or what this rather spoilt woman thinks of her.

"Lorenzo. If you haven't found my diamond, what's your plan?" Lucia remains unphased by Elizabeth.

"Where is Mr Romano?" Elizabeth asks.

"Playing on his boat, most probably," Lucia raises her eyebrows.

"He did threaten to kill Peter Jones, didn't he," the Commissario says, raising his eyebrows at Lucia.

"Wouldn't you? He bought an expensive diamond, and now it's gone." Lucia takes another sip of her cocktail as Godric's whisky arrives. "But he would never kill for me, Lorenzo darling. Professor Green, Lorenzo, what would you like? Where are my manners?

I was just mesmerised by this beautiful young man." Lucia gets up from her chair as the butler opens the door for her to exit the room. As she does, staff wait for her to pass through, then bring a platter of treats to the table for her guests to eat and take drink orders from Lorenzo and Elizabeth. The Commissario immediately fills his plate with meats and cheese while Godric looks at the artichoke hearts and tries one with some dipping sauce. Elizabeth is already full from earlier, until she sees some bittermints from her favourite chocolatiere so opens one to eat with the peppermint tea that has just been placed before her.

"Here," Lucia returns with a small box and places it in front of Elizabeth. "I have two. See, this is what he does. Max buys me the same pieces because he forgets. So, you have it. I know what it's like travelling light when abroad. You must have had to leave your jewels at home." Lucia looks at Elizabeth's over-long linen trousers with mud around the bottom, her blouse which looks like it has seen better days and a pretty green cardigan with bees embroidered. "Every woman needs a little sparkle."

Elizabeth opens the box placed in front of her. Inside is a beautiful bracelet of tiny flowers, mainly daisies, and each flower has a jewel.

"Are they emeralds?" Elizabeth looks more

closely at the flowers.

"I certainly hope so, or Maximilius's a cheapskate."

"And diamonds? I cannot possibly accept this."

"Please don't insult me. It's a gift." Lucia waves her hand about as if she often gives such lavish things away. "They're not the crown jewels from the Tower of London."

Godric looks at the bracelet and is also a little shocked as it seems expensive. He gestures for his nanna to try it on, helps her with it, lifting it out of the box and clips it around her wrist. It looks lovely and suits Elizabeth's tiny frame.

"I cannot accept bribes," Elizabeth replies.

"I thought it would suit you, and it does. There, that's all," Lucia looks at the gift and nods. At this moment Ock walks in—Lucia's son. The young man who was most unpleasant at the supper Stefano invited them to yesterday evening.

"You still giving away my inheritance to every person you meet on the street? That's my girl." Ock kisses his mother on the top of her head and then looks at Elizabeth. "Isn't that dog dead yet?" Ock then breaks into speaking Italian with his mother.

"We can both speak Italian, you know," Godric smirks. "And no, we're not a pair of hangers-on." Godric stands up and shakes Ock's hand with a huge grin. "But, if you threaten my dog again, I will kill you. And I won't even need a diamond in return." Godric delivers his words rather like a joke but squeezes Ock's hand tight to make him realise he means it. Godric then stands between Patty and Ock until Ock moves away.

"It's okay. You sit with your grandma. I'm not staying long." Then Ock pulls at his mother's arm again and tries to pull her up from her seat. "Mamon, can I have a word in private?"

"Darling, Ock. I've missed you," Lucia says as she stands and nods. The two of them walk out into the grounds and stand by the pool, out of earshot.

"Can we press charges for threatening behaviour to an animal?" Elizabeth asks the Commissario.

"Why, what has he done?"

"He keeps threatening Patty," Godric says, stroking Patty's head.

"We can't press charges unless he has actually hurt your dog. And this dog looks so happy." The Commissario smiles at Patty, who has been brought a plate of sausages, rice and peas straight from the kitchen.

"I think it's time for us to leave," Elizabeth says to Godric.

"But I cannot leave. Not with all this food to eat. It would be rude," the Commissario replies.

"Yes, let's go." Godric stands up. "This is a beautiful place, but the temperature has suddenly dropped." He watches Ock in the garden, still whispering to his mother.

Lucia notices and returns.

"You're not leaving already, are you? I wanted to ask you about London and the hip Carnaby Street."

"I think that was the sixties. Were you a model?" Godric asks.

"What in the sixties?"

"No, I didn't mean–" Godric blushes.

"I know," Lucia laughs. "But I was, in my late teens, before this one came along." Lucia watches Ock checking his phone.

"And now, Stefano's daughter is too. Your son's girlfriend, Sophia?" Elizabeth asks.

"You'll have to ask Ock. He's running our fashion empire." Lucia puts her arm around her son.

"And what do you do?" Elizabeth looks around the house.

"Swim." Lucia laughs, "Paint. D'you have time to look? Don't leave yet, please, I beg you."

Godric and Elizabeth realise it would be a huge faux pas if they left now that she has pleaded, so nod and smile. They follow Lucia, as the Commissario tucks into more food, kept company by Ock who does the same. Lucia walks along a long corridor until they come into a grand ballroom. The parquet floor covered in paint splatters. At one end are huge canvasses. On them are large trees, blurred a little, and a lot of green angrily painted lines.

"Look at those! Amazing!" Godric walks over to one, finishing his whisky.

"Quite big," Elizabeth says, really taking a dislike to the paintings. She has seen better pictures created by elephants in rescue centres.

"They keep me out of trouble. I have an exhibition this Tuesday. You must come. And you must have one of my paintings!" She says to Godric. Then she walks over to a desk.

"We're travelling light. In a small car, tiny. We couldn't fit anything else in," Elizabeth explains.

"I can send it ahead to your home if you give me your address?"

"We really don't have space at home either," Elizabeth adds. We don't live in a mansion like this.

"Then this will have to do," Lucia walks back with a painting three inches square and hands it to Godric. He looks at it and sees another tree and more sharp green lines.

"Well, that will fit. Thank you," he says staring at the painting. "I will treasure it." He looks at Elizabeth and smiles.

"I have something better for you. Stay there." And Lucia disappears for a few minutes.

"You don't actually like this stuff, do you?"

Elizabeth asks Godric. "And if I couldn't bring my flower press, why do you get to take that piffling thing home?"

"I find Lucia quite the woman," Godric smirks. "But, I'm not sure even I, who knows very little about art, have space for this." He looks down at the painting.

"Why is this woman being so generous to strangers?" Elizabeth looks down at her lovely bracelet. Lucia returns with a bag from an expensive clothes boutique.

"Now, you don't have to say yes to this, as you need to keep space in your little car for my art. But I thought you might like this jacket. I bought it for Ock. I saw it in a little shop in Rome. He hates it." Lucia pulls out a classy looking jacket from tissue paper so that Godric can try it on.

"Really?" Godric feels the soft linen, which is tight-fitting, but stretchy.

"Ock doesn't want it, and it doesn't fit Max. So, please take it."

Godric loves it instantly. It is perfect for the holiday, and already he feels more Italian. Their age difference must be fifteen years, but he feels a connection. He drops his shades from his head and poses to make Lucia laugh.

"Thank you. If you're sure?"

"It's going to waste," Lucia insists.

"I think I look handsome, don't you?"

"I think you do." Lucia beams.

"Won't the Commissario be jealous?" Elizabeth stirs.

"Don't worry. I have a casserole for him," Lucia replies quickly, uninterested right now in the Commissario. Her eyes glued to Godric.

"Well, we really must be going. We cannot take any more time away from your day, or accept any more presents. I really cannot keep this," Elizabeth replies firmly, taking off the bracelet.

"I insist!" Lucia grabs Elizabeth's wrist and stops her from removing it. "This is Florence thanking you for finding the poison that killed the diamond thief. This is a small gift. I insist." Lucia smiles.

They make their way back and see that the Commissario is still eating.

"Are you going to help the Commissario find my diamond?" Lucia asks Elizbeth in earshot of the Commissario.

"No, my help is now concluded," Elizabeth replies, "And we can continue with our holiday. If Lorenzo can keep Giuseppe away, that is."

The Commissario stands, and as he does, the butler brings over a dish covered in silver foil.

"Well, I hope you will come to my gallery exhibition. Do come. I will put you on the guest list. There'll be food, champagne, and good company."

"For lunch," Lucia explains to Lorenzo, handing him the dish. "I know how you like cook's casserole."

"Lucky me," the Commissario replies, wiping his mouth with a napkin.

"Oh, and take this for Patty." Lucia opens a drawer full of dog collars and quickly puts one around Patty's neck. "It fits perfectly. I lost my little one last year." Lucia then looks up at Godric. "I wish I had one to go around your neck, then I'd keep you here. You're so handsome." Instead, she squeezes Godric's arm again. Godric goes a little red. Ock fake shudders, watching from across the table. Lucia moves away to say goodbye to Lorenzo.

"I think we've been love-bombed," Godric whispers to Elizabeth as they leave the house with the Commissario.

"Yes, and doesn't that make you wonder what she's up to?"

*

Outside, Commissario Bianchi stops and holds his casserole.

"May I leave you to make your own way to your hotel? I have to take this home before I return to the station, or one whiff and it will be gone."

"Of course. I wasn't joking in there," Elizabeth glares at him.

"You're not a joking woman," the Commissario is distracted by the smell of the food and inhales deeply.

"That's me done now." Elizabeth inwardly sighs, knowing the Commissario was teasing her for being so serious. Why are people so tiresome?

"Can we keep the car permit for a few more days?" Godric asks tentatively.

"Of course. Will you be at Lucia's gallery exhibition? It's bound to have good food."

"We'll see. If there isn't anything else we fancy, maybe," Elizabeth replies, uninterested.

They watch as the Commissario walks away, continually sniffing the casserole.

"Do you think he'll make it as far as home?"

"I hope he goes home, stays there for a long time, and leaves us alone."

"D'you think these are real diamonds?" Godric looks down at the sparkly collar Lucia put around Patty's neck.

"I don't know, but we should put it with our valuables until we can take a closer look. We'll have to give all this back," Elizabeth replies. Godric takes off the collar and puts it in his wallet. It is clear that the collar does have diamonds, albeit small, in the decorative detail.

"I'm keeping the jacket. Just the jewels, right?" Godric asks.

"Okay, just the jewels."

"I'm surprised someone like that actually noticed her ring was missing?" Godric comments.

"She didn't. It was in a museum exhibition display in an upmarket art gallery. She had lent it to them. Apparently, she wanted to gift it, but her husband wouldn't let her," Elizabeth explains.

"It's like she's trying to give everything away?" Godric puts his hands in the pockets of his new jacket, looking down and admiring the cut. He feels something and pulls it out. It is Lucia's card with a handwritten message.

"What is it?"

"It says, '*God. Come for tea. Just you. Tomorrow? Call me, darling. Lucia Romano xx*'. What does that mean?"

"Does she fancy you?"

"She has some vital bits missing for my taste, unfortunately. But, might she have clues?"

"You mean more presents?"

"Yes!"

"Stop cooing over her. She could be the murderer."

"How could such a wonderful woman be a killer? She's so glamorous!" Godric fawns over the thought of going back for tea. "She has such a beautiful house. Did you see the swans in the moat in the back garden?"

As they walk away from the gates of the property, which are now locked, they notice one of Stefano's daughters in tears on the pavement not twenty feet away up ahead.

"Is that Sophia?" Elizabeth asks under her breath. Sophia spots them and hurries away in the opposite direction before jumping in a car and driving away. Elizabeth looks back at the house and notices Ock looking out the window behind lifted curtains. When he sees Elizabeth, he drops a curtain and disappears.

"When you said you would see about the exhibition, maybe we should go. Lucia was very kind," Godric suggests.

"I don't want to get involved with any of the people involved with this diamond ring theft." Elizabeth insists.

"But you're happy to spend the afternoon with Stefano?"

"He'd no more steal a diamond as sell off his olive grove."

"How can you be so sure?" Godric asks as they continue along the pavement.

"Instinct," Elizabeth replies. She wonders if her instincts are to be trusted.

34 STENCH AT GIUSEPPE'S

Elizabeth and Godric have one last chore before they can leave Florence for good and continue their holiday. However, they immediately regret visiting Giuseppe Esposito's apartment to find his passport. As the crow flies, his flat is not far from Lucia Romano's house, but that is where the similarity ends. Down a narrow alley, over a betting shop, and only accessible via a decrepit metal fire escape on the outside of the building, Godric carries Patty as they climb up the steps and through the smallest door.

When they get inside, it feels more like a home for a family of rats than a human inhabitant. Curtains hanging off their poles, fast food containers scattered in rotting piles, newspapers open and thrown on the floor. Collectables and figurines stand on dusty on shelves. An ashtray is perched on the arms of a chair, spilling over nearby. They stand momentarily, wondering where on earth Giuseppe would keep his passport.

"Even on my worst days, my dorm room never looked like this. Bravo, Giuseppe, you win the sloth of the decade. We will never find a passport in here." Godric holds his shirt over his nose as Patty starts rummaging beneath his feet. It is hard to decipher, but as Elizabeth's eyes wander across the stench, she notices a miniature painting in a frame containing green lines.

"Isn't that like the one Lucia gave you?" She looks at Godric, who nods.

"Now I don't feel so special." Godric huffs, rescuing a small olive bonsai tree, clearly struggling in the gloom. "Somehow, I don't think this deserves to stay here. It looks older than the apartment." The studio apartment is so acrid and horrid that they have to leave. But not before Patty has grabbed something which looks rather fishy. Godric hands Elizabeth the bonsai.

"What the hell. Is that a fish?" Godric pulls out half a rotten fish Patty has lifted off a plate. Patty chews the last piece that Godric cannot retrieve from her mouth, and licks her lips. "Oh, no, Patty. You can do better than that."

"We cannot stay in here. Let's go," Elizabeth pulls Godric away. "As you say, we won't find a passport here."

"Let me go first, in case you fall, nanna. This is insane."

They slowly descend the staircase without any passport, Godric holding a fishy-smelling Patty and the bonsai again, and Elizabeth another miniature painting with green lines. Who is this Englishman, living in squalor, fearful for his life?

35 A TOUR OF SIENA

Having left Giuseppe's and having dumped all Lucia's gifts and the bonsai and paintings back in their apartment, Elizabeth and Godric are greeted by Stefano at their door with a large bunch of irises for Elizabeth.

"I wanted to come and profusely apologise for my behaviour last night. I was not in my right mind."

"You hit a man," Elizabeth puts her nose to the irises and is pleased that they smell how they are supposed to. She takes another deeper breath.

"Yes."

"That's poor show," Godric says, unimpressed.

"Yes. There's no excuse. None. I'm so sorry."

"Well–"

"Only, I so wanted to ask if you would see it in your hearts to let me show you Siena, by way of an apology."

"We can see Siena. We have a car," Godric replies.

"Might I at least be your driver?" Stefano asks Godric. The idea of getting a free pass on having to remain the sober driver pricks Godric's ears, but then he thinks of Stefano's van. Ugh.

"I'm not going in that van again."

"No, I brought my car." They walk to the window and see a huge crowd gathering around Stefano's Maserati GranTurismo.

"Different set of wheels you have today?" Godric narrows his eyes.

"I wanted you to travel with more comfort. It was the least I could do." Stefano bows his head. "I'm truly sorry, but when it comes to that man." Stefano sighs. "But, let's leave that behind. We have beautiful weather. It could be a good day."

Elizabeth disappears into the bathroom. When she comes out, Godric notices his nanna has brushed her hair and pinched her cheeks.

"We will come with you on one condition, that you promise this will be relaxing and that we will all enjoy ourselves." These are the only words Elizabeth says before walking out of the apartment, holding Patty.

"Siena here we come." Stefano raises his eyebrows at Godric. "There is no tour guide who knows more about Siena."

"You promise?" Godric frowns, unsure

about this man.

The journey by Maserati is fast, with Stefano at one point giving Godric an opportunity to drive his car. This puts a whole new spin on the day for Godric, and all his concerns about the man immediately melt away. Stefano is cool! Elizabeth seems quieter than usual, content perhaps to look out the window and nod. Only once having to say, 'Oh my god slow down, Goddy', but otherwise almost fatalistic about Godric's unnerving driving.

Once they arrive in Siena, park the car, brush down their hair and unhook their fingernails from their car seats, Stefano takes them back to Piazza del Campo. This time, the stop for afternoon tea is much more relaxed, if a little busier. Godric offering to drive them back, Stefano ordering him a double single malt to ensure he doesn't. Afterwards, Godric asks if there is a CD shop.

"Our little car is a bit behind the times when playing music for our travels," Elizabeth explains.

"I think we might have one music shop left. Bit of history there. I'm old enough to have played vinyl the first time around. What do you like?"

"Hip hop, grime."

Stefano screws up his face and looks at Elizabeth, then laughs. "Surely you're not buying any of that while your nanna's in the car. No, a bit of Andreas Bocelli, perhaps."

"You like opera?" Elizabeth asks.

"Very much," Stefano touches Elizabeth's arm excitedly. "There is an outdoor performance," Stefano looks at his watch, "in a few hours with some primo divas. Early evening, so all the older people can get to bed at a sensible time." Stefano pretends to be old to Godric, pulling a face and hunching his back. Then adds, "Would you like to go?" He looks at Elizabeth, hopeful. "Aurelia doesn't like the opera. It would be a nice treat for me."

"I'm not sure Godric–"

Godric can clearly see that his nanna wants to hear some opera. He smiles and nods. Where is this going? Why is this man being so nice to his nanna?

"When in Rome," Godric interrupts, adding his approval.

"I'll get the tickets. I know a guy, who knows a guy," and Stefano winks and touches his nose. Godric is surprised his nanna is not firing questions at Stefano about his friendship with Peter. Ordinarily, the man would not have been able to get a word in edgeways. Godric wonders why Stefano really hates Marco. Is it as simple as he's dating his daughter? Could it be the land that his nanna mentioned Stefano was worried about? Godric supposes that might be enough. Someone who can punch like Stefano.

Why is his nanna even entertaining today? When she is done with the case. He never saw his grandpa punch anyone. It is unforgivable. So, why is she even here?

"You okay, Bunny?" Godric notices something is wrong with his nanna.

"More than okay. You're here." Elizabeth looks at Godric for perhaps a moment too long and smiles. Another smile that does not go up to the eyes. Why does Godric feel too exhausted to take any action? He feels unsettled. He watches as his nanna acts out of character. Quiet. Persuadable. Something is most definitely wrong.

*

The hours pass, and Elizabeth's feet ache from all the walking. Stefano has taken them up towers, out of the city gates to get a great view of all the homes balanced on the hill. He introduced them to a friend who had a large home with the best view where they stopped for more drinks. They milled around the shops, and Godric bought more sweets. Elizabeth could swear the car was beginning to smell like a confectionary shop. Poor Patty's legs were so tired that Godric picks her up to carry. When they finally walk into the Piazza Del Duomo, right outside Siena's Cathedral, Elizabeth is happy to see chairs lined up below a stage and Stefano greeting a man who ushers them right to the front row.

"Terrible seats. We can see up their noses," Stefano grins, "I hope you enjoy," Stefano hands out programmes to them both. And, rather than a full-on opera, it suggests they have a tea time of seemingly famous opera singers from Siena and further afield. The opera singer Godric and Elizabeth saw the other day makes an appearance. Frequent intervals with ice cream vendors walking through the chattering crowd break up singer after singer.

"Opera for softies," Elizabeth smiles to Godric.

"Well, it's easy to be here," he replies kindly, having been bought a hamper of food and alcohol by Stefano from a delicatessen immediately opposite.

"It is a shame in the circumstances," she replies quietly to Godric.

"What?"

But Elizabeth sighs and does not answer. She does not really know how she feels.

"Try to relax now," Godric tries to calm his nanna. But Stefano hears.

"Elizabeth, what can I do?" He asks.

But Elizabeth shakes her head.

"Are you relaxed, Stefano? What can anyone do?" Elizabeth replies, not sure she wants to pursue the conversation.

"I'm upset about Peter," Stefano shakes his

head as an ice cream vendor walks past again, and this time he holds up his hand. "You know, he was my friend. My wife has her horses. I had Peter. We spent hours talking about olives. I don't know why he would steal and then jump off a tower?" Stefano turns to the vendor. "D'you have anything vegan?" She nods, and Stefano holds out three fingers and passes them down the line, one to Godric. Then he hears himself and how his last words sounded to Elizabeth and laughs at himself. "Peter wasn't bored by what I had to say."

"Thank you," Elizabeth takes the ice cream. "He was pushed. He was poisoned." Elizabeth watches as Godric pulls the ice cream man back to ask about some for Patty. The man points, so Godric gets up to buy Patty some dog ice cream at the counter. Elizabeth turns and watches them go. Watching her family leave, suddenly the air feels thinner. She struggles to catch her breath.

"Yes, but how many people are on the planet who can talk about the Morailio olive for days, months?" Stefano continues to talk directly at Elizabeth about Peter, his eyes light up, "and discuss every detail of the Frantoio olive tree. It has its origins here. It is the best olive oil, a great olive to eat. We chose this olive, and it did not let us down."

"Frantoio?" Elizabeth does not have the energy to shut the conversation down.

"Peter. He already knew so much before he came. He had done his research." Stefano looks up at the Dome of the Cathedral. "You know, I feel very guilty. I haven't been to see his wife."

"Peter Jones's wife?" Elizabeth looks out for Godric, worried that she cannot see him.

"Yes. Yes. In Florence."

"The police, they have been all over his flat. Her home. So many times, I hear." Elizabeth shares what she knows with Stefano bites into the vegan chocolate flake stuck in the top of his ice cream.

"Not only has she lost her husband, but she has had to deal with all that alone." Stefano then licks around the bottom of his already dripping ice cream. "She came from England to stay with him when his research grant was extended. From what he said, I don't think she wanted to be here initially. But, as luck would have it, he said she settled. Something finally changed for her, and she fell in love with Tuscany."

"You know her? You were not in love with her, were you? Was this a lovers spat?" Elizabeth does not want to start asking these questions. Where will they lead? But she cannot stop them spilling out of her mouth.

"Ha! Well, if you really want to know, she used to come to dinner with Peter to ours. She seemed happy. She was always laughing. But, since Peter's death, I didn't know what to say.

And now, well, I just feel guilty I haven't been to see her."

"What is she like?" Elizabeth replies.

"Mia. Her name. Oh, very English." Then Stefano hears what he has repeated. "I don't mean that in a bad way. She likes tea, listens to the world service radio, wears long dresses with lacey collars." Stefano moves his hand up to his collar and wiggles his fingers. "She likes Marmite. Bleugh."

"Is that what you think of English women?" Elizabeth asks.

"Oh no, not you. You are not a typical English woman."

"I like Marmite. You should try it with peanut butter on toast in the morning."

"Well, you are–" Stefano starts to speak but then pulls a face at Elizabeth's suggestion.

They become so engrossed in each other that for a moment they miss the opera singer walking up to the stage and are surprised into silence when a large man with a huge barreled chest, belts out the first note of Giacomo Puccini's '*Nessun Dorma*'. Elizabeth and Stefano turn to listen, unsure of what just happened between them. Elizabeth looks at Godric's seat, but he and Patty still have yet to return. She panics. She scans the piazza and visibly relaxes, spotting him in a café across the square, Patty drinking, but wonders why he did not return. This makes Elizabeth agitated by Stefano.

Godric and Patty are her priority. How has this man made her not notice their whereabouts?

When the song has finished, the atmosphere among the crowd erupts in applause. The opera singer begins to leave the stage. There is a pause between Elizabeth and Stefano. Elizabeth fills the void.

"I must see if Godric's okay. But do you have Peter's wife's address?"

"Of course."

"I think I will go to check on her, as it is in Florence, and she is from Cambridge," Elizabeth sighs. "What if she's in danger?"

"You think she's in danger?"

"I think we must head back soon," Godric says from behind, looking at them both. "Patty is pooped, as is my Bunny. And, I'm too tits to the wind to be useful to anyone."

*

Stefano drives them back via San Gimignano.

"Let me take you for a final nightcap. Just five minutes. It's on the way," Stefano walks them up the Via San Giovanni, with all the medieval buildings on either side of the narrow street and back into the hotel he previously took them to. This time they notice the sign outside. The 'Bel San Stefano'. Twinkling farm lights, twilight, and a bright full moon rising across the valley can be seen as they sip their nightcap in the bar.

"Again, this beautiful place you have here."

"Did they name this after you?" Godric asks before walking across to take photographs of the night.

"Maybe," Stefano brushes under the carpet just how wealthy he really is.

"Hey, isn't that–" Elizabeth looks at the photographs on the wall in the restaurant.

"Peter, yes." Stefano looks at the picture of Stefano and Peter, sitting at a table in this dining room, eating. In the photograph with him are his wife, Aurelia, and Mia. "There's Mia." Stefano gets up and taps the photograph.

"You look like good friends in this picture? I didn't see this one last time." Elizabeth looks at the photograph, and them all gathered around one side of a table, with arms linked over their shoulders.

"Dreading there will be a funeral soon, I presume. So final, so real." Stefano looks deeply into Elizabeth's eyes, holds her glance, then breaks away and smiles at Godric, "To know you both. And you, Patty. Well, it's been a breath of fresh air." Stefano cheers, then pats Patty on the head.

This man, with the smile the spit of Elizabeth's poor dead husband, with such a gentle disposition, with the same craggy wrinkles around his eyes showing years of kindness, in a fleeting moment making

Elizabeth feel almost not alone. She knows he is not Gerald. Knows she does not even know him or anything about him. So why does she feel so sad thinking she might never see him ever again? He, thousands of miles from her home, across the other side of Europe. Why did they meet? How did they come to collide?

"Let's visit Mia together. I'm free tomorrow morning while Godric is sleeping off his enjoyment."

"Yes! That is fantastic!" Stefano seems so pleased to have another opportunity to see Elizabeth. Beaming. Then realising they are off to meet a widow, he tones down his response. "I mean, obviously, it is very sad," smiles at Elizabeth, "but good to go together." Stefano cannot hide how pleased he is. He walks over, grabs Elizabeth's hand, and holds it unexpectedly while passing his number on a card. Elizabeth is shocked by the intimacy, which does not go unnoticed by Godric, who then chooses to hold his nanna's other hand to try to make her feel more comfortable without ruining the moment.

Godric narrows his eyes at this man as he watches Stefano hold a smile from ear to ear. Godric may have drunk far too much whisky and enjoyed very much driving the Maserati, but does not trust this man. Who has all that money and wears scruffy shoes to the opera? No good can come from him and his obsession with the English, especially as Stefano's last English friend is now in the morgue.

Godric glances at his nanna and how her smile goes all the way up to her eyes. Godric feels unnerved by this. This is not his nanna. Not the woman always in control. Come to think of it, why has she not grilled Stefano within an inch of his life, like she always does? He is always apologising to people on her behalf. Why has he not had to make excuses to Stefano?

*

"Goodbye," Elizabeth says, still smiling, Stefano squeezing Elizabeth's hand gently and then letting go as they part outside Elizabeth's hotel back in Florence. Godric hugs his nanna as they watch Stefano get into his car and wave from an open window as he creeps along the street, knowing he will now surely get a ticket. Elizabeth stares for a moment at the car leaving, letting the unusually warm spring evening wash over her. Florence streets are quiet, except for a delivery truck removing empties and rubbish from the main piazza. A few orange and yellow beams of lights in apartments and hotels cast shadows on the walls. Godric picks up Patty and puts her inside his jacket as she is clearly tired now from the day. He kisses her head.

"What do you think, Patty? Opera, treats,

sunshine, cuddles. You happy?" Patty snuggles her head further inside his jacket, happy to doze from the slightly overloaded day. Godric cannot stop thinking about what was between Stefano and his Bunny. "That was actually an enjoyable time with Stefano."

"Love you, Goddy," Elizabeth replies. "You're a good grandson."

*

They just make it inside as fireworks light up the sky in anticipation of the start of Easter Sunday, too far away to hear. Elizabeth stands for a moment in the doorway of their hotel, her mind elsewhere. Around her, intermittent fizzing stars bang and crack in the sky. Finally, without thinking, she walks across to the nearby fountain in the Piazza della Signoria. Florence feels so alive, so unsettling.

The piazza is quiet, but for a few lovers, still strolling through the streets, hand in hand, coming to pause and imagine their dreams. Elizabeth stands close, letting the water from the fountain spray across her face, trying to remember coming here all those years ago with Gerald. She closes her eyes, attempting to conjure the moment and replay it in her mind. But the memory is down a dark tunnel and won't return. She shuffles closer and closer to the fountain until she leans over the edge in an attempt to recall that moment.

Then drops her head over the side. The water now loud in her ears. It takes her a few seconds to hear the voice.

"Madame, are you okay? Madame?" A male voice. Is that Gerald? Elizabeth can feel her hair getting wet. "Madame?" She senses a hand on her shoulder. Gerald? She opens her eyes and turns. It is a young man with his girlfriend. Both looking at her with worry across their faces. "Are you okay? Is there someone we can call?"

"Call Gerald. Call him. Tell him I love him." She looks, searching the young man's face for any hope. Anything. But he just seems confused. Elizabeth looks down and shakes her head to infer she is okay. She sees their feet move away slowly. Now her back is getting wet. She is frozen to the spot.

*

Elizabeth walks into the bathroom when she gets back to dry her hair and change her wet top, not saying much. But only minutes after, there is a knock on the door. Godric opens it. It is the Commissario.

"You've been invited to a midnight party." He walks in jovially. Happy it is nearly Easter Sunday.

"Oh, welcome yourself in. We're already asleep, as are our feet," Godric replies, completely uninterested.

"No walking required. I have a chauffeur outside." He holds up a bottle of champagne and three glasses. "This comes from the hostess. I have been instructed to come and get you."

"Patty doesn't like fireworks," Godric replies again. "What dog does?"

"No fireworks. They've stopped. There's a curfew at midnight." The Commissario listens and points to look outside the window. "Sleep when you're dead." He raises his eyebrows. "Holiday, no? Come on. It is five minutes away. Still in the city. At Lucia's midnight garden. She only opens it once or twice a year. It is magical. I think you'll love the plants."

Godric's mood shifts when he hears the hostess is Lucia. Finally, someone is speaking his language. When back at home in England, he is used to his evenings starting at midnight, and secretly is now itching to go. He looks at his nanna.

"Maybe for half an hour? Just for a nightcap? She did mention it today when she called." Godric looks at his nanna, who is leaning against the bedpost. "Lift there and back?"

"She called?" Elizabeth asks, a little surprised. "You didn't say."

"During the opera. You were talking."

"Ah. Well, it seems it is the night for nightcaps." Elizabeth pauses, looking at

Godric's face. It is clear that he won't go without her. She then looks at the Commissario. "You drive me back when I want to go?"

"You have my word," the Commissario replies.

"How big is this garden?"

"Gigantico, and it's on top of a hill. You'll love it."

36 LUCIA'S MIDNIGHT GARDEN

Elizabeth wonders why Lucia Romano wants Godric and herself at the midnight garden tonight. Is Lucia the murderess and perhaps wants to keep Elizabeth close, to convince her of her innocence? Elizabeth wants none of it. It makes no sense, and after the tour of Siena with Stefano, which lasted much longer than anticipated, she can barely keep both eyelids open. She knows Godric wanted to come to this party so much, which was certainly the main reason she failed to refuse. But it is unfair on this little dog.

When they arrive, the house is quiet. Even the piano playing a long a corridor is faint and the only sound she can hear. Very few people, perhaps twenty at the most, are just happily sitting around, quietly chatting. Maybe they, too, have been walking all day. Elizabeth spots a man in a hammock asleep. Party is not the word. Hmm, it makes even less sense why they are both there. That is until Elizabeth sees Lucia and Godric lock eyes. It is unmissable. Almost like old friends, Lucia rushes up to Godric, kissing him on both cheeks, not noticing Elizabeth at all. There you have it. Elizabeth is completely used to people falling in love with Godric. Although it is usually men. She decides to find a quiet corner for herself and Patty.

The Commissario did not lie about the garden. On a large lake, right in the centre of Florence, a man is lying in the middle of a row boat, his feet dangling over the side. Further still, tucked behind an arch Elizabeth finds a scented garden. With aromatic herbs, climbing jasmine and roses. Although it is spring, early blooms have begun, and the lavender stems are just shooting up. Much earlier than England. She sits on a swinging lounger, and lets Patty sleep on her chest. Elizabeth can only just see back up to the house, where Godric is still chatting with Lucia. Lucia's hands are all over her grandson. She watches the Commissario walk towards her to deliver a cup of peppermint tea. When he arrives, he sits at the other end of the swing chair and rocks it a little too violently.

"You need to keep still, or this will spill. And don't wake Patty."

"Ah, of course." The Commissario now

stops the swing chair from moving at all, which displeases Elizabeth, as she had just the right amount of gentle swing before. Patty jumps down and stretches out on a chamomile lawn below. The Commissario pulls biscuits in wrappers out of his pockets and places them beside Elizabeth's drink, unwrapping his own. He leans back, causing the swing lounger to abruptly start swinging again and tea to spill on Elizabeth. "This is comfortable, isn't it? You know, my doctor told me I have gout. He said I should eat less red meat. Perhaps I should become a vegan like you."

Elizabeth wipes tea from her blouse and says nothing, waiting for the point.

"Godric said you were with Stefano today."

The Commissario

says.

Elizabeth puts her tea and biscuits on the floor and shuts her eyes.

"Was he surprised when you told him it was murder? You did tell him, didn't you?"

"I might have mentioned poison. I cannot remember. We didn't speak much about it." Elizabeth keeps her eyes shut.

"You know that is a police secret." The Commissario waggles his head and starts to fiddle with the frills on the roof of the swing chair. But Elizabeth just shakes her head. "So, was he?" the Commissario repeats.

"Why are you hassling me?" Elizabeth

asks.

"I've invited you to a midnight garden on Easter Saturday night. I'm being friendly. And what about Giuseppe?"

Elizabeth shakes her head, then hands the Commissario the death threat note from Giuseppe Esposito from her bag. The Commissario takes his time to read it, then puts it in his pocket, leaning back in the swing to rub his belly and move the swing again with his legs, making Elizabeth start to feel sick.

"How do you know he didn't write this himself? He's English, home of the Bard," the Commissario raises his eyebrows. Right now, Elizabeth could not care less. She then pulls out a clear plastic bag, inside which is a painting from Giuseppe's home.

"Giuseppe also had this in his flat."

"You went to his flat?" The Commissario is surprised.

"He asked us to. It's one of Lucia's. What is he doing with it?"

Elizabeth hands the painting to the Commissario.

"Thank you." The Commissario frowns, appreciating and noting that she bagged it for evidence.

"Is my grandson safe?" Elizabeth asks pointedly, looking back at Lucia.

"Listen. We've checked out their alibis, and they were not in Florence or San

Gimignano when the theft occurred," the Commissario picks his teeth, looking back up at Lucia.

They both notice Godric and Lucia walking down the garden to join them. Lucia is full of enthusiasm when they arrive.

"We just have a small gathering on Easter Sunday. Usually, family and a few friends. But do come!" Lucia says, beaming, holding Godric's arm, and looking mainly at Godric. Elizabeth ignores Lucia's half offer of hospitality and instead addresses her grandson.

"You want to stay for a while, Goddy? I need to take Patty home."

"If you're sure, Bunny?" Godric looks concerned.

"Our driver will take you back. Here." From out of Lucia's pocket, she hands Elizabeth a gift box.

"Not another gift," Elizabeth replies ungratefully.

"But you'll return to England and say that the Italians are so generous," Lucia smiles.

"Will I?" Then Elizabeth looks at Lucia. "Or that your son, Octaviarius, made Sophia cry. Stefano's daughter. We saw her outside your home."

"Oh, young ones and hormones," Lucia shrugs.

"She seemed very upset," Godric looks at

Lucia.

"He's a beast sometimes. Just like his father."

"His father's a beast?" Elizabeth asks.

"Aren't all men, sometimes?" Lucia looks back at Elizabeth.

"No," Elizabeth replies.

"Oh, not Godric. He's an angel," Lucia corrects herself, putting her arm around Godric's neck. Elizabeth sighs. She puts the box in her pocket.

"Had you ever met Peter Jones, Lucia?"

"Why d'you ask?" Lucia replies.

"Did you?"

"I don't see that has anything to do with anything," Lucia shakes her head, surprised by the questioning and tone at her own party.

"Your son is dating Stefano's daughter, and he was good friends with Peter Jones. So, your son must have met Mr Jones?"

"Yes. I believe Ock knew him," Lucia replies.

"And did you?" Elizabeth asks.

"I have told Lorenzo this already, but yes, our paths did cross a couple of times at one or two parties."

"Your parties? Like this? Intimate?"

"Everybody knows everybody in Florence, Professor," the Commissario explains.

"Are you friends with Stefano?" Elizabeth persists with her questions to Lucia, irritated by this woman flirting with her grandson.

"No. That man. Don't mention his name again," Lucia replies, affronted.

"But your son and Sophia?"

"I do not approve. That is all I have to say on the matter," Lucia replies, "Godric, will you join me for a cocktail? Professor Green, I hope you enjoy your gift." Lucia turns to Godric, "I have one for you in the house."

Godric's eyes light up, and then he looks at his nanna, who nods for him to go.

*

Inside Lucia's limousine, which takes Elizabeth and Patty back to their hotel, Elizabeth opens the present Lucia just gave her. Inside is a set of keys with a note, "When in Florence, you are my guests at Villa De' Fiori. It is close, empty, and yours for as long as you would love to stay. Lxx'. Elizabeth dangles the keys. What?

37 EASTER SUNDAY

Elizabeth meets Stefano at the Scoppio del Carro. She feels a little hurried, as she had already been out earlier to take Patty before most were awake and before the fireworks began. A little reassured that she has left Patty now sleeping and tucked up safely inside the apartment, with Italian breakfast television blaring to block out any sounds and Godric, having come home late, asleep by her side. Compared to the first time Elizabeth met Stefano, it is clear that he has made an effort with a clean shirt and washed his hair.

"How are you, Elizabeth?" Stefano leans in to kiss Elizabeth's cheek, but she holds a hand to shake instead. She sees that Stefano notices this and handles it charmingly, taking her hand gently.

"Intrigued by the invite," Elizabeth smiles.

"Well, you're so close, and it's a big tradition in Florence. For over five hundred years, in fact."

The two of them walk towards the Santa

Maria Del Fiore. A large wooden cart is already on its way from Porta al Prato and is due to arrive in the Piazza del Duomo shortly. Stefano looks up at the Duomo. "You know, I never really come down here. What is it they say? Never a tourist in your own home?" Stefano stands underneath the Duomo.

"How's Sophia?" Elizabeth asks as they wait for the spectacle, a little packed in the middle of a growing crowd.

"Sophia?"

"Her fight with that Ock boy?"

"He's nothing but bad news," Stefano spits out his answer.

"I wish animals were not used to pull things," Elizabeth says, noticing oxen who have arrived in the piazza, covered in flowers. They watch as the cart is now detached, and the soldiers and oxen then leave the piazza as bells in the tower start to ring. Shortly after, a hush descends beneath Florence's largest and most iconic Dome. A cardinal lights a fuse, and a few seconds later, the cart, full with fireworks, erupts into a ball of crackling, fizzing, whirring, banging and popping. "I hope the oxen are far away by now!"

"It's supposed to ensure we have a good harvest!" Stefano shouts over the banging. Elizabeth remains silent, her face unhappy, so Stefano suggests an alternative. "Let's go and get breakfast." Elizabeth nods, relieved to be walking away from the throng who appear to be enjoying themselves, laughing and smiling, and fireworks shooting up and exploding, leaving smoke trails in the air. "What would you like to eat?" He asks.

"Plants," Elizabeth replies. "I hate fireworks. They upset the birds, the animals and insects. They should be banned."

Stefano takes Elizabeth through Piazza di Santa Maria Novella to a restaurant which he clearly has been to before. The manager nods to him. "What would you like?" He asks Elizabeth, pulling out a chair under vines trailing over a tenda da sole.

"Tea and toast."

"Yes, yes," Stefano replies, looking anxious about whether he can get toast and quietly mumbling in Italian to the waiter. "Jam?"

"Marmalade?"

Then Stefano leans into the waiter, holding his fingers close together to indicate thin toast. The waiter nods and walks away.

"Thin toast for the lady?" Elizabeth smiles.

"Well."

For a while, they watch the morning go by, comfortable in each other's company and the silence between them. Finally, Elizabeth's mind needs answers.

"Why doesn't Lucia like you?"

"No small talk this morning, then?" Stefano smirks.

"You want me to stay for my toast?"

"The marmalade here is," Stefano kisses his lips.

"She stopped the conversation dead last night when you came up."

"You saw her last night? We were together last night," Stefano asks.

"Are you going to deflect continuously?"

"Damn," Stefano shakes his head and smiles. "I'm going to have to tell you all my secrets, aren't I?"

"If you want us to be friends."

Stefano nods and fiddles with his coffee spoon then looks up at Elizabeth from under his eyebrows. The waiter brings over some toast.

"I very much want us to be friends. Good friends." Then Stefano smiles and looks down at his toast. "My fingers are too big for such dainty toast." He shakes his head and picks up a piece of toast with the crusts cut off. "Her husband. Let's just say we don't see eye to eye."

"How so?"

"I'm more of a traditionalist." Stefano juts out his chin, the corners of his mouth turning down.

"You're going to have to stop talking in riddles."

"It is a glorious morning. We're sitting here, eating toast."

"Not yet," Elizabeth replies.

Stefano shakes his head, looks to the sky, then

at Elizabeth and shrugs.

"He has fingers in many pies. Fashion, finance, jewellery, real estate. Building on land which has never had homes on before. Motherland. Green land. And, well, I fought one of his monstrous property development plans in the courts, and I won. It cost him a lot of money. They don't speak to me."

"What land, where?"

It is Stefano's turn to be silent.

"Where your grandpa grew olives? That beautiful view?"

Stefano nods.

"Just like Marco. They keep nipping at my land around the edges. In cahoots, probably. The two of them." Stefano pulls a face at the margarine he offers Elizabeth before taking the butter himself. "What will we do, build on everything until it's all gone? There are still a lot of brown field sites in the city that could be built upon for homes. There are many empty homes too that could be filled. Never mind the olives. What will happen to the bees!?" Stefano shakes his head. "So, I guess I'm persona non grata."

Elizabeth sees Stefano cross again. She feels the bees on her cardigan that Godric bought her. She thinks of Godric and wonders if he is still asleep. How much she loves him. What is she doing with this stranger who reminds her of her ex-husband, eating toast?

Stefano smiles again, and there it is. Gerald's beaming, twinkly smile, lazy on one side. She closes her eyes, and for just one moment, she is back with the love she holds most dear in her heart.

38 COLOMBA PASQUALE FOR THE JEWEL THIEF'S WIFE

After Stefano has insisted on paying for Elizabeth's marmalade toast, they walk around the piazza for her to see the festive flower displays on plinths and in small green bedding borders and window boxes, all put out, especially for Easter Sunday. Stefano spots a delicatessen and pops in, coming out with a Colomba Pasquale, explaining they cannot turn up empty-handed. He also pops a bar of vegan chocolate in Elizabeth's pocket.

It is a short stroll to the apartment where the wife of the dead jewel thief still resides, but not an easy climb, what with it being on the fifth floor and the lift being broken. Elizabeth and Stefano laugh as they have to pause a couple of times on the staircase, Stefano offering a hand to pull Elizabeth up. Meanwhile, Elizabeth seems highly preoccupied with a big ginger tom cat looking down at them from his perch on the very top floor bannisters. Elizabeth wanting to say hello, but Stefano knowing she would have to climb another three flights to do that and persuading her against it, so instead she just closes her eyes for a moment by way of a cat greeting.

"How do they do that? Perch in such dangerous spots and not fall?" Elizabeth stares.

"Nine lives?"

They are both out of breath when they arrive at the front door. Elizabeth stares at the small woman with a dark brown pixie haircut and high fringe, wearing a pretty flowery dress, who greets them in the doorway. The woman's face pale and unimpressed by their laughter.

"Bongiorno Stefano," Mia says, her eyes red from perhaps crying about her dead husband. Stefano kisses both Mia's cheeks and then explains.

"This is my new friend, Elizabeth." Then he lifts his cake, "We come with Easter sugar."

"Are you police?" Mia asks Elizabeth, eyeing her suspiciously.

"Most certainly not," Elizabeth frowns.

"You're English?" Mia visibly changes, hearing the accent, happier to see them both. "And the only visitors I've had since Peter died, apart from the police, so please forgive me," she pauses, "and Peter's really annoying friend, Giuseppe, who won't leave me alone." Mia looks at Stefano. "And I'm sure I'm being followed by Lucia's cronies." Mia stands aside, inviting them into the flat, taking the cake from Stefano. Then Mia walks out onto her apartment-width balcony, where she is already taking coffee and drops the gift on the table—the view of the River Arno, with boats chugging up and down not two hundred feet below and people standing, looking out at the water before they continue mooching around Florence's beauty.

"I must apologise. I've left it too long. Aurelia is out with the horses today. I just popped into the city to pick up one or two things for this afternoon's party. You're very welcome to come, but I understand if it is too much. We did think about cancelling it, actually." Stefano pauses, "I thought the funeral would be sooner, and we could see each other then. It's just awful. I'm sorry. Why did I say that?" Stefano pats Mia's arm, realising that bringing up the funeral is the worst. "Would you like me to do something to make Giuseppe leave you alone?"

"He keeps turning up." Mia shakes her head and sighs deeply.

Elizabeth, meanwhile, looks around the apartment. The walls are a little crumbly around the edges, but it has a feel of nostalgic Italian grandeur. High ceilings with cornices.

Fading wallpaper, scuffed floorboards but large rooms.

"You look–"

"Like I need some rest?" Mia interrupts Stefano, touching his arm back. "I'm not sleeping. I don't know what to do with myself."

"Mia, I should have invited you over before. Would it be easier if you came to stay with us?" Stefano replies, concerned.

"That's very kind. But what if they release the body soon, and try to get hold of me? I need to be close. And I don't want the police ransacking this place again when I'm not here. It is all I have left of Peter. And I don't want to impose on Aurelia." Mia's eyes fill with tears, which she hurriedly brushes away with her handkerchief.

"Is that Devon or Dorset?"

"It's a mix." Mia smiles at Elizabeth clocking her accent.

"Did they take anything?" Elizabeth asks.

"They took the lot." Mia's voice is dull. "Peter's laptop, research papers. His lifelong work, actually. They just scooped them up and put them in sacks. He'd ordered them, filed them, all his papers. I had helped. They must be in a mess now. What am I supposed to do? I said if anything happened to him, I'd make sure his research was taken up by a postdoc, you know, so it would be published eventually. Now what? Oh–" Mia shuts her eyes and, without looking, takes a cigarette out of a packet on the table, lights it and then takes a drag. Elizabeth is stunned that she does not singe her fringe. Mia then opens her eyes. “It’s all too much for me.” She touches her lip with her finger, perhaps removing a spec of cigarette, then looks at Elizabeth. “You know, they even took his shoes? I mean, his shoes?”

“It sounds a lot,” Elizabeth replies, without pausing in case her own grief surfaces, and asks, “Did they take anything of yours?”

“I don’t have anything to take.” Mia shrugs her shoulders a little. “I’ll get a knife.” And before either Stefano or Elizabeth can say they have no space to eat cake, Mia disappears into the kitchen. When she comes back with ice cream, Stefano’s eyes light up.

“Alright, now you’re talking,” he says as he picks up a spoon and opens the tub. Then realises this is not the time. “Actually, maybe later.” Stefano drops the spoon on the table and sits in one of the balcony chairs instead.

“Will you go back to England now?” Elizabeth asks, deciding to sit down next to Stefano.

“I don’t know. We have the house there, but it doesn’t feel like home anymore. Peter felt like home.” Mia looks around. “I can still feel him here.” Mia picks up an Easter card Peter sent her. “They didn’t take everything.” She shows it to Elizabeth. The card has a childlike drawing of rabbits sitting in a basket, surrounded by flowers. Elizabeth notices a few Easter cards for Mia at the end of the table, lying flat. She picks them up, pretending to admire the front, but peeking inside, she notices one is from Giuseppe, another from Aurelia, but says nothing.

"Will you take Peter back?"

"Excuse me?"

"Home, to Cambridge."

Mia does not answer.

"You're very welcome to lay Peter to rest on the farm, Mia."

Mia looks at Stefano, her eyes bloodshot, so Stefano continues. "We have the grove near the house. I know he liked the spot. There are orange trees. Orange blossom."

"The police won't release his body yet," Mia looks into Stefano's eyes for help, perching on the side of an armchair beside the doors to the balcony.

"What d'you think made Peter steal the diamond, Mia?" Elizabeth asks, looking directly at Mia, waiting to read her facial expressions.

"I thought he was going to the library," Mia tries to compose herself, taking a long drag from her cigarette.

"The library?"

"He told me he was studying." Mia responds. Elizabeth holds her glare, waiting for Mia to explain. It works, and Mia's words come tumbling out. "I was as shocked as the rest of Italy, okay? When I saw him on the CCTV. He hadn't come home, and he wasn't answering his phone. I even went to the library looking for him. I walked up and down the stacks on five floors. Five. Who goes to the library these days?"

"People who read," Elizabeth replies. "So, you were clearly watching television that evening to hear the news? Yet you have no television here?" Elizabeth looks around the small flat.

"I went for a nightcap when I couldn't find Peter. I was in a bar. They had the news on during half-time of a football match. I don't know who was playing. I wasn't watching. But I saw Peter's face. They were so quick to identify him? I don't know how?"

"Because he was working there. He had taken a cleaning job. Didn't you notice?" Elizabeth asks.

"He was telling me he was at the olive farm when he was actually at Bella Dinostrade's. I mean, who's flipping heard of it?"

Her face red with anxiety, Mia looks for someone to tell her they have heard of the fancy gallery. The intercom interrupts, buzzing from a street caller. She stands up and peers over the balcony.

"Ugh. Again." Mia sees Giuseppe stand back and look at her, and then he waves. She points she is going to buzz him up. Giuseppe is sweaty when he arrives and out of breath, holding some irises. "Sit. Have coffee." Mia collapses back into her chair, a little more composed, still holding the flowers.

"Professor Green, I'm so glad you're here," Giuseppe coughs out his words.

"You know each other?"

"Yes, yes. Professor Green is helping the police and was retrieving my passport." Giuseppe pulls a note out of his pocket and throws it on the table as he plonks himself in a chair opposite Mia and next to Elizabeth.

"Wait. You said you were not police?" Mia looks angry at being lied to.

"I'm not."

"I don't understand."

"Elizabeth is my friend. Please, let's calm down. She is a very good woman," Stefano immediately puts his hand up to protect Elizabeth in case Mia does something she regrets.

"She's an expert in poison." Giuseppe claps his hands, pleased to have Elizabeth on board. "She's going to find Peter's killer!" Giuseppe excitedly tells Mia, then turns to Elizabeth, "Did you get my passport?"

"No, I did not. The place was a mess," Elizabeth frowns at Giuseppe.

"So, you are working with the police?" Mia responds to Giuseppe's explanation, her anger turning to hope. "The police have done nothing to find his killer. They're just interested in the diamond." Mia's eyes are now wide, her body leaning in towards Elizabeth. "Apparently, it's worth more than life." She then turns to Stefano. "I'm glad you're here. Really."

"Me too," Stefano looks kindly upon Mia.

"Well, I've met the Commissario, and he's not only interested in the diamond. He wants to find out what happened to your husband," Elizabeth explains.

"Only as a way to find the diamond," Mia replies.

"I cannot argue with that," Elizabeth acknowledges Mia's point. "But, either way, they're looking to find out what happened to Peter."

"Giuseppe. What are you doing here?" Stefano tries to steer the conversation away for the sake of Mia.

"I thought you would be alone," Giuseppe looks at Mia, ignoring Stefano. "My friend befriends this man, and now he's dead. I always wondered if something bad would happen to Peter from knowing you. I didn't realise just how bad. Did he not like your ideas for olives enough?" Giuseppe scowls at Stefano. "Nowhere's safe out there. I've had another one of these. You wouldn't know anything about this, would you, Stefano?" Giuseppe taps the piece of paper he threw down on the table moments before.

"What?" Stefano looks bemused, then replies, "I know nothing about your comings and goings, I'm happy to say."

Elizabeth carefully picks up the side of the note and opens the page from the corner.

> *I know what you have. You need to meet me at the top of the Duomo at nine tonight and leave it there. If you do not, you will not be here to see the sunrise.*

"What d'you have, Giuseppe?" Elizabeth asks, after translating the note from Italian and reading it out loud.

"Does someone think you have the diamond?" Stefano asks, about to pick up the note, but Elizabeth stops him, folds the note, and places inside a serviette for safe keeping, so she can take it to the police.

"Oh, you're going to give that one to Lorenzo?" Giuseppe asks, adding, "He's done nothing since the last one I gave you. I have no bodyguard, no police protection. Nothing. They will come for me next, and I will be dead, I tell you. Dead!" Giuseppe squeals as the perspiration from his forehead starts to trickle down his face. He wipes his face on his jacket sleeve. "I thought I'd be safe here with you. Can I stay on your couch?" Giuseppe pleads to Mia.

"Out of the question?" Stefano replies, seeing Mia's face. "Don't put Mia in the line of fire."

"Oh!" Giuseppe squeals. "D'you think I will be shot?" He grabs Stefano. Stefano then abruptly stands, shaking off Giuseppe.

"Will you just stop shouting? That's not what I mean. Just stop leaning on Mia." Stefano frowns. Mia pushes Giuseppe a coffee cup across the table.

"I've been followed." Giuseppe looks up at Stefano pouring coffee, then glancing at the cocktail trolley in the corner. "Can we make it Irish?"

Mia gets up, returns with some whisky for Giuseppe, and pours a drop into his coffee. Giuseppe drinks it and takes a deep sigh.

"How many notes have you had now?" Elizabeth asks.

"I've lost count." Giuseppe glugs back the coffee whisky combo. "You have one already, this one. Too many."

"So, five, eight, ten?"

"I don't know. I don't know. D'you think with these wits as they are," Giuseppe points to his fragile state, "that I can count?" He finishes his drink and lifts the pot. "That coffee was nice. Is there any more?"

"I'll make some more," Mia offers.

"Not for me," Elizabeth says.

"Nor me," Stefano smiles. "We shouldn't trouble you much longer. I'm so glad we came to see you, Mia."

"How's Cambridge?" Mia asks Elizabeth, aware her house guests might be leaving imminently, leaving her alone with Giuseppe. "I mean, I said I don't think I will go back, but I suspect Cambridge is as beautiful as it was when I left."

"Reports from home suggest that it has been dry but a little chilly," Elizabeth replies, aware she is now talking about the weather. "There was a frost two days ago, which is to be expected, but I hope we don't get many more as it always holds my garden back in June, and I do so love summer flowers." Then Elizabeth stops thinking about home to avoid feeling homesick, instead asking Mia, "Where in Cambridge is your home?"

"Home is nowhere anymore, but we have," she corrects herself, "I have a house in Orchard Street. It's all shut up right now."

"I want to go back to Ely. I will be safer there," Giuseppe says to himself as he gets up to pour more whisky into his cup. "I just need my passport. Please, Professor Green. Please get my passport."

Elizabeth watches Giuseppe walk over to the cocktail trolley, not replying to his pleads. Above Giuseppe's head, she notices a photograph on the wall of two families around a table eating. She can see Stefano and Aurelia, Mia and Peter and Stefano's children, and one or two guests she does not recognise.

"More photographs of the four of you," Elizabeth looks at Stefano. He follows her line of sight and sees the photograph where he has his arm around Peter, their two wives standing behind them, beaming.

"We would eat at least once a fortnight together, I suppose?" Stefano stares at the photograph, and then at Mia, perhaps waiting for her to confirm. She nods and looks sad.

"Did either of you know about the diamond? Had you heard about it before–" Elizabeth looks at Mia and then at Stefano. Stefano shakes his head.

"Who cares about diamonds?" Mia says, "I'm not a magpie. Peter's death is for nothing?" Mia stands frozen to the spot, having got up to make coffee a while ago but not moved. "Now, when I go out, people just give me dirty looks. There goes that woman who was married to the jewel thief of the biggest robbery in Italian history. She must know something." Mia looks at Elizabeth with watery eyes.

"People often think no smoke without fire," Elizabeth stares at Mia.

"What did he want a diamond for? He was a Cambridge Don, for chrissake?" Mia shakes her head, confused.

"Are you good friends then?" Elizabeth asks Giuseuppe of Mia.

"I was good friends with Peter. We met sometimes, didn't we," Giuseppe says to Mia.

"Actually," Mia pauses, shaking her head, "Peter didn't much like you, Giuseppe," Mia replies, looking at the floor. "He said you were always hanging around with bad ideas."

Giuseppe looks at Stefano and Elizabeth, wiping the sweat from his forehead.

"When did he say that?" Giuseppe blurts, his face refuting the statement and a little perplexed.

"He went for beers as he pitied you. You're alone in Florence. Don't have other friends. Peter was too nice."

"You're upset. That's not true."

"Upset?" Mia shakes her head. "My husband is dead. He's dead!" Mia screams and walks out of the living room into her bedroom. The three of them look at each other. "Please leave me alone, Giuseppe!" Mia shouts back.

"I'm not the one she should be upset with?" Giuseppe says, looking at Stefano. "You were always taking him away. Always whispering to him. Getting him to do things for you."

*

Elizabeth stands outside Mia's apartment building with Stefano. They watch Giuseppe walk off in the opposite direction, before crossing the road to stand by the River Arno.

"Not a bad place to own an apartment," Elizabeth looks around and takes in the atmosphere. Tourists are meandering on either side of the road, not a stone's throw from the Ponte Vecchio bridge, as boats chug up and down, carrying goods or more tourists. "Can I borrow your phone?"

"Of course. Mia seemed on edge."

"Thank you. I was quite surprised by her ability to get out of bed."

Elizabeth takes Stefano's phone. "Do I have to dial anything to phone abroad? I will reimburse you."

"No, and it's okay, don't do that." Stefano shows Elizabeth what she needs to do to make a call, then lights a small cigar. Waiting for her to make her call, he turns his head away and moves ever so slightly away to give her privacy. He need not have bothered, as once Elizabeth has dialled, she walks across the road again and back into the gardens of the apartment building to be out of earshot.

"Bob?" Elizabeth listens to Inspector Bob Abley from Cambridge Police Station tell her how he's glad she called and is happy she called him back. "Shh, I'm borrowing someone's phone."

"Who's phone? They now have my private number." Bob Abley sighs.

"Yes, well, you should have thought of that if you are going to bother me on holiday. There is something you need to do for me now."

"Raynott said–"

"Have you got a pen? Peter Jones and his wife, Mia. Can you check them out?"

"I might have already checked them out," Bob replies a little sarcastically. "He's from Cambridge. He allegedly stole this diamond. That's why I've been calling you."

"Right. So, are they who they say they are? Was he actually attached to the university? And she seems to be from Devon or Dorset."

"Yes, and yes. He has nothing on his record. Neither does she. They moved over there for his research. We have all the papers. It checks out. She moved up here from the West Country when her father got a job working for the council about forty years ago. She must have stayed once she grew up. There's nothing out of place."

"How long have they been married?"

"They met in the nineties at least, according to their property records. Could be earlier. Both their names are on the deeds of the Orchard Street property since '97. Married recently, in 2020. I always knew marriage was unlucky. Do you know that Maureen is remarried? Did I tell you? Ink wasn't even dry."

Elizabeth shuts her eyes, feeling for Bob and his recent divorce. Then she thinks of her own marriage to Gerald and how happy it was. Opening her eyes, she notices Stefano leaning against the wall, smoking and watching her. So, she decides to wrap up the conversation.

"And if you're so up on this case, what about Giuseppe Esposito?"

"A loner. From what the neighbours over here told us. Cherry Hinton. His flat has closed curtains. We've no reason to get a warrant. Or, do we?"

39 THE GIFT OF VILLA DE' FIORI

Godric wakes up to explosions of fireworks outside the window and lifts the duvet for Patty to climb under. After ten minutes, everything goes quiet again, so he calls the concierge, who assures him the fireworks are now over until this evening. He decides to go searching for breakfast with Patty. He wanders across the Pont Vecchio Bridge to see if he can sneak into the Boboli Gardens, but is turned away. Hungry, and with no green space close by, Godric sighs. He is just wondering what to do next, when he is tapped on the shoulder by Lucia.

"What are you doing up here?" Lucia asks, joyed to see him.

"Failing at even the simplest of ambitions. I'm still jet lagged."

"Jet lagged?" She smiles.

"Well, you're one hour ahead here. It's already lunch when I'm still looking for breakfast."

They arrive at Lucia's and walk out onto the terrace. The sun pouring down on his face. The butler bringing Patty some chicken and rice. Immediately, Godric relaxes.

"We found her in a bush in Patigno. Her owner died. She was living rough." Godric looks lovingly at Patty.

"Poor little thing." Lucia kisses Patty's head. "I'm already missing the both of you when we aren't together. You do realise you'll have to be my friend forever. I will be knocking on your door in Cambridge." Lucia looks at Godric.

"Forever is a long time," Godric smirks.

"Is it? It wasn't for Peter Jones and my diamond."

"Well, we don't seem to be leaving Florence yet."

"How so? I thought you said last night that your nanna was done with helping the Commissario?"

"She's out with Stefano Brambilla this morning. He's invited her to dinners, the opera, and tours of Siena. It's as if someone wants to keep us busy. To look the other way," Godric ponders.

"Stefano's trouble. Will do anything to protect his olive trees. Anything. Trust me."

"As it happens, I'm already growing rather fond of you. And not just because you gave me a beautiful jacket. And, believe me, we are travelling so light I will have to lose my hairbrush and a pair of jeans to make space in the car."

"And why are you growing fond of me?" Lucia's face opens up, revealing her pure joy at hearing Godric's words.

"Oh, definitely just the excess," Godric replies, trying to keep it light. "Neither of us knows when to stop." No sooner has Godric stopped talking when a member of staff brings through Godric's cooked breakfast orders.

After eating, they walk Patty around Lucia's gardens.

"Is Max away?" Godric asks. "Don't you get lonely?"

"When you have a helicopter and jet, God, you're never far away. But we have grown apart over the years, I suppose. Funny, once, he would do anything for me. Sometimes I do feel vulnerable, I guess? But there's Ock and the staff, so..." She looks up at the house.

"Well, I can protect you today. So long as you protect me from your angry son."

"Ock is a good boy. His father just spoils him."

"You know I'm closer to your son's age, and I would say there is more going on there than being spoiled. Threatening to kill a dog. Twice." Godric is adamant that something is going on with Ock.

"He can be hard, but he's not broken the law or got into trouble. Isn't that all a mother can hope for?"

"You don't think he stole your diamond, do you?" Godric asks. "Are you completely sure?"

"I know you don't much care for him, but darling, are you trying to frame him?"

After a walk in the garden, they wander back up to the house and sit in garden chairs, Patty with her own in the shade. Time drifts by.

"Have you been to Portofino?" Lucia asks. Godric shakes his head, so she continues. "Promise me one thing? That you'll visit? We have a home there. Just above the bay, in the hills. My father gave it to me as a twenty-first birthday present. I'll give you the address. I'd love you to see it."

"That's very kind of you. Thank you. I'm sure my Nanna would love visiting. She went on holiday there with my grandpa once, but I haven't booked anything as it was rather, well, pricey."

"Did your nanna like the keys?"

"Keys?" Godric asks.

"I gave her, well, for you both, a set of keys to my smaller cottage further up the hill. I thought you might like to stay there as it has a garden and would be nicer for Patty?"

"Lucia, that's too much. We couldn't." Godric looks at Lucia, grateful but also confused. "Why are you being so kind?"

"It's empty and going to waste. Please, stay in a little more comfort. If only for Patty?" They wander inside towards the bar. A mixologist appears wearing a white jacket. "What would you like?" Lucia asks as Godric stares behind the bar at the Art Deco mirror and all the expensive-looking spirit bottles and crystal glasses.

"What are you drinking?" Godric replies, rubbing his hands together and watching the talented barman go to work.

"Something tall with a kick," Lucia looks at Godric, trying to make the analogy obvious, "How about a mint julep?"

"Make that two."

"Do you think your nanna will find my ring?"

"I'm afraid she's done now. With the police, I mean. She found the poison," Godric replies, watching the mixologist throw ice into the air.

"Rather dramatic, isn't it? Snake venom? What a way to die." Lucia wonders about Elizabeth as she sips her Mint Julep.

"The killer must have wanted to send a warning. You know, like the–" Godric realises he is in Italy and thinks twice about what he says next.

"He was poisoned and then pushed?" Lucia interrupts.

"Quite the dramatic place, Tuscany." Godric sighs, now feeling flat.

"It can also be wonderful. Come with me to the Uffizi. Let's see Da Vinci, Vasari and Botticelli! We can hide Patty in your jacket," Lucia suggests enthusiastically.

"Alright. Then, I'd better be getting back." Godric studies Lucia's face. It has an innocence about it, and also terrific skin. As he sips his drink, he wonders if she can really be as innocent as she looks.

40 THE FIGHT

"Come back here!"

"Get off me!" Stefano shouts.

"You started this!"

Bystanders watch as Marco Conti and Stefano Brambilla throw punches at one another. Stefano has blood rolling down his cheek. Some of Marco's restaurant and wine shop staff have come out to watch, clearly having been asked by Marco not to stop the fight. Tourists wonder if they should call the police but are told by locals to stop interfering.

"Leave Isabella alone."

"What can you do to stop me? Eh?" Marco circles, waiting for Stefano to give him his best shot. Stefano takes a run at Marco and shoves into him with such force that they stumble over a wall and into a chicken coop, feathers flying everywhere.

41 STEFANO BRAMBILLA'S EASTER SUNDAY PARTY

Elizabeth and Godric meet back at the hotel apartment and discuss Lucia's offer of the use of her cottage. A quick online check reveals Villa De' Fiori, along the Costa S. Giorgio, is a rather grand home.

"And she wants to give us her home to use in Portofino as well." Godric beams. It is clear to Elizabeth Godric wants to stay on for a while, and is aware their hotel apartment rental time is ending. In truth, now the Commissario is off her back, Elizabeth is enjoying feeling closer to Gerald here in Florence. When she wanders the streets and piazzas, she remembers walking around with him all those years ago.

And then, there is Stefano, who somehow brings Gerald closer. She still cannot put her finger on it. Is it as superficial as his smile, his manner, the flick of the back of his hair? Or is it in his bones, his soul? No one could replace

Gerald. She tries to picture Gerald and sees Stefano. Elizabeth shakes her head. She does not want this to end but cannot have Stefano usurping Gerald. No, he brings Gerald back to life. She is not entirely sure that she feels comfortable with her own excitement. Seeing Stefano again this afternoon, her happiness to be invited to his Easter Sunday 'twenty-four-hour party bash', that runs right through to Easter Monday 'and then some', which she remembers Stefano explaining just this morning. She does not even like parties.

Elizabeth looks at Godric, who is crinkling up his face. It is plain he would like her to say yes to staying in Lucia's villa.

"Please don't shake your head at the idea. It might be great? We can see more sights, and be back free to enjoy ourselves. That's why we came away from Cambridge in the first place, wasn't it?"

"Alright, a few more days. But, I'd rather go to Stefano's party, than Lucia's later. I know she mentioned she was entertaining. I'm sure she wants you to go."

"That's fine. We have just seen each other. I can survive."

Elizabeth is uncertain but also pleased that Godric can be very persuasive when he wants to be, which might come in handy. But then she wonders if he is just very persuasive to her, as she knows she would do anything for him.

"We can't rush back home anyway. We have to stay weeks for Patty's passport to be valid with her vaccines to kick in."

"That settles it then."

"I'll cancel our place in Siena. We have seen quite a bit of it already."

"I'll be pleased if we never have to talk about a certain diamond death again."

"Ditto that."

*

Godric drives up a hill behind the Boboli Gardens to Lucia's Villa De' Fiori. There are no locked gates or butlers, but when they enter the house they hear a member of Lucia's staff packing the fridge and freezer with goodies.

"This will do, I suppose," Godric's eyes pop at the champagne and whiskey on the side as they walk in.

"Are you driving us to Siena if I drive us back?" Elizabeth reminds him.

"Yes, of course. Thank you." Godric averts his eyes at all the booze in the box below his feet, then smiles at his nanna. "Lucia was asking a lot about whether you will be helping to solve the case. She had looked you up online. I bet you haven't even looked you up online."

"Whatever for?"

Once settled, they leave for Siena and Stefano's Easter Sunday party. Godric doesn't pry why his nanna took up the invitation or why she enjoys Stefano's company. But, although he wants to see her happy, he is also nervous about what they are driving into.

*

When they arrive at Stefano's home, many cars are already parked in the driveway, and along the road outside the property. A parking attendant waves to them, takes their keys, and leaves with their Fiat.

"I hope he actually is a parking attendant," Elizabeth comments.

"If he wanted to steal a car, d'you think it would be ours?" They survey dozens of supercars, adding up to millions of pounds. "Not bad for olives."

"Gerald always said you never see a poor farmer," Elizabeth replies, appraising the wealth.

They walk through the open front door. To the left of the large hallway, they spot Stefano's daughters, Sophia and Isabella, laughing over a photograph on their phone. Elizabeth notices the Commissario and Sergeant Rossi eating from a buffet. Stefano's wife, Aurelia, is leaning against a fireplace, looking stunning and laughing with a man Elizabeth does not recognise.

From behind them, they become aware that Mia has also just entered. As they get a little stuck in the hallway by all the guests, Aurelia comes over to greet and perhaps rescue them all.

"Mia, Professor Green, Godric," Aurelia smiles.

"I feel like the world's eyes are on me," Mia replies nervously.

Aurelia shakes her head. "I was just about to go for a swim. Come? Escape the crowds? I have a spare costume somewhere," Aurelia puts an arm around Mia and ushers her out of the kitchen and into the garden. Elizabeth watches them go and then scans the kitchen where Aurelia left them with drinks. In such a bustling crowd, it is hard for Elizabeth to think straight. Her eyes fall on the Commissario again, who spots Elizabeth and walks over.

"What are you doing here? Apart from eating?" Elizabeth asks him.

"I'm off duty, and Angelou too. We just popped over, in case of trouble with Marco. Stefano was seen being beaten up in San Gimignano but doesn't want to press charges." The Commissario looks at the Sergeant, who nods as he drops some ice in what looks like an alcoholic drink.

"Oh no! Was he beaten badly? Where is he?" Elizabeth feels her stomach sink.

"I don't think so. Things are always over women."

"Are they? I mean, were they really

fighting over his daughter?" "You know, Lucia and Max are convinced Stefano is a bad egg," the Commissario sighs.

"He's not, though, is he," Elizabeth says confidently. "I would have thought more of you to pander to their whims, especially while you are his guest. And isn't this just Maximilius wanting to take Stefano's land and destroy it?"

"They are at war over land. It's a long-running feud, that is true. I don't think my being here today will make the slightest difference on that count. But, if my presence keeps the peace for a few hours, then it isn't a bad way to while away the afternoon, no?" The Commissario smiles at his Sergeant, who is holding up a pastry he knows his Commissario likes.

Elizabeth drifts away from the Commissario. This is a much bigger party than she thought it would be. She feels claustrophobic. She imagined sitting down for lunch with Stefano and talking intimately, like they had in Florence. She can see him now, outside in the garden, huddled with Giuseppe, deep in conversation. He has not even noticed her.

Elizabeth looks to her right but sees Godric has wandered off. Feeling alone in a crowd, she wonders what she is doing here. Yet she can hardly turn around and go home without Godric. And where is home now? She does not know anymore. Home was where Gerald was, and she is utterly devastated to have lost that, feeling like she is chasing a ghost to try to keep him with her. She does not know what she expected from coming here. But all the excitement has evaporated. All these people in front of her feel both grey and too loud. Their screeching voices piercing her ears. She does not like that she is staying in Lucia's house. Why is this woman being so generous? Why do they not like Stefano? What is Lucia playing at befriending her grandson? From all the noise and jostling, Stefano appears in front of Elizabeth. They lock eyes for more than a second.

"I'm so glad you came," Stefano beams, unable to hide just how pleased he is to see her. Elizabeth spots Stefano's black eye.

"What were you talking to Giuseppe about?" Elizabeth feels both flustered and angry at Stefano, for taking so long to find her.

"I caught him stealing cheese and wine. He was putting it in his bag. I told him to put it back into the kitchen, and that would be the end of the matter."

"Cheese and wine?"

"Yes, well-known nourishment on Easter Sunday. He wasn't even invited?" Stefano pauses. "It's really good to see you. Honestly."

"I don't like parties. They don't seem to suit you either?" Elizabeth looks at Stefano's black eye.

"That makes it all the more special that you came," Stefano says nothing about his eye. There is quiet between them until Stefano takes Elizabeth's hand and leads her through a door into an orangery. Patty following on the lead. All around are delicate panes of glass, and the sweet smell of citrus and sugar envelopes their senses. But Stefano does not stop. They leave the orangery, Stefano still holding Elizabeth's hand as they step into the garden briefly before arriving at the biggest glasshouse Elizabeth has seen outside of the Cambridge Botanic Gardens. Once inside, Stefano shuts the door behind them. They walk along a gravel path, under palm trees and exotic plants, until they arrive at the very back and an expensive looking suite of wicker sofas and chairs and a bar. The air is warm and moist.

"I was hoping you'd come. I prepared these just in case."

Stefano walks behind the bar, takes a cocktail shaker out of a freezer compartment, and pours two mint juleps. Then he lifts a needle on an old vinyl record player which plays 'Casta Diva', Bellini's *Norma Act 1*. "Do sit."

"This is much more relaxing," Elizabeth bends down to stroke Patty.

"Are you hungry?" He asks. Elizabeth shakes her head, Stefano smiling. "Good, because I have no snacks. They attract ants." He passes a cocktail to Elizabeth.

"I'm also driving."

"Ah," Stefano picks up a shaker and makes a fruit cocktail instead. "Here, try this. Pomegranate. Lots of antioxidants. You'll live forever."

"Do you get bananas?" Elizabeth observes, looking at a large plant. Patty finds a puddle of water left over from the plants being watered and starts to lap it up.

"For sure. More than we can eat. We need to find hungry monkeys."

"And Summer Lady's Tresses, *Spiranthes aestivalis.* These are extinct in the UK now. Habitat destruction. Wetlands. You are keeping them warm and wet. Quite the labour of love. Pretty flowers when they come."

"I'm so glad you like it here. I've nursed these species for at least fifteen years. I learnt about them when I was in Kent."

"Well, I'll be–" She is surprised. "I like it here very much." Elizabeth nods to the busy house. Moments after the words leave Elizabeth's mouth, Stefano takes her hand again and encourages her to sit beside him.

"Let's stay here all afternoon. I feel eighteen again," Stefano looks at Elizabeth. "This–"

"You're much younger than–"

"Elizabeth. I don't want you to think I invite anyone into my greenhouse."

"Especially not greenfly," Elizabeth replies, and before she can stop him, Stefano leans over and steals a kiss from her lips. Elizabeth's eyes open wide, and they watch Stefano about to steal another when Marco comes storming in, looking for Stefano, screaming at the top of his voice, oblivious to what just happened.

"So here you are. Hiding!"

Stefano jumps around to face Marco, his face changing to one of extreme anger.

"Leave my house immediately. You're not welcome."

"Your daughter invited me. She loves me," Marco rages.

"Get out," Stefano says quietly.

"You have to sign the land agreement. I'm entitled to it. It will be mine, old man. She'll marry me. She's your oldest daughter. It will all be mine eventually. Accept it."

"Over my dead body," Stefano replies gravely.

"You will cut your own daughter off?"

"Get out," Stefano flails his arms at Marco.

"This is not over," Marco replies, choosing this time not to retaliate, instead feeling his lip for blood, hit by one of Stefano's waving arms.

After Marco has left, Stefano is extremely flustered and pulls a phone from his pocket. He speaks to his security and asks them to find Marco and escort him from the premises.

"I think I've had enough of this so-called

party," Elizabeth says, shocked by Stefano's physical altercation.

"Wait, Elizabeth."

"Does everything have to turn into a fight?"

"You know, Marco is a bad man. He will be the death of me and then watch the vultures circle and trample on my grave until they get what they want."

As Elizabeth opens the glasshouse door and finds herself in the garden, she takes a deep breath and is relieved to see Godric on the terrace not far away. Stefano follows behind, trying to get her to turn around, apologising, and begging her to return and sit. His words are drowned out by the blades of a helicopter circling and descending onto the lawn. Ock steps out of the chopper and sees Sophia. Before he walks to kiss his girlfriend, he heads for Elizabeth.

"Mother sent me to lend you the chopper. I think she thought you might hate the party?" Ock hands Elizabeth an envelope. Elizabeth opens it and reads a note from Lucia. Stefano is by her side, beginning to realise what is about to happen, as Elizabeth looks up at the helicopter and over to Godric and Patty.

"What? You can't leave. No. Don't go like this."

"My mother says you know about the diamond. Where is it?" Ock asks Stefano.

"Stop. Just stop." Stefano pleads with Elizabeth, trying to shrug away Ock, pushing him to the side.

"She says you know." Ock walks off to greet Sophia, who has run down the lawn to jump into his arms. Stefano gets out a handkerchief from his pocket and wipes his brow. Elizabeth looks back at Stefano, sweaty from rushing to try to catch her.

"Are you picking a fight with him now too?" Elizabeth asks Stefano, picking up Patty to make her feel safe from the noise of the whirring helicopter blades.

"Elizabeth."

Godric spots Ock has given his nanna something. He excuses himself from speaking to some olive farmers and walks across the lawn to join her.

"Bunny?"

"It's for us. For Portofino?" Elizabeth starts to walk towards the helicopter, so upset from what just happened in the glasshouse seeing this as her escape. Godric shrugs at Stefano and follows.

Before Elizabeth knows what she is doing, she is climbing in. Stefano grabs her arm, trying to stop her, but Godric pushes Stefano away and climbs in after his nanna, with Patty now snuggled inside his jacket. Elizabeth asks the pilot if he has ear protectors for a dog. He nods, getting out some child-sized ear protectors. The pilot nods and he takes off, leaving Stefano staring up, along with the other guests, at the helicopter's rapid departure.

As Godric looks down at the people getting smaller, he turns to his nanna while putting on his headphones.

"This is impulsive of you?"

"It had better be going to Portofino."

"That is where we're headed, Ma'am," the pilot replies, listening to their conversation. Godric points at a noise breaker that makes the conversation private between himself and his nanna.

"Stefano seemed pretty upset. What was that about?" Godric asks.

"It felt all wrong." Elizabeth looks down at Stefano, who has not taken his eyes off the helicopter. Should she have left like this?

42 PORTOFINO

"You don't think this helicopter is a present from Lucia, do you?" Elizabeth asks Godric, as they cross Tuscany with speed, Stefano and Aurelia's house long gone.

"Perhaps the pilot comes with?" Godric replies, giving his nanna a knowing look.

Eventually, they arrive at the picturesque Italian fishing village on the Riviera, not far from Genoa. Each home in Portofino is a different burnt orange brick with blue awnings or green and white shutters. Smart streets full of nostalgia and whiffs of old Hollywood glamour lead down to a small slip and two dozen open-top fishing boats not more than ten or fifteen feet long, bobbing gently beside a solitary ice cream hut and postcard stand.

The helicopter lands in a garden above the water behind the first row of smaller properties. They should not have been surprised when they realise they are being lowered into the grounds of the most prominent house in the bay. As the butler comes to greet them and a vegan lunch awaits them on a grand terrace overlooking the boats, it is clear Lucia phoned ahead. The helicopter then takes off and leaves them stranded in luxury.

"Ah, are we're being managed? We're now stuck." Elizabeth raises her eyebrows at Godric. "Here we are, out of the way. And, it would seem with no mode of transport at our disposal. Hmm."

"Where would you rather be? At that awful party full of drunk people, or here, in this peaceful, beautiful bay. Maybe Lucia is our fairy godmother."

"Is she? Or is she the wicked witch?" Elizabeth surveys the length of the lawn, the giant palm trees lining either side.

Momentarily leaving the vegan banquet, and curious about the house, they walk through a number of cool, splendid rooms until they are met by Lucia's second under butler, who proceeds to inform them that Master Romano is on his boat in the harbour, as he has decided to watch the concert from there this evening, so they have the house to themselves for a few days, including for this evening's event.

"Evening's event?" Elizabeth asks.

"A concert, Madam. The country's most famous tenor will sing for an Easter

Sunday celebration. Guest performances, an orchestra." The English under butler informs.

"Right. I guess we are doing that, then?" Godric looks at Elizabeth, who opens her eyes a little wider and shakes her head in happy surprise. She remembers how she and Gerald watched a concert in Portofino many years ago. Not from a big house on the hill. They were staying in a modest hotel on the quay. It had a lovely breakfast room, just yards from the water's slip, where they could watch deliveries coming in on little boats.

"Bunny, look!" Godric has found a pair of binoculars and nudges his nanna, pointing at the large boat owned by Maximilius where the under butler had previously pointed towards, which is less a boat and more like a luxury ship with its triple decked dark glazed windows. She takes the binoculars and sees what looks like Lucia's husband with at least two beautiful women.

"Has she sent us here as her spies?" Elizabeth says to herself, in no doubt.

"No, that man over there, on the pontoon, drinking cola and watching the boat while reading the paper, Madam. He is Lucia's spy," the English under butler explains laconically, having overheard Elizabeth.

"Let me look." Godric pulls the binoculars away from his nanna and points them at the spy. "Oh, yes! Definitely a spy. Who wears a pocket handkerchief?" Then Godric looks at the butler and notices he has a pocket handkerchief in his top pocket too. Elizabeth takes the binoculars.

"He's got a package. Hang on. He's got a small box. He's giving it to one of the women. She's opening it." Elizabeth goes quiet. "It just glinted! She's put it on her finger!" Elizabeth looks at Godric wide-eyed.

"What if it's the ring? The stolen ring?" Godric asks.

"It's big. Hang on. She's gone inside. Damn." Elizabeth exhales dramatically, her eyes straining behind the binoculars, desperately trying to get a peek below deck through any of the windows, but they are dark glazed. Animated, she looks at the under butler. "We need to get on that boat."

"It is Master Romano's private party. We're not to disturb," he replies.

"Then we need to hire a row boat and go alongside at night when he's asleep."

"We will be obliged to tell our master of your intentions if you're serious," the head butler has now come through, and is more aggressive in his response.

"Of course, she's serious. Not serious, I mean," Godric replies.

"He's spotted me," Elizabeth says, looking back through the binoculars. "He's holding up binoculars to look at me. Yes, he can see us. He's waving at me." Elizabeth says, still looking at him through the binoculars. "Wait a moment. He's beckoning us down?" Elizabeth smiles. "Looks like we can be overt." Elizabeth pulls a face at Godric to convey why not take the opportunity.

"Put the champers on ice. We'll be back for the concert!" Godric rubs his hands together, quite excited about boarding a rather large piece of luxury.

When Elizabeth, Godric and Patty arrive at the bay, Maximilius has already sent out a tender to pick them up. Elizabeth thinks of '*Some Like It Hot*', as the driver wears a captain's hat on crookedly, and a wide a big grin all over his face.

"Welcome aboard, fellow binocular enthusiasts. Were you spying on me for Lucia?" Maximilius welcomes them with open arms when they arrive.

"It's quite the luxurious dinghy you have there," Godric tries to deflect, looking back at the highly varnished craft. Maximilius puffs on a cigar, the sweaty skin on his forehead brown like a conker, and his vest and tracksuit bottoms making him look anything like a fashion empire multi-millionaire.

"Well, come and have a drink before the show. You're welcome to take one of our fleet out tomorrow. My skipper can steer the sister ship." Maximilius points half-heartedly to a large ship-sized launch moored further away from the harbour.

At this moment, the woman Elizabeth saw taking the shiny ring from Maximilius, walks up onto the deck from below.

"Where is your beautiful new ring?" Elizabeth asks. The young woman wearing a tiny bikini who then looks at Maximilius.

"I just gave Lola a birthday gift. But it's too loose, apparently." Maximilius rolls his eyes.

"You thought I had fat fingers?" The young woman leans into Maximilius and pecks him on the lips with a kiss.

"No, Baby. Don't complain. We'll get it fixed."

"Doesn't your wife mind?" Elizabeth asks.

"Would you like a glass of champagne, Professor Green?" Maximilius ignores her last comment.

"D'you have any stout?" Elizabeth looks at the bartender, who nods.

"And a whisky," Godric shouts across, "a kind one."

For a while, the group make pleasantries, sitting out on deck, watching the sun set behind the hills and the people who begin to gather in the bay area in preparation for the concert. But Elizabeth hates small talk at the best of times. After Godric has explained how they came to be here, Maximilius has commented on his wife's overly generous nature, they've talked of the concert, the weather and how warm the water is at this time of year, Elizabeth cannot help herself probe this wealthy owner of the missing diamond.

"Do you know Stefano Brambilla? Your wife doesn't seem to like him."

"Of course." Maximilius puffs on his cigar.

"What do you know about him?" Elizabeth presses.

"Our worlds don't have reason to collide. Fashion and jewellery with olives. Not a winning combination."

"So you don't know him. Nothing about land fights?"

"Look. I live in Portofino. He lives outside Siena. We don't talk. Yes, of course, I know him. He's always harping on about land. I have no interest in his land."

"Oh really?" Elizabeth is confused, adding, "Why does your wife not like him?"

"I have no idea what goes on in my wife's head. I'm only her husband."

"But Stefano was friends with the jewel thief, and your son is dating Stefano's daughter? And I'm sorry, but Lucia specifically said she wasn't keen on Stefano. So why the family ties?"

"I pay my taxes so the police can do their job. And, my son's trousers rule his brain."

"Yet you still put him in charge of

your fashion empire," Elizabeth says pointedly, adding, "And does he take after his father?"

"He's never been in an office in his life. He just wears the brand. He doesn't run it." Then he realises what she has said, "These are my friends, you are my guests, and I love my wife. Enjoy your drinks. Portofino is a place to come to leave all mundane thoughts aside." Maximilius waves his hand as if to throw his cares into the water. "Be merry, eh?" He raises his glass and toasts them both. After a while, Elizabeth stands.

"Might you have a toilet I can use?"

"One to your left below deck, Madam. Or a larger restroom straight through to your right," a butler discreetly replies.

Elizabeth wanders through the inside of the boat, with its polished goldplate and white leather seating, reeking of new money. Looking back at Maximilius and his guests, she sees that Lola has been joined by another young woman, both now flanking Max on either side. Godric is nursing his whisky and leaning against the edge of the boat enjoying the lazy, beautiful atmosphere of Portofino, Patty asleep on his lap. None of them are watching Elizabeth, so she disappears into a room off the hallway.

She enters what looks like Lola's room and immediately spots a ring box open. A large diamond ring is cushioned inside. Elizabeth sighs. Darn. It is not the stolen ring. A different shape rock and not even red. Something about it even looks like it might not be real. Lacklustre perhaps. She wonders what Maximilius has told these women to get them to stay with him. That his marriage is over? Why would he flaunt it so blatantly? Did Lucia really have a spy, or was her butler back up at the house just joking? It is clear that Maximilius wants to keep the encounter as brief as possible without being impolite as after their drink, the tender driver jumps down into the small boat, ready to take Elizabeth and Godric back ashore.

Later, as Elizabeth and Godric sit on the balcony of Lucia's grand home on the hill, and a tenor starts to sing *Senza Fine* below, Elizabeth watches the small boats bobbing in the bay. She can picture Gerald dancing with her beside the audience sitting around tables by the stage, just inches from the harbour water, right there under the stars. Every day, Italy brings another bittersweet moment.

Godric takes his nanna's hand. She looks far away, unreachable as she was on Valentine's Day. Godric feels helpless. He knows he himself is only inches from his own anxiety overwhelming his every day. The music travels into his chest, and he fails to stop his tears. They look at each other, ducks out of water. What now? Godric shakes his head and wipes his cheeks. He squeezes his nanna and kisses her head.

"See, beauty still exists." He leans in and kisses her again. "I remember when I'd done absolutely no revision and was heading for a fail last year in my exams. It was you who told me to go bravely into the unknown." Godric squeezes Elizabeth's hand. "You don't always have to be the strong one."

Elizabeth puts her head on her grandson's shoulder and shuts her eyes as she listens to the rest of the song. Her tears starting to meet her cheeks. "It's the music," Elizabeth says quietly.

Godric pulls the blanket further up his nanna and hugs her. They listen to the music as the lights on the bay twinkle.

"You'll find someone," she says quietly to her grandson. "It might take a little time, but don't give up."

"I don't deserve to be happy. Why am I alive, and they are dead?" Godric asks the universe.

"Of course, you deserve to be happy, Goddy. Don't ever tell yourself anything else. It was a terrible tragedy, what happened on Valentine's Day. You are not to blame."

Elizabeth wonders what Gerald would think of her breaking down when her grandson needs her. He would tell her to be happy. But how can she be without him? She wonders if he would like Stefano. But she shakes her head and frowns. What was she thinking? She puts the thought out of her head, immediately feeling guilty that it crossed her mind. But Stefano is so kind. She wonders if Gerald has come back to her in Stefano. Her mind races, her heart aches painfully, and her body feels like it is breaking into pieces in sheer panic. She tells herself to snap the hell out of it. Focus.

"D'you think Mr Maximilius is hiding anything?" Elizabeth asks, while the next song, *Era Già Tutto Previsto,* is being introduced.

"At least two affairs. Probably at the same time. Lucia is such an angel," Godric replies. "He's not half as scary as people made out he might be."

"Often the scariest people come in sheep's clothing. The cliché is not for nothing. And she knows you'll report back. If she hasn't locked us up here forever that is. You honestly think she's innocent in all this?"

"Yes, and not because she gives us things." Godric looks at Elizabeth's beautiful bracelet still around her wrist. "It matches your cardigan. The bees can feed from the little daisies."

43 BLACK STALLIONS

Stefano feels tired and confused. Now the early hours of Monday morning, Easter Sunday was a blur of excess drink and more. The Brambillas are notorious for their Easter Sunday celebrations which seem to never end. And just like tradition, here he is in the early hours of the morning, looking for an escape from the guests that have yet to leave. He staggers from the house, wanting to catch his breath and escape the non-stop revelry. He is getting too old for this. The fresh air pulls him up suddenly, making him dizzy. Shaking his head, he hears a ruckus coming from his wife's stables. Is she opening a circus? Horses cry out over the music still blaring on inside the main house.

He wanders around the outside grounds, having heard whinnying in the distance, and he can hear one of them knocking against their stable. What has disturbed them? He is in no mood for this, not after Elizabeth left hours ago. He bumps along a garden wall, telling himself he should not have drunk so many cocktails after she had gone. Stefano did not mean to feel so much for a woman he had not long met. But he cannot stop thinking about her. And to think that she has left for Lucia's, is staying as her guest. He hates the idea. She will be dripping poison in Elizabeth's ear.

Stefano arrives at the stables as the party noise continues in the distance. He wonders if one of the guests has left something in a stable which is upsetting the horses. Not liking the sound of their distress, he heads for the entrance. When he gets inside, a couple of the horses have managed to get out of their own stables and are kicking against a door to try to get in with others. Their eyes are wild, and they have clearly been whipping themselves up into a panic.

Stefano, not a keen rider, trying to think on his feet, wonders if the easiest thing would be to let the loose horses in with the others. Then he can get Aurelia to return them to their correct stables. They are not wearing any reins, and they certainly look distressed. Stefano bends down to unlock the stable door and watches the horses rush in. Before he can bolt it tight again, he feels firm hands on his shoulder and back, pushing him in with the horses and locking him on the wrong side of the now crowded stable gate. This would not have been a problem had the three horses not already been spooked, or there was more space inside. But with hardly enough room for the horses to turn, the three horses rise up in fear of proximity to one another and from having Stefano behind them. In extremis, Stefano is accidentally kicked and falls to the ground. He screams for help but is unable to get up and under the feet of scared horses, and stands no chance. He is kicked and trampled until he closes his eyes in pain.

44 THE OLIVE MAN

Elizabeth and Godric sit on the middle deck of Lucia's boat, which has been temporarily moored for them to enjoy a morning brunch before leaving the bay. More luxurious than Maximilius's yesterday, the middle deck is perfect for Patty, as it has an indoor and outdoor section where she can wander between sunshine and shade. For now, Patty has decided to sit on Elizabeth's lap. With her feet up on a white couch which stretches the entire length of the back of the deck and offers fantastic views of Portofino shimmering in the morning sun, Elizabeth feels she could get used to this for a while. The buildings, familiar faded oranges and reds, and the lush green hills beyond, today feels like a holiday at last.

Godric places his phone, wallet and sunglasses beside his nanna, smiles and then does a backflip over the low rail into the sparkly azure. As soon as he is out of earshot and has dived below the aquamarine waters his phone starts to vibrate. Elizabeth can see Lucia's name but decides to let it ring. Why ruin the harmony of their morning? Elizabeth watches Godric surface as one of the crew unties a jet-ski from inside the back of the boat, jumps on and races out to Godric, only to help Godric safely onto it before swimming back to continue with his staff duties.

Godric starts to circle the boat on the jet ski, waving to Elizabeth. Elizabeth's mind wanders to where they will go next. Perhaps she will suggest they head to San Marino after all. It is good to be by the water. Calming. Godric's phone buzzes again. Irritated, she looks, and this time it is the Commissario. Her heart sinks. Will they ever be free on this trip?

After some time, Godric eventually returns for refreshment. He grabs a towel, checks his phone and the missed calls alert, and then sighs heavily. Elizabeth notices his fingers are like prunes.

"We're on her boat. I guess I should phone her back." As Godric listens to the voice message, Elizabeth watches the muscles in Godric's cheeks drop as he listens to Lucia. He sits down slowly, leaves Lucia hanging on the other end of the phone, and then looks at his nanna gravely. "It's Stefano. He's dead?" Godric watches his nanna's face freeze, helpless to make her feel better. "Lucia says the Commissario is looking for us and wonders why we left. Apparently, he would like to speak with you urgently."

"I'm putting you on speaker, Lucia."

"Don't come. You're much better there staying on holiday and out of this mess. I know I didn't like the man. He was impossible. But I wouldn't want him dead." Lucia pauses. "Oh, I can't believe it. Another tragedy." Lucia's voice is lower and slower than usual.

"I want to get back. Our car is there," Elizabeth replies, making no sense, in complete shock. She slumps, resting forward in the seat, using her arms to keep the weight of her body from falling to the ground.

"Your car? Darling, we can get your car to you if that's what you want, but really, stay up there for a few days. It smells of foul play, doesn't it? I mean, with Mr Jones dead and my diamond missing? Who dies from being trampled by horses?"

"You mean the helicopter ride was one way?" Elizabeth says, then quietly to Godric. "She's keeping us here. Out of the way. To throw shade on us." Elizabeth's breaths are shallow, and Godric can see her skin is already turning clammy.

"I can hear you, Elizabeth. But I think coming back right now is not the best thing. The Commissario wanted to talk to you, and it didn't sound good."

Godric walks over to a bar, opens a fridge, grabs

a water, and rushes back to his nanna, still listening to Lucia on his phone in his hand.

"What?" Godric asks. "What are you talking about? What does that even mean?"

"I'm just saying."

"Sip this," Godric beckons his nanna to sit up and take the water, fetching a cushion to prop her up.

"Stay up there. Honestly, try to enjoy your holiday."

"I want to get back!" Elizabeth sits up, clearly unwell.

"Listen, Lucia. You flew us out here. Please don't make this feel uncomfortable. I can't believe I'm saying this," Godric looks around at the beauty in the bay and the luxury boat, "but we want to get back to Florence!"

*

Godric asks the captain to turn the boat around and take them back to shore. Godric seems to be on the phone almost the entire time it takes to return them to dry land. He does not explain to his nanna what has been said, but Elizabeth can hear his side of the different conversations. Godric glances back at his nanna now and then, as she sits on the sofa at the back of the boat, sipping the water. He has put Patty back on the lead and is now holding her close, as both engines roar at the back, throwing spray up onto his nanna.

"Bunny, let's go and sit in here," still holding the phone in one hand, he helps his nanna up, and they walk further away from the engines into the centre of the boat. Elizabeth slumps back down in complete shock. As Godric tries to focus on his nanna, he can hear Lucia still talking about how there must be two murders now. Godric repeats how they need to get back and please can she send back a helicopter.

"Yes, darling, okay. Sophia has it. I will tell her to give it to you. She is looking for Ock, who also disappeared suddenly from the party after they announced their engagement."

Elizabeth can tell Godric is not okay, yet is shielding his nanna as much as possible from the grim news. As she sips her water, her face white as a sheet, she reaches out a hand to him. Godric grabs it quickly and sits down beside her.

"We'll get our holiday." The words come out of her mouth to try to get through to her grandson who is wiping away a tear. Godric picks up Patty and nods. There are no words.

*

It is not long before they hear the helicopter flying over Portofino. With nothing to pack, they wander outside. Just as Lucia had said, Sophia jumps out, tears streaming down her face.

“Is Ock here?!” she shouts over the rotator blades whirring, looking around.

“No, we’ve not seen him at all!” Godric helpfully shouts back. Elizabeth wonders why this young woman would not have simply called ahead. “So sorry for your loss,” Godric adds.

“He proposed! Ock did.” Sophia shows them her ring. “When my father heard we got into a fight, and now he’s–”

“Another fight,” Elizabeth says to herself under her breath.

“I blamed Ock for my father’s death, and then he left.” Sophia looks around, as the blade slows to a stop, and the frenzied swirls of grass in the lawn calm.

“Would anyone want your father dead?” Elizabeth asks, curious to know why the veil has suddenly dropped from Sophia’s eyes. Who wouldn’t blame Ock for most things?

“What? It was the horses. I didn’t blame Ock. He wouldn’t kill a bird.” She looks down, clearly distressed. “Ock’s mother sent this for you. Take it,” Sophia, seeing Ock is nowhere close, cannot stand talking here, instead marches up the lawn to look for her true love, leaving Elizabeth and Godric holding Patty beside a now quieter helicopter. They watch Sophia run towards Lucia’s Portofino home like it is her own. How the wealthy are so comfortable in the presence of privilege.

But then, perhaps Lucia is keen for her son to marry into such a rich family too. Perhaps they will get Stefano's land after all? Elizabeth looks up at the calmed blades of the chopper.

"Shall we?" Godric asks. Elizabeth then looks across the lawn as Sophia grows smaller in the distance. She had no energy to cross-examine Sophia or ask her why she has flown to Portofino to find her unpleasant boyfriend rather than comfort her mother and sister after the death of her father. Elizabeth wonders why Sophia did not ask her what she thinks about her father's death or why she loves a seemingly awful young man. But then, Elizabeth wonders why most people make the decisions they take.

Elizabeth follows her grandson, too weak to resist the pull of finding out what happened to Stefano. Why did the Commissario call Godric? She will hear his thoughts soon enough.

On the ride back, they sit with Patty in silence, the beautiful Tuscan views beneath them, this time going unnoticed. Godric shuts his eyes. Elizabeth wonders what he must be thinking, if he wishes for a different nanna, that has nothing to do with death.

45 WHAT HAPPENED IN THE GLASSHOUSE?

The helicopter lands back almost exactly where Elizabeth had watched Stefano from the lawn as they left for Portofino after pleading for her not to leave. Only this time, the guests have gone, and she can see police cars parked out the front of Stefano's home.

Godric and Elizabeth land, only to witness an argument taking place, albeit one way, between Aurelia and Giuseppe.

"It's only Vinsanto and Quaresimali. Stefano said I could take them," Giuseppe shrugs.

"Don't you dare! He told you not to steal. He told you to put them back and to leave. What are you even still doing here?!" Aurelia shouts.

A police officer has hold of Giuseppe's bag and is rummaging around it, holding the wine and biscuits under his arm.

Elizabeth wanders off in the opposite direction. She cannot be close to shouting. Not now. She walks over to a fountain and notices there is a freshwater pump. She opens the clip holding Patty's bowl to her belt, then pours some fresh water for Patty.

"Patty is our canary today," Godric says, watching the fight and the police. Elizabeth says nothing. She looks at the olive trees, which form a circle around the fountain. Some of them look very old. She knows how they feel. Elizabeth notices Patty biting at her paw. Even the dog is feeling stressed. Elizabeth and Godric sit for a moment by the fountain. Both feeling detached from what is in front of them by the news.

They were just here, just at a party. Then they heard a beautiful concert and went out on a boat. The water sparkled. And now Stefano is gone. They notice that in between the argument continuing on the terrace and a few cleaning staff tidying away what is not considered evidence, the Commissario appears. Suddenly, she feels a sense of dread as he notices them and starts to head their way. Godric can feel it too, and puts his arm protectively around his nanna. In a strange country, far from home. Elizabeth picks up Patty and checks her paw she was licking, trying to pretend that this policeman is heading elsewhere.

"Professor Green!" the Commissario shouts.

Elizabeth looks up and nods.

"Before you say anything else, can you please not shout? We didn't expect to be here right now," Godric replies, unhappy about the situation.

The Commissario holds up his hands. He joins them, sitting down on the bench by the fountain.

"He said he liked Easter. That it was the best time. That's what he said," Elizabeth says quietly, stroking Patty, who has settled to sleep. The Commissario can feel the mood of Elizabeth and Godric and adjusts his own.

"You grew quite close, the both of you. With Stefano," he says quietly.

"I only knew him a few days," Elizabeth reminds the Commissario, asking, "How did he die?"

"He bought Aurelia a new horse, a stallion. As it happens, she was trying to integrate it with the other horses. She said she had locked the horse in. So, we are not entirely sure what happened yet or how the horse came to be out with the others, or how the horse managed to trample Stefano. But we will get to the bottom of it." Lorenzo looks over his sunglasses at Elizabeth, "We always do."

"What was he doing in the stables?" Elizabeth asks.

"I was going to ask you if you saw anything?" The Commissario replies, "Before you left?"

"Wait a minute! You bring us into this, ask for our help again? Oh no. No, no, no! I'm fed up with this. You cannot continue to use my nanna like this. It has to stop!" Godric's emotions get the better of him, and he starts to tremble with anger, standing up and pacing.

"I thought you wanted no shouting?" the Commissario reminds him.

"My grandson is right to protest. This really does feel like harassment. I can tell you Marco appeared, and I saw them argue again." Elizabeth sighs. "For a moment, it crossed my mind that perhaps Stefano had stolen the diamond, together with Marco, and they were arguing about that. Not Isabella or land. But I just don't believe it. Stefano was a good man. He isn't your diamond thief."

"Yes, and steal a diamond for money? Not Stefano," the Commissario huffs hollowly. "Stefano was the wealthiest man I know. You can walk from Siena to Florence and not leave his land. He didn't need a diamond. If anyone has financial issues, it is Maximilius. He owes years of backdated tax."

At this moment, Aurelia walks over. Her face etched with red lines from tears.

"Professor Green. Stefano told me that you're a clever woman. That you helped him make sense of losing his friend, Peter. Nothing happens as an accident around here. I want you to find the person who murdered my husband. Please. For Stefano. That's all I ask." Then she turns to the Commissario. "And I want you to get my daughter back from the clutches of that man, Lorenzo. You promised me you'd try. Try harder."

"We will be paying Marco Conti a visit, rest assured. But she is a grown woman, Aurelia, and not breaking the law."

"She is still my baby."

"I need to see where Stefano died, please," Elizabeth interrupts and starts to wander off towards the stables. Godric follows, and so the Commissario excuses himself to Aurelia, then catches up and holds up some police tape across the lawn so that they may pass. They walk for a while in the same direction Stefano took the night before. Elizabeth frowns at a plant pot knocked over, unaware Stefano had staggered into it on his way. Aurelia's words ringing in her ears. If there is one thing you can do, just find Stefano's murderer. Finally, they arrive at the stables.

"You say he was crushed to death?" Elizabeth looks around, trying not to let her emotions get the better of her. The police tape preventing them from going any further into the individual stall.

"Well, when he was found, he was on the

floor face down over there, and there were a lot of bruises which were horseshoe-shaped, and a bite on his right shoulder," The Commissario replies quietly.

"A bite?" Godric asks.

"Yes, from a horse."

"Oh." Elizabeth steps back a little, unsteady on her feet, taken by surprise.

"Bunny. Shall we get some air?" Godric asks. Although a shallow breeze runs through the stables, it is dark and feels like the walls are closing in.

"Our pathologist will be checking thoroughly." The Commissario makes it plain no stone will be left unturned. Elizabeth's heart sinks. Now she has seen where Stefano died, noticed the blood in the hay. This man who reminded her of Gerald. Who stole a kiss, who made her feel like a woman again, made her feel both guilty and closer to Gerald than she had felt for a long time. Now he has gone too?

Thoughts rush through her head. Why had Ock fled? Was it really because Sophia had blamed him for her father's death? Why then flee? What was he arguing with Stefano about? Did Marco leave the party when Stefano asked? Or did he come back? And what had Marco been doing at the party, uninvited, anyway? Was it really about Isabella? And Maximilius. Is he really in debt? Did they fake the theft of the diamond and try to frame Stefano?

Who had pushed Peter off the tower? Who knew about snake poison? It all grows more confusing. Then, Elizabeth stares wide-eyed at Patty, throwing up outside the stables. She rushes to her, but not before shouting back at the Commissario.

“You might want to test the glasses in the glasshouse,” then adding to Godric, “We need to take Patty to the vet!” Elizabeth looks down at the little dog, hanging her head and panting.

46 JUST TWO GLASSES

A mad rush to the vet confirmed that Patty had probably eaten or drunk something, but she was okay now. It wasn't anything sinister. Having remembered Patty had drunk from a puddle in the glasshouse, Elizabeth had mentioned this to the vet, who had said it might be possible. Fertiliser or pesticide, perhaps. But more likely just eating some rubbish.

"You thought Patty had been poisoned from something in the glasshouse? But why?" Godric asks.

"Who walks into a packed stable full of horses that have just been introduced? I'm no horse expert. But he would have kept his distance. He was not a stupid man. What if Patty drank what was meant for Stefano, when she drank that puddle by his bar? I wonder if she might have been better off in the bush than being with us right now."

"Patty is okay. She'll be okay. Try not to worry." Godric looks at the little dog. "Was best to be on the safe side, though. But she would have been ill much more quickly if it had been something from the glasshouse. That is too long ago. Chances are, she has just had too many treats. Did you hear the vet? He asked if we were feeding her a rich diet. That's why she might have thrown up."

"We can't keep feeding her titbits from restaurants," Elizabeth replies, relieved Patty is okay.

"Did you hear that, Patty? Everything good comes to an end, little one. Kibble only for you," Godric gently squeezes Patty's paw.

When eventually Elizabeth and Godric get back to Lucia's Villa De' Fiori in Florence on loan to them, they see an invitation on a silver plate by the front door requesting their company for supper tonight.

"Maybe I'll go. We didn't go earlier, did we. I'll make your excuses. It's been a long day," Godric looks exhausted and unsettled.

"Go and drink. You have my permission," Elizabeth knows the day requires any way to get through it.

"D'you think she knows I'm–"

"That you're loving, kind, strong and wonderful? Yes, I'm sure she does."

*

Once Godric has left, Elizabeth walks out into the garden. Lines from the evening sun fall across the lawn as Patty stretches out, exhausted. No matter how cheery her location, Elizabeth's face hangs heavy. She suspects Godric is going to get drunk as a way to deaden reality, but that is not an option for Elizabeth. Elizabeth knows in her heart that she has to help. There is nowhere to hide back in Florence. After an hour, when Patty gets up to sniff, Elizabeth carries Patty all the way to the police station, too frightened to leave her back at the house and lose her. There she finds Sergeant Angelou Rossi returning from a long day shift and about to get supper in the café across the piazza. He greets her with a broad grin.

"Can't leave us alone?"

"Trust me, nothing personal, and I'm not happy to be here, and neither is Patty."

"I could have picked you up in my 308. She's an oldie, but has the power. You can't take Patty in. Here. I'll watch her. I'm not going anywhere." Angelou points to the café and strokes Patty.

"No sausages. Don't let go of her lead. Please, make sure you don't. Can she sleep on your lap?" Elizabeth pulls out Patty's water bowl.

"Don't worry. I have my own dogs. She's safe with me, aren't you, Patty." The Sergeant takes Patty from Elizabeth's arms and whispers into Patty's ears. "Four sausages or five, you say?"

"None. She's been sick." Elizabeth gives the Sergeant a Paddington Bear stare and reluctantly watches them wander across the piazza and disappear inside the café. At least they are inside, she thinks. But no, it is not enough. Elizabeth strides over to the café and enters, finding Angelou choosing a booth at the back near the bar, so that he can talk to the proprietor.

"Only, I cannot lose anyone else. You understand? I just can't. I can't leave her at Lucia's villa. What if a cleaner accidentally lets her out?" Elizabeth picks up Patty, who is inside the café, still on her lead which Angelou is holding, but sniffing around for titbits. She holds Patty close and shuts her eyes. Sergeant Rossi and the proprietor stop talking and wait. Wait for something to happen. Finally, Elizabeth opens her eyes and stares again into the Sergeant's big green eyes. "You understand?"

"I do. I promise. No food. Everything's okay." The Sergeant stands up and pulls a chair out for Elizabeth to sit down. He nods to the proprietor to bring Elizabeth a stiff drink. "Listen. You don't have to go in there. Not tonight. You need a break. A better idea would be to go home. Sleep."

"There are no better ideas. I'm out of ideas." Elizabeth looks at the Sergeant, then takes a swig of the amaretto put in front of her. It is too sweet. Elizabeth puts it back down. "But I have to find what killed Stefano. He deserves that."

"He's going nowhere," the Sergeant says gently.

"He deserves the truth," Elizabeth stares ahead. Patty, still in her grip, licks her face.

"Listen to your dog."

"You promise?"

Sergeant Rossi nods, and Elizabeth leaves for the station.

*

When Elizabeth arrives in pathology, the team is already looking at Stefano's blood reports, his body having been brought back earlier. Elizabeth picks up the cocktail glasses from the corner, now in plastic evidence bags.

"Have you looked at these yet? I mentioned it to the Commissario."

"He was crushed by horses. We have better things to analyse. Look," the chief pathologist, Roberto, pulls back the sheet on Stefano's dead body. Unprepared for the sight of a badly bruised and trampled corpse, Elizabeth looks away, wanting to be sick at the glimpse of Stefano like this. She steps backwards, trying to get her footing.

"He said if you cut him open, you'd find olives running through his veins." Elizabeth remembers Stefano saying it to her. It makes

her feel sad. Then she has a thought. "I think you should look at the glasses," she repeats, holding her nose from the smell of death. "I said I told the Commissario."
Roberto shakes his head but points to a junior team member to take a look. It is not long before he gets to work, swabbing the glasses and running tests, together with Elizabeth over his shoulder, suggesting various poisons for him to search for. Elizabeth notices for the first time how beautiful the glasses themselves are. Stefano must have brought out his very best for her. She stops herself from thinking too much about Stefano. No good will come of it.

While they are working, the Commissario walks in to hear the latest. In no time at all, the junior pathologist mumbles that he has found traces of flunitrazepam.

"Rohypnol would explain why he walked into a stable full of horses and introduced a new fired-up stallion to two mares in close proximity, wouldn't it?" Elizabeth looks at the Commissario, who is just taking in the news. "Impacting his central nervous system. A psychoactive mind-altering substance, travelling to the brain and affecting the way he behaved, no doubt." Elizabeth points. "Blue glasses, masking the colour. He didn't choose the glasses after all. Hmm." She says to herself.

"Dulling the senses," the Commissario suggests, having encountered this drug many times, but usually in rape cases. "What do you mean, didn't choose the glasses?"

"Exactly. Making him amenable." Elizabeth looks at a glass. "Oh, nothing. I thought he'd chosen them. They're very pretty. But they also happen to be usefully blue."

"What would we have done without you?" The Commissario looks a little confused.

"He made a drink for us both. Pre-prepared. He led me into his glasshouse where they were already in his freezer. Well, the cocktail mix was, in a shaker. All he had to do was pour. Like a picnic for two."

"We only found the flunitrazepam in the glass with his DNA." The junior pathologist confirms.

"I was driving, so I couldn't drink the cocktail he'd prepared. He poured mine away. He must have rinsed the glass before pouring me some juice."

"So, the killer was happy to kill you as well?" The Commissario scratches his head. "That's risky, isn't it? Of the killer."

"The cocktail was in the shaker. Had Stefano poured some from the shaker in both glasses, I guess it would have been in both, yes."

"What did you drink?"

"Pomegranate juice. He said it was good for antioxidants. Perhaps the killer thought he would be alone. I can't suppose they knew he would invite me in."

"Anyone could have been poisoned," the Commissario suggests.

"Stefano told me it was his private bar. In fact, it was well hidden by the plants. I didn't know it was there until we were there."

"That's a lot of information. So much precision in your response. Hmm." Roberto looks at Elizabeth, interrupting. Both look at the pathologist but say nothing.

"Quite," Elizabeth sighs.

"Or, did he know you'd find the poison?" The Commissario, a little confused himself, wonders as an afterthought.

"What? What do you mean?" Elizabeth asks, now very tired and thinking of Patty.

"Maybe he intended it."

"You think Stefano wanted to kill himself? If he did, then I really didn't know him at all," Elizabeth replies.

"Or, maybe you wanted to kill him?" The pathologist, now gruff about Elizabeth butting into his patch and the praise the Commissario is giving her.

"Perhaps he was cornered, knowing we'd find he was the diamond thief. So decided to end it all," the Commissario adds, ignoring the pathologist.

"But he wasn't, was he, the diamond thief? And even if he had wanted to end it, which I truly believe he didn't, who would end it with Rohypnol?" Elizabeth replies. Knowing in her heart that Stefano was murdered. "And, I liked Stefano. I did not kill him." She adds to the pathologist, really uninterested in his fantastical thoughts.

"He phoned here to request an injunction against Marco Conti on his property. Quite dramatic. The day of his death. To ban him from the family home." The Commissario smacks his lips together, explaining to Roberto and Elizabeth. "I just picked up the details. Must have been Stefano's last call. He was slurring his words. It sounded like he was drunk." He has a police report in his hands. "And you told me about their argument, Elizabeth, Marco and Stefano. So."

Elizabeth leaves, wanting to get back to her Patty as quickly as possible. Finding Sergeant Angelou Rossi talking to his friends about cars with Patty curled up in his lap is the best sight. But she is not expecting the Sergeant to drive her back to the villa, which is very kind, and seems to be at least the third supercar the Sergeant owns. Though, they do all look like they are falling apart, this one is worn out. As they approach the drive, Elizabeth explains their living accommodation agreement with Lucia, and the Sergeant replies.

"Be careful. She will get you to stay forever."

"Nothing is forever," Elizabeth replies as she lifts herself out of the old Ferrari 308 and says goodbye.

*

Inside the pathology lab, the Commissario is flicking through the report and standing beside Roberto.

"Why did you say Professor Green could have killed Stefano Brambilla when she is helping us?"

"Who is she? One Englishman steals the diamond. Now we have this Englishwoman. What is she doing here? Don't you think it is a bit of a coincidence that she is in Florence now? And they both knew the biggest family in Florence, and now Stefano Brambilla is dead?" Roberto turns his back on Commissario Lorenzo Bianchi. The Commissario picks his teeth in thought.

47 PETALS ON THE SHEETS

Godric and Lucia sit with their legs in the swimming pool near Lucia's terrace. Ripples breaking the stillness of the water. They are on their umpteenth cocktail of the evening, Godric not having the stomach for food and unsure about having left his nanna to come to Lucia's now that he is here, especially as he didn't like the tone of the Commissario when they saw him at Stefano's. Bossy and expectant, lording it over his Bunny.

"Stefano had a lot of enemies," Lucia finally brings up the elephant in the room. "Your nanna has been helping the police. She must be exhausted." Lucia lifts her legs from the pool. "You look so sad."

"I don't know," Godric replies, ignoring Lucia's comment about his own mental state, the butler already waiting to top up his glass.

"You do love me the most, God, though, don't you?" Lucia pulls a towel around her shoulders.

"I love you very much," Godric leans across and kisses Lucia's forehead.

"We are beautiful, aren't we?" She asks. Godric senses uncertainty in her voice.

"Yes, I am the most handsome man you've ever spent time with. And you are indeed the most beautiful woman." Godric smiles and pretends to look as handsome as he can, which is not hard.

"How many women was he really with?" Lucia lights a cigarette, broaching the question she has been trying so hard to avoid asking about her husband in Portofino. Godric does not wish to upset her, but knows she will not stop until he says something. He wonders too if his nanna was right, and whether Lucia only sent him to spy.

"Only a couple of very unattractive women."

"How unattractive?" Lucia's voice wobbles.

"Oh, they looked like their faces had been smacked into walls. All puffy. Clowns clearly did their make-up," lying, Godric continues, "And no social graces. Stomping about the place like elephants. You're a queen bee. The only one deserving of a crown." Godric knows the lies will be less hurtful than the truth. "How well did you know Stefano, really?" Godric looks at Lucia straight. He has told her the truth about Portofino—Fair's fair.

"I knew him well, a long time ago when we were teens," she admits.

"Did you–"

"Sleep with him? Sure, of course. You should have seen him back then. He was a handsome man. But we were never serious. It was a different time. I can't stand him now." Lucia stops, realising she is using the wrong tense. "He was a thorn in Max's side. I wouldn't wish him dead, though. In case you were wondering." Lucia raises her eyebrows at Godric.

"Wow. What a tangled web you have woven."

"It's all such a shock, to be honest with you." Lucia takes a long drag from her cigarette.

"We need to have more fun. Fun is always the answer to any question."

"You're the son I never had," Lucia smiles.

"You have a son."

"He is his father's son," she replies. Godric thinks of his own mother, how she sent him away for school, and how he cannot remember the last time she said 'I love you'.

"Mothers and sons," Godric says to himself.

*

Lucia and Godric decide to dial it up to eleven and start in a fancy roof bar in Florence, then hightail it on to an exclusive restaurant, until they queue jump into a uber-hip nightclub, Lucia tipping the bouncer, where they dance until the early hours of the morning before their legs start to give way.

Godric creeps back into the villa without disturbing his nanna, immediately feeling guilty. What has become of their holiday? He puts his hand in his pocket and pulls out a solid silver necklace Lucia gave him. On it, the words 'Lucia's very best new friend'. He smiles. Who is this woman who knows how to party? He walks into his bedroom and finds rose petals all over his sheets. Lucia. He wants to do the right thing and look after his nanna, but another side of him just wants to piss it all up against a wall and push the button of self-destruct. He remembers seeing the deaths on Valentine's Day, the petals suddenly reminding him of blood rather than love.

48 THE WIDOW

The following morning, Elizabeth notices Godric asleep on a sun lounger in the garden. He looks cold and ill. She places a blanket over him and watches him for a while, perhaps to check he is breathing. She walks back upstairs to find another blanket and comes back down. There. Two should keep him alive.

She frets why he had not made it inside and leaves with a heavy sigh to take Patty for a constitutional. She does not pay much attention to where they are wandering and soon finds herself not far from Mia and Peter Jones's apartment. Something pricks Elizabeth's curiosity, and she rings the bell. She could just say hello for a moment. It won't be long to return to Godric and feed him healthy food. It is only a short time before Mia answers.

"Hello. It's Elizabeth Green."

"Hello?"

"I was walking by and thought I might knock. You know. Two English women abroad.

I wondered if you might like to have a short stroll with me and my dog, Patty?"

"I'm not sure. I've just had a shower, and, well, the news about Stefano." There is a long pause between the women, Mia not letting her finger go from the intercom, waiting for Elizabeth perhaps to say goodbye.

"Yes, well. I wanted to talk to you about that," Elizabeth leans in further to the speaker.

"I'm sorry?"

"I can't come up because of Patty. I have been working with pathology. It might be relevant to Peter's death."

There is a pause before Mia replies.

"Alright, I will be down in a few minutes. You'll have to wait for me to get dressed."

Mia comes down looking thinner than she did just days ago.

"Are you eating?" Elizabeth asks, keeping Patty away from Mia.

"This way is nice. A small garden up there." Mia points to a street ahead to the right off the main road, ignoring Elizabeth's question.

"Stefano was murdered," Elizabeth shares with Mia.

"What?" Mia stops suddenly, leaving Elizabeth carrying on and having to stop and turn. "I thought he had been trampled by his wife's horses?"

"He was drugged, then led into the

horses."

Mia puts her hands on her knees and bends over, dropping her head.

"I can't catch my breath," Mia walks over to a bench in the grounds outside her apartment, not having got very far, and sit. Elizabeth walks back to join her and sits too. "Please." Mia holds her arm out in panic. Elizabeth can see she has started to hyperventilate. Patty starts to jump at Mia.

"It's likely to be the same murderer." Elizabeth continues, "Breathe slowly," as she sits next to Mia. Mia does not say anything for ages, looking out at the day, not knowing how to process the information.

"It can't be true?" Mia replies fitfully. "Please, the dog. She's–"

Elizabeth pulls back a jumping Patty.

"Just breathe slowly," Elizabeth says.

There is a long silence as Mia struggles to control her breathing.

"It must be related to Peter's murder. Try to breathe slowly."

The two women sit in silence, Elizabeth continuing to stroke Mia's back, as Mia struggles to control her breathing.

"I didn't appreciate you were so close to Stefano. That it would cause you to struggle this way," Elizabeth says quietly.

Mia does not reply for ages until, finally, she lifts her head and looks across the gardens to the river in front of them.

"I have clung to the hope that Peter was in an accident, I suppose, falling off the tower. That all this wretched business was nothing to do with him. It's been going round my mind. Over and over. Then you said the same murderer." Mia stops talking and takes a deep breath, then continues. "I can't let myself think that he was frightened. Frightened at the end."

"What did you know about Peter's project of Stefano's olive farm? Could there have been anything untoward?"

"D'you think I haven't thought about the possibility? Running everything through my mind? Again, and again." Mia stares hard at Elizabeth. "What was he doing as a cleaner? I mean, really? I have no idea. It was so unbelievable. Have the police found that out?"

"I know as much as you. I presume to plot a diamond theft." Elizabeth studies Mia's face. "Did he meet anyone else regularly, apart from Stefano? Might he have been doing something illegal he didn't want to tell you about?"

"He was a university lecturer, for goodness sake." Mia lets out a large exhale, again trying to calm her breathing. "He hadn't even made professor. No one was jealous of his studies. He used to have to fight to get funding every year. As it happens, he thought this might be his last. He wanted to make it important. His research. To mean something."

"You never mentioned before that he was thinking about retiring or struggling to fund his research. Does that give him motive? A diamond for a pension?" Elizabeth looks at Mia, waiting for her reply.

"Doesn't everyone struggle for funding in academia, Professor?" Mia shakes her head, her breathing calming a little. "The police know. They grilled me after his death. Numerous times. Wife of a thief. He had a pension, and his mother left him this flat and another in New York. We have a home in Cambridge. We're not strapped for cash. Just because his research was."

"Where else did he go when you weren't together?"

"Nowhere, really." Mia thinks. "Giuseppe. He would drink with Giuseppe—some evenings, I suppose. Giuseppe would knock for him like they were kids at school. Sometimes Peter would hide," Mia does an impression of Giuseppe. "Can Peter come out to play? And I'd have to say no."

Mia now feels like she is back to her regular breathing.

"No one was forcing Peter to go out with Giuseppe when he did, though, were they?"

"As it happens, I think Giuseppe idolised Peter. Perhaps Peter liked that. Liked to feel important. No one in university life makes anyone feel important, as far as I can tell." Mia thinks. "You think Giuseppe was blackmailing Peter?"

"D'you think Giuseppe wants to step into Peter's shoes? Coming to see you like that?" Elizabeth asks pointedly.

"What? No way. Definitely not. You've met Giuseppe, haven't you?" Mia shakes her head.

"Is he coming to see you today?" Elizabeth presses.

"I've no idea, and I sincerely hope not," Mia looks out at the river.

"He wants to take me to lunch," Elizabeth shares.

"Unlucky you," Mia scoffs. "Strange how he's the one with twenty-four death threats but is still alive. Don't you think?" Mia looks at Elizabeth, then back at the river.

"He does seem to be quite hysterical about it, yes. Did Peter get any threats?"

"Not as far as I know. But what did I know? This whole thing has been–" Mia stops herself from saying a shock.

"Do you know Marco?" Elizabeth changes the subject from Giuseppe. As far as Elizabeth can tell, Marco had a motive to murder Stefano. Land and his daughter, Isabella.

"Who?" Mia shakes her head.

"Marco Conti from San Gimignano."

"Only having been aware of him because he was dating one of Aurelia and Stefano's daughters?"

"Stefano tried to take an injunction out against him just before he died. There is something about that man that makes me curious he knows about the murders."

"Oh. No, I'm sorry. I haven't been over there. Since I heard–"

Peter's death from the tower in San Gimignano hangs in Mia's mind. Elizabeth understands.

"You said you wouldn't go home to Cambridge because of Peter's body not being released?" Elizabeth asks.

"I think he'd rather have his ashes scattered in Stefano's olive groves than gloomy England now, anyway, when this is all over. God knows when that will be." Mia then looks at Elizabeth again, her eyes piercing. "And, what am I going to do in Cambridge now? We made a life here. I didn't even want to come. I feel like an outsider everywhere."

"Cambridge has more sunshine than anywhere in the rest of England. It is certainly my favourite place in the world and far from gloomy," Elizabeth replies, knowing exactly how feeling like an outsider can make one lonely, even in company.

"Then, what are you doing here?" Mia replies half-heartedly.

"Talking to you about murder."

49 UNDER PRESSURE FROM THE QUESTORE

When Elizabeth returns to Villa De' Fiori, she finds Godric still asleep under the two blankets but now looking rather sweaty, so she lifts the blankets away and fetches some water to put beside him for when he wakes. She also opens the parasol above his head to shade him from the sun.

As she walks back inside to decide what to prepare for breakfast, she notices the Commissario is sitting outside in his beaten-up old van. She decides to ignore that fact and instead pours two orange juices and pulls out some vegan croissants from the fridge, and sticks the kettle on. Only when she has made tea and placed all the breakfast things on a tray in the kitchen with a banana and a note for Godric does she leave Patty and wander out onto the drive.

"Did you and Stefano have a competition to win the oldest van award?" Elizabeth leans down to look into the Commissario's window, handing him the other juice and a croissant with a serviette.

"Have you had breakfast?" the Commissario takes the food and drinks down the juice, making a satisfying gasp after the last drop.

Elizabeth shakes her head.

"Strangely, I was about to but was interrupted."

"Get in. I know just the place for some rusticos, with spinach and pine nuts. Fantastico!" He hits his nose.

Elizabeth cannot find a good enough reason to decline, now with Patty rested and Godric still asleep, so against her better judgement, she gets into the Commissario's van, half aware she is drifting through this unpleasant case as if a mere passenger, unable to make a decision to be in or out. As the Commissario mutters on about food, Elizabeth is aware that she is controlled by her habitual curiosity to know more and now her additional desire to find justice for Stefano. Yet, without any zeal for it. Of course, she does not recognise herself but wonders if she would have seen so much of Florence without all this happening. She would not have met Stefano, who made her feel closer to Gerald. Who awakened something and filled the void that so desperately needs filling, to distract herself from the ultimate reality, her reality, that everything is over. Now she is just doing things to pass the time. Time without her love.

Not far up the Viale Francesco Petrarca, then down a narrow street, they come to another small courtyard with locals in two separate cafes, one on either side of the cobbles. Many seem to know the Commissario and nod and smile. Elizabeth experiences déjà vu. He leads them to a most petite café in the farthest corner. Again, Elizabeth wonders if he times his eating on which café is currently basking in the sunshine, as right now the tables are in full sun, which is nice given the morning spring air is still nippy in the shade.

"Are you to take me to all the hidden eateries in Florence?"
The Commissario takes off his sunglasses so as not to appear rude but has to squint.

"I'm under pressure from my Questore. He's a pain in my ear." The Commissario moves his fingers to his ear and waggles them as if he can hear his Questore's incessant talking, and then rolls his eyes. "I need to find the diamond."

"I thought we'd found it," Elizabeth explains.

"What?" The Commissario sounds surprised while at the same time making eye contact and smiling at the café owner.

"When we were in Portofino, we visited Maximilius on his boat, on his invitation. There was a young woman flashing a ring he gave her as a gift. We saw it. But it was a different ring. I thought perhaps he had given it to his lover in secret. But actually, it looked fake anyway."

"Fake? Don't tease me like this," the Commissario leans back, takes a deep breath, and then talks to the owner, who has come over to take their order. He beams at the Commissario and pats him on the back. The Commissario orders without asking Elizabeth what she would like. But she is used to his ways of wanting to take the lead when it comes to food and has yet to be disappointed, so chooses not to take offence.

"Speaking of the Romanos, are you in the clutches of Lucia yet? Staying at the Villa De' Fiori."

"I think I've lost Godric. And we've been invited to an exhibition at the same gallery where the jewel was stolen. "At Bella Dinostrade's."

"Ah, Lucia."

"Handy, if her husband's company is in debt. Coincidence that it was the same place, isn't it?"

"As it happens, she knows the owners. Family friends. That is why she had lent them her diamond for another exhibition. It will be something to do on your holiday, I suppose?"

"We cannot stay in Florence for much longer. You're lucky to live here."

"Florence is beautiful, but I don't live here." The Commissario stirs his cappuccino.

"You know everyone here, though," Elizabeth is surprised.

"I'm a Commissario. They're all nervous of me." Lorenzo laughs. "I'm from Lucca. Come with me. I go soon after this."

Sergeant Angelou Rossi finds them, arriving in his Ferrari, which inches its way down the narrow street. Angelou lifts the car door and steps out, wearing his sunglasses and black leather bomber jacket. He greets them both but remains standing beside his boss.

"You have time to join us?"

"I just came to tell you I had to go and see Maxmilius. He's back in Florence. He called the Questore," the Sergeant replies, shaking his head.

"Ugh." The Commissario looks down at the floor and picks something off his shoes. "See, Elizabeth. I am in trouble. Big trouble."

"Maximilius is taking things into his own hands," the Sergeant explains to Elizabeth. "Private police."

"I told him we're more or less conducting door to door," the Sergeant explains helpfully to his Commissario. "Telling him we are both flat out."

"Good for you," the Commissario replies to his Sergeant. "And when you get through all of Florence, perhaps you could try his boat in

Portofino. I hear it has diamonds in it. Or fake ones."

"He said he will offer a reward at his wife's exhibition tonight."

"Some kind of publicity stunt?" Elizabeth asks.

50 SOMETHING ABOUT THAT TOWER

Elizabeth says her goodbyes to the Commissario, who has found something else to order from the menu, and to his Sergeant who seems happy to watch the world go by, agreeing that she will think about visiting Lucca with the Commissario later, if only to stop him going on about it. Getting to know the Commissario and Sergeant a little better, she feels it only makes her miss her own Bob, Inspector Bob Abley, and home. Although both the Commissario and Sergeant have a certain friendliness, it somehow feels shallow as flaking paint, beneath which is a darker colour altogether more unnerving.

As she turns to look back at them both, sitting in the sunshine on patio chairs in what tourists would see as the most beautiful, historic, cobbled piazza, its high-walled homes, shutters and potted plants perched on every surface, it does not feel like a world she knows. All her senses are gently prodding her, reminding her of the cold edge to all of this, and best not to get too close.

Elizabeth returns to pick up Patty, leaving a still-sleeping Godric, who seems to have eaten the breakfast, but then taken himself up to bed. She decides to pay Marco a visit. Something is bugging her. Why are the police not all over this man? The thought that Marco had shown such physical animosity towards Stefano could not leave her head. And Marco was near the scene when Peter Jones's died. Despite the motive behind the trip, the drive to San Gimignano feels like a breath of fresh air. Patty on the front seat with her head out the window. It all feels a lot like summer.

"You come to pay your bill?" Marco is standing outside his restaurant and wine shop as she pulls up in the little Fiat. Elizabeth climbs out of the car, glad for the milling tourists in the piazza that she can call upon if this gets nasty.

"It's a free country, is it not?" Elizabeth replies crossly.

"And yet, I am never free of you." Marco stands astride, looking down his nose at Elizabeth. But this does not deter her from wanting answers.

"Why did you fight with Stefano?"

"The same reason I don't like you. You both make up lies."

"You fed him the wrong order and then threatened him with the police too? Stefano told me about your land grab."

"Huh. He thought he owned all of Tuscany," Marco sneers.

"You were encroaching onto his land without permission."

"Lies, old lady." Marco shakes his head, folding his arms and nodding to a local who passes behind Elizabeth on his way to something or other.

"Is that why you killed him?" Elizabeth asks.

"You really are dumb as–"

"Were you the last person to see Peter? Did you kill him too?" Elizabeth interrupts. "Sergeant Rossi told me. Said you were there when they picked up Peter's body."

"Hey!" Marco shouts at Elizabeth, making some tourists turn to see what's going on. "Don't throw around more lies. The horses took him to his grave."

"Make no mistake, Stefano was murdered. I came to see you to look into your eyes to see if you did it. And now that I'm here, I can see it is a distinct possibility."

"I swear to God," Marco shouts, up in Elizabeth's face.

"The last thing Stefano did before he died was call the police asking for an injunction against you. Bit strange that. And why are the police leaving you alone? I'm curious. Friends in high places?"

"If you don't go right now, I'll–" Marco raises his hand to Elizabeth.

"Stop that right now! Leave her alone. Go back inside and serve your pizza!" Mia comes rushing across the piazza and over to Elizabeth, "What are you doing? Are you mad?" Mia pulls Elizabeth away from Marco. Marco glares at Elizabeth but nods at Mia and walks back into the restaurant as Mia pulls Elizabeth further away. "Let's keep walking."

"But I've left my car."

"We'll come back for that later." Mia continues to hold Elizabeth's arm and pulls her down an alley towards a different piazza.

"What are you doing here?"

"I've come to look. Maybe after we spoke this morning. Something triggered me." Mia pauses as she walks.

"At the tower?" Elizabeth looks at Mia and finishes her sentence. Mia nods. They both walk towards the tower. A number of tourists are looking up at it, as well as a few at the top peering back down and waving. People eating ice creams, drinking fizzy pop and a quiet chatter that can only be associated with happiness and excitement.

"Will you come up with me?" Mia asks.

"Oh, I've already seen the view. I'm–"

"Please?"

"If it has not escaped you, I'm with dog."

"Isn't having a dog quite restricting?" Mia asks, spotting a bench across the piazza and wanders over with Elizabeth. They sit and look up at the tower. "I haven't been here since." Mia squints as she stares up at the tower, the sun beaming to the left. "It's so high. Oh god."

"Why did you come?" Elizabeth asks.

"I couldn't get the picture of it out of my head. I thought somehow, if I came in the day when people were about, I don't know?"

"Has it worked?" Elizabeth asks.

"No, not really. It's so high." Mia pauses, looking up again. "D'you think he was petrified when he was falling? I read on the internet that some say falling is freeing. That you might even feel a small sense of euphoria. It seems so unlikely."

"Pain signals do travel through and to the nerves fast. But falling from that height? He was likely dead as he hit the ground before he felt anything." Elizabeth replies matter of factly. Mia frowns at the thought.

The two women sit together for a while. Elizabeth is frustrated she did not get more from Marco. Eventually, she stands up.

"I have to go back to my car. My grandson will be wondering where I am. Thank you for intervening back there."

"I'll walk with you."

"You're not going up?"

"I think the moment has gone."

Elizabeth and Mia walk back to Piazza della Cisterna, empty of Marco. Elizabeth gets into the little Fiat. Mia explaining her own car is in the car park. As Elizabeth pulls away, she sees in her rearview mirror that Marco has come out of his restaurant and is walking up to Mia. She watches, shocked, as he grabs Mia's arm aggressively. Elizabeth worries, but Mia shakes him off and walks off. Elizabeth wonders if she should turn around to check if Mia is okay and keeps her eye on them but then sees Marco return to his restaurant. Elizabeth remembers Mia saying she didn't much know Marco. But looking back, something feels like they do know each other. Was she imagining it? And, come to think of it, how did the tiny Mia manage to make Marco stop his fight with Elizabeth?

As Elizabeth looks at the road ahead, she spots the red van. It is very quick, it disappears under an arch, and then turns a corner. She blinks and shakes her head. Deep down, she knows what she saw. She decides to head back to Florence in case Godric is getting worried. It might be for the best all round.

51 SUSPICIONS OF A COMMISSARIO

When Elizabeth returns to Villa De' Fiori, she finds a note from Godric. 'Gone swimming with Lucia. See you later, Bunny. Call me if you need me.' She feels sad to have missed him but happy he has found someone to take his mind off everything. Everything here that has not been good, and everything from home that they still have yet to speak openly about.

There is a second note, this one from the Commissario confirming their lunch in Lucca. 'If you can make it, meet you at 12 outside. I'll toot my horn, and if not, you've missed the best tagliatelle of your life'. Elizabeth remembers she had only left it tentative that she would go. She watches Patty taking a long drink and wonders whether she can pull down the blinds and pretend she is not here. What happened to her and Godric's plan to leave this city? Soon after, she hears the tooting horn.

*

"Is this what you do when you're under pressure? Bunk off? I know someone else like that," Elizabeth says as they approach Lucca in the Commissario's truck, Patty on her lap.

"I wanted to ask you how you knew about the poison in the glasses?" The Commissario glances at Elizabeth.

"You promised me a non-work trip to Lucca, and can you watch the road, please." Elizabeth spots half a dozen large holm oak trees growing right on top of the Guinigi Tower. Like a garden in the sky, it takes her breath away. "What a wonderful place for birds. Quite the structural feat. How have they not been swept away in high winds?"

"They're very romantic," the Commissario replies, slightly irritated with Elizabeth for not answering his question.

When they stop at the bicycle shop and the Commissario speaks to the owner and picks out two bicycles, Elizabeth does not object, as she would like to explore at a slow pace and be a tourist again. Elizabeth places Patty inside a basket hanging over the front of her handlebars, and they cycle around the ancient city wall, with the Commissario explaining how the Romans probably established themselves here as a resting place between

Rome and northern Italy, perhaps Milan. All Elizabeth can think about is how she misses her own bicycle and the familiar streets of Cambridge. She has happy thoughts of walking Patty on Jesus Green in the summer, and part of her longs to speed up time.

They cycle past Roman churches, across the Piazza Via Filume, and through the Piazza Amphitheatre, past the largest flower market Elizabeth has seen, until eventually, Lorenzo stops his bicycle outside a beautiful if a little tumbled down house, which appears to be falling into the garden, or perhaps the garden creeping up into it. Elizabeth can see tree branches poking through what looks like a sunroom.

"Lunchtime." He walks around the back with Elizabeth. Elizabeth's eyes light up. From a long terrace, she can see for miles across the countryside. Bougainvillea and lavender surrounds a large dressed table, already catering for many people. Bowls of salad leaves, tomatoes, crusty bread and different types of pasta in sauces line the centre of the table, with wine glasses and half-drunk bottles in frequent use. "My timing is impeccable." The Commissario kisses his wife and then his mother and grandmother's heads.

"Meet Maria, Nanna P, and Grandma Goaty, who is ninety-four and doesn't look a day over sweet sixteen," the Commissario smiles at the women in his life. Elizabeth sees the love in their faces, and how Grandma Goaty does indeed look like a ninety-four-year-old walnut. Elizabeth smiles for the first time in ages. He points to a chair for her to sit. She is surrounded by who can only be nephews and cousins, all resembling the Commissario in some way, and all with his appetite as plates and serving spoons fly and clang as hungry mouths grab and tuck in.

"Now I understand why Puccini's music is so beautiful," Elizabeth quietly tells herself. It is only a short time before the conversation comes around to the diamond. Elizabeth is surprised that his family are so interested in the case.

"It was terrible news that Stefano Brambilla has been murdered," Maria, the Commissario's wife, says to Elizabeth. "He was such a good man."

"You'd have liked my husband." Elizabeth smiles. "Everyone loved Gerald."

"Oh?" Maria replies, a little confused about the connection. "Where is your husband, Elizabeth?" Maria asks innocently. The Commissario shakes his head subtly, but it is too late. Elizabeth breathes in deeply, trying not to show emotion.

"He's no longer with us, but he's always with me," Elizabeth smiles a little at Maria who looks at her sympathetically, so she quickly looks out across the breathtaking view. The view does not help quell her emotions, and she is glad again for the sunglasses Godric bought her. "I'm with my grandson on holiday." Good, she has found something to take her mind off Gerald.

"Well, my husband always finds the killer, Elizabeth. Always. So he will find Stefano's. You mark my words. And the diamond," Maria points at Elizabeth, which Elizabeth thinks a little strange. She does not think she is the killer, does she?

"It must be stressful having to solve this case," Elizabeth replies to Maria.

"I will find it, then everyone will think I'm a hero," the Commissario tucks into some pasta dish, passing another to Elizabeth.

"A bigger hero," his grandmother replies.

"And something tells me I need to stick close to you to find it. I have a feeling that you know things you're not telling me." The Commissario taps his nose. Elizabeth frowns a little but then sees all eyes at the dinner table have fallen on her.

"Don't make Elizabeth feel uncomfortable, darling," Maria tries to neutralise her husband's tone. "Do have some of the tomatoes. They are slow-roasted. Really delicious." Lorenzo's wife passes a plate to Elizabeth. But Elizabeth declines.

"My pathologist thinks you did it. That

you have the diamond," the Commissario wiggles his eyebrows.

"Why tell me this now?" Elizabeth puts down her fork and slides her chair back across the floor. The table descends to a hush.

"I'm just saying. He thinks you cannot be that clever to find the poisons so quickly," the Commissario explains.

"You pulled me into this case when I needed a holiday. I find the poisons for you. Invite me to this family lunch just to tell me that?"

"I am investigating a double murder. C'mon, what do you expect? You are English. The thief was English. I have to rule things out."

Elizabeth looks at the Commissario's wife, then stands up, picks up Patty, and leaves the house without looking back. That the Commissario even slightly suspects her involvement in this case hits her like a train and makes her so furious she cannot find any words.

52 A FAVOUR FOR A FRIEND

Godric is wearing an eye mask and floating on an inflatable unicorn. Sitting on the edge and drinking a hair of the dog, Lucia has her legs dangling in the water. Last night was fun, but they both overindulged and are now just happy to hang out and let their bodies recover.

"I could get used to this." Godric bobs gently on the water, evidence of a large brunch with empty plates and serving dishes being cleared away behind them.

"Stay. Not just for now. Stay for the summer," Lucia reaches for his hand.

"I have these nasty little beasts called exams. I mean, I tell Bunny I'm a genius. And, make no mistake, I'm close. But I think I have to do just a little bit of prep."

"Come back when they're over, then?" Lucia pleads.

"I'll be on the first plane. Send your jet or a

magic carpet."

Godric's phone rings. Lucia picks it up from the side of the pool and shows Godric the screen.

"Do I have a challenger for the new best friend slot?"

"Absolutely not. Ugh. Why won't he leave us alone?"

Once the phone has stopped ringing, Lucia plays a voicemail Giuseppe has left: 'Godric, I need to meet with you. Please. I'm in danger. Englishman to Englishman. I'll wait at Ricci's all afternoon. Can you come? I need your help."

"No. No way. I'm not meeting you. You utter nutter," Godric shouts at his phone.

"What if he has my diamond?" Lucia asks.

*

Godric meets Giuseppe in Ricci's, his hair still wet and now with a slightly burnt nose from this morning's sun, and only because Lucia pleaded with him to find out what Giuseppe had or knew. Giuseppe looks frantic when Godric turns up, his eyes darting around, assessing every passer-by.

"Where's your nanna?" Giuseppe asks, disappointed Elizabeth is not with Godric, shoving another note across the table for Godric to examine. Godric reads it.

I know what you do, you magpie.
You have collected your last shiny object.

Watch your back. Your time is coming.

"How many of these have you had now?" Godric asks, looking at the waiter "Expresso, per favore."

"Too many. Someone has to take them seriously. I thought your nanna, after Stefano's death, would want to help me. I'm from Ely, you know. I told you, didn't I?" Giuseppe looks around some more, then bites into a huge bombolini, jam squirting everywhere.

"Why don't you go back to the police? There's nothing I can do."

"They sent me this?" Giuseppe pulls out a toy magpie from his pocket.

"Patty would like that," Godric thinks the magpie actually looks cute. "Is that a child's soft toy?"

"No one is taking this seriously. You'll be sorry." Giuseppe bites into his bombolini again, his mouth covered in sugar. Godric pulls a face having to watch Giuseppe chew with his mouth open.

"Aurelia was so cross at me the day Stefano died. But I didn't kill him. I didn't do it," Giuseppe explains as raspberries and sugar dribble out the side of his mouth.

"I think you were stealing from them? My nanna said something about cheese?"

"Stefano said I could have the cheese and wine. It's Easter. Why would Aurelia be so mad like that?"

"Maybe because her husband had just died?" Godric looks around at the other people in the café, who all seem to be having more fun than him. He tries to allow his thoughts to drift away from this, but Giuseppe keeps pulling him back.

"Stefano spent more time with Peter than his wife. Everybody knows that."

Godric gets the attention of the waiter. If he has to listen to this drivel, at least he can order his own bombolini and a double whisky.

"Keep them coming. There's a good man." Godric tells the waiter.

"It was like he was in love with Peter, not Aurelia," Giuseppe says, lifting his drink and nodding intently at Godric.

53 A WOMAN IN DISTRESS

Commissario Lorenzo Bianchi's lunch is cut short for two reasons. One, his guest for lunch, Elizabeth, has stormed out. But second, and perhaps more worrying in his mind, is a call from Aurelia.

"Aurelia's in distress. Marco's at her home and trying to break in," he shouts across to Elizabeth when he spots her on the street, searching for a taxi to take her back to Florence.

How swiftly things change, as Elizabeth's ears prick up on hearing this news. In truth, she wants to know if Stefano really was a good man. Keen not to find her own estimations of this man unravel. Certainly, not to the benefit of one Marco Conti. The Commissario, Elizabeth and Patty get in his van and drive to Siena in silence. Or at least, Elizabeth's reticence is palpable. By the time they arrive, Sergeant Angelou Rossi is already arguing across his Ferrari with Marco, having beaten them from Florence. Other police cars arrived considerably earlier from the Siena department. But despite Marco refusing to leave, without any assault, none have decided to arrest him.

"Why did you not arrest him already?" the Commissario asks his Sergeant when he arrives.

"Huh, we were waiting for you?" the Sergeant replies, annoyed at his Commissario. "I've only just got here too, you know."

"You'll not arrest me. I'm not even trespassing!" Marco shouts.

"Who d'you think owns this drive?" the Commissario replies firmly. "This had better be important. You interrupted my lunch."

"What is she doing here?" Marco stares at Elizabeth. Elizabeth looks at the house and sees that the front door is open. Aurelia is standing in a flowing pool dress and wearing huge black sunglasses. Her face red and puffy. Elizabeth looks around. Something looks different about the driveway. It takes her a while, but then she notices there are no horse boxes parked up.

"Tell him to leave. He won't listen to me. Isabella does not want to see him." Aurelia looks at the Commissario. Isabella appears from behind her mother.

"Isabella!" Marco shouts. "You see what they try to do to us? I love you! This house needs a man! To keep you safe!" Marco shouts, but the presence of the Commissario has convinced him now is not the right time to see his girl.

Once Marco's car drives away, Aurelia steps back out onto the drive to join the others, waving her daughter to stay inside.

"He started to shout at me. Shout about a restraining order? Telling me that I couldn't stop my daughter from seeing him. Not now my husband's dead. That the house would be his. He said I should leave, but he became threatening. Thank you, Lorenzo." Aurelia crumbles in front of the Commissario, grabbing his arm for support.

"It's true. Stefano called us asking for an injunction against Marco on the day he died. We made Marco aware, but nothing had been filed yet," the Commissario replies.

"Where are the horse boxes?" Elizabeth asks.

"Gone," Aurelia sighs. "I got rid of them."

"Got rid of the boxes or the horses?"

"Everything."

Elizabeth fears the worst. Her face conveying her fears.

"We're civilised people here in Siena, Professor. They're with different riders now. They've all been separated. For everyone's benefit." Aurelia looks around, feeling their absence. "I just couldn't look at them anymore. It wouldn't have been fair on them," Aurelia shakes her head. Then she sighs deeply. "I've lost everything."

"I've not heard of horses trampling owners in their stables before like that?" Elizabeth asks, stroking Patty on her lap.

"Me neither. I let my daughters ride them," Aurelia agrees. "One was new and hadn't met the others. If they had been whipped up into a frenzy, they would understandably have been scared. Someone must have scared them. They would not do it alone." Aurelia stares at Elizabeth. "They don't just trample like that." Then she pauses and sighs. "Perhaps drunks from the party. Stefano told me it was getting out of hand, but I didn't listen. I wish I'd never had the stupid party, but he insisted." Aurelia shakes her head.

"What was getting out of hand?"

"People were inviting friends of friends. It was too big. We couldn't keep an eye on guests. Someone had urinated in my bath and–"

"Has the Commissario not told you?" Elizabeth is surprised. What is Aurelia going on about?

"Told me what?"

"That your husband was murdered, Aurelia," Elizabeth explains.

"I had heard rumours, but," Aurelia pauses, "Can it be true?"

"You know? But I haven't told you yet?" The Commissario looks confused, looking first at Aurelia, then at Elizabeth.

"Mia called. Elizabeth told her this morning. But why didn't you tell me, Lorenzo? I wanted to hear it from your lips." Aurelia looks at the Commissario, devastated. "I had the right to know."

"It wasn't something I could do on the phone. We are still double checking everything." The Commissario glares at Elizabeth, who just continues to stroke Patty, still cross at him for even raising the possibility that she was somehow involved.

"I didn't want to believe Mia." Aurelia, now very pale, looks for somewhere to sit.

"We only found out this morning–" Elizabeth tries to explain.

"Alright." The Commissario interrupts Elizabeth, finding her words unhelpful.

"But the horses. It wasn't the horses? I got rid of my lovely horses?" Aurelia looks up at Lorenzo, questioning.

"Yes. It was the horses, but also Rohypnol. Both, in fact. As for the drugging, this bears a remarkable similarity to the fact that Peter was drugged," Elizabeth replies. "Did you notice anything untoward at the party?"
But before Aurelia can reply, she faints, falling right into the arms of the Commissario.

*

Perhaps half an hour later, after many sips

of water, Aurelia sits up on a rather expensive looking settee and nods to her fussing butler that she is now fine. The Commissario walks across the room to sit next to her.

"Are you going to be okay? With your daughter? I can come back later. We will make sure Marco comes nowhere near the house. I'll keep a car at the entrance."

"Thank you," Aurelia takes another sip of her water but then turns to Elizabeth, subdued. "I cannot get the party out of my head."

"Was there anything out of the ordinary that you remember?" Elizabeth asks, noticing Aurelia is looking less clammy.

"Take your time," the Commissario picks up a cold towel the butler has left for Aurelia and wipes his own face with it.

"I don't know. I hardly saw my husband that night, which was strange. We're always checking in with one another when we have people around. But it seemed busier than usual." Aurelia stops to think, then adds, "At one point, he was confronting that friend of Peter's. Giuseppe someone. He'd stolen some wine and biscuits. It was ridiculous. Neither of us had invited him. That was what made Steffy so mad about it. We had an exchange on that. I even saw Giuseppe trying to do it again after my husband had–" Aurelia trails off, not wanting to say the word. "Steffy had said he was going to talk to guests in the kitchen. I hate kitchens at parties, so we didn't really speak again." Aurelia suddenly bursts into tears. "I'm sorry. It's just that he seemed so happy. He loved our Easter party so much. He had booked the band for the morning at breakfast to play people home, and he didn't even get to hear them." Aurelia stares at Elizabeth. "You were with him for a while?"

"He seemed okay, yes. Until Marco came in, and they argued. I think it was over your daughter."

"They were always fighting over Isabella. He wasn't invited either." Aurelia throws her hands up. "My husband was just trying to protect her. I don't like that man. Not one bit." Aurelia looks back at the front door and remembers her altercation with Marco earlier.

"He seems old enough to be her father," Elizabeth replies.

Isabella walks into the room and looks at Elizabeth, then at her mother.

"You think your boyfriend might have had something to do with your father's death?" Elizabeth asks.

"Horses killed my father," Isabella replies defensively, not wishing to imagine Marco had anything to do with it. The Commissario looks at Aurelia to see if she needs help telling her daughter the truth, but Aurelia shakes her head subtly so Isabella won't notice.

"Like I say, we will have a car on your

door for the next few days," the Commissario reassures Aurelia that she will be safe. "We will also need to search the home for the diamond." He looks at Aurelia in grief and feels guilty.

"You think my father had something to do with the jewel theft? I don't believe it," Isabella looks at Elizabeth, then at the Commissario, deadly serious.

"When you find who did this to my husband, bring them to me, so I can shoot them. I have a gun." Aurelia stands, walks to a dresser drawer, and pulls out a small pistol. "I will shoot them." Aurelia's hands are shaking with the pistol. The Commissario jumps up quickly and gently eases the gun out of Aurelia's hand. Isabella is shocked.

"Mama!" Isabella looks confused. Aurelia shuts her eyes, realising her fit of pique may have revealed too much to Isabella.

"Leave it with us, Aurelia." Just as the Commissario finishes his sentence, they all hear a noise outside, and low and behold, Marco has returned and is sitting in his car outside the house. The Commissario walks out with Elizabeth, leaving Aurelia and Isabella at the window.

"You're trespassing. Are you begging to be arrested?" The Commissario says crossly.

"Did you have anything to do with Stefano's death? Are you going to admit it?" Elizabeth asks Marco.

"You're insane," Marco spits at Elizabeth. Isabella storms out and begins to wave her arms and shout at Marco.

"You need to leave. You're upsetting my mother. She knew you didn't like father. You need to go."

"But I love you." Marco rushes to Isabella. Aurelia has followed her daughter, trying to break this up. Elizabeth observes how Isabella looks torn. She wonders what on earth Isabella could see in this man.

"Go now!" The Commissario shouts at Marco.

"Go!" Isabella screams. Marco looks at her painfully but then hangs his head and slowly walks towards his car.

"I will leave. I will leave. But I love you. I know you love me." Marco finally listens and gets back in his car. His car screeches away. Isabella pulls her mother inside, leaving the Commissario and Elizabeth alone.

Elizabeth starts walking towards the stables as Isabella closes the front door, taking her mother in to calm down. The Commissario follows Elizabeth, curious as to what is on her mind. They stand in the now empty stables, a smell of hay and horse manure—expensive looking tack hanging on the back of doors. Elizabeth knows something doesn't add up. Stefano would not lock himself in with horses. Even if drugged.

"He was pushed. I bet he was pushed in with the horses," Elizabeth says to the Commissario.

"She really got rid of all the horses?" Elizabeth and the Commissario turn back to the entrance to hear the voice speaking and see Mia holding a bunch of flowers. Mia looks at them both and sees they are surprised to see her. "Oh, hello. I came to offer my condolences." She shrugs. "Where have they gone?" Mia steps in and looks around.

"Gone," Elizabeth replies. Mia frowns and looks around.

"I can't believe this. Aurelia lived for Stefano and her horses. I'm not sure she will want–" Mia looks down at her flowers and decides to put them down in the stables.

"They will die out of water very quickly." Elizabeth picks up the flowers. "Bachelor's buttons deserve water. Take them to her." She gives them back. Mia shuts her eyes and nods.

The three of them walk back out of the stables. Mia says goodbye and walks up to the house. Elizabeth waits by the car, watching the front door open and Aurelia hug Mia and invite her in, taking the flowers and Mia kissing Aurelia as she puts her arm around her to comfort her. The two women, both having lost their husbands.

Elizabeth then turns to the Commissario and watches as he has words with the police officers in their car, guarding the house. Elizabeth shuts her eyes and can hear crickets. As she stands, she can feel her body sway a little. Is it dizziness, or do her feet feel less than grounded here? She remembers Stefano's smile. For a moment, she can hear him too. His laugh, his banter, the moments when he was not talking and just looking at her. She is here, yet he has gone. It all happened so quickly, like a dream. She thinks of Gerald. Gerald. Her man, her husband. Where has he gone? It feels like too long ago. All this with Stefano has pushed Gerald even further back. This is not what she wants. Elizabeth opens her eyes, determined to think of Gerald. The crickets sound louder and drown out any peace. She opens the Commissario's van and sits inside, happy to shut out all the sounds, willing her mind to conjure up that feeling of intimacy from the past. Sitting inside the old van, she watches as the Commissario crunches across the gravel. She wishes it was Godric and they could escape.

"You still believe I had something to do with all this?" Elizabeth frowns at the Commissario, currently in her bad books.

54 HOW TO GET RID OF MY HUSBAND

After finally managing to tear himself away from tiresome Giuseppe, Godric had gone for a long walk to shake off the bad taste in his mouth. He swung by Villa De' Fiori only to find that his nanna and Patty were nowhere to be seen, nor had his Bunny left a note. So, a little unsure of any proper direction, Godric returns to Lucia. When he arrives, he is hoping to jump straight into the pool again but instead finds Lucia dressed and ready to go.

"Good, you can join me for lunch," Lucia is pleased to see him. "And tell me if he knows where my jewel is."

"It would be good to get the image of Giuseppe's revolting eating habits out of my head. He did not admit to stealing your diamond. He is just about to be killed again, apparently. Oh, and someone has bought him a stuffed toy. A magpie. What's that about?"

Godric decides to jump into the pool to cleanse himself of his last encounter.

"Darling. You're all wet?"

"Come in?"

"Time to eat."

Godric swims a length, and Lucia throws a beach ball at him, but nothing stops him. He has to cool down. Finally, he swims up to the edge. Lucia foolishly gets too close, and he pulls her in. She screams, then laughs as she comes up for air—the two growing closer with each encounter.

*

"Are we walking?" Godric asks, now standing on the terrace, hair still wet and clothes dripping.

"To Rome? No, we might miss the entreés if we do that."

As if by magic, a helicopter lands on the lawn, ready to whisk them away.

"I've already been in a helicopter. Big deal." Godric yawns, teasing Lucia, pretending he is used to the lifestyle already.

"Yes, but have you driven one?"

Godric's eyes prick up, and what follows is a co-piloting experience in a chopper flight with Godric and the pilot chatting the whole way there and making Lucia laugh.

Lucia is relieved when they finally arrive, as although Godric had attempted the steep swerve and the vertical pivot, both manoeuvres were entirely uncalled for, and sent the pilot a little white. The pilot was pleased to land the chopper on a swanky restaurant's rooftop, and suggests Godric deserves a large cocktail for his talents – perhaps hoping to incapacitate and knock any idea of Godric co-piloting the return journey firmly on the head.

Soon both Lucia and Godric have forgotten all about the hair-raising event as they sip bubbles and breathe the warm air of Rome, looking out across the lively Piazza Barberini and its cafes and shops.

"We can go shopping after lunch for sparkly things." Lucia cheers her glass against his.

"May I ask, was the diamond insured? Do you think your husband did it for the insurance?"

"Well, if we are going to go there, and spoil a perfectly delightful lunch, don't you think it's strange how little attention Max has paid me since the murders?"

"Come to think of it, I suppose it is odd that he hasn't rushed to be near you," Godric wonders why Lucia has brought this up. Is she thinking about her husband a lot?

"He doesn't understand me like you do," Lucia sighs, looking down at the tree tops on the street from their table in the roof bar.

"Well, there is that," Godric smiles, chinking her glass with his.

"You cannot go home. I simply forbid it."

"I'm playing at being an undergraduate. Albeit failing miserably. But, there are certain expectations." Godric thinks about Cambridge for the first time today, attempting at every turn to push thoughts back down. He remembers the murders back in February, and a shiver runs through his body.

"I'm leaving him," Lucia announces matter-of-factly, biting into a cherry from a bowl on the table.

"Really?" Godric is shocked. "Why?"

"You've met him, haven't you?" Lucia frowns.

"Yes," Godric acknowledges that it is probably a good idea. "Where will you live?"

"Cambridge." Lucia pauses, perhaps waiting for Godric to declare his love and shout, 'Yes!' But Godric looks at Lucia, waiting for an explanation. "No, darling. Only teasing. I don't know yet, as it happens. I wish he'd leave Portofino, and then I could return home. He seems to be intent on making it his playground. So, I suppose I shall live in Florence for now."

"Your home is so beautiful. You must have friends there," Godric looks at Lucia, wondering if she is happy.

"Oh, there will be fights over the home, I'm sure. He will forget that I have put so much into it. Yes, I do, but not real friends. Not anymore. Oh, I don't know. It is hard to meet someone genuine like you, darling."

The two sit in silence for a while. Godric not wanting to upset Lucia further, but honestly unable to cope with supporting her in this way right now. Lucia, glad to have her secret off her chest. She wants Max out of her life and is ready to tell the world.

"Do you need Bunny and me to move out of the Villa De' Fiori?"

"It has not come to that! I was thinking about trying to steal you away to our place in San Marino before you go. We could disappear for a month to the coast."

"I would jump at it any other time," Godric replies, already feeling a little guilty coming to Rome without his nanna and making a mental note to take a coaster from this restaurant so he can find it to bring his Bunny back before they leave for England.

"That you're here now, I am happy. I will tell Max at my art exhibition. I want to tell him in public so that he cannot hurt me."

Godric looks worried by Lucia's words. He loves his new friend and does not like the sound of that.

55 THE PARK KEEPER

It is tea time when Elizabeth arrives back in Florence from Stefano's olive grove. Elizabeth sits with Patty in Villa De' Fiori by a beautiful pond. She notices something sparkling under the water and for a moment wonders if it might be the diamond but it is merely the glimmers from a water feature bouncing off the bottom. The diamond could be anywhere. Has Lucia stolen her own diamond? She wonders if Godric will ask Lucia about the insurance like she wanted him to.

Once rested, and still no sign of Godric, Elizabeth decides to go out for a wander to shake all the thoughts of Stefano circling her mind. She likes this time of day, around five in the afternoon. Many people are leaving work and going home to their loved ones. The hectic hours of the day have been replaced by a more thoughtful, communal, restful time. Although she has no inclination to make friends with the people of Florence en masse, there is something heartening about seeing the laughter on the faces of people in cafes and couples taking a walk together to compare the day's experiences. A moment of calm before many will start on supper preparations. This is just what Elizabeth needs.

She walks up past the gates in Boboli Gardens. The same gardens she entered with the Commissario and Godric. The same park official is standing in the box and smiles at her. She wonders if he will let her pass with Patty. The queues for entry have disappeared, as the park will be closing soon. Before she can ask, the man clearly remembers her and waves her in.

Elizabeth makes the most of this stolen opportunity and first heads to the Buontalenti Grotto with its fairytale sheep, goats and shepherd. The gardens are peaceful. All she can hear are the fountains and Patty sniffing. After a while, she leaves, wondering what drew her to the Grotta in the first place. She ponders why tourists make pilgrimages to places that they haven't given a second thought to before, or have any understanding of their significance. Perhaps, like her, they are just trying to recapture a mood, a feeling of being on holiday. To visit a place of calm, or to feel happier than they did back home, or to find answers. No such luck for Elizabeth. However, she kisses the wall for luck, remembering Gerald had done so before.

After Patty has checked every smell, they wander together to Neptune. She perches on a bench, enchanted to see this beautiful statue again with plants growing over the mound at its base. Now and then, a breeze wafts spray from the fountain in their direction. They sit for a while, Patty having climbed onto her lap. Very few people are on the paths, so it is impossible not to spot the park keeper heading in their direction on his walkie-talkie. Elizabeth is certain she is about to get a dressing down for having brought in Patty. Instead, she sees his friendly manner as he approaches.

"I'm very sorry but we're closing soon. You will need to leave in five minutes. Have you enjoyed your visit?" Elizabeth looks up at the park keeper, the lines on his face from years of sun crinkle into a smile.

"There are so many more plants than when I came before," Elizabeth observes, looking around at the grounds.

"We do our bit. How many years ago?" The park keeper stops, standing near Elizabeth.

"Oh, decades. With my husband."

"I've worked here for many years. Our paths may have crossed," the park keeper remarks kindly, and Elizabeth believes without motive.

"I suppose that's true." The past comes flying up to hit her.

"The good days." It is as if the park keeper can read her thoughts.

"Quite. But not for the butterflies. Having these wildflower meadows is far preferable to the tightly cut lawns I remember," she suggests.

"Are you on holiday?" The park keeper decides to perch on the other end of the bench.

"We were supposed to be," Elizabeth explains, looking at his clothing and seeing that despite being smart, his uniform looks worn out.

"Ah, my colleague saw you with the Commissario."

"Yes, I'm not a fugitive. I promise."

"We suspected you might be helping with the diamond theft. We thought we'd give you special preferences." The park keeper nods towards Patty. As he reaches to stroke Patty, Elizabeth notices the park keeper's tired skin on his hands, with cuts from pruning.

"Well, yes. My holiday has been interrupted somewhat," Elizabeth admits.

"Your husband cannot be happy. Is that why you're here?" The park keeper nods to indicate he means the gardens.

"My husband is not here with me on this trip," she replied flatly.

"Who can miss a trip to Florence?" He smiles, "Best place in the world."

"He's no longer here." Elizabeth watches

the fountain spray dissipate into the late afternoon air.

"Ah." The park keeper pauses, thinking to himself. "My wife is no longer with us either." Noticing Elizabeth's pain, he introduces himself. "Piero. And my wife was Angelina. We're both pleased to meet you."

"Elizabeth. And I'm so sorry." Elizabeth continues to look toward the fountain, her face sad, unable to look at Piero. "When my husband, Gerald, was here, I felt like there was so much I wanted to do. But now he's gone, I don't know what to do."

"We still have our memories," Piero tries to find a positive thought to share.

"Memories are fading—the cruellest thing. I keep trying to remember where we went, what we had to eat. Which streets we walked down. And then," Elizabeth pauses, remembering, "we walk down a street, and it hits me. I came here or there with Gerald. Like it was yesterday again. And then I wake up, and he's gone again." Elizabeth finally looks at Piero, anxiety all over her face.

"I used to bring my wife to the gardens. After it was shut for the night, or days when closed." Piero smiles. "I had a key. I thought I was being very naughty at the time. Hadn't been here long. But we were young and so in love. I don't think anyone would have cared. We'd sneak back just to be alone together. I still remember Angie when I smell the gardenias."

"Smells from the seasons. Both reassuring and heartbreaking, taking us further away from times when we were happy," Elizabeth sighs.

"For a long time," Piero pauses, "for a long time, I would not allow myself to be happy. Angie was not here. It was unfair. I felt guilty." Piero pauses again. "But then, I got so exhausted. I grew ill. Could hear her wanting me not to give up. It's the only thing that makes me not give up. I do everything for her now." Piero laughs. "I cultivate and prune so she can see. So she can enjoy the gardens. I carry her with me." Piero touches his heart.

Elizabeth adjusts Patty on her lap and holds out her hand to shake Piero's. He smiles and takes it.

"We carry them with us," Elizabeth says, almost to herself. "I cannot talk about things with others. My best friend. She's been such a support. But I cannot burden her by keep telling her how sad I feel."

Piero takes out a packet of bonbons from his pocket. Ordinarily, Elizabeth would not take a sweet from a stranger. Too ingrained from youth. But she thanks Piero with a smile and pops it into her mouth. The explosion of lemon and sugar on her tongue momentarily masks the pain. It all makes sense, she thinks. The senses, the emotions. We are all just bags of them, every day just navigating our way away from pain towards pleasure. And bereft when joy has gone.

"You said 'we' earlier. Are you with her on this trip?" Piero finally asks.

"My grandson." Elizabeth thinks of Godric. "As it happens, I think he has brought me here to try to forget. But it has just brought up everything. It makes Gerald feel closer."

"That is kind of him, though," Piero suggests.

"Oh, yes. Terribly kind. I don't want to burden him, either. He has his own traumas to bury."

"It's okay to have all these feelings. So, we have to look after ourselves." Piero takes something else out of his pocket. A photograph of Angelina. Elizabeth looks at the picture and sees that she must have died a while ago, judging from her age in the image and Piero now. Perhaps fifteen or twenty years ago.

"She's very beautiful."

"Thank you." Piero puts the photograph back into his wallet. "My daughter looks just like her, all grown up now. She wants to go to England, actually. She would have grilled you all about it. We have to move on, don't we, and live in the now, I suppose."

"I did meet a man recently," Elizabeth admits.

"Oh, that's good," Piero says interestedly.

"No, not in that way. I felt like he understood. It was just friendship. Very brief." It suddenly feels good to open up to Piero like this, though Elizabeth is unsure why.

"And you felt like there had been no one else who would ever know you like your husband?" Piero asks, curious to know more.

"It was a surprise. It made me feel better, somehow. Not happy, just better. Like I had lifted the lid on the box. Not climbed out, but I could see over the top." Elizabeth pauses, feeling so comfortable talking to Piero, but aware she does not wish to burden him with her troubles. She sucks her sweet. "I haven't had these in ages. They're delicious."

Piero takes the packet out of his pocket and hands it to Elizabeth.

"Please, take them. They're from the store across from my house. I eat too many." Piero puts them in Elizabeth's pocket. "And where is this man now? You should spend more time with him. If it makes you feel like this."

"He's dead. But thank you for the bonbons."

The park keeper frowns at this sad news.

"At least he met you before he died. That's all we have."

*

When Elizabeth arrives back at Villa De' Fiori in the early evening, she feels happier than she has in a while. She finds Marco, however, sitting outside in his car. When he spots Elizabeth and Patty walking along the pavement nearby, he jumps out and confronts her.

"You'd better be careful." He prods her with his finger, which pushes Elizabeth backwards. But Elizabeth is not frightened.

"Oh, go away, you irritating man. You look so guilty." Elizabeth puffs out her chest and protectively stands in front of Patty.

"Stop trying to pin Stefano's death on me, okay?!" Marco scowls.

"Calm down. If it hasn't escaped you, I'm an English woman on holiday and certainly not an Italian police officer."

At that moment, in the corner of her eye, Elizabeth spots the red van driving towards her. It is heading at some speed as if it is about to crash right into them both. Patty starts to bark furiously, and Elizabeth fears she will be run over.

"You. It's you planting these false ideas in Lorenzo's head. He listens to you, crazy woman. You told Stefano I was bad news and got him to take out the injunction. Stop!" Marco shoves Elizabeth, who falls backwards against a wall. Patty is pulled back with her but regains her little feet quickly enough to sink her teeth into Marco's ankle. Just as Marco towers over Elizabeth and is about to kick Patty, and the van run them all over, he is pulled around and punched to the ground by Godric.

"Bunny!" Godric puts down a box he was carrying and bends down to help Elizabeth. The red van continues past and speeds around the corner, then disappears.

56 LUCKY PATTY

A short while after Godric has sent Marco packing, he stands with his nanna in the kitchen of Villa De' Fiori. Elizabeth finds a bag of frozen vegetables to place over his knuckles.

"Who freezes artichoke hearts?" Godric looks at the picture on the packet.

"You shouldn't have hit him," Elizabeth says, turning to find something for Patty.

"Attacking women. I draw the line," Godric winces with the pain.

Elizabeth looks in the fridge and sees meat left for them by a delivery maid. She pulls a face but then sees Patty looking up at the door.

"You have the most powerful nose. I don't even know how to cook this?" Elizabeth wraps it in silver foil and bakes it. She cannot bear to look at it any longer. "You'll have to wait forty minutes," Elizabeth looks down at Patty, then turns to Godric. "You were with Lucia?"

"Rome for lunch. Can you believe it? It was delicious, and I'm taking you there."

"It's been such a tiring day," Elizabeth shakes her head. "I cannot believe you were in Rome. How wonderful."

"Also, we picked up this." Godric brings over the box he was carrying earlier. He opens it and pulls out a rucksack for his back. He removes a paper covering, adjusts the straps and then places Patty inside. Then he lifts her up and puts her over his shoulders. Patty licks his ear. "Ah, you see, right there. A design flaw." Godric tries to move his ear away from Patty, but she circles behind him to lick the other. Elizabeth laughs. "We saw it in Rome while shopping."

"Don't tell me, another gift," Elizabeth asks.

"I might have paid for it," Godric smiles.

"Did you?"

"No."

"What is it with that woman?" Elizabeth shakes her head.

"She says a Bolognese like Patty is often the breed of choice in Milan. I love her so much."

"Patty or Lucia."

"Can't a man love both?" Godric looks at a very tired Elizabeth. "She said the diamond is insured. Something about once the case is over, then they can claim."

"Interesting. So, she could stand to gain," Elizabeth's mind starts to whirr as she watches

Patty lick Godric's ear.

"She's going to ask Max for a divorce tonight. I don't know if that clouds things." Godric twists his neck as far as it will go each way to entertain Patty.

"Really? I am glad for her. No one deserves his public flaunting of other women." Then Elizabeth frowns. "Did you see the red van?"

"What? When?"

"Just now, outside."

"I was more worried about you," Godric replies.

"It was there. The red van was there." Elizabeth cannot make sense of anything. She shakes her head in disbelief, repeating almost to herself. "It was there."

"I can take Patty, and she can sleep in this too." Godric tries to change the subject to calm his nanna's nerves. "We can all go. But we should sit down and rest first. You've had a nasty shock. Let's make some tea." Godric hugs his nanna, allowing Patty to lean across and lick Elizabeth's face. "I can see Patty is going to like being carried at head height." Godric sees that his nanna is elsewhere with her thoughts. He notices her curls are a little messed up from being pushed over outside. It makes him so cross.

"I can't believe he came to the house. We should tell the Commissario."

"It feels like the Commissario is

protecting him. It seems the man can do anything," Elizabeth decides to sit down on a bar stool. Completely pooped.

"If that's the case, we should make it crystal clear. Report this to Bob."

"Yes, I was thinking the same thing. We might need his help," Elizabeth thinks about what she can ask of Inspector Bob Abley that she cannot find out for herself.

"He got us into this mess." Godric looks at his nanna but knows Inspector Bob Abley probably did everything he could in his powers not to get them involved.

57 IN VINO, VERITAS

Having left Elizabeth and nursing a throbbing ear and cheek from Godric's punches, Marco has driven to his largest vineyard to check up on his finest oak barrels. He has quite a sweat from the day, and hatred for many fills his mood. Isabella is not here. He is banned from her home by her mother. She is not even returning his calls. Everything is getting out of hand and not going the way he planned. Marco kicks at the gravel in his driveway. Isabella had told him that her father had made sure that should Isabella marry him then all the estate would go to Sophia, his dreams of becoming Tuscany's most powerful landowner were slipping away.

He picks up a wine bottle from his desk as he enters his office, opens the top, drinks it straight from the neck, checks his voicemail on his mobile, listens, and then sighs deeply. He is not going anywhere tonight and plans to get blind drunk. It is time to make the call and lay all his cards on the table.

Marco walks down into the cool dark cellar, continuing to neck back wine from the bottle. Beside the wine rack is a barrel still upended, yet to be sealed. He peers into it as he takes another gulp. He is determined to get what is rightfully his. He pulls his phone from his pocket and dials.

"Your pressure won't work." He listens for a while and then reiterates, "Look, I know what happened to Peter. I've said I'm only interested in the prize. You help me get that, or you will go the way Peter did. Do you need me to spell it out?"

58 ART IS LIFE

It is eight o'clock on the evening of Lucia's exhibition. Anyone outside passing along the narrow street right off the upmarket Piazza della Signoria in Florence would see a packed gallery, brightly lit, full of beautiful people with drinks in their hands and trays of canapes held by young women squeezing between paintings and expensive-looking dresses and finely cut suits. All inside the same gallery where a certain diamond was stolen only a week ago.

Maximilius, Ock and Sophia all stand conversing, sipping champagne, him telling everyone about the reward for finding the diamond. An uninvited Giuseppe is also present, staring up at a large painting. The painting, which takes up an entire wall, is a block of red with just a few splashes of orange.

To any art critic, it would be hard not to agree that the exhibition is a success. Red dots are placed below descriptors as gallery staff beam from ear to ear. Lucia has even bought Godric a new smart tech jumper, with the words 'don't start what you cannot fini' lit up, the letters running across his chest like a trader's ticker tape in neon green. Carrying Patty on his shoulders in her new carry rucksack, he looks like part of the exhibition. News photographers take image after image of Lucia next to her work. She is interviewed on camera and smiles as she explains her method and mediums. After the hundredth photograph, she grabs Godric to be in one. Elizabeth watches, frowning, as Commissario Lorenzo Bianchi comes to join her.

"I'm surprised to see Lucia's husband here. Godric tells me they might be divorcing. You say you have ruled out an insurance job?"

"They stole their own diamond?" The Commissario gives Elizabeth a wry smile. "I cannot believe they would break up such a powerful family for that."

"You said that he's in debt? And everything ends."

"Oh, Elizabeth, but she isn't," the Commissario shakes his head.

"Could he have stolen it from her?" Elizabeth questions the Commissario, who thinks about this, having already thought about most scenarios.

"If he did, why return to the scene?" The Commissario plays along.

"To be the doting husband, of course,"

Elizabeth replies, watching Godric in his high-tech top being photographed with Lucia and Patty on his back.

"Hmm, well, we checked his alibi, and nothing linked him to the theft or murders." The Commissario shrugs.

"So, you had the same suspicions?"

"Standard procedure." The Commissario smiles at Elizabeth. But Elizabeth is now scanning the room for possible suspects.

"Why is Giuseppe here?" She asks the Commissario, as they both watch Giuseppe putting two canapes in his mouth simultaneously, then coughing over the floor as he cannot swallow properly and nearly chokes.

"To avoid being murdered? A hair on his head has not yet been harmed," the Commissario chuckles.

"Don't you find that suspicious?" Elizabeth watches Giuseppe pick up some food he coughed out and pop it into his mouth.

"As a time waster. Most definitely. But he does love his food, as do I." The Commissario stops a waitress to retrieve some canapes. Elizabeth hears a car arrive outside, its V8 engine roaring. Sergeant Angelou Rossi enters, wearing his sunglasses and, cool as a cucumber, strides over to his Commissario, who is popping in a small mint and cucumber pastry. Behind the Sergeant is a very teary and hysterical Isabella.

"Good of you to come fashionably late?" The Commissario nods to his Sergeant but immediately cannot take his eyes off Isabella, who stands wide-eyed and dishevelled.

"I just found her in Galluzzo. Wandering. Hysterical. Like this. She won't speak. I thought I'd take her home, but we were closer and suspected her sister might be here. Might get some sense from her?" The Sergeant clearly knows Isabella and Sophia well. He holds Isabella's arm to stop her from wandering away. Elizabeth wonders how these wealthy families of Tuscany are on such good terms with the Commissario and his Sergeant.

"Isn't that blood?" Elizabeth looks down at Isabella's dress and sees spots of blood. She then looks at Isabella's hands, and the blood under her fingernails. The Sergeant seems surprised he had missed it.

"Isabella? Is everything okay?" The Commissario asks, leaning into Isabella's face, her chin almost on her chest.

"He's dead," she whispers.

"What?" The Commissario whispers.

"Marco is dead." Quietly, Isabella lifts her face and just as quickly faints. The Commissario catches her and looks for a chair.

"Can you find me something, Angelou?" The Commissario hurriedly orders his Sergeant, who rushes to get the seemingly solitary chair in the corner of the room. They sit Isabella on the chair, her head between her legs until finally they can find her some water—champagne being the only beverage circulating. After a minute, Isabella opens her eyes, still white as a sheet. The guests too busy with canapes and conversation to notice. Sophia is even unaware of her sister's appearance.

"Did you say Marco is dead?" The Commissario has bent down to Isabella's height on the chair and is talking to her quietly. The rest of the room ignoring him.

"Is that Marco's blood on your dress and hands?" Elizabeth asks looking down. Isabella looks down at her dress, not having spotted it until now. Isabella lets out an almighty blood-curdling scream and then shouts at the top of her lungs.

"Marco! Marco is dead!!"

The room falls quiet. From the hush comes gasps of surprise, followed by shaking heads and wide eyes. Sophia, now hearing her sister's voice, rushes over.

"He's dead!" Isabella cries again.

"Where is he, Isabella? Where is Marco?" The Commissario asks.

"There was wine smashed, and a barrel had been broken open. The vineyard is full of blood!" Isabella breaks into a sob.

"You stay here with her," the Commissario

looks at his Sergeant, who nods. "See what else you can get from her. Call me." Then he turns to Elizabeth. "Okay. Let's go." He starts to rush off and notices Elizabeth has yet to follow. He looks back and stands for a moment. "You coming?"

Elizabeth looks at Godric, who has already spotted her. He nods, twirls Patty's ear, and then points at the door for Elizabeth to go, having also now heard the news. Elizabeth sees someone she thinks she recognises behind Godric but feels her arm being pulled by the Commissario, so she turns, dreading what she is walking into, but in too deep to ignore.

59 GIVEN TWO BARRELS

When the Commissario and Elizabeth come close to Marco's vineyard, they are surprised to be the first—no police cars or pathology vans.

"Looks like we beat the cavalry," the Commissario comments, pulling out his phone to check they are on their way.

Elizabeth, never having been here, is struck by the size. Not entirely on the grand scale of Stefano's farm, but definitely with some air of grandeur. Vines lined the approach, large barrels with decades-old bent-up olive trees standing next to fragrant bougainvillea, climbing a large and beautiful property with geraniums spilling out of window boxes. Artisan tumble-down walls from fallen small brick outbuildings have been turned into features, with wisterias tastefully manicured up their sides.

The Commissario is so used to living in

Tuscany that he takes little notice of the beautiful surroundings. His old battered van, suiting the environment, pulling up near a large double door.

"Did you call it in, Angelou?" The Commissario asks his Sergeant, now on speaker phone.

"I did, but only once you'd left. It's mad here. Isabella turned hysterical. Ran around into the piazza, wailing. I had to grab her. She said she found Marco dead in his cellar. He's in the cellar."

Elizabeth wonders if the Commissario has been here out of hours before, as he seems to know exactly where to go as she follows him to a staircase. He stops suddenly and takes out two pairs of plastic SOCO slippers.

"Put these on. And don't touch anything."

After descending into the gloom, they enter a large commercial wine cellar, with row upon row of oak barrel caskets lining the stone floor until the eye can no longer see. There are a few breaks in the rows, where seats and small bars have been set up. Perhaps for tasting soirées. Though now it feels eerily silent.

Along one corridor, the Commissario stops suddenly and holds up his hand for Elizabeth. She notices Marco's legs and, stepping around a corner, they see Marco dead on the ground by a small barrel table, with wine bottles smashed. The Commissario walks over to Marco to feel for a pulse.

"Cold," he confirms to Elizabeth. Elizabeth looks around and listens, but the deathly silence envelopes, aside from the Commissario's brogues scraping against the concrete as he stands up and walks over to the table. He moves his hands towards a bottle of wine, taking out a plastic glove from his pocket. "And this stinks of murder."

"Could be arsenic. Isabella said she spoke to him a few hours ago," Elizabeth suggests.

"If she is telling the truth." The Commissario nods. "Why do you say arsenic?" The Commissario carefully lifts Marco's jacket with his pen to pull out his wallet.

"It's a possibility. No bullet wounds or gunshot levels of blood. Some around the mouth and on the floor as if he might have coughed it up. It could possibly be poison just like before."

"Yes, but why arsenic?"

"I don't know." But Elizabeth does, so she sighs before having to explain, thinking surely the Commissario should know. "Arsenic disrupts the cellular process that produces ATP, the molecule in charge of transporting energy through the body's cells. If you look, you can see vomit on the edge of that upended wine barrel." Elizabeth looks at the wine barrel, which has a trickle of sick, now congealed, down the side. "It could be another poison, but arsenic is quick. A popular choice among murderers, as you must know."

"Sometimes I think you know more about this case than I do," the Commissario opens Marco's wallet and finds a photograph of Isabella, a receipt for the restaurant Colpo di Fortuna in Poggibonsi and a hand drawn map, pencilled on the side it says Stefano and Aurelia's land, with the name Stefano crossed out.

"I could be wrong." Elizabeth looks over the Commissario's arm and tries to remember the contents of the wallet.

"How often are you wrong?"

"We're all human." Elizabeth refrains from telling the Commissario that she is never wrong.

"Didn't you see him a few hours ago? He was spotted outside Lucia's Villa. Her security phoned it in. We had a tag on him. The CCTV showed he pushed you, and then Godric punched him."

"He did. He came to threaten me to stop helping you." Elizabeth cannot tell if the Commissario is suspicious about her meeting Marco but decides not to pick at that wound.

"Well, our forensics team will be here soon. But it would be extraordinarily helpful if you could help pathology with this case. Given how successful you have been in identifying both Peter Jones and Stefano Brambilla's cause of deaths. And please give one of my Sergeants a statement about Marco's threats to you today."

"I'm here, am I not? Is that not being helpful? For someone you're not paying."

"It was you who found traces of a drug in his glass from Stefano's glasshouse. You were seen drinking with him, heading in there. What were you doing alone with Stefano? I meant to ask again."

"He had invited me to this glasshouse for a drink. I wasn't quite sure why."

"Hmm."

"I will help you with this, but then I really must have my holiday." Elizabeth remains curious to know who murdered Stefano and is not entirely unhappy that Marco is not around to hound her anymore. She looks at Marco on the floor. She supposes she did get the last laugh on the poor table service in his restaurant in San Gimignano after all. She smirks. The Commissario notices.

"Why do you laugh?"

"Not laughing." But Elizabeth knows full well she was smirking and feels a great sense of karma as she looks down at a very dead Marco. "Can I borrow your phone?"

"Sure." The Commissario couldn't care less who Elizabeth is phoning, instead starts to bag up anything he can find ahead of the SOCO's arrival. "If you're going to call, can you do it outside? This is a crime scene."

"Bob?" Elizabeth walks out of the cellar and up into the courtyard. "A man attacked me, and now he's dead." Elizabeth listens. "No, I don't feel calm." On the other end of the phone, Inspector Bob Abley is sitting at home in Grantchester with the golf on the TV. He stands up and starts to pace.

"Where are you?"

"This is absolutely the worst holiday."

"Are you okay?"

"No, no, I'm not. How's Cambridge?" Elizabeth tries to picture home.

"Dry and cold. Surely it's warm and sunny over there? Florence is such a magical place."

"I'm in the middle of nowhere, surrounded by wine, olives and death."

"Are you okay?" Inspector Bob Abley sounds concerned.

"You asked me that. No. But–" Elizabeth pauses. "I don't think I have any choice now. I have to try to find out who is killing people over here. I think the Commissario, this Lorenzo chap, isn't really giving me much choice."

"Right. But don't help if." Bob Abley trails off, not sure what to say, then adds. "I've held off Raynott. He's, I think he's got something else to worry about. The Vice Principal called him in. Students letting down his tyres. He's still driving petrol and they're calling him a climate denier."

"I was going to ask you to find out about this Marco Conti. But I don't need that anymore. He's the one who's dead tonight. But I wondered what else you had on Giuseppe Esposito?"

"Right. Let me go and find the file. I can't remember."

Elizabeth waits for Inspector Bob Abley to come back to the phone. While she waits marked police cars turn up and start to get out of their cars and set up the location as a crime scene. Elizabeth is asked to move further away from the doors. She walks across the gravel and sits on a bench. She can hear her friend rifling through papers.

"Ah, here it is. Whose phone is this, by the way? Have you bought one?"

"The Commissario's. I don't need a phone."

"Right. Well. I've told you everything about Mr Esposito. He has a flat in Cherry Hinton. He knew Peter before he left for Italy. But I guess you knew that. They knew him in the Free Press, where Peter drank before he left. Ah, not sure if you knew that he worked with house clearances. Sold his business when he left the country." Bob Abley pauses. "Are you alright? Did Marco hurt you? It sounded like a strong push against that wall. Good job Godric was there."

"I didn't tell you he pushed me? Or that

Godric was there?" Elizabeth thinks it strange how much Inspector Abley knows about Marco attacking her.

"Oh, perhaps it was the Commissario," Abley replies.

*

Standing with Lucia alone in the empty gallery, with everyone having left a while ago, Godric feels a little anxious.

"I keep telling Bunny she must get a mobile phone."

"Drink this." Lucia hands him a cocktail.

"I think I'd better sober up, Bunny needs me, and I need to get Patty back so she can sleep properly." Godric turns and notices Patty's head on his shoulder. He also increasingly feels like he is neglecting his nanna and wants to do something to help her. All of a sudden, he feels too far away from home. "I don't think I can take any more death. I want to spend some time with my Nanna. This trip was supposed to help her get over–" Godric doesn't finish his sentence. He does not feel like sharing with Lucia. He looks at her for a moment and wonders who she is. Something doesn't feel right about all this.

"Come home with me. We can talk, not talk, whatever," Lucia says calmly. "Help me celebrate this evening. I sold all my paintings!"

"No. Not tonight," Godric looks down.

"I wish Max hadn't come," Lucia replies, feeling awkward.

"You seemed so close tonight. Until he ripped down one of your paintings."

"Did we? It's all an act, Goddy. He does it to wind me up. He did go a little mad at the end. What was that about?"

"Maybe he's jealous of your success?" Godric does not want to talk anymore.

"He knows I want to divorce him. I told him before you arrived. And he's refused to give me one. He said over his dead body."

*

When the Commissario drives Elizabeth back to Florence, they first stop at the police station. Elizabeth is exhausted and wants to go home and says she will walk, but as she gets out of the car, they both see Giuseppe being brought in by two police officers, Sergeant Rossi walking behind.

"Someone has reported he's been stealing from an antiques shop. We checked it out," the Sergeant explains, "Things have gone missing. When we went to his home, there was silverware there. He denies it. We may have found our jewel thief."

"Petty pilfering," Elizabeth says under her breath.

"Excuse me?" The Sergeant looks at Elizabeth tilting his head.

"Strange thing to steal. Bric-a-brac from an antiques shop. If a person steals a diamond worth millions, to then be stealing silverware?"

"Unless they were addicted to the thrill?" Sergeant Rossi defends his thought.

"There's something off about all this," Elizabeth says before walking away, wanting to get back to find Godric.

*

When Elizabeth returns to Villa De' Fiori, she finds Godric and Patty still up in one of the living rooms.

"I was getting worried," Godric embraces his nanna in a big hug and will not let go. Elizabeth think's Patty's tail is going to wag itself off. Elizabeth notices two Oranginas on the table and finally breaks the hug, reaching for one of the curvy bottles.

"Marco Conti won't be threatening any more customers," Elizabeth says, opening a drink.

"He really is dead?" Godric picks up the other Orangina.

"Pretty sure it's murder." Elizabeth looks at Godric, feeling like she is about to drop on her feet. Godric can see.

"Here. Go up. I'll bring you a snack. I got these as I saw them in a little shop on the way back. You remember when we had them in Reims? We were going to sit and enjoy ourselves at five o'clock every afternoon. Wasn't that the plan?"

Elizabeth smiles, then nods—Godric's eyes water, so relieved to see her.

"What has happened to us, Bunny?"

"We're all okay. Look, we have Patty. We are here." Elizabeth looks around, trying to make Godric feel better. The two stand in silence for a while. Elizabeth exhausted but pleased to be close to Godric. Godric feeling out of sorts and not sure why.

"Lucia is divorcing her husband," Godric says, adding, "It all seemed very uneventful, but when you left, he erupted, and he pulled one of her paintings off the wall before leaving."

"Hmm," Elizabeth says, unable to reply with anything sensible. Then remembers. "I think I saw the red van cheese man at the gallery behind you."

"When?"

"As I left. He was standing behind you. Did you see him?"

Godric shakes his head a little. "That has just given me the shivers. I swear to the heavens, hells, and all that's mysterious in the universe." His voice petering out. He plonks himself down in a big red velvet chair, thinking he'll make snacks later.

Elizabeth notices a photograph of Lucia and Maximilius on the dresser and walks over to pick it up, sipping her orangey fizz. Patty already snoring from the sofa.

"So, what is the truth about their relationship?" Elizabeth looks at the photo frame still in her hands. She looks more closely. Neither of them is smiling. "Who frames a photograph like that?" She asks Godric, but Godric is already asleep.

*

Long after Elizabeth has left, and once they have released Giuseppe on bail, pending an investigation about the theft of antiques, Commissario Bianchi walks over to the pathology laboratory for an update on Marco Conti. It is the middle of the night, and he rubs his eyes, wishing he could be asleep. He does not like that his digestive routine has been thrown awry, having been messed up by this case.

"Any news?" The Commissario picks up a document from the side.

"Arsenic," the pathologist Roberto replies, "nothing else in the blood. All the pathology we'd expect from a large dose."

"Well, I'll be damned. Professor Green called it," the Commissario scratches his head.

"What? How?" Roberto is flabbergasted.

"Blood around the mouth."

"That's unusual. That does not present with arsenic." Roberto scratches his head.

"What is she then, a witch?" The Commissario raises his eyebrows. "She called it."

"Maybe she does know more about these murders than she's telling you?" The pathologist sows more seeds of suspicion in Lorenzo's mind. "Has Professor Green got something to win or lose?"

"She liked Stefano, granted," the Commissario's mind starts to work overtime with the fatigue. He rubs the side of his temples. "They were having drinks. Stefano dies, and now this? She disliked Marco Conti."

"There you go," Roberto replies, tired and unhappy about having been called in. "And didn't Godric just punch Marco?"

"Maybe she wanted to get her own back on Marco after he threatened to call the police about her not paying for the food? Angelou told me. I have to speak to Angelou. And what was she doing in Marco's restaurant anyway? There were plenty of other places to eat," the Commissario cannot make sense of his thoughts which are running away from him.

"It does not have the best steak, but it does have the best views. The wine's meh. Overrated." The pathologist dreams of sitting down and eating as well. "When are we going to eat together."

"Micky's will be open?" The Commissario looks at his watch—two o'clock in the morning.

"I should have left Giuseppe Esposito in the cells," he says to himself. "But he would have chewed the night watch's ears off."

60 INKWELLS AND BOMBSHELLS

Elizabeth feels remarkably refreshed when she wakes up in the morning. Patty stretched out across the bed. Without disturbing Godric, who must have eventually taken himself up to bed, they leave and head towards Giuseppe's home. There is something that does not add up about him. Why does he keep attending events he is not invited to? And now, the antique thefts?

When Elizabeth arrives, Giuseppe opens the door and walks back inside without saying a word, then slumps down in a chair, still in his dressing gown. Patty jumps up on the only other clutter-free chair in the room. The apartment looks nothing like one owned by someone with money or a hidden diamond. Elizabeth walks over to the curtains and pulls them open, pushing the windows out wide. Giuseppe lets out a groan, squinting.

"Not only have I had umpteen death

threats, now I'm being framed? All that silverware. Never seen it in my life." Giuseppe angrily waves his arms around with an air of desperation. "I mean, who steals silver inkwells and paintbrushes with silver handles?"

"They found them here," Elizabeth replies.

"Inkwells?" Giuseppe is flabbergasted.

Elizabeth looks around and wonders how on earth the police found anything in this mess, which Giuseppe still hasn't cleaned up from the last time she was here. She peers inside a random pram and notices he uses it to store wine bottles.

"You feel safe here now?"

"I ran out of money to stay at the hotel." Giuseuppe's face full of defeat, and then he frowns. "You said you didn't get my passport? They've taken it now, so I'm scuppered." Then Giuseppe has a thought. "Say, if you came before, maybe you planted the silverware. You could have done it," he says accusingly.

"And my motive for that being?" Elizabeth rolls her eyes. "You're saying you didn't take anything? There is CCTV from the antiques shop, placing you there."

"Ah, but there is no record of me taking anything. The CCTV only shows me browsing," Giuseppe replies defensively. "That's why they had to let me go. It's called 'lack of evidence'," Giuseppe says these words slowly. He picks up a hairbrush from the shelf, starts pulling out hair and dropping it on the carpet.

"Hmm," Elizabeth frowns.

"Oh great, and you don't believe me either." Giuseppe watches Patty grab one of his dried sausage treats and tuck into it. "You should teach your dog not to steal."

"Funnily enough, it's not a priority on my list." Elizabeth, worried the sausage might poison Patty, pulls it from her mouth. "You were a friend of Peter. And now he is dead. You knew Stefano. And he too is dead."

"I did not know Stefano well," Giuseppe corrects Elizabeth.

"Enough to invite yourself to his party. Did you know Marco Conti?"

"I went to Stefano's because the police are not protecting me, and like you, I want to know who the killer is. I was nervous I might get murdered at the party, but I also thought safety in numbers."

"Is that why you stole the food and drank there?"

"I was just saving some for later?" Giuseppe looks at Elizabeth like she is mad. "Everyone is trying to frame me for all this. The police want to find anyone to pin this on. Well, it's not going to be me."

"No, I don't think it is." Elizabeth stands closer to the window to catch some air.

"You think I'm innocent?" Giuseppe gets

excited and happy all at once.

"I don't care about thefts, whether diamonds or silver-handled paint brushes. Of murder, yes. I don't think you have it in you. And I think you're telling the truth about the death threats. You get umpteen death threats, and yet you're still alive. But the fact is, three men are dead, and you were best friends with one of them and had visited the other man's house numerous times. What did Marco Conti know that meant he was too dangerous alive? What do you know?"

But Giuseppe just shrugs.

"I only knew Peter, that's it. I've told you. We would drink together, eat together, talk anthropology."

Elizabeth picks up a card on the shelf. It is a birthday card from Peter, wishing Giuseppe a happy birthday.

"When was your birthday?"

"Two weeks ago. He took me for a meal. Just me and him. It was the last time we spent an evening together."

"Just from Peter? Mia hasn't signed. Yet, you keep visiting her. Is she really your friend?"

"I've only really seen her since Peter died, I suppose? She's the only other English person I know here. I should leave and return to England, but they won't let me now. Why didn't you get my passport for me?"

*

As Elizabeth leaves Guiseppe's, perhaps a little better informed about the case, she is approached by the Commissario's car.

"Professor."

"Are you following me?" Elizabeth picks up Patty to keep her safe and walks over to his window.

"Something told me you'd be here. D'you know Giuseppe? I mean, from your home in England?" The Commissario gets out of his car and starts to walk with Elizabeth. They head down towards the Arno.

"What question is that?" Elizabeth looks at the Commissario, a little cross.

"You went to his house. We saw you. Saturday morning, just gone. What were you doing? You'd just left me, yet you didn't mention where you were going?" The Commissario takes out a packet of biscuits from his pocket and tucks in, offering Elizabeth, who declines.

"He asked us to get his passport. He wanted to leave the country. For the life of me, I cannot understand what he's doing here. Was that a crime? You told me to go to the procession to meet him." Elizabeth looks at the Arno. It seems wide and cold and nothing like the narrow River Cam, with its ducks and swans.

"Stealing diamonds? Murdering Italians?" The Commissario's tone is colder than usual.

"Have you eaten yet? Apart from biscuits. If not, you really should." Elizabeth begins to grow irritated by the Commissario.

"As it happens, no."

"Go and get something, for all our sakes." But the Commissario continues to push Elizabeth to see her reaction, while munching biscuits.

"It just seems a little odd that you called it last night. You were right. Marco Conti did indeed die from arsenic poisoning."

"Well, I never," Elizabeth almost looks pleased with her own powers of deduction. Forgetting for a moment that Marco Conti is dead.

"And, it was painfully clear you had expressed on more than one occasion that you did not care for this man."

"Wait a minute." Elizabeth does not care for the Commissario's thought process or tone. "What are you insinuating?"

"I'm afraid we must ask you not to leave Florence, Professor Green."

"Let me get this straight. You think I murdered Marco Conti because he was going to report me to the police for not paying a bill in a restaurant which I thought was unfair and indeed did pay for the drinks but refused to pay for the meat delivered as we could not eat it?" Elizabeth pulls a face at the Commissario to express how idiotic she thinks he is being. "Not so much flabbergasted as disappointed."

"I'm sorry, but I must reiterate that you must not leave Florence."

"Just stop following me. We're done."

61 YOUNG LOVE BURSTS

Not long after Elizabeth left, Lucia sent a car for Godric, and he was woken by the driver beeping his horn. Still in his robe, his clothes bundled into the car, Lucia brought him back to hers. Now face down on massage tables, the pool pump trickling in the background and the sun warming their backs, ylang-ylang oils permeate the air as Godric and Lucia relax under the hand of expert masseuses. Breaking up this tranquil way to start the day, Ock comes storming in, tears streaming down his face.

"Sophia's dumped me." He flounces down on a chair beside his mother, picking up her drink and downing it in one.

"Really dear, that was my Martini." Lucia looks up and sees how upset her son is.

"She blames me for everything."

"Oh darling, don't be silly. She's just distressed. She's just lost her father. She'll come round. Just be there for her."

"It's your fault. It's your diamond." Ock snipes at his mother.

"Hey!" Godric pulls his face up from his massage table, unhappy how Ock is speaking to Lucia.

"It's okay." Lucia looks at Godric, then turns to her son. "She followed you up to Portofino. She clearly turned to you when she needed someone the most. And you looked very much in love last night at the gallery?"

"Father made everything worse." Ock looks around for something else to drink and steals Godric's, then nods to a butler to get more.

"So, blame your father, darling."

"He told her that she could look to him as a father now her father had gone, and maybe he'd be a better father." Ock shakes his head. "He was completely insensitive. He doesn't see how he hurts people."

"Ha," Godric says, thinking how the apple has not fallen far from the tree.

"You telling him you want a divorce sent him nuclear. He even told me he was carrying me in the business. It's made him lose his senses!"

62 TWO WIVES

Closer to Sienna this morning, Mia has driven out to see Aurelia. The late spring sunshine falls through the trees, casting pale shadows across the warming earth. Birds are chirping in the olive trees surrounding the driveway, lawns are warming and dewy, and the promise of summer is in the air.

However, Stefano and Aurelia's home looks deathly quiet, and Mia wonders if Aurelia has let the staff go. Although it has only been a few days, the place looks uncared for. Mia looks at the huge sit-on lawn mower, abandoned midway through cutting. Silence from the stables is replaced by a radio beneath what looks like a window cleaner having a nap in the hammock, his water pale and squeegee mop beside him, not seeing much action.

Mia gets out of her car and slowly crunches up the gravel path towards the front door. But if hoping for a warm reception, instead she is greeted by Isabella and Sophia with angry faces. Both daughters give her both barrels.

"What are you doing here again?" Sophia screams.

"Get away!" they shout.

"If you hadn't brought your husband here, our father would still be alive!" Shouts Sophia. "Stop bothering my mother."

"I just wanted to see your mother and bring more flowers. She spoke to me just yesterday? I wanted to thank her for her kindness."

"You think your flowers will help my mother?" Sophia grabs the flowers, and throws them on the ground. "My sister is without her lover. We have death everywhere."

"I've also lost my husband," Mia says quietly.

But there is no response. The door is slammed in her face. Mia looks up at the house. She thinks she sees a curtain move. Could that be Aurelia? Mia looks at the flowers out of their posy and scattered across the gravel. She thinks how pointless their short life was, how this makes no sense. She doesn't have the heart to leave them there, so picks them up, one by one and puts them back in their paper covering. She sees a watering can near the stables and a tap. She walks across and fills the can with water. Then, she puts the flowers in the water.

"We don't all have to die today. Not today," Mia says to herself, leaving the flowers in the can in the sun. Returning to her car, she spots a car parked across the drive. She looks at a Ferrari with a shadow of a man in the front seat. She wonders if she is seeing things. Could it be Stefano? Is he alive? No. It is Sergeant Angelou Rossi. Mia looks back at the house and wonders if Aurelia is inside and knows that she is out here, sitting in her car. What if she is avoiding her? She watches for any sign at the windows, sighs, then drives away.

63 THE OLIVE TREE

Annoyed by the Commissario's 'request to stay', Elizabeth immediately leaves Florence in the little Fiat. See what he thinks about that! She takes Patty with her, unsure where Godric is, as she swings by Villa De' Fiori, and he is nowhere to be seen. She pulls out the CD Godric is so fond of and throws it on the backseat, replacing it with Chopin's Fantaisie Impromptu. Her destination takes her a while to find, but she remembers it was somewhere between Siena and Florence, on Stefano's land, on the right-hand side down a little track. The Fiat climbs to the top of a hill and pulls up next to the white cottage—Stefano's secret place.

Elizabeth lets Patty out to stretch her legs and walks down towards the bench with spectacular views across the vineyards and valleys of Tuscany. The views she stared at with Stefano that meant so much to him. She had felt privileged somehow that he took her here. She wonders why he had done that. Did he know he would be murdered? Was he trying to send her some kind of subliminal message?

Elizabeth notices Patty has wandered off behind the cottage. She follows, worried she will lose her, and finds her eating what looks like a leftover burger. Elizabeth sees a brazier still smoking a little, beside a couple of chairs. She peers inside and there, in front of her eyes, is a half-burnt shirt. She reaches down with a stick to pick it out and drops it on the floor, stamping on it to ensure it is out. A man's white linen shirt, with faded gold check criss-crossing. From the top pocket, Elizabeth pulls out a singed piece of paper with printed dates over Easter below the letter 'G'. They make no sense. Inside the shirt collar reads the name 'Peter Jones'.

"Patty, I think you've just earned your keep."

Elizabeth finds a canvas bag in the car, pops the shirt inside, and then pockets the piece of paper.

Finally, she walks back to the bench and sits. Tears spike her eyes. She misses Gerald more than ever. What would he do? She is not even allowed to leave Florence, although she has ignored that so far. She pats her lap, and Patty jumps up and licks her chin. Elizabeth kisses Patty, who smells mildly of smoke and burger. "What are we going to do now?"

The beautiful valley view ahead of her

could not feel more at odds with her mood. A solitary cloud covers the sun and as the warmth temporarily disappears, Elizabeth feels a spring chill blow right through her. Almost as if Stefano's spirit was trying to tell her something. She pulls the piece of paper from her pocket. 'G', for Gerald.

*

After Elizabeth says goodbye to the view from the hill, she heads for Stefano's home. When she arrives, Isabella opens the door. Her eyes puffy from crying. Elizabeth explains that she has come to see her mother but is told that Aurelia has gone shopping with Sophia. Isabella makes no effort to turn Elizabeth away and walks back into the house, leaving the front door open. Elizabeth thinks that knowing Stefano had a soft spot for her might have made Isabella more welcoming.

"Is it wise to just leave the door?"

"It's not like Marco is going to break his restraining order, is it?" Isabella replies sadly.

"I didn't like Marco," Elizabeth admits to Isabella as Isabella pours lemonade. "The Commissario thinks I might have killed him."

"He didn't like you one bit either." Isabella eyes Elizabeth, processing the Commissario's suspicions. "The Commissario's just desperate. He doesn't have a grasp of this, does he?" She says disappointedly, dropping the lemonade bottle heavily and passing Elizabeth a glass. "You know, this has aged me twenty years. I've lost my Papa, my Marco. And my mother is acting like a child, getting rid of all her horses and the staff. I'm having to be the parent. Me. Have you met me?"

"You look like a strong young woman, entirely capable of getting through this. Though, I admit, grief can be debilitating." Elizabeth observes Isabella more closely. Her long brown hair with sunkissed natural highlights, large brown eyes, glowing skin, she looks so young and healthy. Isabella wanders out of the kitchen, expecting Elizabeth to follow, to a room Elizabeth does not remember from the party. The door must have been locked to guests. "This is a nice room."

"It's my mother's space," Isabella explains. "She normally retreats here when she wants to escape my father and our noise. We've been spending most of our time here since my Papa," Isabella cannot finish her sentence. "I suppose it's a place not full to the brim with Papa's things."

"I would have thought it would help to feel close to your father, having his things around you?" Elizabeth is confused by Isabella's response.

"Oh, make no mistake, I want to be close. I sleep with one of his neckerchiefs." Isabella pulls it out of her pocket and lifts it to her nose.

"My Mother has to be in charge of the farm now. Her desk. She has had to take so many calls." Isabella looks across the room to the far corner, over to Aurelia's desk. "Maybe it's her way of coping."

There is a pause as both sip their lemonade. Elizabeth is unsure why she has been brought to Aurelia's private room but perches on a sofa.

"It was you who found Marco?" Elizabeth asks, hoping she might hear more about what happened that night.

"We'd ridden the horses here, Marco's horses. My mother didn't know. We'd sneaked a couple of stallions over. I'd not really been in the mood to ride. Not with Papa having passed. Marco thought I blamed him for what happened to Papa. I know they'd fought. But I didn't blame him. Papa was strict about Marco. Didn't think he was a good man. But he never gave him a chance. I think Marco was sad about it. But we had a lovely afternoon. Honestly, Marco used to make me laugh so much. He was pretending to be Zorro." Isabella pauses and smiles at the memory. "Then, for the rest of the day I stayed home." Isabella looks under her eyebrows.

"You stayed home? Why?"

"Marco wasn't welcome here, so I was going to head out to his vineyard later. I told this to Angelou."

"Isabella, I want to find who murdered your father. Anything, anything you can tell me. I'm not trying to do anything other than find justice for your papa."

"Well, I caught a taxi to Marco's vineyard, as I knew we'd both be drinking later. I just remember paying the taxi driver and him leaving down the drive."

"You told Angelou Marco was dead," Elizabeth prompts Isabella to continue.

"He was lying there. Not moving." Isabella's face is full of distress. "We'd been so happy?" Isabella's face turns grim. "It was strange. I knew something was wrong as soon as I got there. I don't know why. You get a sixth sense about these things, don't you?"

"Then what happened?" Elizabeth asks, thinking back to how she dealt with Gerald's death. "How did you find him?"

"He was slumped over a table, on a stool. I thought he'd perhaps had too much to drink, but when I moved him, he fell. And, as he did, he spat at me. I don't know. I don't know. He was already dead." Isabella pulls a face. "He spat blood."

"It may have been building up in his mouth long after he died from the pressure of a ruptured organ."

"Stop. Please." Isabella drops her head. "No one will talk to me about it, apart from Angelou. My mother doesn't want to know.

Sophia is caught up in Papa and Ock. I don't think either of them liked Marco."

"Where did you go? Why didn't you call the police?" Elizabeth shakes her head.

"I don't know. I walked along the lane then reached the main road. I'd left my phone back at the vineyard. I didn't know what I was doing. I was hysterical. I didn't have a car. Someone stopped and gave me a lift into Florence. I suppose I wanted to find Lorenzo," Isabella explains. "I didn't want anyone to find Marco, not any policeman. I trust Lorenzo to find Marco's killer. Then Angelou found me." Isabella picks up a decanter with brandy in it and pours one. She holds it for Elizabeth, who shakes her head.

"Might you have some water?" Elizabeth asks, feeling the heat build in the south-facing room.

"Yes, of course." Isabella pours some iced water from a tray and hands it to Elizabeth. Elizabeth looks around the room at how many photographs of horses there are. On the walls, in frames on the desks. Isabella spots Elizabeth looking.

"We all love horses. All but Papa. He doesn't really care for them. Didn't."

"How is your mother coping without your father?" Elizabeth wonders if Aurelia feels the same wrench she does. "It is so hard for a widow."

"It is." Isabella pulls a ring out from under her jumper, attached to a necklace around her neck.

"You married Marco Conti?"

"We didn't tell Papa. He would have been so mad."

64 COME HOME

Giuseppe waits for Mia at her apartment. When she arrives, he follows her up the stairs. But at the front door to her apartment, Mia stops.

"You cannot come in, Giuseppe. It's been a stressful morning."

"Just for five minutes. Five minutes. That's all. It's imperative," Giuseppe is sweatier than usual, having coughed and spluttered all the flights up.

"You have to stop coming round. The police have arrested you for theft. I'm sorry, but I just don't trust you not to take anything of Peter's. I think you should direct your attention elsewhere. Now, if you will excuse me, I'm exhausted."

"No, no. Mia. I'm Peter's friend. I didn't want this to happen to him. I'm worried about you. Worried for you." Giuseppe sounds panicked.

"And I'm pretty worried for me too. Especially when I politely ask you to leave,

Giuseppe, and yet you are still here." Mia fiddles with her key, turning her back on Giuseppe.

"Let's go in, and I can explain everything about the arrest. They've not even charged me." Giuseppe wipes his forehead with his shirt.

"And that should put my mind at rest? You assure me that Peter wasn't wrapped up in anything with you, but how can I believe you now? Perhaps you put him up to it. This thieving. It makes me unsure who to trust."

"Perhaps you did!" Giuseppe shouts in temper. "Maybe you know where the diamond is!" Giuseppe throws his arms around violently, spitting at Mia.

"My husband is dead, and all you care about are material things. Go away before I call the police." Mia opens her door and goes to shut it, but Giuseppe puts his foot in it, making Mia jump.

"Come home to England with me." Giuseppe's face all screwed up between the gap.

"This is my home. Peter is here. Please," Mia begs.

"Let's leave on the next plane. As soon as I find my passport!"

"You're being ridiculous. Get your foot out of the door!" Mia now shouts, but Giuseppe ignores her.

"Perhaps you and I could work. I could look after you," Giuseppe suggests. "Yes, I will save us both."

"Move your foot away then, and we can talk," Mia insists. Giuseppe finally steps back and moves his foot out of the door, but as soon as he does, Mia slams the door shut. From behind it, she shouts at him.

"Go home, Giuseppe!"

Giuseppe stares at the door for a minute. He looks through the spy hole, even though he knows he cannot see anything. On the other side of the door, Mia's heart is racing.

"You know, I think it was Marco who wanted me dead. I have not had a death threat since. Why would he have wanted that?" Giuseppe asks. But Mia is done talking to this odious man. She does not move from behind the door until she hears his footsteps walk away, then she takes the largest breath and slides down to the floor in tears.

65 TWO ITALYS

Elizabeth arrives back at Villa De' Fiori and, much to her surprise, finds Godric lying on a sunbed, reading.

"Hello, stranger!" He sits up when he hears her footsteps and gives Patty the biggest kiss.

"Like ships passing. Have you been enjoying yourself in the company of the glamorous Lucia?" Elizabeth is relieved to see him and cannot stop herself from giving him the biggest hug.

"Isn't she wonderful? She's such a natural woman. Like a movie star," Godric sighs.

"Are those stars in your eyes?" Elizabeth raises her eyebrows and perches on a sun lounger beside Godric's.

"She knows Radar Wilkinson, an ex of mine. She said we would have been a match made in heaven. Perhaps I should give him a call? What d'you think?"

"Radar?" Elizabeth remembers with horror Radar Wilkinson's influence over Godric and how heartbroken Godric was when things ended. She also remembers distinctly how Radar moved in a different world. Jets, boats, parties. It was Godric's lost summer, having turned eighteen, and everything was legal, even the illegal things, to Godric. "Hmm, perhaps," Elizabeth remembers Radar's sneers at her home when he visited once and how he put his shoes on her settee.

"Lucia wants to take me to the Amalfi coast. I told her we had other plans. I don't need to hang out with Lucia. I want to be with you." Godric gives her a long and knowing look. "I think I've just been trying, you know, to bury my head from recent events back home." Godric thinks back to Valentine's Day. "But we can make some new plans of our own?"

"Whatever you can to get yourself through it. There's no wrong action. It's good that you've been spending time with someone you like. Maybe, so long as it doesn't lead you back to Radar?"

"Shall we just leave? Let's just go. We have nothing to pack. We could go now. Let's go to the Amalfi coast. Just us. Why not?" Godric sits up, hopeful that Elizabeth will agree to his spontaneous suggestion.

"Ah, well, there might be a slight chink in that plan. I've been asked by police not to leave Florence."

"What? That parking permit is not worth it. I really want to take you," Godric reaches across the loungers to hold his nanna's hand.

"No, you don't understand. I'm not allowed to leave. Apparently, I'm a suspect."

"Wait, what the–" Godric stands up in shock.

"I was right about the type of poison that killed Marco," Elizabeth interrupts. "I named it. So now they think I could have done it. I didn't like the man. I kept telling everyone how much." Elizabeth pulls a face. "Perhaps honesty isn't always the best policy." She smiles at Godric. "God forbid I could just be good at knowing my poisons."

"No." Godric is dumbfounded. "But this is madness!" Worry crosses his face.

"So now, it is my interest to solve the case, if but to clear my name."

Godric picks up his phone and dials. The person on the other end of the line picks up.

"This is all your fault. You got us into this mess. You get us out!" Godric listens to Inspector Bob Abley, who clearly does not know the latest news about Elizabeth. "They bloody think Bunny did it! That's what! Millionaires, weird guys with bric-a-brac collections. Any of them could have done it!" Godric fumes. "Yes, you'd better ruddy well call him now. Now!" Godric hangs up on Bob Abley and starts pacing. "I'm going to go down there and find that greedy Commissario and give him some of my best thoughts!"

"What can Bob do?" Elizabeth sounds resigned, perhaps too tired to fight this time.

"Get off the golf course and sort this out now. Fly over here to get you out of this mess!" Godric shouts out across the garden to anyone who might be listening.

"Oh, it's not going to be Bob. It will be Superintendent Raynott that got us into this mess. The fact of the matter is that neither can help me now."

They both realise it will only be Elizabeth's powers of deduction that can get her out of this, not a gannet of a Commissario or a golf ball obsessed Inspector.

Out of the realisation, Elizabeth suddenly has a sense of dread. She does not like this predicament one bit. And all the more for putting her grandson and now Patty in jeopardy. What will they do if she gets arrested? Would the Commissario really do that? Would he go as far as embroiling Godric in the case? Godric did punch Marco. Elizabeth does not have to wait long to find out what mood the Commissario is in, as he has let himself in the house, much to Elizabeth's annoyance.

"Aren't guests supposed to knock? In case one would rather not entertain?" Elizabeth frowns at the Commissario.

"I do not come as your guest, Professor Green. I need to speak with you urgently."

66 MAXIMILIUS ROMANO IS DYING

Elizabeth is standing in front of a bed in a hospital. Not any hospital, a private one with bells and whistles and handsome-looking doctors monitoring the patient's pulse every fifteen minutes under subdued lighting and expensive cotton sheets.

"He was choppered in from his boat in Portofino."

Elizabeth does not understand why a patient would have to come all this way, but the Commissario explains, "This is our best hospital."

"Where was he found?"

Elizabeth listens to Maximilius's laboured breathing.

"In the bathroom of his boat," The Commissario replies.

"Who found him?"

"A cleaner of all people." The Commissario sounds confused. How can someone so wealthy be left alone and not found by anyone beforehand. Where were his staff?

"What's so strange about that?" Elizabeth does not understand.

"We have the cleaner in custody. She's a young woman," the Commissario replies reassuringly.

"So, you suspect a cleaner was trying to kill Mr Romano here?" Elizabeth shakes her head.

"Well, a cleaner stole the jewel, so there is a pattern with cleaners." The Commissario looks at Maximilius's motionless body.

"Right, right. That makes complete sense when you say it aloud," Elizabeth replies sarcastically. "What else?"

"There wasn't a mark in the bathroom. It was spotless. Someone, perhaps the cleaner, though they are admitting nothing, must have wiped the evidence of what is killing him away."

"What do you mean?" Elizabeth observes Maximilius lying in bed, with many medical contraptions monitoring his heart, oxygen levels and more.

"They even left the cleaning box out, with all the bleach and cleaning fluids."

"So, he was in a bathroom below deck?" Elizabeth asks.

"It's weird. They'd even cleaned the toilet."

"We're looking for a murderer who can't

pass a dirty toilet," Sergeant Angelou Rossi says, lurking behind Elizabeth and two nurses. One nurse brings in fresh white puffy towels to the exclusive en-suite hospital room.

"Why did you bring me here? You have a police force. I thought I was under suspicion. I thought you were bringing me in to question me. This is such an imposition of my freedom. I shall be speaking to my Inspector again."

"We thought, well, Angelou thought," the Commissario looks at Angelou who mouths, 'You're welcome', "You're so quick to deduce all the other poisons that–"

"Hang on. You tell me not to leave Florence, then ask me back on the case to identify the poison?" Elizabeth is flabbergasted.

"You did leave Florence, though, didn't you? At the first opportunity," the Commissario tries to defend his defenceless position.

"And, you had me tailed? Yet, you still value my opinion about potential murders?" Elizabeth looks back at Maximilius. "People have been called idiots for less."

"You think this is a possible attempted murder?" the Sergeant asks.

"What am I, psychic? I've only looked at the man. "I'm not helping you. Leave me alone." Elizabeth leaves the hospital room, refusing to entertain the prospect of being a pawn in the Commissario's hand.

"Alright, alright. I was tired. My pathologist caught me off guard. Put ideas into my head," the Commissario says as he follows Elizabeth into the corridor. "Have you ever made a mistake?"

"Don't be ridiculous." Elizabeth looks at the Commissario and raises an eyebrow.

"Please, Elizabeth. I'm very sorry. Please, take a look at his charts. Not for me, for my Sergeant. He said he looked after your dog."

"He only looked after my dog while I was helping you, Lorenzo." Elizabeth sighs, and turns around, having lost all respect for this Commissario. "I will only, I repeat, only help if you drop all this nonsense that I could be in any way," Elizabeth raising her voice when saying 'any' "in any way responsible. You have caused untoward stress for my grandson." There is a pause, longer than Elizabeth would have wanted, and then she sees the Commissario nod. "Excuse me, what now?"

"Okay," the Commissario replies.

"Pardon?"

"Okay, okay. I do not think you have anything to do with the murders." The Commissario replies.

"Then why did you say so?"

"I thought I just said? I was tired, my pathologist." There is another pause as Elizabeth waits for more. The Commissario adds, "Can we please talk about this after?

A man is dying." But Elizabeth still does not budge. "Okay, I didn't want you to leave either. There, that's all of it. I'm sorry, I made a mistake!"

"Alright, no need to shout. So, Max was in a bathroom that had just been cleaned." Elizabeth walks back into the room and looks at the charts.

"Yes, that's right, below deck as you said," the Sergeant replies, glad to see Elizabeth back.

"Were there windows in this bathroom?"

"No," the Sergeant answers.

"Has anyone checked for chloramine poisoning?" Elizabeth asks.

"What?" The Commissario chimes in.

"The cleaner, young, you said, most probably mixed toilet cleaner with bleach. It releases chlorine gas or chloramines. Can kill, actually, but judging by his symptoms, I'd say he was lucky." Elizabeth walks over and opens all the windows. "He needs oxygen."

"What? Is that it?" The Commissario is confused.

Elizabeth walks out of the hospital room without looking back, muttering to herself about men, and if they only cleaned a toilet every so often, they'd know what she was talking about. She hears a voice behind her.

"Elizabeth, stop. What do you mean toilet

cleaner with bleach?" the Commissario asks.

"Look it up! I cannot be here with you."

67 AN APOLOGY

Sometime later, after Godric and Elizabeth have had a reasonably calm tea together and Elizabeth has filled Godric in on the latest developments, after what happened with Marco and now the Commissario, Godric insists he will no longer let his nanna out of his sight. Approximately half an hour later, once Godric has put on his dog carrier, they knock for Mia as Elizabeth has a hunch.

"Hello, Professor Green?" They both hear Mia's voice on the apartment intercom at the street front door.

"May we come up? We come bearing gifts or at least something of interest," Elizabeth replies. They hear the buzzer, and it isn't long before they are at Mia's apartment, as the lift is working now.

"Hello?" Mia is a little thrown by Godric's appearance as she opens her door and lets them into her apartment. She vaguely remembers him from Stefano's party. "I thought it was just you, Professor Green?"

"My grandson is keeping me company this evening."

"Good evening." Godric looks at Mia and gives her a small packet of biscuits. "We had these in our kitchen and thought you might like them."

"I'm gluten-free."

"Ah, well, they are delicious, so I might keep hold if that's the case." Godric pockets the biscuits.

"Right." Mia looks at them both, wondering why they are here.

"I found Peter's shirt." Elizabeth pulls out the shirt from the bag in front of Mia. "I was in half a mind not to come. The police seemed to know when I came last time and accused me of meddling or worse. That I'm involved somehow?"

"I think they have someone watching the apartment. Probably to check up on me," Mia replies, walking over to the window and looking out to look for police watching her apartment. "Where did you find it?" Mia then comes back and looks at the shirt with interest, catching the smell of smoke, wrinkling her nose.

"Was it a favourite of his?" Godric asks, trying to hide his distaste for the gold thread faint check on the white shirt.

"On Stefano's land," Elizabeth replies, not giving the game away as to where.

"Ah. Perhaps he left it when they were out together," Mia slumps into a chair, ignoring Godric's question but instead asking him about England. "You don't seem to be having much of a holiday together, then?"

"It started well, but I'm beginning to miss home a little," Godric replies.

"I'm sorry you miss home, Godric. I don't have a home. Not anymore." Mia sips her drink, not even bothering to offer them anything. "Is that why you came? To bring me back Peter's shirt?"

"Have you been able to make friends?" Godric asks.

"Oh, I have to give the shirt to the police. I'm afraid you can't have it?" Elizabeth tells Mia, putting it back in the bag instead of handing it to Mia.

"I've very little faith in the police in finding my husband's killer. They seem only to be interested in diamonds." Mia says wearily. She is about to question why she cannot have the shirt when her buzzer goes. "That had better not be Giuseppe again." She says crossly. Mia gets up to listen to her intercom.

"Hello darling, it's me."

Mia looks and sees it is Aurelia.

"Full house this morning. Come up." Mia buzzes up Aurelia. It isn't long before Aurelia is standing in the doorway.

"This is just the worst day." Aurelia

smiles.

"Come in," Mia walks into her living room. Aurelia sees Elizabeth and Godric.

"Hello, Elizabeth, hello," Aurelia says, her face puffy, forgetting Godric's name, and then turning to Mia. "I just came to apologise for my daughters turning you away like that. I had no idea you drove all that way."

"What are you doing here?" Mia asks Aurelia.

"You came to see me, so I was just being polite." Aurelia looks at Godric as she speaks to Mia, a little embarrassed. "Honestly, I don't know what to do with myself. But then, I know you understand." Aurelia pauses, acknowledging Mia's grieving.

"I'm sorry for your loss." Mia looks at Aurelia for a long time, then walks back over to her drink, her fists clenched, now crying.

"Are you okay, Mia?" Elizabeth asks, seeing Mia's tears flowing.

"Still, there is so much on the farm that needs my attention. Stefano did everything. I had to get away. I'm making things ten times worse." Then Aurelia sits, uninvited. "The two widows. To lose him like this is a real shock." Aurelia touches Mia's arm. "I always thought I'd go first. Break my neck and fall off a horse. He was built like an ox."

"I'm sorry, Aurelia. I don't know what to say," Mia replies awkwardly. "I just want to curl into a ball and disappear myself."

"So, you didn't notice the shirt missing?" Elizabeth asks.

"What? No." Mia replies, "The police now think Professor Green is meddling in the case and involved," Mia explains to Aurelia.

"What has that got to do with the shirt?" Godric replies defensively. "And, for the record, they don't anymore."

Mia walks out onto the balcony, so Elizabeth follows, while Godric walks into the kitchen to see if there is anything good to eat. But all there is in the cupboard is a jar of jam, safety pins and a bar of chocolate. He pulls a square of the chocolate, which tastes good, then leaves a little disappointed.

"Isn't that Giuseppe?" Elizabeth points to a bench below Mia's apartment, in a small garden lined by lime trees.

"Oh." Mia looks upset, "I don't know whether to call the police. He's been there all day," Mia pauses as she looks at Giuseppe. "I'm more convinced than ever that he told Peter to steal the diamond. Maybe he thinks Peter hid it here? He has been harassing me, it's scary."

"But Peter was murdered on the roof of the tower in San Gimignano. Surely, he had the diamond with him?"

"I suppose, but what if he came here first? The police have this image sensor tool, and even waved it over our floorboard. There's no diamond here," Mia says.

"Oh gosh, I had no idea." Aurelia watches Giuseppe below. All of a sudden, Giuseppe looks up at the balcony. Mia hides and grabs Aurelia's arm.

"Please tell him to go away," Mia says as they watch Giuseppe march towards the door.

68 FOUND JEWELLERY

"I don't want you coming here at any time." Lucia pushes Maximilius back outside the front door.

"We need to talk." Maximilius stands there, waiting for his wife to see reason.

"No, we don't." Lucia shakes her head, then looks at one of her staff and opens her eyes wide, indicating she gave clear instructions to keep her husband off the property. The employee shrugs back, clearly aware that they both still pay his wages.

"I cannot believe you really want a divorce." Maximilius smiles. "Let's at least talk about why, sensibly, over a drink?"

"I do." Seeing she cannot keep him out, Lucia drops her shoulders and walks towards her office. Maximilius follows.

"Hey. I thought these had been stolen too?" Maximilius spots a pair of earrings on a table in Lucia's office.

"What gave you that idea?'

Maximilius frowns. He walks over to her desk

as Lucia picks up the divorce papers her lawyer has drawn up.

"Just sign these. Let's make this civilized. Shall we? There's a very generous settlement in there," Lucia hands Maximilius the papers.

"And these?" Maximilius holds up tickets for the exhibition, which included her diamond. "You said you didn't go?"

"I didn't. I was sent them, okay? Stop rifling through my desk. It's so tiresome."

"I told you it was a bad idea to exhibit it. But you had to ignore me. If it hadn't been for that bloody ring, we would not be talking divorce." Maximilius picks up a folder marked Peter Jones. "And this?"

"I had him investigated. So what?" Lucia pauses. "If you must know, I wanted to know if you had anything to do with it."

"What, after he was dead?"

"Er, yes. I didn't know who he was before." Lucia shakes her head.

"And you didn't hire him to steal it and then had to bump him off yourself?" Maximilius laughs.

"Max. Stop. It's over." She looks at him, knowing this will hurt but aware that they both know the reality, that they have been living separate lives for a while now. "You can't hurt me anymore."

"Is this a test? You asking me for a divorce

to get me to tell you how much I love you? That you mean everything to me? Okay, I'll say it if you really want me to." Maximilius chucks the divorce papers down on a chaise longues.

"I don't want that. I don't." Lucia picks the papers right back up and hands them to Maximilius again. He rolls his eyes and refuses momentarily to take them before sighing and snatching them back.

"And who is this fop you're treating like your latest puppy dog?" he asks, his tone colder now.

"He's not a fop. He's ten times the man you are," Lucia replies defensively.

"You know you're barking up the wrong tree. He came onto my boat. Not the man for you, I'm telling you." Maximilius pulls the documents out of the envelope and looks at the front page of his divorce.

"Not everything is carnal. You wouldn't understand." Lucia picks up the phone. "Darling. Can you come around? Oh, she can come too." Lucia listens to Godric telling her he cannot leave his nanna.

"What's the matter? No one love you?" Maximilius asks.

Lucia covers the phone.

"I don't love you. Please go."

Maximilius tuts and leaves with the papers, unhappy that his plan backfired.

*

When Elizabeth and Godric leave Mia, Godric gets a call from Lucia, so they agree to go and see if she is okay, having heard her tone and learning Maximilius is there. But when they arrive, Lucia is already alone again. She rushes into Godric's arms and beckons them into her home.

As Lucia embraces Godric and offers him a drink, it does not take long for Elizabeth to find the file that Maximilius chucked down onto the settee, all about Peter. Elizabeth opens it and starts rifling through the notes.

"I hired a P.I. when the diamond was stolen." Lucia sees Elizabeth studying the file. "It's all routine stuff. Max just found it and as much as accused me of stealing my own diamond and being in cahoots with this man. If cahoots is the right word?" Lucia looks at Godric as if he has just come and saved her like a white knight. "Thank you for coming. You were so quick."

"We were close," Godric smiles.

"It says he was a fox hunter," Elizabeth comments. "God, please no. I bet you don't have that here."

"Oh, we have hunting. Wild boar. But I don't do it."

"Is the correct answer," Godric hugs Lucia.

"I think Stefano used to hunt?" Lucia

suggests to Elizabeth.

"Oh no, he didn't. He showed me all the netting he put up around his estate. He did tell me the only marital argument was over wild boar." Elizabeth puts the folder under her arm. "May I borrow this?"

"Sure," Lucia replies.

"Can you change the locks?" Godric suggests.

"You read my mind," Lucia says, sipping her cocktail, her hands still trembling.

"We can stay for a bit, can't we?" Godric looks hopefully at Elizabeth.

"Yes, okay. I can look at this now," Elizabeth nods.

"Why don't we go and sit somewhere more comfortable," Lucia ushers them out of her office and into a large living room filled with plants, which also overlooks the garden. Elizabeth likes this very much.

"Why didn't you show me this room before?" Elizabeth nestles down into a comfortable settee with the folder on Peter and a peppermint tea. Godric and Lucia go to sit at the cocktail bar, and start drowning Lucia's sorrows.

69 ALL THAT GLITTERS

When Aurelia finally leaves Mia's apartment – and after he watched Elizabeth and Godric depart earlier – Giuseppe decides to follow Aurelia home. If Mia won't entertain his calls, then maybe Stefano's wife will. Perhaps he can speak reason to her. Someone needs to believe him, believe the death threats. He needs help, and if Peter was obsessed with olives, then perhaps that is where he will find the answer. He has tried everything else.

Giuseppe stops briefly on the way to buy some flowers from a garage, hoping they will persuade Aurelia to open the door. He has lost her car, having been following her, but he need not have worried. When he arrives on the driveway, Aurelia is still outside and welcomes him in.

"We need to talk," Aurelia suggests.

"Music to my ears," Giuseppe says as he

plonks himself down on her white couch, his legs sweating.

"Perhaps we should sit on these chairs at the table. There is a breeze from the French doors," Aurelia looks at her expensive couch and leads Giuseppe towards some open windows in her drawing room. She picks up a plant spray bottle and subtly gives her couch a squib of water, hoping to remove any lasting stain then rushes towards the table, and pulls out a chair, plopping a towel on top of Giuseppe's seat that had been hanging by the window ready to use by the pool.

"This is very nice. Ooh. Iced tea!" Giuseppe sees a large jug on the table. Ice cubes rattle as he pours himself a glass. Aurelia observes his selfish act, not considering whether she might like something. It makes it easier to be cold towards him. "I don't suppose you have any whisky?" He asks.

"Stefano liked a whisky." Aurelia sits beside Giuseppe, without offering him any whisky. "On the rocks, he'd say. He was drinking a lot of it before he died. Always in that glasshouse of his. Making drinks."

"Oh, his glasshouse? He didn't just grow olive trees in there?" Giuseppe looks past the orangery through the double doors.

"Sometimes I think he liked that place more than me. His favourite place, he'd say. He spent a lot of time out there, with his whisky and ice. Always the whisky." Aurelia sighs.

"He loved you very much," Giuseppe lies, not having known Stefano or cared for him and having his own suspicions that Stefano was indeed behind Peter's death. "He told me he could not have done all this without you."

"He had a funny way of showing it sometimes. He was always speaking about that Englishwoman, Elizabeth, before he died. You know, I think he had a crush." Aurelia sounds a little surprised.

"Surely not. You're much more beautiful," Giuseppe continues, then adds. "My death threats have stopped. Do you think that means they came from Marco?"

"Thank you, Giuseppe, that is very kind. And, perhaps you should tell the Commissario about that?" Then she thinks and adds, "You know, before you go, you should pop into Stefano's study and choose something of his, just as a memento. I don't know what to do with it all. Peter was his closest friend, and you were friends with Peter. There might be something that they both did together in there."

"You mean it?" Giuseppe's bottom lip wobbles. "I miss him so much," he bursts into tears. Giuseppe is thinking of Peter, but Aurelia believes it to be Stefano.

"Okay, okay. He was my husband, not yours."

"I can't help it. Peter was my best friend." Giuseppe continues to cry, and Aurelia, realising her mistake, decides to pour herself some iced tea and let him cry it out. After a while, she continues.

"You need to leave Mia alone. You're frightening her," she says matter-of-factly.

"I've been looking out for her. Did she say that?"

"I invited you in, Giuseppe, to say this has to stop."

"Where are your staff? Peter always told me you had a battalion of butlers. Are you alone?"

"I fired them. They didn't save Stefano. They didn't stop Marco invading our home. I need to find new staff," Aurelia replies. "Ones that will actually protect me."

"I could live here. Protect you. We could protect one another."

"I'm fine, thank you." Aurelia frowns.

"But, you're not fine. You're alone. You can't be alone," A droplet of sweat from Giuseppe's forehead falls on the table in front of him.

"I'm not alone. My daughters are living with me," Aurelia says defensively.

"But they're not here now?" Giuseppe looks around and listens to the quiet house.

"They'll be back." Aurelia is beginning to think inviting Giuseppe was not a great idea.

She stands up and walks behind a couch, trying to act as casually as possible but choosing to put distance between herself and this man.

"But when? The house is so quiet. No one is here but you. It isn't safe."

"I rarely have visitors. I'm secluded here, private. Don't make me regret it, inviting you in like this," Aurelia's voice raises a little, which Giuseppe picks up on.

"It's not safe! If I'm not safe, you're not safe. Peter is dead. Stefano is dead, and now Marco!"

"Calm down," Aurelia looks around the room to see what she can do to help calm this man.

"But how can I calm down!" Giuseppe shouts hysterically.

"Stop shouting. Stop shouting," Aurelia cries, running out of the room. "Leave me alone! Show yourself out! Just go!"

Giuseppe gets up and waits for a while for Aurelia to come back. When she does not, he starts to wander about the house. He walks into the kitchen. Just a sleeping dog on the floor. It looks untidy. Perhaps because the staff have been sacked.

He walks back out and across the hall to Stefano's office. Did Aurelia mean it? To take anything? As he enters, he can smell Stefano. He notices Stefano's old jacket and thinks about taking that. He tries it on. It is a little tight across the chest, but the arms are too long, and it almost hangs to his knees. And anyway, he was hoping for a memento of Peter that Stefano might have kept. He did not like Stefano anyway, and will never forgive him for getting Peter involved in goodness only knows what. Giuseppe wanders over to Stefano's desk and notices paperweights and pens. Perhaps he should take a pen. But then, that would remind him of Stefano, not Peter? What can he take? In the corner is a bookshelf. But he doesn't want to carry a book.

Giuseppe leaves the office and steps outside. Still, without a souvenir, he decides to go and have a look at the glasshouse. Perhaps he can keep one of the plants Peter was studying. He walks across the gravel path, aware that the glasshouse is joined to the orangery and the house. Will Aurelia shout at him to leave? She did not say he could not come around the back. Ah, she is probably crying on her bed. She does not want to see him and does not care about his death threats. No, he will look at the glasshouse, in case there is something there.

Inside, he immediately smells the plants and feels the humidity. It makes him thirsty, and he wishes he'd finished his iced tea. He walks to the end and sees Stefano's small bar. Who puts a bar into a glasshouse? Giuseppe supposes that Stefano was not an ordinary kind of man. He reaches down into the cupboard and finds some gin, vodka and whisky. Giuseppe has driven here but knows he can take his liquor. One for the road, he thinks. He pours a generous measure of whisky into a crystal glass. Then looks for some ice to cool himself down. Aurelia had mentioned Stefano drank on the rocks. He notices the small fridge freezer built into the bar. He opens and reaches in for a tray of ice. When he pulls the tray out and sits it on the wooden bar, he has to blink. Inside one of the squares is something ruby red. Could that be? Surely not. He turns the tray over and taps out the ice. There, in a small square of ice, is a diamond ring. There is no mistaking it. Giuseppe's eyes dart around, and he knocks back his whisky. Up in the corner, a CCTV camera silently follows Giuseppe out of the glasshouse.

*

Aurelia throws water on her face in the bathroom. When she wanders back into her drawing room and notices Giuseppe has gone and is not in Stefano's study when she enters, she looks out the front and notices Giuseppe's car has gone. Leaving the front door wide open, she walks into a small room between her drawing room and the kitchen, a security room. Inside are a bank of cameras. She hits rewind one minute on controls and watches

Giuseppe walk out of the house and back into the glasshouse. She forwards a little and then zooms in and sees what Giuseppe sees. Giuseppe melting some ice under the bar tap. Giuseppe holding a diamond ring up to the light and then pocketing the ring. After glancing around furtively, she watches Giuseppe hurry out of the glasshouse, jump into his car and drive away.

Aurelia picks up a phone and dials.

"Commissario Bianchi please. Yes, Aurelia Brambilla." She listens for a moment and then says, "Tell Lorenzo I have just seen Giuseppe Esposito with a diamond ring in my house. It might be the stolen diamond ring! Yes, to come quickly."

*

Aurelia plays Commissario Lorenzo Bianchi the tape in her house's surveillance room, as Lorenzo munches on a cherry pastry from her kitchen. The Commissario's eyes widen as he sees the moment when Giuseppe runs an ice cube under the tap, watches the ice dissolve, and then holds the red diamond ring up to the light. He then pops in the last of the pastry, and with full mouth explains what is going to happen now.

"My team picked Giuseppe up in his car already in Poggibonsi."

"I told Mia Jones, is that okay?" Aurelia's

voice is shaking. “We had just been with Giuseppe, and he’d been harassing her. I’d allowed him to come in here to try to tell him to stop. He’d followed me. We want to know if there is news of the diamond being found. It will mean Peter could be innocent. Perhaps Giuseppe blackmailed him and my husband? He seemed to know right where to find the diamond. All those times telling us he was scared for his life, had death threats,” Aurelia says, shaking her head. “And he kept asking me if I was alone. If no one was here with me. It was like he wanted to know, oh I don’t know. It was horrible. It gave me quite the shiver.”

“If he has the diamond, we can recover it. This will be an important moment in the case. And yes, it will help us uncover the truth.” The Commissario then looks around for a plate of cherry pastries. “Do you have any more of those? They’re delicious.”

70 GOTCHA ON CCTV

The Commissario calls in his Sergeant and Elizabeth to join him when he returns to Stefano Brambilla's olive grove estate later the same day, particularly Elizabeth because she had been right about Maximilius's poisoning being chlorine related. The Commissario values her opinion now as Maximilius made a rapid recovery with oxygen.

When Godric mentions he cannot leave his Bunny's side and will be joining her at the olive estate, Lucia wants to come too. Lucia also heard from her son, Ock, who through endless calls attempting reconciliation with Sophia, somehow also discovered what had happened earlier at the olive estate with a certain Giuseppe Esposito. Maximilius, on checking himself out of hospital, also calling Ock, and being updated on events, has to hear what this Professor Green has to say about Giuseppe Esposito and his diamond. Elizabeth saved his life as far as he is concerned. And getting his diamond back will be a bonus. Peter's widow, Mia, who has also arrived at the invitation of Aurelia, enters the olive estate home and sits down next to Sophia. Aurelia, having poured drinks for everyone, the sound of ice chinking against crystal, is now fiddling with the buttons on a television hung over a fireplace. By the time Isabella returns home, still in mourning for Marco's death, she finds everyone packed into her mother's private room on sofas and chairs, all with one big fat red diamond on their minds, chatting loudly, each questioning what could have happened as they wait to hear whether the diamond can be handed back to its rightful owner.

A hush descends as the Commissario walks into the room, followed by his Sergeant, Elizabeth and Godric. Once all are in, Sergeant Rossi shuts the door as if to prevent anyone from leaving.

"This is unexpected to see you all here. But, well, actually, it is good. It saves us time," the Commissario says, addressing the seated room, pacing up and down, catching the gaze of each of them. "And– we can confirm, Aurelia, that Giuseppe Esposito has been taken in for questioning, and had a ring on his person."

Aurelia picks up a remote and hits play, cutting across the Commissario. "I knew it!" The CCTV footage begins to play without Aurelia even asking the Commissario for permission, interrupting his next thought. "Let me show you and everyone what I saw," Aurelia holds up a hand to the Commissario to gesture for him to give her a minute, her eyes wide and a little wild. "I couldn't believe Stefano had the diamond all along, hidden in some ice. I've already told the Commissario. Stefano must have been blackmailed by Mr Esposito." Aurelia looks at Lucia and shakes her head. "I do not think he could do something like this. He must have been under great pressure to save our lives!"

Before the Commissario can stop Aurelia, the CCTV tape continues to play, and the evidence of Giuseppe's action pours out for all the room to see. Giuseppe first opening a freezer compartment in Stefano's glasshouse bar, pulling out a tray of ice and turning them over. There are gasps as some in the room see the rare red diamond ring already in a cube. Then more noises and shock as all now see Giuseppe, having melted the ice cube under the tap, holding the red diamond up to the light to examine it.

"My ring!" Lucia stands up. Elizabeth looks anything but impressed with the conversation so far but remains seated on the other side of Godric, quiet as a cucumber.

"Where is it now? That ring is ours!" Maximilius shouts, then wheezes. Ock pours him a glass of water from a large jug on a coffee table.

"Mine. It's mine," Lucia corrects her soon-to-be ex-husband, Maximilius. "Where is it?" Lucia asks the Commissario.

"Okay, everyone, sit down, please." The Commissario glares at Aurelia for already playing evidence and indicates he also means her, then turns to Lucia to explain. "We have a jeweller authenticating the diamond ring at the station right now. We're questioning Giuseppe Esposito." Then the Commissario reminds Lucia, "But if it is your ring, it will have to be held until this case is closed as evidence, as you know full well."

"Why are we here then? Why are you wasting our time?" Lucia asks. "I thought the ring was here?" Lucia slumps back down into the sofa. There are sighs as everyone realises the Commissario did not enter the room with the ring.

"No. Giuseppe took the ring! He ran off with it, took it from the ice cube. He knew where it was and disappeared!" Aurelia shouts, so far having refused to sit. "Shall I play the tape again? We have caught him in the act, right there!" Aurelia rewinds the clip and cues it up again, then presses play.

"We didn't actually invite you all," Sergeant Rossi answers Lucia, ignoring Aurelia momentarily. "We came to speak with Aurelia Brambilla about what Giuseppe Esposito was doing here." The Commissario nods, and his Sergeant continues, "We're surprised you're all here and came so quickly. Did you come by Bentley?" The Sergeant raises his eyebrows at Lucia.

"Giuseppe invited himself here. I had no idea he would follow me from Mia's," Aurelia shakes her head, answering the Sergeant's question to bring it back to the subject at hand. "And have been hiding the ring here. He's a madman."

"Why didn't you stop him? If he had the diamond?" Lucia looks at Aurelia. "And what was it doing here?"

"Do you not see the CCTV?" Aurelia is flabbergasted. "What are we doing here? Is no one watching this? He knew exactly where to find it. He must have hidden it in the glasshouse. Then he left before I realised." Aurelia leans back on a chest of drawers, her head looking at the floor, shaking it from side to side, finding the words hard to say. "He must have been blackmailing Steffy, or, I don't know what."

"This is what I'm trying to establish. Thank you, Mrs Brambilla." The Commissario replies, trying to keep a formality to this situation to equal the gravity. He takes a deep breath, calming people down with his hands and unhappy that so many people have gathered so quickly. "We will get to speak with you one at a time. I would like to speak with Mrs Brambilla. Please all wait outside until my Sergeant invites you back in. One by one, please." The Commissario takes some kind of meat treat from his pocket and peels back the wrapping, hoping this is an end to the missing diamond case.

"Before everybody leaves, I wondered if I might have a quick word?" Elizabeth asks the Commissario. "Or am I still under suspicion?"

"Well, two English people are already now known thieves," Aurelia replies, flashing Mia a glance, perhaps for labelling her husband in the same boat as Giuseppe. "I think it would be a good idea for everyone to go outside, including you, Professor Green, and wait your turn. If you are even who you say you are. Are you even a professor? Did you blackmail my husband to steal the ring? I'm beginning to have such dark thoughts. The Commissario needs to wrap this up quickly to get back to Giuseppe."

"I would be interested, actually, to hear what Elizabeth thinks," the Commissario overrules Aurlelia, Aurelia noticing how the Commissario calls Elizabeth by her first name.

"And my nanna is a professor," Godric corrects Aurelia, "and a very clever one at that."

*

Elizabeth slowly stands as the

Commissario nods his approval, patting her grandson as a thank you for standing up for her.

"We were on holiday," Elizabeth looks down at Godric. "It was supposed to be a lovely time. There have been some special moments," Elizabeth smiles, thinking back to the afternoon she and Godric climbed the steps and looked out at the view across Florence, then looks down at Patty on Godric's lap and smiles that they also found this beautiful little dog to share their futures with. Then Elizabeth looks around the room at the gathered group. "But I have to say, they've all been near ruined by this missing diamond and some of the people in this room."

Elizabeth pauses, then walks over to the window and touches a plant. Then she looks back at the faces of those gathered, noticing some now bored, others confused, the remaining irritated. "You know, I used to think this was a romantic place, full of happy people. We chose Tuscany as it is the epitome of a gentle landscape, wine, sunshine, good food, beautiful views." Elizabeth thinks longingly about what might have been and closes her eyes for a moment. She takes a deep sigh, then opens her eyes and stares at the people in the room again, only this time slowly, one by one. "I really hope that you're not all a cross-representation–"

"I don't see what your holiday has anything to do with anything?" Ock scoffs interrupting. Sophia looks at him and shakes her head, so he leaves it.

"You, in particular. Who is cruel to a dog? The worst kind of behaviour." Elizabeth glares at Ock.

"Yes, I'm not sure where this is going?" Mia looks at the Commissario.

"Continue," the Commissario nods at Elizabeth encouragingly, ignoring Mia.

"I've only been nice to you?" Lucia sounds a little affronted by Elizabeth's words to her son.

"If nice means giving me a gift every single time I see you. Why is that, Lucia? Anyone would be forgiven for thinking that you gave your diamond away."

"Exactly!" Maximilius nods vigorously. "She never looked after it, even offered it to the gallery organisers."

"Why so generous?" Elizabeth asks Lucia.

"I just want to make people happy." Lucia shrugs. "Shoot me."

"Perhaps not the right thing to say in the middle of a murder enquiry," Elizabeth replies, then continues her train of thought, looking straight at Lucia. "At first, I had my suspicions about you. Too good to be true. Too friendly. It would have been so simple if you had stolen your own diamond for the insurance."

"How ridiculous, darling." Lucia laughs, revealing her expensive teeth.

"I know," Elizabeth continues, "that was until I found out just how wealthy you really are. You couldn't give away your fortune in your lifetime if you gave gifts to everyone in Florence for the rest of your life. So, why steal your own diamond?"

Godric is surprised by the extent of Lucia's wealth, his eyes open wide. Lucia shrugs, then looks at her husband.

"And I couldn't find any vendetta or beef you had against Peter? I think you were as curious as I about the whole thing, which is why you hired a private investigator to look into him."

"Yes, darling," Lucia replies.

"You did?" The Commissario looks a little disappointed.

"You have been marvellous, Lorenzo. I didn't find anything," she replies kindly. "I have more pie, too, waiting for you at home." Then Lucia laughs and looks at her soon-to-be ex-husband. "He's the one in debt. That's why he won't give me a divorce."

"Father would not steal your diamond, Mama," Ock shakes his head.

"I know. He's many things, but not a thief. That's why I loved him for all those years," Lucia sighs.

"Loved? You're breaking my heart,"

Maximilius replies, hearing her kind words but knowing she really does want to leave him.

"But I don't trust those who are mean to animals." Elizabeth looks back at Ock. "Why do you do it? Why?" She shakes her head.

"This dog has no manners," Ock glares at Patty. Godric glares back.

"You're simply horrid to animals and should never be allowed to look after them," Elizabeth tells Ock bluntly.

"Huh, like I have time for that. What is this?" Ock looks at the Commissario, who is also unsure where Elizabeth is going with her comments.

"As much as I want you to be the murderer–" Elizabeth continues, looking at Ock.

"Elizabeth! You're my guest," Lucia interrupts, reminding Elizabeth that it is her son she is talking about.

"As much as I wondered if you might have the capacity for murder, and there is evidence that those who harm animals go on to harm humans, so you may well end up in trouble eventually," Elizabeth continues, unwilling to be silenced by Lucia. "In this particular case, however, I found no evidence against you, Ockaviarius. Godric told me you do, in fact, have a trust fund, which gives you no motive to kill for money. And I cannot see why you would murder your girlfriend's father on this occasion. No, it felt too far-fetched to pursue."

"I'm scared and relieved all at once," Ock replies sarcastically, kissing Sophia, who shakes her head. "Who is this woman?"

Elizabeth turns to look at Maximilius. "You knew Marco, didn't you? Were in cahoots with him to steal some of Stefano's land. Poor Stefano told me before he died. So, it might be reasonable to think that you murdered Stefano and Marco. And that perhaps the death of Peter was just a decoy. That this was all about the land."

"Take that back immediately!" Maximilius screams, jumping up and then feeling dizzy.

"Sit down, Sir. Thankfully, for you, there were too many clues pointing in another direction. Though you should consider protecting nature and choosing the company you keep more carefully. Taking more care where you build," Elizabeth reprimands Maximilius, who looks flustered and confused.

*

"Giuseppe found the diamond in the glasshouse, you say?" Elizabeth looks at Aurelia, who looks back impatiently. Aurelia sighs at the Commissario to indicate she has no idea what Elizabeth is doing here.

"Just answer the questions," the

Commissario nods at Aurelia reassuringly. "Professor Green has been right about everything else so far. So let's hear what she has to say."

"I've already told the Commissario," Aurelia answers Elizabeth and decides not to call Lorenzo by his first name. Two can play at that game. "Why are we still sitting here? The Commissario needs to question Giuseppe about what he's done." Aurelia taps her feet.

"Something is not sitting well with me here. I just have to understand, how did Giuseppe, Mr Esposito, know where to look for the diamond?" Elizabeth moves her head ever so slightly to the side, watching Aurelia with a steely glare.

"How should I know? Maybe he spoke to my husband. Why are we dragging this out?" Aurelia again glares at the Commissario.

"So, you think your own husband stole the diamond?" Elizabeth persists with her line of questions. "Is that now what you're saying?"

"Unless I'm not much mistaken, you're not a member of the Italian police, and it was mentioned, was it not, at Mia's just hours ago, that you are a suspect yourself?" Aurelia replies.

"Just humour me," Elizabeth decides to let it go, but Godric won't.

"My Bunny is not a suspect. She has been dragged from her holiday time and time again to help solve this mess. D'you think we want to be here? No, we do not, madam. But my Bunny will get to the bottom of this, so stop trying to interfere with the process and answer the ruddy question."

"No one is talking about my dead husband," Mia interrupts. "Just a diamond ring. That's all I hear about. What about Peter? Has Giuseppe been questioned about that too?" Mia glances at the Commissario, then covers her face with her hands, her elbows resting in her lap. "It's clear Giuseppe was a thief. I can't believe he killed his own friend. My husband." Mia cries. Elizabeth looks at Mia but then back to Aurelia.

"So, you don't know how Giuseppe knew where to look?" Elizabeth asks Aurelia, sticking to her original question. "Was it not strange that Giuseppe came to visit you, Aurelia? You told the Commissario that he came and sat with you, concerned you were alone."

"And?" Aurelia frowns. "Why are we going around the houses when that thief and possible murderer needs to be questioned by you, Commissario? Don't you need to be at the station now if you have caught him? You've seen the CCTV."

"He is being questioned, Mrs Brambilla." The Commissario tries to reassure Aurelia. "Though, I'm also unsure what you are getting at, Elizabeth?" the Commissario looks quizzically at Elizabeth.

"Well, if Aurelia says she does not know what Giuseppe was doing here, then perhaps now is a good time to share that we know he must have come straight from Mia's today, Commissario. Godric and I saw him there, sitting on a bench, as did you, Aurelia, and Mia. Neither of you were concerned about Giuseppe's welfare then? Quite the opposite, Mia was complaining of harassment. That Giuseppe had been scaring her." Elizabeth looks at Mia. "Is that not true?" But Elizabeth does not wait for Mia's reply, instead turning to Aurelia, "So, why the sudden change in hospitality? Welcoming him in, sitting him down? It makes no sense."

"I don't know. I suppose I pitied him. He's pathetic." Aurelia looks at Elizabeth and shrugs, sounding a little more caring.

"So, all alone, you let a man into your home who, not hours before, was accused of harassment by your friend? After hearing that, you invited him in to drink iced tea? Is that not what you did?"

"He helped himself to iced tea if we are being pedantic." Aurelia opens her eyes wide, but Elizabeth stares at her, so Aurelia continues. "I know. It looks odd, but I suppose I felt it was the easiest way to appease him. So what?"

"He didn't break in. You invited him in.

That's the fact of the matter." Elizabeth drums home her point. The group in the room look a bit confused as to why Elizabeth seems to be persisting with this question.

"Like I say, it was easier to appease him," Aurelia states dismissively. "He just wanted to get to the diamond. Clearly, that's why he drove over to come in."

"Hmm. But if he knew where the diamond was, why was he sitting on a bench outside Mia's? Mia said he was sitting there all day. Isn't that right, Mia?" Elizabeth asks. "A little odd, don't you think?"

"I don't know. Did I say that?" Mia lifts her head, tears on her face.

"Yes, you did say that, Mia," Godric supports his nanna. "You were telling us you were fearful of him, that he was harassing you and wouldn't leave you alone. You told us he'd been on the bench outside your apartment all day."

"Thank you, Godric, exactly so," Elizabeth confirms.

"How did I know that letting this man in would lead me to this discovery," Aurelia says, adding, "That my own husband, Stefano, must have known about the diamond?" Aurelia looks at the shocked guests, who are now only really realising that Stefano was involved with Peter and now Giuseppe in the diamond theft.

"Giuseppe will pay!" Shouts Maximilius,

standing up.

"Sit down. I don't think Elizabeth agrees with any of this. Look at her face." Lucia pulls Max to sit back down, seeing Elizabeth frown at Aurelia's version of events.

*

"Hmm," Elizabeth puts her head to one side. "There are just a few more things that don't add up." Elizabeth turns her attention from Aurelia to Mia.

"Mia, you said you didn't know Marco." Elizabeth looks at Mia. "But I saw how you were talking to him in San Gimignano. In my car's rearview mirror. You said you were going to go up the tower, Mia. But you had gone to visit Marco, hadn't you? Did he know something about Peter's death?"

"I was mourning my husband, returning to the scene where he died. It was very emotional for me. Why don't you believe me?" Mia looks hurt.

"Because you lie," Elizabeth replies matter of factly. The room is shocked at Elizabeth's uncaring response but continues to listen, gripped to know where Elizabeth is going next with her accusations. She continues before anyone can interrupt, "I told you that the police accused me of meddling, or worse after I'd been to see you. And you said they had someone watching your apartment, and that must be why."

"Yes, I'm sure the police have been watching me," Mia looks at the Commissario.

"Only they haven't. Sergeant Rossi here ran a check for me. No police were watching your apartment." Elizabeth looks at the Sergeant to thank him, then looks back at Mia. "It was you, Mia, who called the police to complain that I was bothering you. You complained about me. Why?"

"Because all this is none of your business. What are you doing questioning all of us anyway? What right do you have? Just because you're English, you think you have the right to drop by my home to see me at any time." Mia mumbles, shocked at having been found out.

"You lied. To my face." Elizabeth waits for Mia to respond. Mia sinks her head into her hands again.

"Is any of this going to bring back my husband?" Mia says, still looking at the floor.

"Come to think of it. You painted Giuseppe black every time I saw you, Mia." Elizabeth adds. "Am I the only one you tried to warn the police about?" Elizabeth looks out the window. "Look at the birds. Aren't they lovely in your garden, Aurelia?"

"What?" Aurelia replies, confused as to where this is going.

"Was it your idea or Mia's to send

Giuseppe that Magpie toy?"

"What?" Aurelia shakes her head.

"Very clever. You both knew he'd show people. He showed everyone he could the death threats. So why wouldn't he show them the magpie toy? You planted the seed that he could be a thief. The thief."

"What? He stole the ring? We have it on tape," Aurelia replies angrily. "Enough of this!"

"Hmm. I'm not so sure he did. Maybe when the police picked him up earlier, he was on the way to the police station with it?" Elizabeth posits.

"I just want my ring back," Lucia pipes up. "So, are we saying Giuseppe has it or not?"

"You weren't that interested in it when you had it?" Maximilius says, having kept quiet for some time.

"Wait a minute," Godric pulls Lucia back. "Let my nanna finish."

"Why are you talking to my mother and Mia about magpie toys?" Sophia asks Elizabeth.

"Who shows someone they've been sent a magpie if they're a magpie?" Elizabeth continues, looking at Aurelia and then at Mia.

"What?" The Commissario is now confused.

"Eh?" The Sergeant agrees.

"Why are you listening to this woman when you should be leaving to speak to Giuseppe?" Mia asks, past her wit's end.

"Birds get such a bad reputation. They're just good at finding things." Elizabeth huffs.

"Think about it." Godric continues. "He showed people all the death threats. But what thief you know would say, 'Hey, look, someone sent me a toy that makes me look like a thief'? If he was guilty, why would he show a magpie someone sent him?"

"I'm confused," Ock leans back in his seat.

"We went to Giuseppe's apartment. Godric and I," Elizabeth continues.

"It was a mess," Godric adds.

"We saw no silver, nothing worth anything there. It was all rubbish. He was some things, messy, perhaps depressed, but there were no signs he was a thief."

"I don't know what you're talking about. Silver?" Aurelia replies.

"Oh, but I think you do, and Mia too. I think you know much more about the so-called stolen silver items found in Giuseppe's apartment. And buying a small painting of Lucia's and putting it in Giuseppe's apartment too. Was that supposed to try to frame him as well? That he knew her, had her art. Was preparing for the jewel theft? We saw Lucia's painting at Giuseppe's when Godric and I visited his home."

"My art? Everyone is a fan. I cannot help it. I do suffer when I create them. They have been called masterpieces," Lucia blows on her fingernails.

"Don't worry. I retrieved it. It is safe with the Commissario," Godric smiles at Lucia.

"Hopefully, cheering up the station," Lucia sighs happily.

"I'm sorry, Commissario, but I grow impatient to be reunited with my diamond," Maximilius interrupts.

"My diamond," Lucia replies again, correcting her soon to be ex-husband.

"Can we all shh!" Godric shouts, "Bunny, please continue. People look at the Commissario, who then adds.

"Perhaps you should get to the point you're trying to make, Elizabeth?" The Commissario says encouragingly.

*

"I found it odd, when Aurelia, you visited Mia, that you called her darling in such an affectionate way and didn't bring her anything." Elizabeth begins to explain, sticking to the facts. "When Stefano visited Mia, he brought her a cake. When Giuseppe visited, he brought her flowers. You were overly familiar and brought Mia nothing."

"Elizabeth," the Commissario interrupts, "Make your point."

"I think you both know each other better than you're letting on. Much better, in fact." Elizabeth looks back and forth between Mia and Aurelia. "I also think it is strange that you're making such a fuss to point the finger at Giuseppe. You show us all the CCTV without the Commissario giving you permission. You label your husband, Aurelia, as a thief? Why jump to this conclusion, or say Giuseppe is already guilty? You paint them black so quickly. Anyone could have put that diamond in the ice cube."

"For crying out loud. It's on CCTV him stealing the diamond in plain sight." Aurelia is exasperated.

"Very interesting. When, exactly, did you install the CCTV?"

"What?" Aurelia shakes her head. "For goodness sake," Aurelia starts to pace. "Is this going to take forever?"

"Not before Stefano's death, that's for sure, or there would have been CCTV of what happened to your husband that afternoon in the same glasshouse where Giuseppe is filmed," Elizabeth replies.

"It was installed after Stefano's death, exactly, as I was worried about what might happen around the property. It made me feel more secure. And good job too!" Aurelia raises her voice.

"And yet, you let your staff go? Your grounds keepers, your house staff. People who could see what is going on around here. Be witnesses. Observe things like diamond rings being put in ice." Elizabeth starts to walk towards Aurelia.

"This has nothing to do with you?" Aurelia says firmly, leaning back into the wall.

"I didn't know you let go of all your staff, Mrs Brambilla?" the Commissario asks.

"Isn't it convenient that CCTV caught Giuseppe?" Elizabeth says, now standing close to Aurelia, staring at her.

"I'm glad it did! Thanks to Aurelia, we could see exactly who stole the diamond!" Maximilius waves his hands about.

"Quite," Elizabeth raises an eyebrow, hoping everyone will catch up and spotting that perhaps the Commissario now finally has. "And I presume you got rid of your horses for the same reason as the staff."

"Horses don't talk," Aurelia replies dryly.

"No, but it does make you look like the martyr, doesn't it," Elizabeth adds. "And, you want nothing to do with Stefano's things? We are in a room now which has nothing of Stefanos. I surround myself with my husband's things. Why have you banished them all?"

"Commissario, what's going on here?" Mia asks. "Is this woman going to bring out her crystals next?" Mia glares at Elizabeth.

"Let me tell you what I think is going on here." Elizabeth walks to the dresser and pauses. "All the photographs of Peter and

Stefano always had both of you in the background."

"Photographs?" The Sergeant asks. Elizabeth picks up a photograph of Stefano, Peter, Mia and Aurelia from the dresser. Aurelia has her arm around Mia, standing behind Peter and Stefano seated on a sofa.

"Of the four of them, yes. Stefano, Peter, but also Mia and Aurelia. In Mia's home, here, in Stefano's restaurant in San Gimignano," Elizabeth explains, continuing, "And here," she hands the photo frame to the Sergeant. "At first, it made me think perhaps Stefano was in cahoots with Peter. I was looking at the men. At Peter. They were always in the foreground, friendly. But Mia and Aurelia were always arms linked, standing behind their husbands."

"You have lost the plot," Mia tells Elizabeth.

"When exactly did you fall in love with each other?" Elizabeth looks to Mia and then to Aurelia. "Why didn't you just leave? Why set your husband up to steal a diamond, Mia, and then plan to let him get framed while you run away with the diamond and Aurelia?"

There are gasps from the others.

"Mama?" Sophia looks at her mother. "Why is she saying these things?"

"Giuseppe told Godric that Stefano spent more time with Peter than his wife." Elizabeth continues, glancing briefly at the Commissario.

"I did wonder why Stefano was so friendly to me. Perhaps he was lonely?" Elizabeth muses to herself. Neither Mia nor Aurelia say anything, while Elizabeth continues, "I was speaking to a park keeper in the Boboli Gardens, talking about how sad I felt after Stefano passed. He said his family must be very sad. But I never saw it in your face, Aurelia? I know what sadness feels like, looks like."

"Did you ever look at my face? You were too busy flirting with my husband," Aurelia scoffs. Elizabeth purses her lips to hide the sadness she feels for Gerald even still, and the pity for Stefano who had no one to love him so, then continues.

"And you, Mia, you had safety pins in your cupboard. I saw one in your hand to make yourself cry." Godric looks at his nanna.

"Yes!" Godric confirms. "There were unwound safety pins on the table."

"But the first thing went wrong. Perhaps Peter recognised you both, so you had to push him off the tower. Did you mean for the poison to kill him? Or to disarm him while you ran off with the diamond? I'm curious," Elizabeth asks Mia and Aurelia.

"Is she saying Aurelia and Mia murdered their husbands?" Lucia quietly asks Godric.

"I think she's saying exactly that," Godric replies, hearing this for the first time too.

"I'm not entertaining this," Aurelia shakes

her head. But Elizabeth is determined now to rattle through her suspicions before she is stopped.

"Then things started to unravel. Perhaps because you have never been serial killers before? I suppose one needs practice to get good at this sort of thing. Stefano saw you were getting very cosy and heard you talk about Peter? Maybe you were nervous Stefano had twigged what you had both done? Perhaps you both were disappointed that Stefano didn't seem to care about your possible affair with Mia, Aurelia? He just wanted to spend time with his daughters." Then Elizabeth looks at Mia. "And, you had not worked out the implications of murdering your husband, had you? Only, once Stefano twigged, he had to go too."

"This is slander," Aurelia says quietly.

"You killed your husband!" Lucia is aghast as the penny drops.

"Shut up! He was my husband. Mine. Not yours." Aurelia frowns at Lucia. Elizabeth interrupts Aurelia.

"Is that why you chose the diamond as the object to steal, Aurelia? Petty historic jealousy?" Elizabeth looks at Lucia to explain. "Godric told me about your fling with Stefano in your teens," then looks back at Aurelia. "Did you want to get your own back on Lucia? Had Stefano still got a soft spot for her?"

"It's all lies," Aurelia starts shaking her head, her drink wobbling in a trembling hand.

"Then, you realised that once Stefano was dead, you had the land and didn't have to run away together after all. The original reason I suppose for stealing the diamond was so you could live the lifestyle you were living only elsewhere. The horses, the pools. I can see it."

"Why are you talking about Mia and my mother like this, accusing them of horrific things? They are both widows. Widows!" Isabella says in an outburst. Elizabeth knows what she is about to say will devastate Isabella, particularly wondering if she ever told her mother that she had married Marco and is also a widow. To lose her father, killed by her own mother, and now to hear what Elizabeth is about to say. Elizabeth looks at the anguish on Isabella's face but knows she cannot stop now.

"But now, you had a new opponent. Marco. When you found out he had married your daughter, Isabella, and that Stefano had changed his will to leave everything to his daughters, Marco had to go too. You'd already murdered your husbands. Why not murder your daughter's husband too?" Everyone gasps and looks at Isabella, including Aurelia.

"You married Marco?" Aurelia pretends she doesn't know.

"Mama, why would she say these nasty things about you?" Isabella asks, in tears.

"Marco was going to tell you when you had calmed down about us. He said you weren't ready to hear it from me. But you knew all along?"

"Are you going to let this woman make up lies about me? Haven't I suffered enough?" Aurelia looks to the Commissario, ignoring her own daughter. "There is no evidence for any of this because it's not true!"

"The Commissario found a map in Marco's wallet." Elizabeth looks at the Commissario, "When he found Marco's body. That is right, is it not?".

"It was like a treasure map," the Commissario says quietly. "Stefano's land. Or, rather, your land," the Commissario looks at Aurelia.

"When I heard that Isabella had secretly married Marco and that he had intentions of gaining all of Stefano's land, I wondered who might want him gone?" Elizabeth admits. "We saw the ring on his finger. He had his marriage papers with him when he died. And it could not have been Stefano." Elizabeth finds explaining quite tiring. Godric hands her a glass of water and she takes a sip.

"I must admit, this is all making sense. I have seen Mia and Aurelia in town together, shopping, holding hands," Lucia replies, shocked.

"Shut up! Shut up!" Sophia shouts out.

"My mother would not do anything so beastly," Sophia starts to cry in panic.

"Okay, Soph, don't shout at my mother. She's not done anything," Ock puts his arm around both his mother and his girlfriend to hold them close, also a little in shock, having spent time himself with Aurelia at Sophia's home.

*

"Is this how you treat mourning widows?" Mia snaps at Elizabeth, now angrily, standing up, pacing, her tears gone. "You came to my house, sat at my table, and then you turn on me like this? No wonder the police suspected you. Is this some complicated ruse to try to throw light off yourself?"

Elizabeth pauses, then asks Mia. "You remember you told me Giuseppe had death threats?"

"He had twenty-four. I mean, he's been making it up, clearly," Mia spits.

"I'm curious. How did you know how many death threats Giuseppe had?"

"What? What are you talking about?" Mia frowns, rubbing her forehead.

"You said the exact number of death threats now. And you said the same amount when I visited you before. Twenty-four. How did you know that?"

"He must have told me?" Mia looks

confused.

"It's just when Godric and I would ask him, we thought he must be lying about his death threats as he could not remember how many."

"Maybe he just felt closer to me. His best friend was my husband," Mia replies.

"Maybe," Elizabeth pauses. "But then I found this in the pocket of the white shirt I showed you," Elizabeth pulls out a piece of paper from her pocket in a plastic bag. She looks at the Commissario to excuse her for not sharing. "It didn't make sense to me, not until today." Elizabeth hands the piece of paper carefully to the Commissario in the bag. "Commissario. What number is on that piece of paper?"

"Twenty-four."

"The paper has a G on. G for Giuseppe. The shirt was half burnt in a fire up on Stefano's land. The brazier was still smoking. When I came back to Florence and showed it to you in the bag, you didn't even ask why half of it was missing or who had burnt it. Because it was you, Mia. You knew how many death threats Giuseppe had, as you sent them. It was all planned to make Giuseppe look guilty. Death threats, but no death. Magpie toy and thief." There are gasps again from the room, and Mia shakes her head and starts crying again.

"You're making this all up. Inventing such a crazy idea. Why can't you leave me alone." Mia sobs.

"Commissario, you should let us give our statements faster than this and get onto chasing the real suspect, Giuseppe!" Aurelia shouts, adding, "Maybe Giuseppe was trying to get rid of some evidence?" Aurelia says helpfully.

"Is that right?" Elizabeth replies wryly. "Whoever wrote that piece of paper sent the threats. You will be able to check against the handwriting."

There is a gasp from the room.

"Perhaps it was Marco," Lucia suggests helpfully.

"Already dead as the brazier was still smoking," Elizabeth replies. "And, if Marco wanted Aurelia's land after he married Isabella–"

"He wasn't money grabbing. He just wanted us to start a family," Isabella interrupts. Aurelia, tries to comfort her daughter by placing a hand on her shoulder, but Isabella flinches.

"Who had most to lose?" Elizabeth looks at Aurelia. "Was Marco blackmailing you, Aurelia? Did he already know what you had done to your own husband and Peter?"

"Are you suggesting I killed my daughter's husband to stop him from taking my land?" Aurelia says, flabbergasted.

"And because he knew you murdered

your husband. I can imagine Marco may have put that together." Elizabeth replies matter of factly. "Yes. He saw you that day Peter fell from the tower. The police said Marco was there shortly after they turned up. At first, it made me suspicious of him maybe having killed Peter. But he had no motive. What I didn't realise until recently is that he saw you, didn't he, Aurelia? He saw you in San Gimignano the night Peter was murdered. And then again when you left the scene."

*

Aurelia ignores Elizabeth and instead protests that the focus of the conversation should be elsewhere.

"Why are we not concerned about Giuseppe? He is the one who has been arrested with the diamond. I don't need to listen to nonsense." Aurelia stares hard at the Commissario. "You need to go and deal with the real criminal. Now!"

"We have detained Giuseppe Esposito, but he has not been arrested yet," the Sergeant corrects Aurelia. "Just being questioned." The Sergeant picks up his phone.

"I don't think the diamond you picked up with Giuseppe is the real diamond," Elizabeth suggests. "And please stop crying, Mia. We all know you have a safety pin in your hand."

Ock grabs Mia's hand, peels it open, and picks

out the pin. More gasps from the room as Mia pulls away and tries not to look guilty.

"What?" Maximilius leans forward in his seat. "That too? The diamond is not real?"

"What?" Lucia looks at the Commissario for confirmation.

"I think I know where the real diamond is. I think you'll find it somewhere where Patty found the shirt, up on the hill, where no one goes," Elizabeth explains. "I suspect both Mia and Aurelia here are fidgety because both were planning on running away together and retrieving the real diamond, with all of you descending on the house here and waiting for the fake diamond Giuseppe took. We scuppered their getaway plan. To getaway before the diamond was revealed to be a fake."

"As I say, we have a jeweller there right now to check the diamond." The Commissario looks at his Sergeant, who is listening to someone on the end of the phone and shakes his head. It is clear he has just heard the news that the diamond is not real.

"Fake," the Sergeant mouths while he continues to listen on the phone.

"Where is the diamond?" Maximilius asks the Commissario.

"This is utter nonsense," Mia rubs her face and has started to go red.

"The police will find the diamond. They will be able to check Marco's phone. You have covered your tracks so badly. Better to admit what you have done." Elizabeth glares at Mia.

"Your bloody dog," Mia replies, scowling at Patty.

"People who don't like animals." Elizabeth stares at Mia.

"I didn't mean to do it–"

"Shut up!" Aurelia interrupts Mia.

"What's the point?" Mia replies to Aurelia. "We're in love," Mia admits, then looks at Elizabeth. "The first time I saw her, I couldn't take my eyes off Aurie."

"You killed both your husbands. Perhaps Peter wanted to keep the diamond for himself. He didn't know you loved Aurelia and that you had just used him. He had to go. And then Stefano. Like I say, he must have worked it out, realised what you had done," Elizabeth speculates.

"No," Mia shakes her head.

"Did he know that his wife was in love with you? He was so very kind to you. That day. At your apartment. He wanted to bring you cake," Elizabeth replies.

"We didn't kill Stefano," Mia says slowly.

"But you drugged him." Elizabeth corrects Mia.

"Yes," Mia says quietly.

There are more gasps in the room.

"Aurelia wanted to tell him we were leaving. But we didn't mean to kill him. Just have him not explode at us," Mia explains. "We didn't know he'd walk into the horses."

"But you gave him enough drugs. You pushed him in," Elizabeth looks at Aurelia.

"He didn't love me. He didn't care that I love Mia," Aurelia admits. "He neglected me, so yes! I pushed him!"

There are more gasps, and Mia looks a little surprised at Aurelia.

"I have never been involved in a case where the murders have been so badly executed. Apart from Marco's," Elizabeth continues.

"No!" Isabella stands up. "Mama! No! Tell me no!"

Aurelia lights a cigarette, walks towards the window, aware her time is up.

"We didn't mean to kill them, apart from Marco. Marco, we had to kill. He was going to take everything, and then it would have all been for nothing," Aurelia says flatly.

There is a shock in the room, and Isabella lets out a guttural scream. Elizabeth sits back down next to Godric, who pours her more water.

"I think now you can let people out to be questioned separately, Commissario," Elizabeth looks at the Commissario, then at Godric and nods. "Perhaps we can have our holiday now."

71 GOODBYE FLORENCE

It is time to say goodbye to Florence, and Elizabeth and Godric find themselves standing with Patty beside the little Fiat 500 in the driveway of Villa De' Fiori. With his own Fiat 600T van, Commissario Lorenzo Bianchi has come to wave them off.

"We found the diamond," the Commissario explains. "Thanks to your deductions. We had to turn the little cottage on the hill upside down, but we found it. In a bottle of olive oil on Stefano's desk, sitting on top of tickets to an opera show he must have attended in Siena before his death. The bottle was covered with Aurelia's fingerprints but none of Stefano's. His prints were only on the tickets."

"Poor Stefano," Elizabeth remembers the concert well.

"And we have Marco's phone records. Mia was the last person he phoned the night of his death. He texted her, asking why she wasn't more worried that he knew her secret and what had happened to Peter. Marco was guessing they had also murdered Stefano. And that they must hand over the land or they'll go the way their victims did. He told Mia to meet him at the vineyard. It was the last message he sent. We also found traces of what poisoned him in Aurelia's kitchen."

"Is that enough evidence?" Godric asks.

"Mia called Marco back. It's on her phone records. With traces of poison in Aurelia's kitchen. Yes, when added to the death threats to Giuseppe, the brazier fire you found, and that it was Mia found stealing the silver from that antiques shop a week earlier. We looked back through the CCTV in the shop. I'd say that is irrefutable, especially with their confessions."

"Huh, that was just a hunch about the antiques shop," Elizabeth replies, watching Godric load Patty into the back seat of the Fiat 500.

"A good one. I suppose she thought it would be wiped. We have released Giuseppe. He said he will go back to the UK with Peter's remains."

Elizabeth can see that Godric is ready to go. She looks one more time at the Commissario's face, knowing exactly what he will be doing in less than an hour.

"I can't say it's been entirely enjoyable, but I wish you many good meals in the future," Elizabeth narrows her eyes at the Commissario.

The Commissario bends down into his van and pulls out a basket of food.

"My wife, she made me bring this. As a peace offering. She said I behaved badly towards you, Elizabeth. I did."

"You did," Elizabeth offers no forgiveness to this man in front of her. But also feels no malice or hard feelings.

"We have no space," Godric replies with a perfunctory manner, leaning his head out of the car window to look at the treats, unhappy that the Commissario did not go out to bat for his nanna and was always too interested in food. "But we can pull these out." Godric pulls out bread, olives, nuts, crisps, tomatoes and wine from a fancy basket. Everything apart from the basket itself. The Commissario smiles, holding an empty basket.

"If you come back to Florence, please do come and help us," the Commissario suggests to Elizabeth. "We are forever in your debt, and you would always be welcome at the station to offer your expert opinion."

"I can assure you, that will never happen," Elizabeth smiles, pleased with her polite revenge, then sad that this man never really got to know her and perhaps forgiving him a little for having a boss rather like Inspector

Abley's Super in Cambridge in the shape of the Questore. "But we are good. It is all good," Elizabeth continues with her knowing smile, mainly for her own pleasure.

The Commissario nods a 'fair enough' and leaves in his van. Like ships crossing, a chauffeur pulls up with Lucia inside a limo. She opens her window.

"Darlings! You got me my diamond. Thank you."

"What are you going to do with it?" Elizabeth asks, curious.

"I'm donating it to the needy. Anything to stop Max getting it in the divorce," Lucia beams, her very white teeth dazzling Elizabeth's eyes a little.

"The needy?" Godric asks.

"Yes," Lucia smiles, getting out of the car and walking straight over to Godric to kiss him on the cheek. "You'll come back after your exams?"

"Immediately," Godric assures his new friend.

"I don't know how I will manage without you," Lucia pulls a sad face.

"You'll get a grip," Elizabeth says, a little irritated with the baby voice Lucia has put on. Godric pulls the keys to the villa out of his pocket and gives them to Lucia.

"Keep them, and here are two blank tickets for you, Elizabeth. No name, no expiry. Just punch in your details and enjoy. I've already given God one for himself to pop over. Invite a friend."

"You really are the most generous person, aren't you," Elizabeth replies. Then uncharacteristically adds, "Thank you for making Godric's stay more enjoyable–"

"Than yours?" Lucia interrupts. "I expect you're looking forward to going home."

"I am, but it seems a long way off yet, and part of me is so tired now."

"Then let me fly you home. We can deliver the car," Lucia says brightly.

"That's very kind but completely unnecessary," Elizabeth says. "And, every part of me wants to be away relaxing, without murders to solve for a change."

"We're looking forward to visiting places at a more leisurely pace as we did before we came to Florence," Godric chips in. "On our way home."

"Well, I have something for you," Lucia pulls an envelope from her jacket pocket.

"You have to stop this nonsense," Godric looks at Elizabeth, who rolls her eyes.

"The keys to my place in Annecy, this time on the lake. You can spend more time on your way home, perhaps. You said it was your favourite place, God?" Lucia smiles, then kisses his cheek. "Consider it a thank you for finding my diamond."

"It is my favourite place," Godric beams, happy to accept this offer.

"I miss you already," Lucia hugs Godric, then sighs. As they are departing, Patty sticks her head out of the window.

"Say goodbye, Patty, you're coming home with us now," Elizabeth says to Patty, looking up at the villa, pleased to be leaving Florence behind.

*

Elizabeth asks Godric to drive her to the Boboli Gardens one last time. She has to deliver something. Godric drops her off and says he will wait with Patty. Elizabeth smiles but does not explain. In her hand, she carries an envelope and is hurriedly scribbling the park keeper's name on the front. Entering the gates, it is not long before she arrives at a pergola covered in lilac wisteria in bloom. Unexpectedly, she spots the park keeper just through the gate.

"It is nice to see you again," the park keeper, Piero smiles.

"Piero! Oh, I'm so glad I found you. I was going to leave this at the gate, but I haven't had time to write you a note."

They step aside from the line of visitors entering, the wisteria hanging just feet from their heads, bees buzzing in the glorious spring air.

“You’re leaving?” Piero takes the envelope Elizabeth holds out and opens it.

“What’s this?”

“I don’t need them. They were a gift. So, I thought you could make that trip you always wanted to and bring your daughter to visit England.” Elizabeth watches his hesitancy. “I think your wife would like you to take them. I really have no use for them. I would hate for them to go to waste.”

“But I can’t accept these? That is far too generous.”

“No. I insist. Someone on my visit has taught me more about generosity and its importance. Please.” Elizabeth smiles, not waiting for his reply. He looks down at two first-class plane tickets from Italy to the UK, then back up at the enigmatic woman walking away.

*

When Elizabeth returns to Godric and Patty, she is ready to leave the city. Everything they need is in the little Fiat 500.

“Everything okay?” Godric asks.

“Today is a new day, and I have a feeling it’s going to be good.”

“Sure is.” And with that, they leave Florence without looking back.

72 WHAT'S IMPORTANT

On the way home, Elizabeth and Godric do visit Lucia's home in Annecy on the lake. With its infinity pool, floor to ceiling windows and outdoor fire pit it becomes hard to leave. Watching the spring sun setting each night, they finally get the stress-free time they deserve and stay for a few nights. But inevitably the real world pulls them back and Godric realises he now cannot drive back all the way with Elizabeth and Patty, as his exams loom and he has done no revision, so they agree he will fly back from Chambery while Elizabeth takes the Fiat 500 back through the Channel tunnel.

They pull up in the car park and say their goodbyes. Godric leans into the back and pulls out two Oranginas.

"Five o'clocksees."

They open their bottles and drink.

"You know, we rescued Patty at the

wrong time, in the wrong place, but she's rescued us both back." Godric kisses Patty goodbye. "Take good care of her."

"Who are you talking to? Me or Patty?" Elizabeth raises her eyebrows.

"Try Daft Punk. For Patty's sake. Something upbeat. None of that Liszt. Don't be getting melancholy. I'll see you in a week or so." Elizabeth can feel her eyes starting to water.

"Alright. I'll try. If you insist," Elizabeth pretends to sigh heavily.

"I don't like leaving you," Godric tells his nanna.

"I'm a grown up. We'll be fine," Elizabeth replies.

"Will you call me if you need anything?"

"I'm not frail or vulnerable. Stop it. Don't miss your flight. You have exams to revise for," Elizabeth pretends to frown.

But they both know they've been through so much this year that has knocked them off their feet.

"Do you a deal? I won't worry about you if you don't worry about me," Godric insists.

"Well, that's a silly deal."

"Love you, Bunny."

"Now go. She's paid first class. You don't want to get downgraded."

"Can they do that?" Godric walks away, looking back and grinning.

*

Elizabeth decides to drive slowly back to the coast, as she still has just under two weeks or thereabouts before she can take Patty across the border to England. She travels through the centre of France and stops off in Avallon, where she finds it remarkably easy to pass afternoons sitting in squares, watching the world go by. She stops again in Vezeley, enjoying views across the valleys and cafes to sit and read the one copy of The Guardian she can find. When she finally drives to the coast and Le Touquet, she plays Daft Punk for the entire journey, thinking how lucky she is to have such a wonderful grandson in her life.

Things feel brighter still when she finds a hotel situated right on the beach, with a room where Patty can step straight out onto the white sand. It is clear Patty's toes have never had so much fun, and Elizabeth spends hours throwing a tennis ball for Patty to fetch, not tiring of the simple pleasures. This routine goes on for days, and Elizabeth's French even begins to improve as Patty brings locals and tourists alike up to speak and say hello. Elizabeth knows full well, she is never alone with a dog.

It is on a Tuesday, two days before she can take Patty home. They must get Patty's final pills this afternoon in order to cross the border. Elizabeth strolls along the promenade. Patty sees a dog on the other side of the street and starts barking and wagging her tail. It is most unlike Patty, and there is nothing Elizabeth can do to calm her excitement. The other dog begins to pull his owner out into the traffic, to try to reach Patty and somehow breaks free, the lead having slipped through the man's fingers. In split seconds, observing the heavy traffic, Elizabeth hands Patty's lead to a woman beside her who is watching the whole commotion. Elizabeth then rushes out into the road to rescue the other dog who has escaped to say hello to Patty. But, as Elizabeth runs, she doesn't see a car heading right for her. In seconds, Elizabeth grabs the other dog as a red van zooms past and hits the car about to knock Elizabeth over. Elizabeth stumbles, now holding the lead of the dog she caught. The man runs out to retrieve the lead and thanks Elizabeth profusely for saving his dog. Elizabeth does not hear the man. Instead, once she sees Patty is okay, her eyes lock onto the red van. It is clear to all bystanders that the red van drove right into the side of the car to stop it from running Elizabeth over. The man gets out of his van and rushes to Elizabeth to see if she is okay.

"It's you?" Elizabeth says, shocked and confused.

"Are you okay?" The man asks, pulling

Elizabeth up and reuniting her with Patty. "Let's sit on this bench and just see if you are okay."

"I have to take Patty to her appointment for her final examination and tablets. I can't be late." Elizabeth winces at her wrist.

"D'you need a hospital?"

"No, it's fine. Just sore."

"Let me take you both to the vets."

"Bob paid you to look out for me, didn't he? And you're a P.I.?" Elizabeth tells the man.

"I owed your good old Inspector Bob in Cambridge a favour. He's a good man, you know. Mike. Pleased to meet you," the man introduces himself.

"Your van?" Elizabeth looks across the pavement the other way from the beach and can see that one side of the front of the van is completely crumpled.

"It's hired."

"We've been calling you Fromage Man. We've seen you everywhere," Elizabeth explains.

"I was only meant to follow you to see if the car was going to make it and if Godric would be able to drive on the other side of the road." Michael chuckles to himself. "As it turns out, you have a pretty good grandson."

"I was right. Huh," Elizabeth replies.

"Bob was worried Godric would drink and–"

"And you–"

"Yes, I was going to take you home." Mike pauses. "But you kept getting into scrapes, so Bob would keep extending my contract. And then, when you started working for the Italian police, my budget came out of Bob's official expenses. I went legit. As your bodyguard." Mike laughs. "At one point, I had some tips on that Marco chap and wanted to let you know, but you figured it out yourself."

"So that's how Bob knew about Marco pushing me against a wall. You've been keeping him in the loop!" Elizabeth shakes her head, thinking about her friend back home worrying about her. "You could have told us. You freaked us out on more than one occasion."

"If I had, you would have told me to stop following you or set the Commissario on me."

"And now, we have Patty. And you to thank for saving me in Reims. That van nearly knocked me over then," Elizabeth remembers. "And just now."

"Most people aren't murdered. It's more common to get knocked over, it is true." Mike laughs. "Come on, drink up, and we'll get you to that vet appointment, so my job will be done when I can watch you head back to England." Michael flags down a taxi from the road, and they stand up from the bench. Elizabeth looks at this stranger, who turned out to be her guardian angel and feels she has learnt a lot from this holiday. It is time to start living again. Elizabeth holds Patty's lead tight.

"Time to go and start living, Patty."

* * *

THE END

Thank you very much for reading *Holiday Mystery*, Book 6 of the series The Cambridge Murder Mysteries.

Titles available in The Cambridge Murder Mystery Series:

Book 1: Poison

Book 2: Cursed

Book 3: Blood Moon

Book 4: A Christmas Mystery

Book 5: Valentine's Day – Kiss of Death

Book 6: Holiday Mystery

Short Stories and Novellas in the Cambridge Murder Mystery Series:

Christmas Eve in Grantchester

Green *(available by subscribing to my newsletter)*

Other titles by Charlot King:

Animal Tales: Woof

Animal Tales: Pup

For more information on the other books in the series please do visit www.charlotking.com where you can also subscribe to Charlot King's VIP Club. If you'd like to follow what Charlot King is up to you can find her on Twitter: @queencharlot. And, if you enjoyed this book, Charlot would be so very grateful for a review on Amazon and Goodreads as well as telling all your friends. Much appreciated! Thanks again, and very happy reading.

Printed in Great Britain
by Amazon

30996502R00320